M000282655

NEW BEGINNINGS AT SEASIDE BLOOMS

WELCOME TO WHITSBOROUGH BAY BOOK 2

JESSICA REDLAND

Boldwood

First published in Great Britain in 2020 by Boldwood Books Ltd.

Copyright © Jessica Redland, 2020

Cover Design by Charlotte Abrams-Simpson

Cover Photography: Shutterstock

Every effort has been made to obtain the necessary permissions with reference to copyright material, both illustrative and quoted. We apologise for any omissions in this respect and will be pleased to make the appropriate acknowledgements in any future edition.

A CIP catalogue record for this book is available from the British Library.

Paperback ISBN 978-1-83889-166-4

Ebook ISBN 978-1-83889-168-8

Kindle ISBN 978-1-83889-167-1

Audio CD ISBN 978-1-83889-244-9

MP3 CD ISBN 978-1-83889-717-8

Digital audio download ISBN 978-1-83889-165-7

Boldwood Books Ltd
23 Bowerdean Street
London SW6 3TN
www.boldwoodbooks.com

I searched for Steven and found Mark instead.This is for him xx

PART I

ONE YEAR AGO

1

'Come on, Jason. Ring.' I frowned at my iPhone as I paced up and down in the lounge, my stiletto heels echoing on the wooden floorboards. 'Or text. I don't care which. Just make contact. Please.'

My heart leapt as the phone beeped, but the text was from one of my best friends instead.

✉ From Elise
Happy birthday Sarah! Last year in your twenties so make the most of it. Wish you weren't so far away so I could give you a birthday hug so sending one by text instead. I've hopefully timed your present to arrive today. Hope Jason's got you a fab gift… proposal maybe? Have a great evening xxxxxxx

I stretched out my arm to admire the sparkly silver bracelet she'd sent.

✉ To Elise
Just got home and your parcel was waiting. Way too generous as usual… but absolutely gorgeous!

Thank you so much. Not sure where he's taking me
but hopefully it's somewhere nice this time. I'm
all dressed up with nowhere to go! Would be lying
if I said a proposal hadn't crossed my mind.
EEEEEEKKKK!!!! You'll be first to know if he
does xxx

My hands shook slightly and I felt a flutter in my stomach as I
typed in the words. Could tonight really be the night? Maybe. The
timing felt about right and he'd been talking about making plans
for the future. We'd been together for two years and two months
and had lived together for most of that time. Aside from occasional
bouts of thoughtlessness on his part and a tendency to drag me to
the gym or on a twenty-mile hike way more often than a person
should have to endure in a lifetime, we were very happy together
and I assumed that a proposal wouldn't be too far away.

Another text arrived but it still wasn't Jason.

From Clare
Sorry for not texting earlier. Dim Daz borrowed
my phone then drove to Essex with it. Bloody
muppet. Anyway, better late than never… happy
birthday you old fart. Can't believe you want to
spend the evening with your eejit flatmate rather
than me. Hope it's not McDonalds this time! Maybe
he'll really treat you & do Pizza Hut?! Keep
Saturday night free if you want your card & gift
or I'm keeping them xx

She'd added several laughing emojis to the end of the text.

'Your Auntie Clare is being very rude, as usual,' I said to one of
our kittens, Kat, who'd appeared to demand a fuss. 'Flatmate
indeed.' But I couldn't help smiling. Only Clare could get away with
a comment like that.

To Clare

Thanks. Was beginning to think you'd forgotten
me! I promise to keep Saturday free for you.
Dread to know what sort of abuse I'd get if I
don't. Not sure where MY BOYFRIEND is taking me.
Still waiting to hear. McDonalds was a misunderstanding and you know it! Laters xx

✉ From Clare
Misunderstanding my arse! My final guess of the
evening… The Griffin

I shook my head. So our two-year anniversary hadn't gone quite
to plan, but it was my fault really. I should have known that saying,
'I'd love to go out for a meal to celebrate; how about The Kam Po? I
could meet you in The Griffin after work,' was far too vague for
Jason. I ended up nursing the same glass of Pinot Grigio for ninety
minutes before finally accepting he wasn't coming. Trudging home,
I found him in his gym kit playing on his Xbox. 'You been working
late?' he asked. 'You should've texted me. I got you a McDonalds on
the way home, but it'll be cold now and there's nothing else to eat.'
He returned to his game and I went to bed hungry. I kept hoping
he'd realise his mistake but he never did and, by then, it felt too late
to say anything.

I checked my phone again now. Nothing. It couldn't happen
twice, could it? No. It had been *his* idea this time. Some of my
friends from work had suggested a birthday meal, but Jason had
insisted on taking me out himself. I'd gently reminded him a couple
of days ago and he'd assured me it was in hand and I wasn't to quiz
him any further or I'd spoil the surprise. He said he'd contact me
last minute with a location to meet him so I could enjoy the excitement of speculating about where we were going. This was certainly
last minute and excitement wasn't quite the feeling I'd describe.

It was now after half six. Sod it! I couldn't do this anymore.

✉ To Jason
This is killing me! Where are you taking me? I'm

```
all ready and awaiting my instructions! Please
tell me you haven't forgotten xx
```

I hoped that reading my birthday cards again would distract me. It didn't. A little voice in my head kept telling me he *had* forgotten and Clare's joke about McDonalds or my local might not be far from the truth. Perhaps he was frantically phoning round restaurants right now and that's why he hadn't been in touch. Another text arrived and, finally, it was from him. *Please don't say McDonalds...*

```
⊠ From Jason
South Kensington Tube Station. 1915hrs. Table
booked for 1930hrs xx
```

Butterflies stirred in my stomach. *Oh my God! South Kensington. Could it be...?*

I hastily shoved my phone in my bag, pulled on my coat and left the flat, legs shaking as I strode towards the tube station. It was just a coincidence. There were hundreds of restaurants in South Kensington and we could be going to any of them. With Jason's track record, it could be McDonald's. But what if...?

He'd taken me to Luigi's to celebrate me moving down to London shortly after we started seeing each other. During dessert, the man on the table next to us proposed to his girlfriend. It was such a moving and romantic moment and, on the way home, Jason said that he could imagine proposing there too. But that didn't mean he'd booked a table there tonight to propose to me, did it?

When I reached South Kensington tube station, it took all my willpower to stand still on the escalator when all I wanted to do was to shove past the travellers, run up the steps, and skip across the concourse screaming, 'Yes, Jason, I *will* marry you.'

I spotted him by one of the exits. My breath caught as I saw what he was wearing. Classically tall, dark, and handsome, he looked particularly hot in the three-piece suit he'd bought for his brother's wedding last summer. After his firefighter uniform, it was my favourite outfit on him. Although, to be perfectly honest, with a toned body like his, I preferred no clothes at all.

'Happy birthday.' He bent down and gave me a soft kiss. I breathed in his musky scent and those butterflies went crazy. 'You look good.'

'Thank you.' I whipped open my coat like a flasher, revealing the LBD I'd agonised over wearing for fear I'd be over-dressed.

He wolf-whistled and I flushed from head to toe. 'I approve. Although you may be a little over-dressed for what I have planned later tonight.'

I flushed again and Jason laughed as he took my hand in his. 'Shall we?'

'Where are we going?' I tried to sound casual but failed abysmally. *Please say Luigi's. Please.*

He winked at me, grinning widely. 'It's a surprise.'
Oh my God!

It could only have been three minutes, but I swear that walk felt like an hour. My sweaty hand kept slipping from his, I stumbled several times and I even hiccupped, causing Jason to ask if I'd been on the wine before leaving the flat.

The Italian flag and deep green canopy of Luigi's loomed ahead of us. My breathing quickened and I mentally prepared myself: *must not look gutted if we walk past, must look happy wherever he takes me.*

But we didn't walk past. We stopped. We went in. He gave his name and we were led to a table towards the back where a bucket of champagne on ice was waiting for us. Champagne. Proper Champagne. Jason always said that supermarket own label Cava was overpriced. Which could only mean... Oh. My. God!

I put my glass of champagne down as Jason pushed the candle aside and reached for my hand across the table a few minutes later.

'You really do look gorgeous tonight,' he said.

'You don't scrub up too badly yourself,' I whispered, barely able to speak for anticipation of what was coming.

His dark eyes twinkled as he gazed at me over the table. 'Thank you. I thought I should make a special effort. It's a special occasion, after all.'

Eeeeeekkkkk!

'I haven't given you your birthday present yet.'

A shiver of anticipation ran through me. 'No, you haven't.'

'If I know you, you'll have spent all day trying to guess what it is.'

'Me? It never entered my head.'

Jason laughed. 'Yeah, right. I think you'll like it. I was going to wait until the end of the meal but I'm too excited about it to wait. Is it okay if we do it now?'

I nodded.

'There are a few things I want to say first,' he continued.

'Your water, sir.' A waiter inconveniently appeared. *Bottled water? Not tap? Crikey!* I willed the waiter to be quick. 'Would you like me to pour, sir?' he asked.

I silently pleaded with Jason to say no before I wet myself with excitement.

'It's fine. You can just leave it. Thanks.'

'Happy Birthday,' Jason said when the waiter finally left.

'Thank you.' We clinked champagne glasses.

'Now, where was I?'

'You wanted to say some things?'

'Oh yes. Do you remember the night we met?' He reached for my hand again.

'Of course. Best night of my life.'

'We said it was fate that we met, remember?'

'It was meant to be,' I agreed. Neither of us was supposed to be in Nottingham the night we met. I'd been drafted in last minute to make up numbers on a friend of a friend's hen do and Jason had spontaneously decided to visit an old friend there after his weekend plans fell through.

After a day of never-to-be-repeated-because-it-was-so-terrifying 'fun and frolics in the great outdoors', the hen party donned fairy wings and net skirts and embarked on a pub crawl. We ended up in an eighties club where I spotted Jason on the dance floor looking very cute and very out of place in a thick jumper. 'Aren't you hot?' I shouted over the music.

'I'm used to the heat,' he replied. 'I'm a firefighter.' Oh behave! I had an obsession with firemen so that one line told me all I needed to know. Then when I found out he lived in London... Well, I was moving there from Manchester two weeks later. It had to be fate.

'Can you remember what I said attracted me to you that night in Nottingham?' Jason asked.

'My fluffy wings?'

He laughed. 'The outfit certainly helped. But there was something that made me get your phone number at the end of the night.'

I shrugged.

'It was that you'd spent the day on a gorge-walking adventure. Any woman who'd spent the day abseiling, climbing and walking through waterfalls was worth getting to know better.'

Oh! That was unexpected. I thought I'd told him it was a one-off for the hen do and I'd never have agreed to make up the numbers if I'd realised what was planned. Maybe I hadn't. Probably wasn't the moment to confess it now.

'I've never had a girlfriend who enjoys being outdoors and keeping fit as much as I do,' he continued. 'I can't believe I've found someone who loves to go to the gym...' Didn't he realise I tolerated rather than loved going to the gym? Obviously not.

'... who enjoys mountain biking...' Eek! I'd better not confess that my mountain bike hadn't actually been stolen but was hiding in Clare's garage because I'd have a coronary if I ever had to put myself through the extreme torture again that Jason described as a 'gentle leisurely ride'.

'... and hiking. It's such a dream come true. I love that you have the same passions as me.' He looked at me all dewy-eyed across the table and I tried to hold his gaze with confidence while my pulse raced. Oh no! I'd anticipated a proposal speech to be all about how happy I made him and how much he loved my company. Actually, that's effectively what he'd said, but I so hadn't seen it coming from that angle. I knew honesty was the foundation of a good relationship, but these were only little white lies, weren't they? I mean, I did regularly accompany him to the gym, but mainly because he worked shifts so I'd hardly see him if I didn't. And I did go hiking, but that's because I loved being in the countryside, not because I liked to trample twenty miles across it. Perhaps the time for confession wasn't when he was about to propose. It wasn't like that was all we had in common. We did loads of other things together. The gym and all that stuff was such a small part of what we did... wasn't it?

Thankfully Jason's scary fitness speech had ended. 'You know you mean the world to me so I wanted to make you really happy on your birthday. I racked my brains trying to think of the perfect gift. I wanted to give you something you really long for so... here it is. The one thing I know you really, really want...'

He reached into the pocket of his suit jacket. My heart leapt as he produced a small green velvet ring box. 'Happy birthday, Sarah,' he said, placing it in front of me.

'Is this—?'

'Open it and you'll see.'

With shaking hands, I eased open the lid. My stomach lurched as it opened wider and wider to reveal... What the...?

There wasn't an engagement ring inside.

There wasn't even a pair of earrings.

There was a small key.

I looked at Jason, then at the key, then back at Jason again. A thought struck me. He hadn't got down on one bended knee yet so maybe this was the start of an elaborate game to find the ring. It would be locked in a tin in a suitcase in a safe or something like that and I'd have to follow a trail of rose petals and fairy dust. How incredibly romantic.

He handed me an envelope. The first clue maybe? I tore the seal open and scanned the contents. Maybe not. My fist tightened, crumpling the edge of the paper.

Dear Mr Wilkes & Miss Peterson,

We're delighted to confirm your six-month premium membership at The Fitness Factor. This is a fantastic investment in your health and wellbeing. Your exclusive membership guarantees a place in our most popular classes – no waiting lists for you – as well as a weekly premium-members-only pool session and climbing wall session.

And you'll have exclusive use of your very own lockers for the duration. We're pleased to enclose your keys.

Finally, we'll be launching an exciting programme of outdoors adventures next year on which premium members will have priority booking.

Thank you for choosing The Fitness Factor. We look forward to welcoming you both as premium members very soon.

Your Fitness Factor Team

He hadn't, had he? Surely he hadn't bought me a gym membership for my birthday. A joint membership. A gift for him too. I felt nauseous as that random speech about keeping fit and the great outdoors suddenly had a context.

'What do you think?' Jason shuffled in his seat with obvious excitement. 'Is it the perfect gift or what?'

'It's great,' I said, my voice sounding an octave higher than usual. 'Thanks, Jase.'

'You're welcome. I knew you'd love it. How many times have you said you wished you had your own locker so you didn't have to remember to take your shampoo and stuff when you go for a swim or sauna?'

Cue flashback of us leaving the gym a couple of weeks ago. I mustn't have zipped my bag up properly because my shower gel clattered onto the tiled entrance floor, spurting citrus gunk everywhere. 'Do you know what I wish for right now...?' I said.

'I know six months is a big commitment,' he continued, 'but as we've been living together for two years, I didn't think it would be too big a step.'

I felt my shoulders sag and the energy seep from my whole being. So that's what he meant about plans for the future. A six-month gym contract. Not a lifetime together. Tears pricked my eyes and I rapidly blinked them away.

'That's not the only present I've got for you,' Jason said.

Maybe? He reached under his seat for something then pushed a sports shop carrier bag across the table with 'Love, Jason' scrawled across the front in marker pen. Maybe not. I peered into the bag and reluctantly pulled at the shiny leopard-print material. Oh. My. God. 'A leotard?'

'You'll look fantastic in that.' I really think he believed it.

I tentatively dangled the offending article over one finger and clocked the size 8–10 label. I wanted to scream at him: *When have I ever been a size 8–10? When have I ever liked leopard-print? When have I ever indicated that I'd like to wear a leotard instead of a baggy T-shirt and leggings? After more than two years together, don't you know me at all?* Yet all I said was, 'Thanks, Jason. It's lovely,' trying to sound as though I actually meant it. I suspected the accompanying smile looked more like a grimace, but Jason clearly didn't notice. He looked so pleased with himself.

'I knew you'd like it. I was only going to get you the gym membership, but when I was in the shop the other day, I spotted that in the sale and thought it was so you.'

How? How could he possibly think a leopard-print leotard was so me? I couldn't bring myself to look at him as I hastily shoved the Devil's gym kit back into the bag.

'Firefighter Wilkes!' A booming voice startled me. 'You come to my restaurant.'

'Mr Crocetti!' Jason stood up and embraced a large man wearing chef's whites.

'Luigi, please,' he insisted. 'And who is the *bella donna*? Your wife?'

'God, no!' Jason said. 'We're not married. She's just my girl-friend, Sarah.'

I stared at Jason, mouth open. '*God, no*'! Did he really just say that? And '*just* my girlfriend'? He did. He said, 'God, no!' That would mean the idea of getting married to me was... I couldn't finish the thought.

'*Buona sera,* Sarah.' Luigi reached for my hand and kissed it. 'Your man here, he save house. He save rabbit. He is hero.'

'He did what?' My head felt fuzzy. I needed some air, but I had a wall on one side and a loud Italian on the other.

'He save house. He save rabbit,' Luigi repeated.

'I was on a shout today,' Jason explained. 'Small fire in Luigi's garage. Their pet rabbit was overcome by smoke but I did mouth-to-mouth and—'

'He save rabbit. *Bambini* so happy. I say to him come to my restaurant any time. On the house. You choose anything. He suggest tonight. I say of course.'

'Thanks Luigi,' Jason said.

'Enjoy.' Luigi leaned over and patted my arm then pointed at Jason. 'Hero,' he said, bowing. Then he headed towards the kitchen.

I felt the colour drain from my cheeks as I stared at Jason. 'It's free?' I whispered. 'The meal? Champagne? Tonight?'

'I know. How great is that? Don't get mad at me, but I hadn't got round to booking anywhere so the timing was perfect. Like I could afford to bring you here again if it wasn't on the house.'

He grinned at me, clearly thrilled with himself and oblivious to the impact of his actions. I lowered my eyes to my hands, which were hanging limply in my lap, and focused on the bare engagement finger. It was never going to be a proposal. It was a last-minute freebie and I was such a stupid fool. Sighing, I covered my left hand with my right one.

'Are you okay?' Jason asked. 'You don't look very well.'

'I thought you were bringing me here to—'

'To what?'

I looked up from my hands. He genuinely looked flummoxed. He'd forgotten what happened here last time and what he'd said.

'Sarah? To what?'

'Nothing,' I muttered. 'It doesn't matter. Would you excuse me?' I stood up slowly, holding on to the table, fearing my legs wouldn't hold me. 'Must go to the ladies before the food arrives.'

Humiliation and disappointment burned at the back of my throat as I stumbled through the crowded restaurant. I fought hard to keep it together until I made it to the ladies, but I'd barely closed the cubicle door before the first heaving sob shook my body. Slumped on the toilet, I didn't care who heard. Anguished cries echoed off the marble walls and cocooned me in my pain.

Eventually the tears stopped flowing and the shaking subsided, but the pain in my heart remained. I blew my nose and wiped wearily at my wet cheeks. How stupid had I been to think he'd brought me here to propose? How could I have got it so wrong?

I rose slowly, dropped the pile of soggy tissues into the toilet pan, flushed it and watched the tissues disappear along with my hopes and dreams. The words he'd said to Luigi echoed in my mind. Not his wife; *just* his girlfriend? Where the hell could we go from here? Not up the aisle, that was for sure.

But a nagging voice in my head said, 'Don't get angry at him, Sarah. This is *your* fault. You've had over two years to tell him you don't love the gym or hiking or mountain biking like he does. What do you expect? The poor guy genuinely thought he'd bought you something you'd love because you led him to believe that you loved working out as much as him. This is your doing; not his.'

I didn't want to listen to that voice.

PART II

ONE YEAR LATER

2

I stood on the pavement staring down at the lower-ground-floor Victorian flat that Jason and I had rented for the last three years and twenty-three days. The keys dug into my palm while I watched the changing light of the TV screen flickering through the voile-covered window. A cold wind tugged at my coat and tickled my nose. I shivered and sniffed. Then I sniffed again, breathing in the unmistakeable aroma of a fresh, garlicky, homemade lasagne. Jason made a mean lasagne when we first met. He cooked a lot in the early days but now the freezer was packed with ready meals.

A feeling of nostalgia overcame me for those early happy days. Maybe the smell was coming from our flat. Maybe he'd have remembered it was my thirtieth and cooked as a birthday treat. Yeah, right. And he'd have done the washing up and vacuumed the flat. Was that a pig flying past? Jason was between shifts so would have spent a couple of hours at the gym followed by a bike ride and would now be lying on the sofa, game controller practically welded to his hands.

How had a whole year passed since the disastrous non-proposal? I'd returned to the table that night to find Jason tucking into his starter. If he noticed my red eyes and tear-stained cheeks, he never said a word. My sudden loss of appetite was embraced as more free food for him and my silence on the train home was put down to fatigue following a tough week at work. Had he really been that clueless?

I sat down heavily on the top step, trying to muster the strength to go inside, and rummaged in my bag for my phone. Instead of making me smile, my Facebook newsfeed full of birthday wishes acted as a depressing reminder of all that was wrong in my life: 'Happy 30th birthday. Hope Jason's taking you somewhere nice.' 'Happy 30th Sarah. Can he top Luigi's this year?' 'Hope you've had a fabulous day and that Jason has a weekend of pampering planned.' Chances of that: zero. Especially as he hadn't even acknowledged it was my birthday when I'd left for work that morning. Mind you, barely acknowledging each other had become our existence and I was exhausted from it.

Could I face another year like this? I didn't want to die all alone like my Uncle Alan, but was this really better than being alone?

A text arrived.

✉ From Elise
Our Jess and Lee are back from Rome and they're engaged!!! I'm at Minty's with them & Gary. Her diamond's bigger than mine. Outrageous! Look forward to speaking to you tomorrow to find out all about your big birthday night out xxx

My shoulders drooped even further. Elise's little sister was engaged? But she was six years younger than me. She couldn't be getting married. Not before me. But she'd clearly met the right person whereas I... I looked up at the window and shook my head. It was time.

Standing up, I brushed some dust off my skirt and made my way down the stone steps. I unlocked the door, stepped inside the hall, took a deep breath and announced as brightly as I could, 'Jason? I'm home.'

No answer. Just the sound of machine-gun fire. My hand moved towards the knob on the lounge door but I drew it back and headed for the kitchen instead. Perhaps a little Dutch courage first.

Given that the flat smelled more of sweaty socks than lasagne, I was right in my prediction that he wouldn't have prepared a meal. An overwhelming feeling of weariness took hold of my whole body as I slumped against the kitchen doorframe and surveyed the carnage. How did he do it? Useless, lazy, slobby... The damp washing festered in the machine. The A4 note I'd stuck to the front of the machine stating in large marker pen capitals, 'Please hang us up' lay on the worktop covered in crumbs and a coffee cup stain. Mugs languished in dull beige liquid in the washing up bowl. Banana peels, empty crisp packets and part-drunk glasses of squash obliterated the worktops.

I grabbed a half-empty bottle of wine from the fridge and took a large swig. A little shocked with myself for drinking from a full-size bottle of wine – what next, vodka out of a paper bag? – I reached into the cupboard for a glass, poured the rest and took a long glug. 'Happy thirtieth birthday, Sarah. Shaping up to be just as crap as your twenty-ninth.'

Stomach rumbling, I opened the fridge again and began rummaging. What could I eat? I settled on a jar of crunchy peanut butter even though I don't actually like the stuff. Spoon in hand, I heaved myself onto one of the uncomfortable stools at the narrow breakfast bar. Whoever designed the stupid things – undoubtedly a man – definitely didn't have size 16–18 bottoms in mind.

I gazed around the kitchen. A pile of cards and a couple of small packages lay next to the breadbin. Feeling like there was nothing 'happy' about my birthday, I left them where they were.

Twenty minutes later, Jason walked into the kitchen, yawning and scratching his bits. 'You're home.'

'Looks like it.'

I watched his eyes flick from me to the empty bottle of wine to the peanut butter. He didn't pass comment anymore but I knew what he was thinking whenever he caught me mid-binge: *No wonder you're fat. You were slim when we met. You went to the gym. You cared about your appearance. Now look at the state of you.*

'You've still got your coat on,' he said.

'Have I?' I hadn't realised. The only things I was aware of were how hungry I still was, how I had peanut butter welded to the roof of my mouth, how the wine had gone straight to my head, and how I'd lost all feeling in my left buttock. My right one probably wasn't far behind.

'What time is it?' he asked.

'Nearly ten.' I watched him reach for the fridge door and wondered why I used to think he was out of my league. He was certainly tall and dark but was he handsome? Not really. It was true what they said about personality. That fit body, which I once hadn't been able to keep my hands off, did nothing for me anymore. I was also blatantly aware that, after a year of comfort-eating, my body did nothing for him either... except perhaps repulse him. Working late for the past year to avoid facing up to the reality that Jason wasn't The One after all meant I got home too late to cook, so I lived on a diet of chocolate, crisps, doughnuts and takeaways. This took its toll on my bank balance, my figure, my confidence and our relationship. We argued constantly at first. Then we started ignoring each other so I ate more to comfort myself and... well, it was a pretty vicious circle.

He closed the fridge door. 'What's for dinner?' He flicked the top off a bottle of lager. It dropped to the floor where it lay on the tiles next to a tomato stalk and what looked like a blob of salad cream. He wouldn't pick it up. He didn't care. And, at that very moment, I realised that neither did I. I slid off the stool, reached for my post and said, 'I can't do this anymore, Jason.'

'Do what?'

'Live like this.'

'I haven't had time to clear up.'

'I don't mean the mess.' I looked up from my post and fixed my eyes on his. 'I mean our relationship. I want us to break up.' The minute the words left my mouth, I felt liberated. I felt light as a feather. I felt... Oh crap, he was about to protest.

'Are you serious?'

'Yes.' *Stay strong. Don't say it was just a suggestion. Don't agree to try again. You can do this. You may as well end it and be alone because what you have right now is not a relationship. You're like flatmates who don't even like each other.* 'We're not right for each other. This last year hasn't exactly been relationship heaven, has it?'

Jason stared at me, completely poker-faced. I willed him to say something. Agree. Protest. Shout. Cheer. Just do something. He gulped the rest of his drink down and banged the empty bottle on the worktop. Then he flashed me a dazzling smile and said, 'Well, thank God one of us finally had the guts to say it. Sarah, you're a life-saver. Do you fancy getting last orders in down at The Griffin? Don't look so shocked. Come on. I'll buy you a birthday drink.'

So that was that. Just over three years together had ended. No tears, no recriminations; just two drinks, a packet of Scampi Fries and an amicable conversation about what idiots we'd been to let it drag on so long. We agreed to give notice on the flat and sell the car, and I'd get custody of the cats.

I couldn't have felt more relieved that the ordeal was finally over although it had been so easy that I couldn't stop kicking myself for not having the guts to end it sooner.

Jason kissed me goodnight – a gentle peck on the cheek – then hailed a cab to a friend's house to avoid a night on the sofa and to give me some space to think.

Which is exactly what I did. In fact, I lay awake most of the night thinking. And worrying. About the important stuff like where I'd live, how quickly we'd sell the car and how we'd detangle our finances, as well as the little things that suddenly seemed important at 3 a.m. like who'd keep the tea-light holders we'd bought in Greenwich Market last summer and whether I'd have to pay Jason for his share of the cat scratching post.

Rain tapped gently on the window, then with more ferocity. The rhythmic drumming eventually sent me into a troubled sleep where I reverted to my thirteen-year-old self, shivering outside Uncle Alan's flat.

'Uncle Alan? It's only me,' I shouted through his letterbox.

Drops of icy rain from the overflowing guttering splashed onto my head and trickled down my neck. I sniffed as a large drop ran down my nose, then instantly recoiled from the letterbox, clutching my nose, as a stench akin to rotting meat hit me. Urgh! He must have left the chicken out of the fridge again. I held my breath as I lifted the flap again. 'I'm going to let myself in.'

Tucking the carrier bag containing the Sunday papers under my arm, I fished in my jeans pocket for the spare key and unlocked the door, bracing myself against the overpowering stench. My stomach lurched and I pressed my hand over my nose and mouth, thankful that I'd skipped breakfast.

'Uncle Alan?' I called through my fingers. 'Don't say you can't smell it this time.'

A few flies buzzed round my ears and I swatted at them with my hand. Placing my bag down in the hall, I slowly removed my waterproof and hung it on the peg next to the beige mac that he never left home without. My hands shook slightly as I eased off my wellies and called again, 'Uncle Alan? Are you being a grump again today? I won't help you with the crossword if you are.'

Heart thumping, I waited for his response. Nothing.

I swatted a few more flies before creeping down the hall towards the lounge at the back of the flat. 'Uncle Alan?' I paused just before the lounge doorway and listened again. Over the rain, the thunder, and the flies, I could hear the thump, thump, thump of my heart.

With my hand still over my nose and mouth, it took all my strength and courage to step from the hall into the lounge because the sinking feeling in my stomach told me that our regular Sunday routine was about to be broken forever.

The curtains were partially closed so the lounge was in darkness. I tentatively felt along the blown vinyl for the light switch. As my fingers reached the plastic casing, a flash of lightning lit the room like a floodlight. And that's when I saw him. Lying there. Over the thunder I heard a scream. A girl's scream – a terrified, pained sound.

I sat upright now, heart thumping, as a flash of lightning lit my bedroom. 'Uncle Alan?' I whispered. When the thunder crashed, I shivered and dived under the covers, clutching my teddy bear, Mr Pink, reminding myself that I was thirty years old, not thirteen. I needed to think positive thoughts. I needed to picture him alive instead. I needed to focus the routine we used to have. At 10 a.m. every Sunday, I'd announced my arrival through the letterbox, let myself in and headed for the lounge where I found him reclining in his favourite chair, dunking a plain digestive in milky tea. With a life controlled by diabetes, that plain digestive was his one weekly treat. A strawberry milkshake and a couple of chocolate digestives would be waiting for me. I admired his restraint at never succumbing to the chocolate ones himself. We'd have our drinks while I told him about my week at school and what I'd been doing in my after-school clubs, then I'd help him with the crossword. I say help but I certainly wasn't the brains of the partnership; my reading saved him the faff of putting on his glasses and my writing spared the arthritic aches in his hands. His body may have let him down but his mind was sharp with a million facts and details.

Another flash of lightning lit the room and, with it, a vision of Uncle Alan flashed into my mind – the lightning revealing the swollen face, the marbled yellowy-grey skin, the soiled trousers – and I shuddered. I wished I hadn't been the one who found him that day. But if I hadn't, it would have been Mum, Dad or my brother, Ben and I wouldn't have wished the gruesome discovery on any of them either. If only I could erase that image from my mind and picture him instead as the grump with a heart that I knew him to be, with a big frown but twinkly grey eyes that teared up each time I hugged him goodbye.

I blinked back my own tears that came so easily every time I thought of him. I should have visited more often. Once a week wasn't enough. He needed me. He had nobody but our small family. I wiped at a rogue tear and admonished myself. I was young, I did my best and he appreciated it.

Cowering under the duvet, my mind flitted between the day I'd found Uncle Alan and my current predicament with Jason.

When the storm finally subsided at dawn, I'd only reached one conclusion: I didn't want to be alone all weekend. The only close friend I had in London was Clare and she was away at a work event in Birmingham, which meant that home – the seaside town of Whitsborough Bay in North Yorkshire – was the place to run. Unfortunately, I'd picked up a voicemail from Mum to say that Dad had whisked her to Paris for the weekend and she hoped Jason had planned an equally romantic weekend for my birthday (oh, the irony). I couldn't therefore stay with my parents. I could turn to

Mum's sister, my Auntie Kay, though. There was no need to ring ahead because I knew exactly where she'd be. She was practically married to her business and never, ever took time off.

After throwing some clothes into a small case, I travelled the underground then caught the first train out of King's Cross.

I took one final deep gulp of fresh seaside air, then pushed open the door to Seaside Blooms – a florist's that Auntie Kay had opened twenty-five years earlier. The little bell tinkled joyously. I've always loved that sound, so welcoming and so intrinsically associated with home.

'Sarah! What are you doing here?' Auntie Kay gently put down the bridal bouquet she was arranging. She wiped her hands on her apron as she rushed out from behind the counter.

'Surprise!'

She launched herself at me. 'I was going to ring you tonight so it's perfect you're here.'

As I hugged her tightly, the floodgates, which had surprisingly stayed closed the night before, burst open.

'Sweetheart, what is it? What's happened?'

'Jason,' I whispered.

'Is he okay?'

'It's over.'

'Oh sweetie, I'm so sorry.'

The shop bell tinkled. Keeping my back to the door in case it was anyone I knew, I released Auntie Kay and rummaged in my bag for a tissue.

'Morning, Mrs Bates,' she said. 'Cathy will be with you in a moment. Cathy?'

Cathy appeared through the arch from the back of the shop, smoothing down her apron over her ample curves. She beamed when she saw me. 'Sarah! Kay didn't say—'

'Sarah's paid us a surprise visit,' Auntie Kay interrupted. 'But we just need a chat in The Outback. Can you see to Mrs Bates?'

'Of course.' Cathy, who'd obviously spotted the tears, gave me a sympathetic look and lightly patted my arm as she bustled past.

Auntie Kay bundled me into The Outback – the name Ben and I had given to the office/storage/kitchen area behind the shop after Auntie Kay's fondness for saying, 'I'm just going out back to make a cuppa' – and sat me down on her battered leather desk chair. She perched on the desk and waited while I composed myself.

'Sorry about that,' I said. 'I thought I was fine but maybe saying it aloud made me realise it was real.' *And that I'm alone. Again. Like Uncle Alan.*

'Who ended it?'

'Me.'

'Can I ask why?'

'You can, but maybe later. Is it okay to stay at Seashell Cottage tonight?' I had a key for Mum and Dad's but would far rather stay at Auntie Kay's cottage in the Old Town than be alone.

'Of course it is. There's always a bed for you there.'

Feeling much calmer, I gave my eyes another wipe and pushed some stray curls behind my ears. 'You've got a wedding today?'

'It can wait. You know I've always got time for my favourite niece.'

'I'm your only niece.'

'I'm sure you'd still be my favourite even if there were a dozen.'

I smiled. 'I wouldn't have disturbed you but apparently Mum and Dad are in Paris for the weekend.'

'Ah yes. The romantic break. Your dad surprised her with the tickets yesterday. Apparently it's thirty-five years since he proposed.'

I sighed. 'All right for some. Jason never whisks – whisked – me away on romantic weekends.'

'Then it's probably just as well you've ditched him. It's time to find someone who will.'

I shook my head. 'Maybe not just yet. I think I need to find me again first.' Even though that meant being alone for a while. Panic started to well and I repeated the mantra I'd developed when I was twenty-two and distraught by the break-up of my first serious relationship. *Alone as in single... but not lonely. I have friends. Alone as in single...* I stood up and took a deep breath. 'How about you get back to your bouquet, I'll make us all a drink and then I can give you a hand with the flowers?'

'Are you sure you don't mind?'

'I'm sure. I'll enjoy it.'

'Your help would be a godsend,' she said. 'There should have been four of us in, but Wendy's at a wedding and Gemma was a no-show. She says gastric flu but I say hangover. She's on a final warning and we're way behind. Bridesmaids' bouquets or buttonholes?'

'Buttonholes please. I've not slept so I don't think I'm awake enough to do justice to the bouquets.' The truth was I was worried about messing up. The situation at home had started to affect me in my job as a Marketing Assistant for a high street bank. I'd made a couple of careless mistakes recently and had been given a lecture on not bringing my personal problems into work. My confidence was at an all-time low.

As if sensing my crisis of confidence, Auntie Kay said, 'Tired or not, I know you can do this. You are, and always have been, the most naturally talented florist I've ever had the pleasure to train and you've got the qualifications to prove it. You could make those bouquets in your sleep with your hands tied behind your back. But I'll let you off seeing as you've had a traumatic birthday. You can start on the buttonholes, but if it gets busy I'll need to promote you to bouquets. And I need all the details about Jason while you work. I can't wait till later.'

A couple of hours later, Auntie Kay studied the three bridesmaids' bouquets, two children's posies and eight buttonholes I'd created. 'Tell me again why you don't work here. These are stunning. Those classes in *that* London have certainly been worth the money.'

It made me laugh when she referred to my home as '*that* London' in the same tone of disgust she might use to describe '*that* sexually transmitted infection'. She'd only visited me there once and I was left in no doubt that she thought it was one time too many. I'd never quite sussed whether it was specifically '*that* London' that she hated or the fact that I lived there instead of at home.

'I haven't done bouquets in a while,' I said. 'I'm quite pleased.'

'You should be. You say you've been to your flower club more often over the last year...?'

I nodded. 'Great Jason-avoiding activity.'

'Well, it has paid dividends. Hey, Cathy, come and look.'

Cathy ambled over. 'Sarah, they're gorgeous. You know what you should do?'

'No. What?'

'You should move back home and work for your auntie.'

'Did you two rehearse that?' I said, planting my hands on my hips in mock-indignation, but I couldn't help smiling. It was so lovely to feel wanted, especially after the past year with Jason when I'd felt anything but.

'I've no idea what you mean.' Auntie Kay looked at me all wide-eyed and innocent. 'But it's a good idea. Are you sure you don't want to?'

'Yes, Auntie Kay. I'm sure. Because—'

'I know, I know...' She winked at Cathy. 'Because floristry is just a hobby even though you're twice as talented as most professional florists I know. Because you don't live here anymore. Because you love *that* London. Because your job's there. Because Jason doesn't want to move.' She paused then added dramatically, 'Although Jason's out of the picture now, so...'

'Auntie Kay! This isn't my home anymore. I moved away twelve years ago.'

'And you could move back just as easily. I'd even brave another trip to help you pack your stuff. Cathy could hold the fort here, couldn't you Cathy?'

'Piece of cake,' Cathy said. 'Just name the date.'

'Stop it you two.' I put my hands over my ears and started humming until Auntie Kay made a zipping action across her mouth, lightly slapped her wrist and mouthed 'sorry'.

'I should think so too.' I took my hands off my ears.

'You'll change your mind about moving back here soon.'

'I doubt it. Thanks for the effort, though. I'd probably be offended if you didn't keep trying to convince me to stay. I'd think you didn't want me anymore.'

'Come here you.' She hugged me again. 'I'll always want my favourite niece around.'

'Hello. Is this a bad time?'

I hadn't heard the bell above the door tinkle so the male voice startled me. I looked round to see a man in a navy morning suit. He looked to be in his early thirties and was about six feet tall with thick dark hair, which he wore slightly spiky at the top. Very nice.

'Nick!' Auntie Kay gave him a kiss on each cheek. 'Goodness me, you scrub up well. Let's have a look at you.'

'Thank you.' Nick did a slightly awkward twirl. 'I think you're being generous, though. Don't most people look good in one of these things?'

In my opinion, yes they do, but Nick looked extra fine in his. My stomach did an unexpected flip as he looked towards me and smiled. For a fleeting moment, I was oblivious to anything except him and those blue eyes that twinkled like the ocean on a sunny day.

'You don't think I look like a blue penguin?' he asked, still holding my gaze.

No. Just a gorgeous hunk of loveliness. Whoa! Get a grip, Sarah. The guy's about to get married. Look away. Now.

Thankfully Auntie Kay spoke and Nick broke our gaze. 'Don't put yourself down. Some men look ridiculous in one and I've seen hundreds of them in this business. It really suits you. You're looking very handsome.'

She turned to me. *Oh no. Don't you dare.*

She dared. 'Isn't he, Sarah? Isn't he looking handsome?'

My cheeks burned. 'Yes stranger-who-I've never met, you look very "handsome" as my auntie puts it.'

Nick laughed, put out his hand and shook mine enthusiastically. 'Auntie? Then you must be Kay's niece, Sarah. I've heard loads about you. I'm Nick Derbyshire.'

'Hi Nick.' I reluctantly let go of his hand.

'Are you nervous, Nick?' Auntie Kay asked.

'Terrified. Especially about the speech. I wish I didn't have to speak first.'

'The groom doesn't usually speak first,' I blurted out. 'The Father of the Bride does.'

Nick smiled proudly. 'I *am* the Father of the Bride.'

'But... but you can't be much older than me.'

'I'm thirty-two.'

'Then you must have had your daughter very young.'

Auntie Kay laughed. 'He hasn't got kids. It's his sister's wedding.'

I frowned. 'But...'

'Our dad died when I was ten and Callie was six,' Nick said. 'I've been the father figure as well as her big brother so she asked me to give her away.'

'Oh, that's so lovely. I'm sorry about your dad, though.'

'Thank you. He'd have been very proud of Callie today.' He turned to Auntie Kay. 'Are the flowers ready?'

'Let me show you.' She led Nick to a large table behind the counter. 'Sarah did most of them,' she gushed, turning round and grinning at me. 'She's so talented. Aren't they gorgeous?'

My cheeks burned again. Could she be more obvious?

Nick turned and smiled at me. 'Very gorgeous.' There was something in the way he looked at me that made me think he wasn't talking about the flowers. *He can't mean me... can he? I'm far from gorgeous. I'm fat. My hair's a mess. My eyes are red and... no, he definitely means the flowers. I'm being silly. Hallucinating due to lack of sleep.*

The bell tinkled and a younger man in a matching suit poked his head round the door. 'Sorry, Nick. I'm on double yellows,' he said.

'Okay, best get going then.' Nick handed a box to the man then grabbed the other.

Auntie Kay pulled the door wide open for them both. 'Send my love to Callie,' she said. 'Tell her I want to see the photos. Good luck with the speech. They say you should picture your audience naked. Helps with the nerves.'

'Not a pleasant thought. You haven't seen my Uncle Clive.' He screwed up his face and shuddered. 'I can't dislodge that vision now. I may be traumatised for life. And on that note... thanks again for these, Kay.' He turned back and gave me a big smile. 'It was lovely to meet you at last, Sarah. You're exactly how I imagined. Hope our paths cross again.'

I smiled and waved, trying to ignore the butterflies in my stomach. *Calm down, Sarah. You're only having a reaction to him because you're now single and it's allowed. You're bound to be attracted to the first good-looking man who does you the courtesy of speaking to you. Especially when he's wearing a morning suit and has eyes the colour of the ocean and... stop it.*

Auntie Kay closed the door and made her way back to the counter. 'Such a lovely young man,' she said.

'He seemed pleasant enough.' I tried to sound nonchalant. I'm not sure if I pulled it off.

'He is. Very pleasant. Very lovely. You remember Alma Sutton who lived next door to me when you were little? She was Nick's grandma.'

'Small world.'

'He's such a sensitive young man, too. He comes in every year on New Year's Eve to pick up three bouquets of white roses and three loose stems. On New Year's Day, he puts a bouquet on the graves of his grandma, granddad and dad and he throws the single ones into the sea off Lighthouse Point to remember each of them.'

'That's very sweet and thoughtful of him.'

'He's single, you know.'

'Isn't he a bit young for you?'

'I don't mean for me.'

I planted my hands on my hips and gave her a mock-stern expression. 'I know exactly what you mean and I'm choosing to ignore it. I've already told you I'm not ready for dating and, even if I was, someone who lives four hours away wouldn't be top of my list.'

'You could move back home.'

'I think I'd need a slightly stronger reason to move back home than you trying to play Cupid.' I sighed and shook my head.

Auntie Kay didn't retort. Instead, she fiddled with my grandma's engagement ring, twirling it round and round on her finger. I narrowed my eyes at her. 'Are you okay?'

She stopped twiddling and took a deep breath. 'I said I was going to ring you tonight. It's time to tell you why.'

My stomach flipped but not in the nice way caused by Nick earlier – more of a foreboding way. I'd assumed she was going to call to ask me about my birthday, not because she had news. And possibly bad news if this rare display of nerves was anything to go by. Thoughts of terminal illnesses swam round my mind.

'You're making me nervous,' I said.

'Give me a minute.' She disappeared into The Outback and returned a few moments later clutching a bright red ring binder, which she handed to me.

'What's this?'

'You said it would take a slightly stronger reason for you to move home than a bit of matchmaking. Well, I've got one. You know how I always said you'd inherit Seaside Blooms when I'm gone and Ben would get Seashell Cottage?'

'Yes. And I always told you not to be so morbid.' *Oh God! She* is *ill. No!*

She twiddled with her ring again. 'I've changed my mind. I don't want to leave the business to you in my will. I want to give it to you now.'

'What?'

'I've had an unexpected opportunity to travel around the world with my friend Linda and I've decided to take it. I want to retire and I want you to become the new owner of Seaside Blooms. Pretty much immediately.'

4

'So you've finally had the sense to dump that eejit?' Clare unwrapped her scarf, slipped off her coat and handed me both. 'Could you not have left it there? Why pack in your job as well?' Without waiting for an answer, she marched into my bedroom.

I hung her coat up then followed her. She was stretched out on the bed, high-heeled brown suede boots dumped in the doorway. I tutted and moved them to the side.

'Don't you ever wear jeans like a normal person?' I asked, taking in her expensive-looking soft cream fitted jumper and short brown cashmere skirt. 'That doesn't look very practical for helping me pack.'

Clare propped herself up on her elbows. 'My role is to lie here and direct. Packing's a good chance for a clear-out so we'll start with your clothes. I'll tell you what you can keep. Don't look at me like that. I'm doing you a favour, so I am.'

'In what way?'

'By the time I'm finished, you'll have a lot less crap to fit in the van tomorrow.'

'How rude.'

'Although you won't need to worry about any of it if I can convince you to change your mind and stay.'

'I'm sorry.' I pushed her legs to one side so I could perch on the

bed. 'You know I'll miss you loads but this is too good an opportunity. I had to take it.'

She sighed. 'I know. I'm probably the one who should be saying
sorry.'

'For what?'

'For being such a crap friend.'

'Because you've been sulking all week?' I stuck my tongue out
at her.

'I've been a lot more crap than that.'

'You've been seeing Jason behind my back,' I joked.

She sat upright. 'Jesus! Are you mad? When I said I couldn't
stand him, I wasn't hiding some deep carnal lust. I genuinely
couldn't stand him.'

'Okay. Point made.'

She slumped back onto her elbows again. 'But I have been a
crap friend because I haven't been there for you. I've known how
miserable you've been at work and with Jason for the past year and I
haven't said anything to encourage you to talk about it.'

'You knew? How? I never said a word.'

'You didn't have to. I knew because I know you, Sarah. We've
been friends for twelve years and we lived together for three of
those. You don't know someone that well and not notice when
they're miserable.'

'So why didn't you say anything?' I demanded, feeling quite
miffed that she hadn't spoken up. 'You normally blurt out exactly
what you think so why keep quiet when your opinion might have
made a difference?'

She grimaced. 'Because of all this.' She pointed to the chaos of
part-packed boxes and crates spread around the room. 'I figured
that if I encouraged you to talk about your worries, you'd finally
come to your senses, ditch your man Jason and quit your job. So I
selfishly kept quiet because if you had no Jason and no job, why
would you want to stay in London with me? Especially when,
despite your protests, I know you've never really settled here. And
now I wish I *had* said something because you're leaving anyway and
I feel like a great big pile of crap for ignoring you when I knew you

needed me. So I'd understand if you're mad at me and want to throw me out.'

I slowly shook my head. 'If I was mad at you, I'd have to be mad at my parents, our Ben, Auntie Kay, Elise and everyone else I know because, if you noticed, any of them could have noticed and brought it up, yet nobody breathed a word. It wasn't your responsibility to force it out of me. If I'd wanted to talk about it, I'd have talked about it.'

'So we're good?'

I smiled reassuringly. 'We're good.'

Clare exhaled loudly. 'That's a relief. I could do with a drink after all that heavy stuff. Can I suggest you open a bottle of wine then tell me everything? Jason, job, floristry – the lot.'

'It's only eleven. Are you sure you don't want a coffee?'

'Wine please.'

When I returned with two glasses, Clare was fussing Kit and Kat who'd wandered in from the cold.

'About time too.' She held out her hand. 'It's like the Sahara in here.' She took a long gulp. 'That's better. Now take the weight off your feet and tell me all about the ditching of your man.'

'The packing?' I protested.

'The packing can wait. If you lend me a T-shirt I may even help you but first I need to know everything. Start with that gobshite.' She patted the bed and I obediently sat beside her.

'I might have made out that things were okay with Jason and me but, seeing as we're being honest about stuff, the past year has been seriously grim…'

Ninety minutes later, we'd emptied the bottle and Clare was up-to-date.

'You make out like it was some major decision about the shop,' she said. 'But you hate your job, you hate London and you're suddenly single. Surely your Auntie Kay's offer was a no-brainer. I doubt many people get handed a successful business for free doing something they absolutely love.'

'I don't *hate* any of those things. I just don't love them anymore.' Clare raised an eyebrow. 'Okay,' I said. 'It's semantics but it was a really tough decision. There were pros and cons to each.'

'Don't tell me you got your Post-it notes out.'

I rolled off the bed and opened my wardrobe doors. Stuck to the inside of the left door were a stack of brightly coloured Post-it notes listing the pros and cons of staying in London and, on the right door, a Whitsborough Bay list. I pointed to them. 'Busted!'

Clare picked up her glass again, drained it and then put it back down. 'I can't believe you make all your major life decisions through Post-it notes.'

'It helps structure my thinking.'

She shook her head. 'I trust I'm top of your pros list for staying here?'

'Of course. In capitals.'

'I should think so too.' She squinted across the room. 'I don't believe it. You've colour coded them this time, haven't you?'

'And my pen colours,' I said, realising too late that it probably wasn't something to be proud of.

'That is so pitiful, I could cry for you. Remind me again why I'm friends with you?'

I smiled. 'Because nobody else will put up with your bolshiness.'

'Fair point.' She stood up and headed towards the wardrobes then turned around again and nodded at her glass. 'I'm empty.'

When I returned, she was standing in front of the wardrobe looking down the lists.

'I see Elise is at the top of your pro list for home and your con list for here,' she said without turning around.

'And, as already stated, you're at the top of my con list for home and my pro list for here,' I said.

'I suppose.' She shut the wardrobe doors. 'I could have helped you move your stuff home, you know. You didn't have to enlist her.'

'Her uncle has a van. It made sense for her to drive it down rather than hire one and have the dilemma of where to return it to.'

'When's she coming?'

'Tomorrow at lunchtime. She'd have come today but there's some family thing she can't avoid.'

'In that case, I'll reluctantly help you pack today providing you keep the wine flowing, but you'll have to manage without me tomorrow.'

'Fine.'

'Fine. Glad we've got that sorted. Will you start packing now or are you going to waste the rest of the day gossiping?'

I opened a drawer and threw an old T-shirt to her. While she changed, I pulled a chair over to the wardrobe to climb on, trying to push aside her negativity towards Elise. It hurt that my two closest friends hated each other and I was always stuck in the middle.

Elise had been my best friend since our first day at primary school. I'd retreated to a corner of the classroom, sobbing my heart out after my mum left me. The teacher had obviously lost patience in trying to soothe me and had left me to it. After thirty minutes or so, I had no tears left but was too scared to join any of the other children playing, so I'd sat with my head buried under my jumper until a gentle voice said, 'Will you play in the sand pit with me, please?' I'd pulled my jumper off my head and looked up to see a pretty little redhead standing over me with a bucket and spade in one hand and her other hand outstretched to take mine.

My friendship with Clare had also been forged while I was in tears but many years later on my first day at Manchester University. My parents had just left me in the dark, grotty room that was to be my home for the next year. Surrounded by boxes and suitcases and wondering where to start unpacking, the enormity of leaving home to live in a huge city hit me and a feeling of absolute loneliness engulfed me. I suddenly pictured myself like Uncle Alan, all alone, with no friends and nothing to do but sit in the library studying. The floodgates opened. I jumped when an Irish voice declared loudly, 'Jesus, I thought my room was a shit-hole but yours definitely wins the prize for dump of the year.'

I looked up to see a tall girl leaning against the doorframe. She was the most stunning female I'd ever seen in real life: legs up to her armpits, long blonde hair so shiny that she looked fresh out of a shampoo advert, and eyes as green as emeralds. 'I'm Clare O'Connell.' She didn't wait for me to give my name, just continued talking. 'Have you never heard of travelling light? Jesus, how many suitcases and boxes does one girl need? You'd think you were here for ten years at a time, not ten weeks.' She moved over to a crate holding my CDs and started rummaging. 'At least your taste in music is okay.

Oh, wait. I spoke too soon. This album is a bag of shite.' She picked out a CD – can't remember what now – and tossed it in the bin. Through my tears, I stared at her then at the bin. I didn't know whether to shout at her or laugh.

'It'll take you forever to get all this crap in order and there are far better ways we could be spending our time right now. We're off to the pub.'

'Are we?' I'd never met anyone that confident and didn't know how to react. She was scary... but also quite exciting.

'Might as well start as we mean to go on,' Clare continued. 'Grab your purse, wipe that snot off your face, and let's go. First beer's on you and you'd better not tell me you don't drink pints. Or even worse, that you don't drink at all. Because if that's the case, we're not going to be friends.'

'I drink, but...' I tailed off. I didn't dare confess I'd never had a pint in my life. University was going to be full of learning experiences and perhaps drinking pints was one I should embrace.

Six hours and way too many pints of Irish ale later – another new learning experience – Clare and I started a lifelong friendship. I also started a horrendous hangover.

I'd automatically assumed that my two best friends would bond immediately. Elise visited me at university the following term and I couldn't wait to introduce them. The first hour in the pub seemed to go well but I returned from the ladies to find them in a heated debate about the value of marriage. It had been handbags at dawn ever since.

'Ready,' Clare said, pulling me back to the present. 'You can start passing stuff down.'

I handed down boxes and crates from the deep top shelves.

'What's in all of these?'

I shrugged. 'Haven't a clue. Mum and Dad brought them down last year. They got sick of nagging Ben and me to clear out our old bedrooms so they could re-decorate so they did it for us.'

Clare looked at the pile she'd just created. 'It's all your child-hood crap then? Are we going to find naked Barbie dolls with shaved heads and dodgy old school photos?'

'Possibly. A lot of it can probably be ditched.'

Clare knelt on the floor and started rummaging through a crate. 'This one's boring,' she said a few minutes later.

'What's in it?' I looked up from the box of old board games I'd found.

'Mainly old schoolbooks. I want an interesting box.'

'I'm not sure any of them will be interesting. Why don't you try that cardboard one?'

Clare crawled over to the box, ripped off the parcel tape and started rummaging. 'Ooh, what's this?'

I looked up as she pulled out a rolled-up piece of pale pink paper with a dark pink satin ribbon tied round it, like a scroll.

Oh no. She's found my—

'"Life Plan of Sarah Louise Peterson, age almost fourteen,"' she read as she unfurled it. 'You have got to be jesting.'

I put my hands over my eyes and felt my cheeks burn my palms. Trust me to direct Clare to the most embarrassing box in the world ever. She wanted interesting? She'd just found it.

Life Plan of Sarah Louise Peterson, age almost 14

Age 20–21: Meet gorgeous, kind, generous, funny, rich boyfriend with dark hair and blue eyes

Age 22: Get engaged (Update Age 22: Big fat fail. Single now. Try 26???)

Proposal: On a red dragon boat on the boating lake in Hearnshaw Park. (Update Age 22: proposal abroad – Venice? Rome?)

Ring: Gold with sapphires and diamonds (Update Age 22: platinum with solitaire diamond)

Age 24: Get married in pretty church. Reception in Sherrington Hall

Dress: Big white dress with puffy sleeves and long train. Wear tiara and veil. Hair piled in curls on top of head. Princess for the day! (Update Age 22: ivory dress with short train, no puffy sleeves and perhaps not so BIG! Yes to sparkly tiara. Still want to be a princess!)

Bridesmaids: Lots of bridesmaids wearing peach frilly dresses with big sleeves (Update Age 22: Eek! Just Elise and Clare. NOT peach! Definitely no frills or big sleeves)

Age 26: First child – boy

Age 28: Twins – one of each

Age 30: Fourth child – girl

(Update Age 22: 2 children. What was I thinking?! And might need to revise age due to engagement fail)

Animals: A dog, 2 cats and a rabbit

Home: Cottage in Old Town with sea views, garden, roses round the door – just like Auntie Kay's

Life: Will live happily ever after with husband who adores me just like Mum & Dad and have children who are funny, clever and beautiful. Will NOT be alone like Uncle Alan. Ever.

I swear it took twenty minutes before Clare managed to finish reading it out loud – essential for maximum humiliation effect – because she was laughing so much.

'My sides hurt,' she said finally, wiping her eyes. 'I don't know what's most funny – you writing it in the first place or you taking the time to update it in your twenties. *In your twenties.* And you called yourself a princess. *In. Your. Twenties.*'

'It was an important document at the time.' I folded my arms and glared at her. I meant it. Written shortly after I'd found Uncle Alan, my Life Plan had been deadly serious and was my way of avoiding ending up like him. I'd really believed it would happen. 'And I'll just point out that I was an emotional wreck after splitting up with Andy when I added to it. And very drunk. You know I wasn't in a good place after it ended with him.'

Clare nodded. 'I remember. So, Sarah Louise Peterson, aged thirty-and-eight-days, what exactly have you achieved off your Life Plan?'

'Two cats.' I looked towards Kit and Kat curled up on the duvet. Tears pricked my eyes from the overwhelming disappointment of it all. 'How useless am I?' My voice caught in my throat.

'Not useless,' Clare said softly. 'Sad? Yes. Pathetic? Yes. An eejit? Yes. But not useless.'

'I think there's a compliment in there. Somewhere.' I smiled weakly.

'There is.'

We sat in silence for a while.

'What if I never meet someone?' I said eventually. What if I never get married and have kids?'

'Then you don't get married and have kids,' she said, shrugging. 'So what? You can't force these things. Actually, you can, but you wouldn't get your happily ever after. Would you rather be married to your man Jason right now with a gremlin on the way and be miserable, or would you rather be single again with the possibility that it may or may not happen?'

'Neither. I'd rather be single than with Jason. Definitely no regrets there. But I don't like the thought of that being the case for the rest of my life. I always wanted to marry and have a family.'

'That's pretty obvious from reading this.' Clare rolled the scroll up again, put the ribbon round it and gently placed it back in the box. 'I know you won't want to hear this, but you need to get over this ridiculous obsession with getting married. It's not the answer to life, the universe and everything you know.'

'And you'd know that because you've been married how many times?'

Clare closed the flaps on the box and pushed it aside. 'None,' she said, 'as you well know. But that's not the point. I know plenty of married people and, believe me, it's not the happily ever after you seem to have built it up to be.'

'It is for some.'

'Like your parents? I think you'll find they're pretty unique. I know you see them as your role models and you want the same, but surely even you must realise that what they have is *not* the norm.'

'Maybe not. But it shows that true love and true compatibility exists.'

'For a *very* small minority of people. For most people, marriage ends in divorce.'

'Cynic.'

'Realist. And if they don't divorce, they trundle on with neither party making the other happy but not quite being miserable enough to call it quits. Don't look at me like that. It's a fact. And the very notion of having a written plan that says you must be married at a certain age... Really? Seriously, Sarah, if it happens it happens. If it doesn't, it doesn't. Get used to it.'

I sighed. 'The thing is, I know I don't *need* a man to fulfil some missing gap in my life but I *want* to meet someone special. I *want* the happily ever after.'

'Need. Want. What's the difference?'

I thought for a moment. 'Remember our last shopping trip. You didn't *need* those expensive beige shoes but you *wanted* them, didn't you?'

'Beige shoes? I take it you're referring to that stunning pair of nude Manolo Blahniks?'

'Whatever. Shoes are shoes.'

'Wash your mouth out.'

'Do you see my point?'

'I guess so. Although I still maintain I both wanted *and* needed those shoes.'

'Of course you did. Because you only own two hundred pairs already.' I twiddled with my ponytail. 'There's one other reason why I want to meet The One. As it says on the plan, I don't want to end up like my Uncle Alan.' What killed me about his death was that the autopsy revealed a massive hypo three days before I found him. Three days. Poor man. I tried not to think about how long he'd been on the floor, knowing he was dying, before taking his final breath. All alone. What a horrific way to go.

'It's tragic about your uncle. And I genuinely do get why that would—'

Ding dong.

Clare and I looked at each other.

'You expecting someone?' she asked.

I shook my head and scrambled to my feet.

'If it's Mr Right, tell him his timing's impeccable.'

I flung open the door to find Elise on the doorstep a day ahead of schedule.

5

'I hope that's a surprised face and not a disappointed one,' Elise said.

'Of course it is. Sorry. I wasn't expecting you till tomorrow.' I hugged her. 'I thought you had some family thing.'

'I did, but Gary didn't like the idea of me driving both ways in one day so he insisted I give it a miss. I thought I'd surprise you and help you pack. I hope that's okay.'

'Of course it is.' I bit my lip. 'But I'd better warn you that—'

'Hello Elise. How are you?'

—that Clare is here. Oh crap.

'Clare? What a delight. I'm good, thanks. You?'

'Couldn't be better,' Clare said. 'No hubby today? I thought you two were welded together.'

'We have our own lives too, you know. That's what makes a relationship successful. Oh, but you wouldn't know, would you?'

'Elise!' That was so unlike her. Somehow Clare always managed to bring out a nasty streak in Elise that I'd never seen surface with me or anyone else.

'Doesn't bother me,' Clare said. 'I'd rather have a hundred one-night-stands than get hitched at eighteen to the only man I've ever kissed.'

'Well, it bothers me.' I held a hand up at each of them. 'You've had your childish fun and now you can play nicely. Or you can leave.'

'But—' started Clare.

'But nothing. You can either apologise and be civil to each other in which case you can both stay. Or you can both leave now. Which is it to be?'

'Sorry, Sarah,' Elise said. 'I got lost and I'm a bit stressed.'

'Apology welcome, but it's Clare you need to say sorry to.'

Elise stiffened as she turned towards Clare. 'I'm sorry, Clare. What I said about your lack of relationships was unnecessary.'

Clare ran a hand through her expensively styled bob: her signature move when in the presence of other females. I knew her apology would be insincere, but at least it was forthcoming.

'Thank you, Elise,' she said. 'Although you do speak the truth and I'm not in the least offended as that's how I choose to live my life. I don't need a man as a permanent fixture. Unlike some people.'

Elise casually removed the bobble from her hair. Her long auburn curls tumbled out. What was it with those two and their hair? If they were cats, they'd be peeing up the walls to mark their territory.

'I applaud you, Clare,' Elise said. 'You didn't apologise. In fact, you managed to add another insult in there.'

'Yes, well, if the cap fits...' said Clare with a toss of her hair. 'It's Sarah's last day in London and I want to be here so I'm prepared to call a truce if you are.'

Elise nodded. 'Fine by me.'

'Right,' I said. 'That was delightful as always. Repeat it and you both leave. Understood?'

'Yes, Mum,' Clare said.

'Understood,' Elise said.

'Glass of wine or cup of tea?' I asked Elise.

Elise looked at her watch and frowned. 'Tea please.'

'Wine please,' Clare said, then disappeared back into the bedroom as Elise and I headed for the kitchen.

Drinks made, we found Clare on the floor, ripping the tape off another cardboard box. 'It's like Christmas,' she said. 'Will this be a good gift or a rubbish one?' She peered in and moved a few things.

'Books. Rubbish one. What's in that bag?' She crawled across the floor.

What bag? I only got boxes out. My eyes flicked in the direction she was heading. A large white paper bag with rope handles lay on the floor. *No! Not that.*

But Clare had already pulled the pink box out of the bag. I cringed at the purple glitter lettering sparkling on the lid. '"Sarah's Treasures",' she read. 'Now *this* looks interesting. What's in here?'

'Nothing.' I tried to grab the box off her but she was having none of it.

She prised the lid off. 'Ooh. Hot, hot, hot.'

Ground, swallow me up.

'Are those firefighters?' Elise asked. 'From the calendars?'

'Might be.' In honour of my fireman obsession, Elise had bought me the firefighters' calendar for Christmas four or five years in a row when we were in our teens. At the end of each year, I ripped out my favourites to keep and gaze upon during low moments.

While I lounged on the bed, mortified, Clare and Elise spent the next ten minutes or so debating over whom was the hottest. Boredom finally set in. 'What else is in here?' asked Clare.

'To be honest, I can't remember.' I put my wine down and joined them on the floor. 'I haven't looked in it for years.' They both looked at me with raised eyebrows. 'Okay, I may have had the odd peek at the gorgeous young firemen, but I haven't looked at anything else.' I leaned over Clare and rummaged in the box. 'Concert ticket stubs, cinema tickets, valentine cards.'

'What's this?' Clare bent forwards and picked up a CD. 'Mix CD of lurve songs from an ex?'

'I don't think so,' I said. 'No one's ever made me one. Does it say anything on it?'

'"Mandy's Party",' Elise read. 'Mandy from college?'

'Must be. I don't know any other Mandys.'

'Only one way to find out,' Clare said. 'Have you got a CD player?'

'There's an old one in that box of games by the window,' I said, pointing to it.

Elise was closest so she crawled over to the box and pulled out a small pink radio/CD player covered in stickers. I plugged it in by the bed and popped the CD in. 'I bet it's something hideously cheesy. Mandy loved novelty tunes so we may need to do some selective listening.'

Only it wasn't music. It was a recording I swear I'd lost twelve years previously. And it was about to completely change my already turbulent life.

6

The CD played static for a few moments before a gentle Cornish female voice kicked in.

'Hello Sarah, my name's Madame Louisa. It's the twenty-second of April. Your friend, Mandy, has asked me to do a reading for all her friends as a memento for her eighteenth birthday. It will be a general reading covering the next ten to fifteen years.'

'Oh my God.' I pressed the pause button. 'It's the clairvoyant CD. But I lost it. How the hell...?'

Elise looked as shocked as I felt. 'We trashed Mandy's house and yours looking for that.'

'I know! So how did it get in there?'

'What is it?' Clare asked. 'Did you say clairvoyant?'

'Yes.'

'From when you were eighteen?'

'Yes.'

Clare rubbed her hands together. 'This should be interesting. And who's this Mandy? I've never heard you mention her.'

'She was a friend at college but we lost touch. She had this clairvoyant party. Her mum was into stuff like that. We'd been drinking cocktails all evening and, by the time I went in, the room was spinning. I had my reading, came out, fell over, threw up and my dad had to collect me. The next day I couldn't remember a thing about my reading. We're talking major alcohol blackout here, but I figured it was no problem because I had a CD. Only the CD had gone missing and remained missing until right now.'

Clare sighed. 'Things don't just disappear then re-appear. You obviously didn't look hard enough and—'

'But we did,' I protested.

'Obviously not,' Clare said. 'Let's hear it then.'

'I don't know if I want to.'

Clare raised her eyebrows at me questioningly.

'She said the reading would cover ten to fifteen years. It's twelve years on now. What if she predicts bad things are about to happen?'

She shuffled her bum round so she could lean against the wardrobe and face Elise and me. 'Or, what if she just comes out with an absolute pile of crap? I know what I'll be betting on.'

'What do you think?' I asked Elise.

'You never know till you try,' Elise said. 'There's always the eject button if you don't like what you hear.'

I looked from one eager face to the other, my two best friends united in opinion for once, but I still hesitated. What if she said I was going to contract an incurable disease aged thirty-and-a-half? What if she said the biggest mistake I ever made was taking over Seaside Blooms and I'd end up homeless and bankrupt? And what if she said I was never going to meet Mr Right or that I'd already met him and let him slip through my fingers? Andy perhaps?

'I don't know,' I said eventually.

Clare sighed. 'Jesus, Sarah. What's the worst that could happen?'

'That's what I'm worried about.' A flashback hit me. 'Uncle Alan,' I gasped. 'I spoke to him.'

'You did what?' Clare asked.

'When I came out of the reading, I told everyone I'd spoken to him.'

'I remember that,' Elise said. 'But you didn't tell anyone what he said…'

'And I couldn't remember the next day.'

'Well, now's your chance to find out,' Clare said.

I took a deep breath and leaned forward. With shaking hands, I pressed play again.

'Let me explain what's going to happen. I'll be using my crystal ball to help me, as well as a guide from the spirit world. I'm recording our discussion so you can listen to what I say on another day in the quietness of your own home where it will be easier to take in. Although I've been asked to give you a general reading, is there anything you'd rather I focus on? Any burning questions?'

'Er no, well, erm... maybe work and men?'

'You sound so young,' Elise squealed, 'and drunk.'

I hung my head in embarrassment at the sound of my childish squeaky voice and the slurred words. This was going to be cringe-worthy.

'Work and men?' repeated Madame Louisa. 'I can certainly make sure I cover those topics. Let's start. I'm contacting the spirit world. I have a lady with me. An elderly lady. She says she's on your mum's side of the family.'

'My grandma?'

'She says yes.'

'Bollocks,' Clare said.

I pressed pause. 'What is?'

'You led her. She mentioned an elderly lady and you immediately let her know your grandma is dead so now she can pretend it's your grandma she's communicating with.'

I scowled at her and pressed play again.

'She says you look like your mum and that, if you find the photo taken at the lighthouse, you'll see that you look just like your grandma too, except you don't have the heart shaped birthmark on your cheek that she has.'

Goose bumps pricked my arms. I wasn't familiar with the light-house photo – I'd have to ask Mum about that – but I could clearly remember the birthmark. I stared at Clare, trying to mentally convey that the birthmark couldn't be a lucky guess, but she wouldn't catch my eye.

'Your grandma says she hopes you enjoyed your drinks but doesn't envy you the headache you'll have tomorrow.

'You're a warm and caring person, Sarah. You're always there for your friends and you're a great listener, doing your agony aunt bit when they're in trouble. Your friends always come to you first with their prob-

lems and you like feeling you can help. Yet, when you have a problem yourself or are worried about anything, you put on a brave face and try to work through it by yourself or you bury your head in the sand, hoping things will get better on their own. This approach doesn't work. As you get older, you'll realise that being more open about your doubts could have prevented you from getting stuck in a rut with your job and your relationship.

'In years to come you'll find yourself in a relationship that should never have lasted as long as it did. It would never have lasted that long if you'd talked to your friends about your concerns.

'You need to hold on to the beliefs you have of love and marriage because you will find it; it will just take quite a bit longer than you'd hoped in your great plan of life. But, when you find the right one, you'll have exactly what your parents have; just like you long for.'

I stopped the CD and looked at Clare then Elise. 'Do you think she could be talking about Jason? And she mentioned my life plan. And my parents.'

Elise nodded but Clare just pulled a face that I knew meant, 'What a pile of crap'.

'Will you just press play, please?' Clare said. 'I don't think we need to be analysing every sentence, do we? And she didn't say "life plan". She said, "your great plan of life" which is very general and very different, so it is.'

'You're very close to your family. I see two mother figures in your life. Do you have a stepmother? No. Not a stepmother but definitely a mother figure. Godmother? I see her surrounded by flowers. Do you know who I'm talking about?'

'My Auntie Kay. She owns Seaside Blooms on Castle Street. She's my auntie and my godmother.'

'I see. She's a very important influence on your life, isn't she? She'll be pivotal when you reach your thirties but I'll come back to that later. We'll return to the more immediate future for now. You're going to university after college. You're currently planning to become a teacher.'

'Did Mandy tell you that?'

'No. As I said, the spirit world and the crystal are guiding me.'

Clare raised her hand and I pressed pause again. 'Well, that was a load of old tosh.' She pointed at Elise. 'She's the teacher, not you.'

Elise and I exchanged looks.

'At the time the CD was made, I *did* want to be a teacher,' I said.

'But you did business studies. You wanted a job in marketing or PR like me.'

'I know. But I *used* to want to be a teacher.'

'Since when?'

'Since I was little.'

'We both wanted to be teachers,' Elise said. 'I wanted to teach English and drama but Sarah wanted primary school.'

I nodded. 'College released me for work experience after my exams finished and I hated it. As soon as I got my A level results, I went through clearing. I thought business studies would help keep my options open.'

'Can't imagine you as a teacher,' Clare muttered. She held out her glass. 'I need a top up.'

'The bottle's empty.'

'Drink.'

I sighed and headed for the kitchen to reluctantly open a third bottle. I returned to a heated debate.

'It's lucky guesses,' snapped Clare.

'It isn't. It's a gift,' Elise insisted.

'Bollocks.'

'That's intelligent, Clare.'

'It's more intelligent than some charlatan pretending she can predict the future.'

'Just because you don't understand something, it doesn't mean it isn't true,' Elise retaliated.

'And a few lucky guesses don't mean it's true either. Plus she said Sarah wanted to be a teacher when Sarah obviously didn't want to be one so it's not even accurate.'

'She said Sarah was *planning* to become a teacher which, at the time, she was.'

'You're just trying to fit things to—'

They both stopped when I coughed loudly. Elise muttered 'sorry' and Clare just looked at me with sad eyes. Without a word, I topped up Clare's glass then pressed play again.

'You're the sort of person who'll always work hard and make sure they

do their best in their career. You won't become a teacher, but you'll still go to university. After graduating, you'll stay in the city where you studied, then move to London with work a few years later. After many years of the same career in the same company, your auntie will offer you an opportunity, out of the blue, to make a fresh start and make a career out of something you love. It will be something completely different to what you're used to and will enable you to use the creativity that your job stifled. The opportunity will be presented to you when you've reached a crossroads in your life and, even though you're desperate for a change, you'll feel like you shouldn't take it. It will excite you and scare you at the same time. You'll doubt you can do it, but you should know that you have what it takes to be an amazing success at it.'

There was a short pause and I realised that my heart was thumping rapidly. This had to be the weirdest thing ever, listening to someone summarise my life – though at the time, it had been predictions.

'Let's move on to the other subject you wanted to discuss. Men, was it? You haven't had much success with men so far but remember you're still very young. University will be an awakening for you with many intelligent, interesting men. A friend will become very special and you'll be together throughout university.'

I pressed stop and was about to say his name when someone beat me to it.

'Andy,' Clare said. She looked surprised as if she hadn't meant to say it aloud. She quickly added, 'I only said that because you were about to and not because I believe in anything she's saying. Another lucky guess. Lots of relationships start with friendship.'

Nice back-pedalling, Clare. She was right, though. It had to be Andy. Feeling warm and fuzzy as I always did when I thought about him, I pressed play again.

'It will be an intense and passionate relationship. You'll both think you've found The One and that you'll always be together, but it will end after university. It will be very hard getting over him, but, over the years, the hurt will lessen and you'll strike up a friendship again. You'll often wonder about trying again, Sarah, but the timing will never quite work.'

'That's definitely Andy and that's frighteningly accurate,' I whispered. I felt a bit shaky and sat on my hands to steady them. It couldn't be a more accurate summary of Andy and me if I'd written it myself. 'You can't just say that's a lucky guess, Clare, surely?'

'Hasn't everyone had a first love that they always wonder "what if...?" about? That's basically all your woman there is saying.'

'I disagree,' Elise said.

'You would.'

There will be a few more short-term relationships before you meet someone else who you think is The One. He may wear the uniform of your dreams, but he still isn't The One for you. It will take you a long time to accept this but, when you do, the ending will be quick and a whole new chapter in your life will start. This is the person I was talking about earlier.'

'Will I ever get married? All I've ever wanted to do is get married.'

'I know you have. I know you don't want to end up alone like your uncle and you won't. You're nothing like him. In the new chapter of your life, you'll get together with someone very special. He'll have the looks and personality you've always hoped for and treat you with such care and respect. Would you like to know his name?'

'Do you know it?'

'Yes. It is Steven.'

'Steven?'

'Yes. But beware, Sarah, your grandma's saying that it won't all be plain sailing. In this new chapter of your life, there'll be options presented to you and one key moment when you have to pick between two special men – one who meant a lot in your past and one who means a lot in your present – forcing you to choose between the familiar and the unknown. Make sure you follow your heart, not your head. Following your heart will lead you to the true Steven.'

'Can you tell me anything else about Steven? Where will I meet him? When? Will I know it's him straightaway?'

'I'm afraid your time's up, Sarah. All I'll say is that your grandma's telling me you won't get together until you turn thirty and that you must be patient and remain hopeful.'

'Thirty? That can't be right; I'm getting married when I'm twenty-four.'

'We'll see, Sarah. I know that's what your Life Plan says but life doesn't always turn out as we plan. Enjoy the ride.'

'Surely there's something else you can tell me about Steven. How will I know it's him? Steven's a common name.'

'The name isn't that important. Your grandma says you'll just know he's The One. I'm going to give you this CD and I suggest you put it somewhere safe and listen to it on your own in a week or so when you can really think about what I've said. Or perhaps when you hit your crossroads and it finds its way back into your life.'

'Okay. Thanks.'

'Your grandma says night-night and to please send her love to her two little girls and her grandson. She also says your mum will be devastated in the future when she can't find your grandma's bracelet. It's not lost. It's under the sofa. Goodbye Sarah.'

'Thanks again.' I could hear the sounds of chairs screeching on the CD, telling me I'd got up to head for the door.

'Oh, Sarah! Stop a moment. I'm getting a message through for you from the man I mentioned earlier. Your uncle.'

'Uncle Alan?'

'Yes. He says he's so sorry that you were the one who found him. He'd give anything to not have scared you like that. He wants you to know that, although he may have been grumpy sometimes, the time you spent with him meant so much to him, and... Sorry, Sarah, he's gone now and this doesn't make sense to me. He says he still has one every week, but now it's a chocolate one. Do you know what he means?'

'A digestive. A chocolate digestive.'

With very shaky hands I leaned forwards and pressed the stop button before slumping back against the bed. 'There's no way she could have made that up,' I said. 'No way at all.'

7

'I still can't believe you're here,' Auntie Kay said while we waited at the counter of The Chocolate Pot on Monday morning. 'And so quickly. I thought you'd have to work a month's notice.'

'I did too, but I was owed a stack of holiday so my manager agreed to a week.'

'That was lucky.' Auntie Kay paid and handed me a cup of hot chocolate and a bag with a croissant in it. 'Saves us rushing to cram everything in before I fly.'

'I felt bad about abandoning Clare so quickly. I'm worried about her being lonely.'

'It's sweet that you worry about your friends, but I'm sure she'll be fine.'

We headed slowly up Castle Street towards Seaside Blooms. I smiled as the autumn sun warmed my face and breathed deeply to take in the fresh sea air. Instead of feeling stressed at the unknown that lay ahead, I felt content and relaxed. Definitely the right decision.

'Good to be home?' she asked.

'So far, so good. It feels almost as if I never moved away.'

Arriving in front of Seaside Blooms, Auntie Kay handed me her drink and pastry while she rummaged in her bag. 'You should invite

Clare up here soon if you're worried,' she said. 'Make her feel like she's part of your new life. Let her escape from *that* London.'

'I've already invited her up for the weekend. She said I have a new life and need time to settle in, but I managed to convince her. I hope she doesn't cancel on me.'

'I'm sure she won't, sweetie. She probably just needs a bit of time to adjust to life without her best friend on her doorstep. Can't be easy knowing that Elise is on your doorstep instead. They don't get along, do they?'

'Never have done.'

'Classic case of the green-eyed monster.'

'Jealousy? Of what?'

'You, of course. They've both been part of your life at key moments and both are jealous that they have to share you with the other.'

I mulled this over while Auntie Kay continued to rummage in her bag. It would certainly explain the ridiculous need to be the first to hear information and the constant snipes at each other. But it seemed so juvenile. 'I just assumed it was a personality clash. Perhaps you're right.'

'I think there's something in your theory too,' she continued. 'They're definitely chalk and cheese and, in their case, I think opposites repel rather than attract. They're a great balance for you, sweetheart, because you're somewhere in the middle. Gotcha!' She finally found what she'd been rummaging for: a small bunch of keys attached to a plastic daisy. She handed them to me. 'These are yours now. Are you going to open up?'

'I'd be delighted to.'

'Are you ready for new beginnings at Seaside Blooms?'

'After the year I've just had, I couldn't be more ready to start afresh.' I handed her the food and drinks, and grinned as I unlocked the door to my shop. *My* shop. It didn't feel real. The little bell tinkled delicately overhead as I pushed open the door and allowed Auntie Kay to step past me. She stooped down to pick up a small pile of post on her way, giving me my first clear view into the shop. I gasped. What the...? 'Auntie Kay, what have you done? It's empty.'

'I know. Surprise!'

'Why?'

'Because I want you to make it yours and you wouldn't do that if it had all my fittings in it. You've just said you couldn't be more ready to start afresh and this is definitely starting afresh.'

I looked for somewhere to dump my drink but she'd even had the counter ripped out. There was nothing except grubby-looking lino and bare, scuffed white walls.

'Say something,' she said. 'You're making me nervous.'

'I'm in shock. You said something about closing the shop for a month or so while I got sorted out but I assumed you meant opening a bank account and changing names with the suppliers. Not this.' That earlier feeling of contentment and relaxation was replaced by a feeling of rising panic.

'This isn't quite the reaction I was expecting. I thought you'd be pleased.'

'I am. Sorry. It's just that there's so much to do and I don't know if I can afford it. I've only got a few grand in savings, which won't go far. When Jason sells the car, I'll get my share, but I don't know when that will be.'

'Don't worry about the money side of things.' Auntie Kay gave me a reassuring smile. 'Do you really think I'd rip the fittings out and not leave you with any money to replace them?'

'No! Absolutely not! You can't give me any money. You've already given me the shop, which is way too generous as it is.'

She laughed. 'I thought you might say that. How would you feel if we called it a loan?'

I was about to object but, without the money to kit the place out, I wouldn't have a business to run. 'Are you sure?'

'Yes, and I don't want you to pay anything back until you've been open at least six months and found your feet.'

'Thank you so much.' I hugged her then looked around the empty shop again. 'Where do I start?'

Auntie Kay laughed. 'With a vision, of course. What do you want to sell?'

I frowned. 'It's a florist's so I'm kind of thinking flowers and plants could be on the right lines.'

'Come on, Sarah, where's your imagination? If I know you, you'll have given this loads of thought. I bet you even bought a new notepad. Where is it?'

I laughed as I unzipped my bag and pulled out a gorgeous new A5 notepad with a silk beaded cover and soft pastel pages. 'Guilty.' I'd been fantasising all week about the changes I'd love to make. I'd rushed out at lunchtime on the day I resigned to buy a pad and spent the next few evenings filling it when I should have been packing.

'I knew it. Let's have a look.' She flicked through page after page of scribbled ideas, drawings, paint swatches and photos I found online. 'You want to sell gifts?'

'I was thinking maybe a one-stop shop for all occasions. Buying flowers for a new mum? Why not get a card and a teddy here too?' I tailed off. 'It's too much, isn't it?'

She handed me the pad. 'What you've done in here is exactly what I expected of you. It's fresh. It's different. And if one person can bring it to life and make a success of it, it's you. I can't wait to see how it looks.'

'You're not offended?'

'Of course I'm not offended. My business is finished, over, ended.' She drew a cross in the air with her hand. 'This is now a new business with a new owner. You've got to imagine this was something else before... like a hairdresser's. You've had to rip out all the sinks and mirrors and you're about to turn it into a florist's from scratch. The only thing I'm leaving you with is my till because it's new, my supplier details because you'll need those, and any bookings from January onwards. I've transferred my last few bookings for the year to Evie Chandler who runs Blossoms on Park View. Her lease runs out in March and it's being taken over by a charity shop. The rest is up to you.'

'What about the staff?'

'A bit depleted. Gemma failed to show for work on Monday so I told her not to bother coming back. Pat left a couple of months ago. Wendy was due to retire at the end of the year so I've paid her till then. My Saturday girl left for university. That just leaves Cathy and

Trish, my delivery driver. I've not promised them anything but I'd strongly recommend you take them both on.'

I nodded vigorously. 'Definitely. I'll call them this morning. Will that be enough staff? Mum said she doesn't want a permanent job but she's happy to help out for a few months.'

'I'd take her up on the offer and find yourself a Saturday kid. Give it a couple of months to work out who else you need and when. Evie's volunteered to help if you're ever stuck. I think she's keen to keep her hand in.'

'That's kind of her,' I said. 'Okay, sounds like we have a plan.'

Auntie Kay headed into The Outback. I took a slurp of my hot chocolate as I slowly turned in a circle looking round my 'blank canvas', my mind racing with ideas. *It's going to look fabulous. The lino can go for a start. And that horrible strip lighting. I want solid wood floors and ceiling spotlights. A large granite counter over there with loads of room to create…*

'You're visualising it, aren't you?' she said, coming back into the shop.

I nodded sheepishly. No matter what she said or did, I couldn't help but feel guilty that I wanted to change what she'd lovingly created.

'Has it sunk in yet that this is yours?' she asked.

'Not in the slightest.'

'Then claim it.'

'What do you mean?'

'Stand in the middle of the shop and say, "this is mine". Don't look at me like that. I haven't lost the plot if that's what you're thinking.'

'It's *exactly* what I was thinking.'

'It doesn't get you out of doing it, though.'

Deciding I might as well humour her, I put my drink and croissant down on the floor and walked into the centre of the shop. 'This is mine,' I said, pulling a face at her.

'Rubbish. Louder.'

'This is mine,' I repeated, a bit louder.

'Louder.'

I smiled and shook my head at her. '*This is mine.*'

'Again.'

'*This is mine.*'

'Arms in the air. Jump up and down and shout it again and again.'

'*This is mine,*' I yelled, jumping up and down like a cheerleader. '*This is mine.*'

'Has it sunk in yet?' she asked.

'No. Should it have?' I wandered back to her.

'No. I didn't think it would. But it was funny to watch.'

'Auntie Kay! That's mean.' I gave her a little shove.

'I couldn't resist. So, what are you going to do first to create your dream premises?'

I shrugged. 'I don't know. I really wasn't expecting an empty shell. Maybe I could get the walls skimmed? There seem to be a few bits of damaged plaster where the shelves were.'

'Great plan. No time like the present. There's a *Yellow Pages* in The Outback.'

I raised my eyebrows at her. '*Yellow Pages*? Seriously? I thought they stopped printing those years ago.'

'You're not in *that* London anymore,' she said. 'We still get them around here, although it may be a couple of years since I got the last one.' She pointed towards a phone in the corner. 'The landline's still connected. There's a handset there and another on the desk. I suggest you get calling.'

I glanced at the phone and tutted. 'That reminds me. I need to get myself a new mobile but I can't justify the cost, even with your generous loan.'

'What happened to yours?'

'It was a work one so I had to give it back. I feel like I've lost a limb.'

'It's your lucky day, then,' Auntie Kay said. 'I'm treating myself to a new phone for my holidays so you can have my old one.'

'Really? Oh, that would be amazing. Thank you.'

'Pleasure. Right, I'm off. I'll come back late this afternoon to see how you're getting on.'

'You're leaving me?' *Panic!*

'I have a holiday wardrobe to buy. Linda and I are off to York.'

'But—'

'But nothing. You need me out of your hair so you can be creative. See you later.' With a tinkle of the bell she was gone.

Locking the door behind her, I headed into The Outback and my eyes flicked to a small pile of envelopes and leaflets lying on the desk.

'That must be the post Auntie Kay picked up when we came in,' I muttered to myself. 'Let's see. Pizza flier. Not now, thanks, just about to have my croissant.' I dropped each item on the desk as I discarded it. 'Electricity bill. Auntie Kay can have that. Floristry magazine. Good for a bit of inspiration, must get it transferred into my name. Business card for Steve Higgins, Window Cleaner. Bank state— Hang on a minute, business card for whom?'

8

I grabbed the card and stared at it. Steve Higgins. Steve. Steven. Before I had time to think about whether or not it was a good idea, I picked up the desk phone and dialled his mobile number. What was I going to say? He could be my destiny. I didn't want to mess up our first conversation. I nearly hung up but the ringtone changed signalling voicemail. Phew.

'Hi, this is Steve Higgins, window cleaner.' *Sounds nice. Friendly.* 'I'm sorry I can't answer.' *Polite. Always a good sign.* 'I'm probably up a ladder right now...' *Sense of humour. Up a ladder. Just like a fireman. Swoon.* '... but leave your name, number and a message and I'll get back to you as soon as it's safe. Bye.'

He had a strong confident voice with a slight North Yorkshire accent. Nice. Leave a message? Don't leave a message? Dilemma.

'Hi Steve. We've never met...' *Crap. I should have hung up. What a rubbish line. Must try to recover it.* 'My name's Sarah. Sarah Peterson. I'm the new owner of Seaside Blooms on Castle Street. It's my first day and I've just been sorting through the post. You dropped a card through the letterbox...' *Friendly and confident. Business-like, but with a fun tone of voice. Well recovered.* 'I need you...' *And completely ruined again. What is wrong with you?* 'I mean I need a window cleaner. Can you stop by? I'm here all day.' *Disconnect now. Quickly. Before you utter another word.*

I hung up and shook my head. 'I need you.' What the hell was that? And now I'd invited him to stop by. He could be *the* Steven Madame Louisa talked about and I'd asked him to come to the shop when I was wearing scruffy clothes and no make-up. *Well done, Sarah. That was clever.*

After a year of not caring, my appearance suddenly mattered very much. I'd never been one for designer clothes, unlike Clare, but I had always taken pride in my appearance. The non-proposal and steady weight gain had put paid to that. I didn't feel good so why bother to look good? My hair was long, dark, and naturally curly. I used to spend ages teasing it into new styles I found on YouTube or taming it into sleek shiny locks with my GHDs, but scraping it back into a ponytail seemed so much easier. I'd never been one for spending ages on my make-up, but I used to make a bit of effort. A bit of effort was soon replaced by virtually no effort: a dusting of loose powder to take the shine off and a slick of mascara. Frizzy hair in a ponytail and the natural look weren't going to attract *the* Steven, were they?

I glanced at my watch. I didn't have time to get back to Mum and Dad's to change so there was nothing for it; I had to go shopping. I downed the last of my hot chocolate, looked sadly at the untouched croissant and grabbed my bag.

* * *

Carrier bags in hands, my pulse raced as I power-walked back down the precinct towards Castle Street. Glancing at the clock outside the shopping centre, I did a double-take. *No! I can't have been gone an hour and a half. It's not possible.* But the mountain of carriers dangling from my aching arms told me it was. Clothes, make-up, shoes. I'd even bought some new lingerie. Okay, so Steve Higgins wasn't going to see my underwear at our first meeting but *I'd* know I was in a matching set of bra and knickers for the first time in a year and I'd feel good, which would come over to him as sexy and confident, therefore creating a good first impression.

I hastily unlocked the door. Another business card lay on the mat. *Don't say I've missed him. Not after all this effort.* I picked it up and turned it over. In neat capitals on the back it read:

DONE YOUR WINDOWS FOR FREE AS TRIAL
IF HAPPY WITH THEM, LEAVE MESSAGE & I'LL COME BACK ON
MONDAYS BEFORE YOU OPEN. LET ME KNOW IF YOU PREFER A
DIFFERENT DAY
STEVE

I dropped my bags on the desk in The Outback, cursing myself for being so stupid. What on earth had got into me?

Mondays were fine but I couldn't face calling him just yet in case I messed that up too. I couldn't face calling any plasterers either.

Auntie Kay had stripped the shop bare but she hadn't touched the stock cupboard so I'd start on that. Surely that couldn't go wrong.

I took one more look at the bags. What a waste of time and money. Not to mention dignity.

* * *

Elise called at the shop after school.

'I wish Auntie Kay hadn't disappeared to York for the day.' I flopped back on the desk chair and pouted. 'She could have saved me from making a fool of myself and spending a small fortune that I could have invested in the business instead.

'I feel your pain,' Elise said. She adjusted her position on the desk slightly, knocking over a pot of pens in the process. 'Oops. Sorry.'

'It's fine. Leave them. I need to sort the whole desk out. The Outback is a bit of a mess. Like my love life.'

Elise laughed. 'Whoa! That was a little dramatic, don't you think? Should I start calling you Clare?'

'I'm being pathetic, aren't I?'

'Not pathetic. Just someone who wants to meet Mr Right and there's nothing wrong with that, but give it time. It's only your first full day at home.' Elise leaned against the wall again. 'Maybe he wasn't *the* Steven anyway. It's a common name. You might meet a few before you meet the right one.'

'Maybe. Do you really think it's going to happen? Or do you think Clare's right about the CD being a load of rubbish?' I realised I'd crossed my fingers.

'I think she used slightly stronger words than "rubbish",' Elise said, rolling her eyes at me. 'But to answer your question, everything else was accurate so why not that? I find the sudden reappearance of the CD on the weekend you move home a bit mysterious and perhaps even magical, so I can't help thinking it's all part of something amazing that's about to happen to you.'

I smiled and sat forward. 'I keep thinking that too.'

'Have you listened to it again?'

'Three times. Everything's so accurate. The only unexplained bit is that stuff about the lighthouse picture and the bracelet. I remember Mum losing the bracelet years ago so that definitely happened but, as for finding it... Mum caught me with the sofa pulled out last night, all the cushions off it, and the carpet pulled up. I was too embarrassed to tell her about the CD so I made out I'd lost my earring then felt really stupid when she pointed out I was wearing a pair.'

'No bracelet?'

'No. Just 73p in change and a wine gum.'

'And the photo?'

'I asked her, making out that I could vaguely remember it from childhood, but she wasn't aware of one and neither was Auntie Kay. They both said I resemble Grandma, but they've always said that. I'm assuming there's something about this photo that shows the resemblance more clearly.'

Elise shrugged. 'Maybe it will suddenly show up and you'll know for sure. Just like the CD did.'

A shiver of delight ran down my back. 'It all seems so magical, like you said. *The* Steven could still be the window cleaner, but if he isn't, how do you think I'll meet him?'

'He could be a customer,' Elise suggested.

'I'm not so sure.'

'Why not?'

'What will the shop mainly be selling?'

'Flowers.'

'And who do men buy flowers for?'

'Their wives or girlfriends? Oh, I see. Good point.'

'It probably isn't the best choice of business for meeting my future husband.'

'What about someone buying flowers for his mum?' Elise suggested.

'Maybe. Although I suspect most men our age would order online or they'd buy from a supermarket. Where does Gary get you flowers from?'

Elise shrugged. 'I'd be able to tell you if he ever bought me flowers.'

'Oh. Sorry.' Oops!

'Don't be. Men!' Elise smiled but it didn't reach her eyes. I was on the verge of asking her if everything was okay at home but she continued talking. 'Perhaps you'll just meet him on a night out in town. I promise we'll have lots of those. I'm so excited to have you back home after all these years.'

'I'm excited to be back,' I said. 'Hey, does Gary have any single friends called Steven?'

I watched Elise's lips moving as if she was listing all her husband's male friends. 'I don't think so,' she said eventually. 'One of the doctors at his surgery is called Simon but that's the closest. I can double check with him if you like?'

'Would you? But be subtle. I'd rather only you and Clare knew about my little search.'

'Okay. Discretion it is. Ooh, I know a Steven from school.'

'Really? What's he like?'

'Married with three children and twins on the way. Don't think it'll be him somehow. I don't think I know any other Stevens, or at least none above the age of consent.' Elise picked up a pen and clicked the end on and off a few times. 'Back to Steve the window cleaner. Any plans?'

I sighed. 'I rang him just before you got here to confirm

Mondays were fine and, thankfully, got his voicemail. I guess I'll just have to wait until next Monday when he does my windows and make sure I'm in early and looking my best.'

'Wait till next Monday? No chance. I bet you do a recce round town tomorrow to see if you can spot him.'

9

I pressed the bell to stop the bus at the top of town the following morning. Elise knew me far too well. As soon as she'd said it, I realised I couldn't wait a week before eliminating Steve Higgins as *the* Steven. Alighting a stop early, I was going to walk up and down some of the side streets in the hope of spotting him and finding out if he was old, had no teeth or had hair sprouting out of his nose or ears.

The bus pulled into the stop and I yawned as I got off. This searching for Steven thing was tiring. I'd been up since six experimenting with different outfits just in case I did spot him, which was pretty pointless because there was no way I was planning to speak to him. I'd finally settled on my favourite jeans and a plain navy tunic-style top. Very flattering.

I spotted a couple of window cleaners outside an estate agent to the north. Eek! I hadn't thought about Steve Higgins being part of a team.

I tried to walk slowly and casually towards them without staring but how can you check out your potential destiny if you don't actually look at him? Then a thought struck me. Unless he was wearing clothes emblazoned with his name, how the hell would I know if he was Steve Higgins or not? Duh! It seemed that ill-considered plans were becoming my forte.

One of the men was doing something at the back of the van. Perhaps that would have a name on it. The other one was up a ladder with a baseball cap obliterating his face.

'So did you get your end away last night?' shouted the one on the ladder, looking down at his colleague, before starting his descent. What sort of question was that to be shouting out at half seven in the morning? The other one shut the van doors, snorted loudly, then spat on the ground. Ew! Dirty, disgusting man. Well, if that was Steve Higgins, then he wasn't the Steven for me. *My* Steven wouldn't do something so gross.

I quickly crossed the road, preferring not to stick around to hear the answer to the question. Glancing back, I checked the writing on the side of the van and my shoulders sagged as I read, 'Steve Higgins Window Cleaning Services'. Pants. I looked back at the two men again, just to be certain. Baseball Cap lit a cigarette and the other one spat on the ground again before lighting up too. No. Not for me.

I turned around to take the shortest route to the shop, feeling disappointed yet at the same time glad I had closure instead of spending the week building him up into some sort of demi-god.

* * *

Ten minutes later, I unlocked the door to Seaside Blooms and stood in the middle of the empty shop, smiling. I'd wasted yesterday but I wasn't going to waste today. When I got back home last night, Mum told me that Auntie Kay had phoned to say she was staying overnight in York but would be back by lunchtime and was looking forward to a progress report from me. I needed to make sure I had something to report and I'd start with sorting out a plasterer.

Locking the door again, I made my way into The Outback and, while I waited for the kettle to boil, I sat at the desk and opened the *Yellow Pages*.

Places of Worship... Planning Consultants... Plant & Machinery Hire... Got it! Plasterers. Three pages. Let's see... AA Plasterers... Ace Plastering... Aidan & Steve's Plastering Services... Ooh. Aidan and STEVE.

I sat forward on the desk chair, a flutter of excitement in my stomach. An unexpected source of Stevens. I lay the directory flat on the desk as I poured over the advert for Aidan and Steve. 'Plastering, artexing, coving, skimming. Aidan and Steve each have over twenty-five years' experience...' I stopped reading and sat back. Twenty-five years' experience? Even if they'd started out straight from school, that made them both over forty. I didn't envisage myself with a man ten to fifteen years my senior.

Oh well, plenty more fish in the sea or, in my case, plenty more Stevens in the phone directory. Interesting. I ran my finger down the page again. Ha! Stephen Lewis. No hint at his age. Oh, and Steve Pinder. And Steve Walters. Surely it was best practice to get three quotes.

I picked up the phone then paused. What person in their right mind selected their plasterer on the basis of their name? What the heck. The circumstances were exceptional.

An hour later there was a knock on the door. I'd left messages for the two Steves, but Stephen Lewis answered his phone on the third ring. He said he had a day off and was coming into town anyway so he'd pop by in an hour.

I wasted that whole hour getting ready. I re-did my make-up and faffed with my unruly hair. I washed the mugs Elise and I had used yesterday and picked up the pens she'd spilled over the desk. I even squirted some bleach down the toilet. Don't know why I did that. My final act of insanity was ordering coffee and muffins from The Chocolate Pot. They don't deliver but, determined not to make the same mistake of leaving the shop and missing Stephen, I persuaded the owner, Tara, to make an exception because we were, after all, only seven doors apart.

Opening the door, I beamed at the attractive man, probably in his mid-thirties. I eagerly took in the short dark hair (freshly cut), clean clothes (nice smell), bright blue eyes (beautiful) and friendly smile (dreamy). Exactly how I'd described on my Life Plan. *OMG! He could be* the *Steven.*

'Sarah?' he asked.

I nodded, dumbstruck by his beauty.

'Stephen Lewis,' he said. 'We spoke earlier about a plastering quote.'

Stop staring at him. He's speaking. Answer him.

'I am at the right shop?' Lines of confusion dented his perfect forehead. 'It was you I spoke to earlier, wasn't it?'

Speak! 'Yes, er, sorry. Miles away. Come in.'

'I hope you don't mind me bringing the kids with me.'

Kids? I reluctantly peeled my eyes away from his face and looked down. Two small children clung onto his legs. How had I missed them?

'And the baby,' he continued.

There's a baby too? Sure enough, there was a lime green pram next to him. How had I missed that? It was practically fluorescent.

'This is Josh and Luke.' He affectionately rubbed the heads of the two limpets. 'They're two.'

'Twins?' One word at a time was about all I could manage.

'Identical.' He beamed proudly. 'And the little angel in the pram is Caitlin. She's eleven weeks.'

I reluctantly peered into the pram. 'Cute.'

'My wife and I think so.'

Of course. Why wouldn't he have a beautiful wife and beautiful kids? He was beautiful. Even if he wasn't married, he was so out of my league, it made me want to cry.

'I'm really sorry about the kids. I know it's not very professional. I rang around everyone I knew but nobody was free and I couldn't miss out on the chance of some work. I promise I don't bring them with me normally. I can come back later if you prefer.'

I shook my head, opened the door wide, and tried to sound cheerful. 'Everyone in.' *Ooh, two words. Big improvement.*

'Something smells nice,' he said.

Oh crap! The coffee and muffins. I glanced guiltily towards the pasting table I'd found in The Outback. Resting on it was a plate of carefully stacked muffins alongside the pair of steaming coffees that I'd transferred out of the paper cups into proper mugs. *Quick. Think of something. Anything.*

'Er, yeah. Elevenses,' I said.

'At half nine?'

'Late breakfast. Early elevenses. I was up early. It's for my... my... my mum. She's here. Well, she's not here. She's coming. Soon. One of the coffees is for her. And a muffin. If she wants one. Not that I'm going to force her. She doesn't have to have one. But they're not all for me either. Mum can have them all if she wants. I don't mind. I'm not precious about them.' *Maybe more words weren't such a good idea.*

'Right.' Stephen gathered the twins closer to him. 'So, you wanted a quote for some plastering?' He slipped off his coat and laid it across the pram – *oh wow, look at those tanned muscles* – and dug out a notebook and pen. 'What exactly do you want doing?'

'Doing?'

'Plastering?'

'Of course. Plastering.' I swept my arm around the shop. 'How much for all of this?'

He wandered over to one of the walls and stroked it. Lucky wall. He really was yummy. A dreamy 'hmm' escaped from my lips.

'Sorry?' he said.

I cleared my throat. 'Muffin crumb. Lodged in my throat. Just clearing it. Ahem. Ah, that's better.'

He looked at the plate of untouched muffins then back at me again. 'O-kay. The walls aren't too bad. Just need a quick skim. Do you want me to do your back?'

'Yes please.'

'Can I see it?'

'My back? Now?'

'Now works for me if that's okay with you.'

I looked at the twins who were chasing each other round the shop. 'What about your children?'

'They're fine here, aren't they? I don't think even they can do much damage in an empty shop.' He laughed.

'Are you sure you want to see my back?'

'Unless you only want a quote for plastering the shop part.'

Oh! Out the back. Not my back. Why would he want to see my back? Especially in front of his kids. He has a wife and three children. Sarah Peterson, what is wrong with you? You must sound completely deranged. Wrap it up and get rid of him.

'Actually, the back's good,' I said. 'I don't need the back doing. Just the shop. How much for the shop?'

'What do you want doing with this archway?' He stretched a

tanned arm towards The Outback entrance, flexing his muscles as he did. Then, just to torment me even more, he walked past me towards the arch with a tantalising aroma of musky aftershave trailing in his wake. My pulse quickened and my legs weakened. *What are you doing to me? Just say the words and I'll lock the kids in the loo and you can have me right here, right now on the lino.*

He ran his hand round the arch. 'Any ideas?' he asked.

Plenty, but they're all X-rated and probably best not shared with you right now. I shook my head, trying to dislodge my wicked thoughts. 'No. No ideas. Just leave it.' I moved towards the door. There was an awkward silence. 'So, thanks for coming.' I opened the door, grateful for the cold blast of air to cool my flushed cheeks.

'You're welcome.' He reached for his coat and put it back on, flexing those muscles once more. 'Don't you want to know how much it will be?'

'How much what will be?'

'The plastering.' That look was there again: half-scared, half-sympathetic as if he was unsure whether I was mad as in dangerous or mad as in simple.

A nervous giggle spilled out of my mouth. 'Sorry. I... er... thought you'd already said. How much?'

'About £750 to £800.'

'Great. That's fine. Thanks. Bye.'

Stephen hesitated. 'I could start tomorrow if you want. I had a couple of jobs fall through so I'm free and I could really use the work.' He glanced towards the baby.

'Sorry to hear that,' I said. *But I can't have you working here, you beautiful unavailable man.*

Stephen pushed the fluorescent pram and ushered the twins out the door. He turned around just before I could shut the door and, almost in a whisper, said, 'So, do you want me to do it then?' He looked terrified. I felt awful. Surely he didn't want the job after meeting me, but clearly times were tight and he had a young family to feed.

'Er... a few people to see,' I said, trying to sound positive. 'I'll be in touch. Bye.'

I pushed the door shut and leaned against it. Could that have been any more embarrassing? Muffins and coffee? Doing my back? Oh. My. God. Cringe, cringe, cringe.

I stomped into the kitchen area with the mugs and tipped them down the sink before returning to the shop where I stuffed a large chunk of muffin into my mouth. Oh well, one down, two more Steves to go. If I could face them.

Early that afternoon, Steve Walters called me back to say he was snowed under until Christmas, then he was getting married. He could give me an appointment in February, at a push, when he was back from his honeymoon.

Forty minutes after that, Steve Pinder called me to say I must have a very old copy of the *Yellow Pages* because he'd retired five years ago. I closed it and looked at the front. Yep, eight years old. I *knew* they didn't print the damn thing anymore. I tossed the directory at the wall, taking a large chunk out of the plaster. Definitely needed plastering now.

10

'You grab a seat; I'll get some drinks.' Clare rummaged in her bag for her purse while I headed for a couple of comfy armchairs in Minty's on Friday evening.

My favourite bar was on a side street at the top of town. Leather sofas, brightly coloured armchairs and an eclectic mix of wooden chairs and stools jostled for space around homemade tables erected from railway sleepers, driftwood, and beer barrels. Old pictures and adverts promoting the area across the past century adorned the wall, interspersed with paintings of local scenes by local artists, including some by the owner.

'I'm surprised,' Clare said as she re-joined me with two glasses of wine.

'At what?'

'It's really nice in here.'

'And that surprises you because...?'

'I don't know. I think I expected somewhere a bit rough. Northern seaside resort and all that.'

'How rude! We're not all completely unsophisticated up north, you know. We do have a few nice bars and even one or two posh restaurants. We also got electricity recently. And indoor toilets are starting to become popular. It's all very exciting.'

'All right, you've made your point, so you have.' Clare took a sip from her wine. 'So, will you be sharing your game plan?'

'My game plan?'

'Your plan to snare your man Steven.'

'I thought you didn't believe in all that.'

'I don't but it's pretty obvious that you do, so let's say, just for a moment, that your clairvoyant woman isn't a raving eejit and is actually right. You're about to finally fulfil your childhood fantasy of meeting this perfect being, getting married, having one point seven children and living happily ever after. We now believe he answers to the name of Steven. How are you going to make sure you meet him?'

'I don't know. I figured it would just happen naturally. If it's meant to be, it *will* happen.'

'"Naturally"?' Clare raised an eyebrow. '"If it's meant to be, it will happen"? Don't give me that bollocks.'

'What do you mean?'

'This is *you* we're talking about. The girl with the Life Plan. The girl who uses Post-it notes to make the key decisions in her life. The girl who was practically peeing her pants at that clairvoyant reading. Waiting for something to happen naturally is not part of that girl's DNA.'

I took a sip of my wine and frowned. For the first time in my life, I didn't have a plan. I'd assumed he'd just appear and, after my window cleaning and plastering episodes, I figured the less interference from me, the better. 'Maybe he'll be a customer?' I offered half-heartedly.

'Yeah, sure he will. He'll sweep you off your feet while he's buying a bouquet for his wife to celebrate their wedding anniversary or the birth of their first gremlin.'

'Baby.' Clare and babies don't mix. I've always wanted children although I admit I'm not one of those women who goes gooey around them like Elise. I do, however, think Clare's view of them is a little extreme.

'Gremlin,' she growled. 'Okay, let's not worry too much about where you'll meet him. Let's imagine it's happened. What are you going to say to him?'

'Say?'

'Will you be blurting out that he's your destiny and proposing on the spot or will you be playing it cool and risking him walking out of your life?'

'I... I dunno. I hadn't really thought about it.'

'You haven't thought about much, have you?'

I felt a jolt of panic. Clare was absolutely right; I needed a game plan for this or I could blow it big time. How crazy would I look if I mentioned the reading to any Stevens I happened to meet? They'd run a mile.

'I need to listen to the CD again at some point.'

'Really? You promise you won't get mad.'

'I promise.' Clare nodded with vigour but her mischievous smile contradicted her.

'What are you scheming?'

'Nothing. I swear to you. I've decided I'm going to humour you this weekend and go along with this whole meeting Steven thing because I know it's important to you. But I want it to be noted that I still think it's a big steaming bag of shite.'

'Point noted and well made, thank you.'

'Good. Will we get started then? Do you think any of that lot are Stevens?' Clare nodded towards the bar.

I shuffled round in my chair. A group of three fairly attractive men stood by the bar, laughing as they waited for their drinks.

I turned back to Clare. 'I'd like to think the dark-haired one might be.'

She frowned. 'They've all got dark hair.'

'Exactly.'

Clare giggled. 'That was quite funny. For you. No time like the present.' She swigged back the rest of her drink then stood up.

'Where are you going?'

'To introduce us to the nice young men at the bar.'

'You want me to come with you?'

'Of course. Or did you think I was going to drag them over one by one so you could do a name-check?'

'No. But—'

But Clare wasn't listening. She'd already picked up her bag and coat. I reluctantly reached for my coat. Then I heard one word that froze me to the spot.

'Steve!' The tallest of the trio waved in the direction of the door.

I slowly turned towards the door, stomach lurching.

Clare grabbed my arm. 'I guess that answers our question,' she whispered.

It must have started raining as 'Steve' held a dripping coat over his head. Could he be *the* Steven? I swear the whole bar must have been able to hear the thumping of my heart.

'Move your coat,' I whispered. 'I can't see your face.'

'Steve! Over here.'

I held my breath as he finally removed the coat then shook out his blond hair.

Clare squeezed my arm. 'Not bad,' she whispered. 'I know you prefer dark hair but he's pretty cute.'

'Not bad,' I whispered back. 'Not bad at all.'

Steve headed towards the group.

'I can't believe you're late for your own bloody stag do,' shouted one of the men. 'You'd better not be late next Saturday, Steve, or my sister will lynch you.'

Bollocks.

'I'm guessing he'll not be your man Steven then?'

'No. I'm guessing not.'

'Good. Because I have an absolute gem of an idea for how to meet him quickly.'

'Sounds intriguing.'

She took a deep, dramatic intake of breath before announcing enthusiastically, 'A dating app.'

I couldn't remember the last time I'd heard her sound so excited about something. And I couldn't remember the last time I'd felt such a huge anti-climax. 'Tinder? Seriously?'

She shook her head. 'Not necessarily Tinder. There are plenty of others. And I haven't finished. That's not the grand idea.'

Thank goodness for that. 'So what is?'

'I believe you make your own decisions and control your own destiny. Clairvoyance would imply it's mapped out for us already which means we're not in control. If you believe the CD, you just have to wait for Steven to appear. How about trying my way and making him appear?'

'How?'

'By targeting Stevens on the app. It's a fairly common name so it's possible you could fall for a Steven if you date enough of them. You therefore fulfil the crazy prophecy except you're in control. You've made it happen. Now, tell me, is that a grand idea or is that a grand idea?'

'A dating app?'

'Weren't you listening to me? I'm talking about *targeted* app dating. I'm talking about seeking out profiles that only belong to Stevens. Don't you think that's genius?'

'I'm not sure.'

'You're not sure?' The high pitch made me flinch and quickly look around the bar to make sure nobody else was looking.

'Maybe I'm just tired,' I suggested. 'It's not a *bad* idea. I just didn't imagine that's how I'd meet him.'

'Well I think it's a brilliant idea. It surely can't hurt to try.'

'Do you really think it'll work?'

'Christ, how would I know? I don't do long-term relationships so I'm probably the worst person in the world to be giving you advice. But, as we've just discussed, you're probably not going to meet Steven at work and the first one we encounter on a night out is on his stag do. Do you have any better ideas? Apparently one in four relationships start online.'

'One in four?'

'I knew you'd like that stat.' Clare grinned. 'So why not try this? For whatever stupid and misguided reason, I think you're convinced that woman is right and Steven's your destiny. I know you and I know you'll get yourself into a right state constantly wondering when you're going to meet him. I say don't wait. Get out there, control your own destiny, and search for Steven yourself. There must be loads from North Yorkshire registered on dating apps and, if none of them are right, then I think you should admit defeat and accept your clairvoyant was wrong. Could you do that?'

'I'm not sure.'

'Sarah! Where's your sense of adventure?'

'Can I promise to think about it?'

Clare stared at me for a while. 'You have until tomorrow morning,' she said at last. 'Because tomorrow we register you. I'm going to the bar. You can start thinking about it while I'm gone.'

I watched her head to the now-packed bar, men gazing adoringly at her as she passed and women narrowing their eyes with instant dislike. It happened everywhere she went. I leaned back in my seat. Online dating, but only targeting Stevens? Interesting idea. Maybe I hadn't given her enough credit for it. Logic would say that the more Stevens I met, the more likely I was to find *the* Steven. Going through the *Yellow Pages* definitely wasn't the way forward, especially when my copy was eight years out-of-date. Maybe online dating was the way to go. I took another sip of my wine. One in four? Yes, I definitely liked that statistic. Couldn't do any harm looking.

'Decision made?' Clare asked, reappearing with our drinks a few minutes later.

'Go on, then. I'll give it a try, but it's going to have to be online rather than an app.'

'Why?'

I reached into my bag and cringed as I held up the phone that Auntie Kay had 'kindly' gifted me.

Clare recoiled in disgust. 'What the hell is that?'

'My new mobile.'

'New? Jesus! Didn't those things go out with the ark?'

'New to me, then. I told Auntie Kay that I couldn't justify splashing out on a smartphone and she said I could have her old one. I hadn't appreciated it would be quite so old although I should have guessed with her being such a technophobe.'

Clare took the battered Nokia from me and winced at the weight. 'This is bad.'

'But it will have to do. For now, anyway. There's broadband at home and I've got my laptop so I'll give your online dating suggestion a go. I think.'

11

I smiled at Clare's text and put my phone back in my pocket. Daily nag? More like five times daily!

It was the Wednesday after Clare's visit. I'd had the shop plastered on Thursday and Friday last week then spent the last couple of days painting ready for the floor to be fitted. Mum had helped me paint and it had been lovely to spend two solid days with her. I was really close to my parents but hadn't realised how much I'd missed casually chatting to Mum about nothing in particular. It felt so good to be back in Whitsborough Bay and surrounded by my family again.

Auntie Kay arrived at Seaside Blooms, as planned. She'd been so busy getting organised for her travels that I hadn't seen her since the beginning of last week.

'Wow! It looks fantastic in here now that you've painted.' She turned in a small circle on the paint-spattered lino. 'I can't believe how big it looks. I should have done this years ago.'

'It looked great when you had it. All I've done is freshen it up a bit.'

'Thanks, sweetie. That's very kind of you, but we both know it was looking a bit shabby.' She moved to one of the walls and ran her hand down the smooth plaster. 'Nice job. Who did you get to do it?'

My cheeks flushed and I quickly turned away and put my bag down on the pasting table. 'Some bloke I found in the *Yellow Pages.*' After my disgraceful attempt at flirting with Stephen Lewis, I phoned round another eight plasterers (avoiding Stevens) the next morning and discovered none of them were available for several weeks. I then had a major attack of the guilts. Stephen had seemed like a lovely guy and he clearly needed the work. It was hardly his fault he was so damn gorgeous that I couldn't put lustful thoughts out of my mind. I bottled any verbal contact, texting him to say he had the job and he should pick up and drop off the keys with Tara at The Chocolate Pot.

'He's done a great job,' Auntie Kay said. 'And I'm loving these cream walls. So much warmer than the white.'

'Thanks,' I said. 'Clare's coming up again the weekend after next to draw some abstract flowers on the walls. She's good at stuff like that.'

'Sounds lovely. Is she okay with your move home now?'

'I don't think she'll ever love the idea but I think she accepts it. Cup of tea?'

'I thought you'd never ask.'

'I've got a question to ask you while the kettle's boiling.'

Auntie Kay followed me into The Outback. I filled the kettle in the small kitchen area and switched it on. 'What do you think about online dating?'

She stiffened. 'I've told you before. I don't want to meet anyone so don't start that again.'

Crumbs! Hit a raw nerve there. 'Not for you, silly. I mean for me.'

'Oh. Why didn't you say so?' Her voice had softened, but the fiddling with Grandma's ring told me she was on edge. I've always thought it was a shame that Auntie Kay was single. Before leaving home for university, I set her up with the divorced dad of a school friend. She spotted the set-up and traced it back to me. It's the one and only time she's ever shouted at me and boy did she shout. I asked Mum why she got so mad but she told me it was Auntie Kay's business and she'd tell me if she wanted to. It became a taboo subject after that.

'I thought it was obvious I meant for me.' I threw teabags into the mugs. 'Why would I suggest you start online dating when you're about to leave the country?'

'Good point. Sorry for snapping. I thought you said you weren't ready to start dating again so soon after Jason.'

'I don't know if I am. It's a scary thought after we'd been together so long, but I want to meet someone sooner or later and I don't think it'll happen through work. Clare came up with the online dating idea. Do you think I should give it a try?'

Drinks made, I ushered Auntie Kay to the desk chair then perched on the desk.

'I don't know anything about online dating,' she said, leaning back, 'but if you want to start dating, I know the perfect man for you.'

'Really. Who?' *Please say he's called Steven.*

'It's someone you've already met.'

I shrugged. 'Who?'

'Nick Derbyshire.'

The name sounded familiar but I couldn't quite place it.

'You must remember him,' she said. 'Alma Sutton's grandson. He came in for the flowers for his sister's wedding.'

Oh yes! The man with the eyes like the ocean. I definitely remembered him. My pulse quickened as I pictured him in his morning suit, looking at me intently.

'You said he was handsome,' she said.

'I didn't.'

'You did.'

'Only because you made me.'

'But you do think he's handsome, don't you?'

'I can't say I was paying that much attention,' I lied. 'If you recall, I'd just jumped on a train after dumping Jason. Checking out other men wasn't high on my list of priorities that day.'

'Well, he *is* handsome.' She looked so proud you'd have thought she was his mum. 'And he's single. And he's lovely. And he has his own business which is doing pretty well.'

'If he's that handsome and lovely and successful, why's he single?'

'Sarah! That's a bit harsh.' She playfully slapped at my leg. 'Perhaps he's like you – hasn't found the right person yet.'

'Perhaps.'

'So it's agreed?'

'What is?'

'I'll set you up on a date with Nick.'

I put my tea down with such vigour, it slopped everywhere. 'You'll do no such thing.'

'But you just said—'

'I said the word "perhaps" in agreement that Nick may, like me, not have met The One yet. How you interpret that as "please set me up on a date with him" is beyond me.' I took a tissue out of my pocket and dabbed at the spilt liquid.

Auntie Kay took a long noisy slurp of her tea. 'We'll see.'

'I mean it,' I said. 'He seems nice enough and I admit he's easy on the eye but I don't want to go out with him so don't you dare play Cupid.'

'Okay. Okay.' She put her hands up in surrender. 'I won't set you up on a date with him. It's a missed opportunity, though.'

I narrowed my eyes and gave her the meanest scowl I could manage.

'Fine. I'll shut up. I just don't get why you won't even consider one evening with him.'

'Because I don't want to.' *Because he's not called Steven.*

'You sound like a five-year-old when you say that.' Auntie Kay held my gaze with her eyebrows raised.

Damn! How did she do it? She knew there was more to it. I hadn't intended to tell anyone else, but she'd always been such a good listener. Oh, sod it. The accounts could wait. 'If I tell you something, will you promise not to tell anyone else. Not even Mum...?'

* * *

'So that's why you won't let me fix you up with Nick,' Auntie Kay said when I'd finished, 'Even though I can tell you fancy the pants off him.'

'Auntie Kay! I do not. Can we focus back on Steven? What do you think?'

'Honestly?'

'Honestly.'

'I get it. I do. I understand why you'd believe and I want to be supportive of you but I'm just not convinced by the whole clairvoyance thing.'

'Why?'

'Personal experience.' Auntie Kay started fiddling with her ring again.

'You've seen a clairvoyant?'

She seemed in a daze, fiddling with the ring and staring into nothing.

'Auntie Kay? You've seen one?'

'I must have seen about twenty after...'

'After what? Auntie Kay? After what?'

She blinked and looked back at me. 'I need to show you these accounts, don't I?'

'The accounts can wait. Why did you see twenty clairvoyants? What happened?'

'Nothing. Did I say twenty? I meant twenty of us went to a spiritualist church once. Load of nonsense. Right, it's just after eleven. I'm all yours till half twelve then I'm meeting Linda for lunch to plan our next shopping trip. Accounts. Now.' She pulled a couple of files out of the desk drawer.

I desperately wanted to know why she'd visited twenty clairvoyants and what she thought of my search for Steven but I knew from her assertive tone that the subject was closed. If I pushed, she'd find an excuse to leave.

'Whoopee! Bring it on,' I said.

* * *

The knock on the door a few hours later startled me. I rubbed my eyes as I went to answer it. Butterflies fluttered in my stomach when I saw him standing there. 'Nick? Hi.' I'd kill her. Hadn't she listened to a word I said about Steven?

'Congratulations on becoming the new owner.'

'Thank you.'

There was an awkward pause. What was the protocol for visits like this? Should I invite him in? What had she said to him? Did he think it was a date?

'Kay said you need someone to set up your website and asked me to stop by this afternoon to chat about what you want.'

'Did she now?' *The crafty little...*

He looked beyond me into the empty shop. 'Is it a bad time?'

'Sorry.' I swung the door open. 'Come in.'

'Thanks.' He stepped inside. 'I can come back another time if you're busy.'

'No. It's fine. You're here now and I could do with a break from staring at the accounts. Cuppa?'

'Yes please.' He followed me through The Outback into the kitchen area. 'The shop looks good.'

'Thanks,' I said. 'I'm really pleased so far.' I put the kettle on. 'So, I'm guessing you're a web designer or something like that.'

He smiled. Those gorgeous bright blue eyes twinkled with mischief. 'Do you mind if I say something?'

'Is it a nice something or a nasty something?'

'It's sort of an observation.'

'Go ahead.'

'I'm not trying to embarrass you or put you on the spot,' he said, 'but you looked a bit shocked to see me at the door just now. Given that you don't know what my job is, I'm guessing that having me stop by to discuss your website wasn't your idea. I'm therefore wondering whether me being here is more about your auntie trying to do a little matchmaking than you actually needing help with your website.'

My cheeks flushed deeply.

'Sorry,' he said. 'I *have* embarrassed you.'

I shook my head and smiled. 'No. *You* haven't embarrassed me; Auntie Kay has. I told her just this morning not to set me up with y

—' I tailed off and bit my lip, desperately wishing I could retract my words.

Nick laughed, a warm and infectious sound. 'It's okay. You can finish the sentence. I promise not to jump off Lighthouse Point if you don't want to go out with me.'

'It's not that. I mean it's not you. It's... it's complicated. Tea or coffee?'

'Coffee please. White. No sugar.' Nick leaned against the work-top. 'You don't have to explain. I know you've only just split up with your boyfriend. Kay managed to slip that into our brief conversa-tion, which was another big clue that perhaps she was playing Cupid. You probably need some time to yourself.'

I sighed and shook my head. 'It's not that either.' I stirred his coffee. 'Things with Jason had run their course a long time ago. It's just that...'

When I didn't finish the sentence, Nick prompted gently, 'I'm a good listener.'

I sighed. 'Believe me, you don't want to hear my woes.'

'Try me.'

I handed him his drink and studied his face. It would be useful to hear a male viewpoint. It would also be useful to have someone completely independent to tell me whether or not I was being crazy with the whole searching for Steven thing. Auntie Kay had been as much use as a chocolate teapot. But could I really open up to someone I'd only just met?

'I'm not sure,' I said, eventually. 'You might laugh.'

'I promise I won't. If it helps, I volunteer as a youth counsellor and, believe me, I've heard it all over the years. I don't judge. I don't laugh. I just listen and occasionally offer a few words of wisdom. But I can also drop the subject, shut up, and we can talk websites with no pressure. Or I can go.'

I finished making my tea and took a deep breath. 'You're on.'

'Websites, woes or leave?'

I laughed. 'Woes. If you're absolutely sure you don't mind spending the next hour or so listening to me wittering on.'

'It would be a pleasure. But can I make a suggestion?'

I nodded.

'Might your woes be better shared over a beer rather than a coffee? Is it too early for a swift half in Minty's?'

'Best idea I've heard all day and my favourite bar too. Are you sure you've got time? You don't have any other appointments?'

'No. No plans. I'm yours for as long as you want me.' Nick held my gaze and my stomach did a back-flip. Was that a loaded statement?

* * *

'There you have it,' I said. 'Pathetic eh?' I took a swig from my third glass of wine.

Nick had been right. He was really easy to talk to and a great listener. Feeling relaxed – especially after the first glass of wine on an empty stomach – I told him all about Uncle Alan, my Life Plan, Jason, the clairvoyant CD and Clare's suggestion to start online dating. I left out the window cleaner and plasterer episodes. They were definitely on a need-to-know-only basis.

'Not pathetic at all.' Nick touched my hand lightly, making my heart flutter. 'Thanks for sharing.'

'Thanks for listening.'

'You're welcome.'

'So, what do you think?' I asked.

He took a deep breath. 'First thing to say is that I don't think you're mad for believing in the reading. At some point in their lives, I'd say that most people have something they desperately want to believe can happen. I bet 99 per cent of people have dreams of packing in the day job to become a pop star, winning the lottery or simply meeting the man or woman of their dreams.'

I smiled. 'Which one is it for you?'

'All three. Give me a few beers and a karaoke machine and I think I'm Tom Jones. There's nothing like a good rendition of *Delilah*.' He laughed. 'And my attempt is *nothing* like a good rendition.'

I laughed too. *Ooh. I'd like to see that. Especially if it involves some Tom Jones hip gyrating.*

'I never buy lottery tickets,' he continued, 'so that kind of scuppers the first two.'

'Which just leaves meeting The One?'

'I'm in the same boat as you there. Always hoping but it hasn't happened yet.' He took a swig of his pint. 'Actually, that's a lie. I was engaged once. I thought Lisa was The One for me but it turns out I wasn't The One for her.'

'Oh. That sounds like a story. What happened?'

'The classic cliché. She ran off with my best mate. Could have been worse. At least she did it the day before the wedding instead of leaving me at the altar a best man and a bride short of a wedding party.'

'Oh, Nick, I'm so sorry. Was this recent?'

He shook his head and gave a weak smile. 'Years ago. I was twenty-one. She was only nineteen. I'd say we were too young but it seemed to work for her and Alex. Last I knew, they're still together and have two kids.'

'That must have hurt.'

He nodded. 'Like hell. Not only did I lose my fiancée but I lost my best mate too and, over the years, that's been harder to deal with. Alex and I had been inseparable since nursery and, even though we were only ten at the time, he was so supportive when my dad died. I haven't thought about Lisa for years but I still really miss Alex. He was like a brother to me.'

'I'm sorry,' I said again.

'Don't be.' He smiled. This time his eyes smiled too. 'Water under the bridge. The main lasting impact is that it's made me cautious about male friends. For the first few years, I wouldn't introduce any male friends to girlfriends in case it happened again. My closest friend now is female – Skye – and I like not having that threat.'

I tried to imagine how I'd feel if Elise or Clare had run off with Andy or with Jason in the early days when it had been good. The betrayal didn't bear thinking about. 'Poor you.'

'Thank you, but we're meant to be talking about you. You wanted my verdict?'

I nodded, feeling silly for making such a fuss after what he'd been through with his dad then Alex and Lisa.

'Here goes,' he said. 'From what you've said, it sounds like most of what your clairvoyant predicted has already happened plus that stuff about your uncle is pretty compelling. I'm therefore with you when you say why wouldn't she be right about Steven.'

'Exactly. That's what I've been trying to tell Clare.'

Nick screwed his nose up.

'There's a "but" isn't there?'

He nodded and pulled an apologetic expression. 'But I'm also with your friend Clare in that your clairvoyant could be wrong. She could be wrong about the timescales of you meeting The One or she could be wrong about the name. I'd hate you to close yourself off to other possibilities and spend years expecting Steven to walk into your life, feeling disappointed every time you meet someone you're attracted to who has the wrong name.'

'So what do you think I should do?'

'It's entirely up to you but, if you really want my opinion, I think you should do what your friend Clare suggests and register for online dating. It sounds like a great way to find several Stevens, but you're completely in control as to whether you meet them or not. That must be better than hoping Steven will walk through your door wanting a bunch of flowers for his mum.'

'What if she's wrong about the name? How would I know?'

'Give it a timescale. How does three months sound? If you don't find Steven in that time, widen your search and go on a few dates with Neil, Mike or Dave or whoever you like the sound of.'

'You talk a lot of sense. Three months of searching for Steven it is. Or maybe four.'

Nick laughed. 'If, in the meantime, you find a non-Steven who you find yourself attracted to, maybe you should just go with it and accept your clairvoyant was wrong about the name.' He looked at me again with that same intensity I'd felt in the shop. Did he mean him? The idea gave me a warm and fuzzy feeling.

Nick smiled then nodded at the glass I'd just drained. 'Another?'

I looked at my watch. 'I've kept you for over two hours. Don't you need to do some work?'

'I've had four pints and it's not even dinnertime. I don't think I'd be capable of doing anything that I wouldn't have to re-do sober tomorrow so I'm all yours if you want me. But don't let me keep you if you need to do something in the shop.'

I stretched and breathed in deeply. 'I think I'll be pretty useless too so I'm all yours if you want me too.'

We held each other's gaze. We'd both said, 'if you want me'. What was going on? Were we testing the water? Were we flirting? It felt like it.

'Looks like we're stuck with each other then,' Nick said. 'I'll get them in.'

I gently touched his arm. 'Before you go, answer me one question.'

'Anything.'

'Do you have a middle name?'

He smiled. 'Yes.'

'I don't suppose it's Steven, is it?' I chewed my lip.

Nick laughed. 'Sorry. It's John after my dad.'

I twiddled with a strand of hair. 'Just checking.'

His eyes seemed to drink me in as he said, 'I wish it was Steven. I really do.'

12

✉ From Nick
How's the search going for the elusive Steven?
Had a great time with you on Wednesday. Hope we
can do it again soon. Still available to do your
website... if you really want one! Met a Steve
today & thought of you... but he was bald and had
no teeth. Decided not to give him your number!

It was Friday evening and I'd caught the bus to Elise's house after finishing what I needed to do in the shop. I laughed at Nick's message then put my phone back in my bag. 'Sorry about that,' I said to Elise. 'Where were we?'

'Not so fast,' she said. 'I know that smile.'

'What?' I concentrated on curling my legs under me on her sofa in an effort not to catch her eye.

'Don't play Little Miss Innocent with me. That's your "I like someone" smile.'

'It is not.'

'It is too. Who was it?'

'Nobody. Just a new friend.'

'A friend?' Elise raised an eyebrow. 'A *male* friend?'

'Will you stop it with the implications?' I raised both eyebrows back at her. 'It's a guy called Nick. Auntie Kay decided to set us up. She was about as subtle as a brick so we sussed her out but decided to have a few drinks together anyway. Just as friends.'

'Is he single?'

'Yes.'

'Good-looking?'

I blushed. 'Might be.'

'But you're just friends?'

I nodded.

'Why?'

'Why not?' I said. 'He's good fun. I like him. I want to see him again.'

'I mean why are you only friends? You're single, he's single and you get on well. Why not more?'

'You know why.'

Elise shrugged, then I saw realisation dawn. 'Oh. Steven. So, online dating? Much as it pains me to admit it, Clare's idea sounds great. Becky from school met her fiancé online and she's completely smitten. Obviously or she wouldn't be marrying the guy. But before she met him, she had a great time dating. Have you joined up yet?'

'I'm thinking I should focus on getting the shop ready. I only have Auntie Kay for another two weeks and she's so elusive at the moment with all her shopping trips that I'm struggling to tap into all her knowledge. I've got a load of gifts to source before I re-open and—'

'Stop making excuses,' Elise said. 'Do you want to find Steven or not?'

'It's all right for you. You've got Gary.' I nodded towards the stunning wedding photo on Elise's mantelpiece. 'You never had to go through all these dating traumas.'

Elise looked wistfully at the photo for a few moments before shaking her head. 'So tell me why you're *really* hesitating.'

'I've got absolutely nothing against online dating. I know loads of people have met their partners that way. But I've had this little fantasy lately that he'll be a customer buying flowers for a sick relative in hospital and our eyes will meet across a bunch of stargazer lilies and something will just click. He'll ask me what my favourite

flowers are. I'll say white roses because they're so pure and beautiful. He'll ask for a dozen of them to be delivered to someone even
more beautiful than they are. Thinking I've imagined the chemistry,
I'll complete an order form with a heavy heart. My heart will be
thumping as he gives his name as Steven. He'll tell me the message
is, "Please say you'll meet me tonight. I've already fallen for you" or
perhaps something less cheesy, and, when I ask for the delivery
address, he'll say, "Sarah at Seaside Blooms on Castle Street," and...
stop laughing at me.' I threw a cushion at Elise.

'I'm not laughing at you. It's just sweet that you're so wildly
romantic.'

'Pathetic, you mean. And cheesy. Anyway, we've already decided
that he's unlikely to be a customer.'

'So when are you going to register?'

'Not you too.'

'I told you I think it's a good idea so I'm going to nag you.'

'Clare's been bombarding me with texts all week. There's
another reason why I've been putting it off.'

Elise shuffled forward in her chair. 'Spill.'

'I know I'm probably being really silly about it but I'm a bit
embarrassed about the idea of dating when I'm living with Mum
and Dad, especially when everyone I date will be called Steven. In
time, if – when – I meet *the* Steven, I'll tell them the whole story,
but, for now, I don't think I want anyone else to know.'

She raised her eyebrows questioningly. 'You told your Auntie
Kay. Won't your mum be hurt that you opened up to her sister and
not her?'

I bit my lip. I hadn't thought about that. 'I asked her not to say
anything and I don't think she will. And telling her is different to
telling my parents. She's about to leave the country so she won't be
watching my every move, but I'm living with Mum and Dad. If I
don't meet Steven straight away, I don't want them to think I've
turned into some sort of serial-dater. I think I'll wait till I'm settled
with the shop, then look for somewhere to rent in the New Year,
then register.'

'Then you'll be packing to move out. Then unpacking. Then it
will be Valentine's Day then Mother's Day so the shop will be busy,

then wedding season and, before you know it, Christmas again. There'll never be a right time.'

True. I looked at the clock and realised we'd been yakking for two hours. 'It's half seven,' I said. 'Aren't you meant to be having dinner with the mother-in-law?'

Elise gasped. 'Oh crap! Trust me to give her more ammunition against me.'

'Is she really that bad?'

'Worse. Give me five minutes to get changed then I'll drop you off on my way. Gary's meeting me there.'

'I hope you've got your best twin-set and pearls ready,' I shouted after her as she ran up the stairs. Elise's husband, Gary, is lovely and very down-to-earth, but his mum is posh. Or rather she likes to think she's posh. She polishes the silver, uses the Royal Doulton dinner service and constantly name drops, which would be great if she actually knew anyone famous. However, her elite circle consists of the vicar, the Mayor, the Chair of the Rotary Club and Vera Hainsworth who got a recipe published in *Woman's Weekly* in 1982. Not exactly A-list.

I'd been joking about the twin-set but when she re-appeared five minutes later, Elise's attire wasn't far from it. My eyes widened as I took in the beige ballet pumps, tan tights, beige knee-length pencil skirt, fussy white blouse and Elise's beautiful auburn hair tied back in a plait, secured with a yellow ribbon. 'Who are you and what have you done with my friend Elise?'

Elise closed her eyes and gave a little shudder. 'Don't even go there,' she muttered. 'All I can say is that, when faced with a mother-in-law like mine, it's a good idea to pick your battles. Are you all set?'

During the five-minute drive from Elise's house to Mum and Dad's, I tried to explore what she meant, but she just sighed and said, 'It's a long story and not a very interesting one. Once you're all settled and the shop's opened and doing well, we'll go out for cocktails and I'll tell you everything. For now, I'm more interested in you and this online dating idea. Are you going to register tonight or not? There'll always be excuses but *the* Steven's out there and procrastinating isn't going to help you find him.'

* * *

I blew on a mug of tea as I sat at the dressing table in my old bedroom and stared at my laptop screen two hours later. Bowing to peer pressure, I'd found an article on the ten best dating sites, which helped narrow it down although my mind was still in a whirr. Which site? And, even before that, did I really want to go down the online dating route? I knew the stargazer lilies fantasy was something that would only happen in the movies, but I still preferred the romantic ideal of *the* Steven appearing out of the blue rather than finding him online. I also knew that Clare was right, though; I would tie myself into knots waiting for him to appear, jumping every time I heard someone say the name 'Steven'. Would I tie myself in knots any less if I registered with an online dating site? What if I messaged half a dozen Stevens and none of them responded? Would making contact and having it ignored be worse than just not knowing when *the* Steven would walk into my life? *Argh!!!* My head hurt just thinking about it.

I clicked onto my emails instead. There was one from Andy with the intriguing subject line of, 'Have I Got BIG News For You'. My stomach did a flip. Even after all these years of just being friends, I still had a physical reaction each time I heard from him.

Andy Kerr had lived in the same halls of residence as Clare and me in our first year. We were friends at first but I found myself increasingly attracted to him as the first term progressed. I had no idea whether he felt the same until he steered me towards a bunch of mistletoe dangling from the ceiling at the Christmas Ball. We were inseparable for the last week of term but I was worried a month apart over the Christmas holidays would be too much. He'd returned home to Bournemouth and we'd both lined up part-time jobs so meeting up over the break wasn't an option. Fortunately, it turned out that absence really did make the heart grow fonder and, as soon as we got back in January, we officially became a couple, very much in love.

I hesitated before I opened Andy's email message. What if the news was that he'd finally proposed to Kelly after a two-year on-off relationship or he was going to be a daddy? My hand shook slightly as I clicked on the message.

Hi Sarah
Sorry it's been a few months. How's it going?
How's work? How's Jason? Just a quickie to ask
whether you're free any time mid-December. My
contract in Dubai is finally at an end and I return
to the UK for good around then. I'm dying to see
you again. Can I take you out for a meal and catch
up on all your news? Let me know a date that suits
you around all the office Christmas parties etc.
All the best
Andy xx

Hmm. No mention of Kelly or impending fatherhood. Phew.

Hi Andy
Good to hear from you. Great news about your
return to the UK. Is Kelly coming back too? No
work Christmas parties for me — I've left work!
But I've also left London. I'm living back home
and have taken over Auntie Kay's shop. I'm re-
opening at the end of November and I'm expecting
December to fly by in a blur. I'm afraid there's
no chance of me coming to London, but if you ever
fancy a trip to North Yorkshire…
Sarah xx

From Andy:
Here was me thinking I was about to go through a
major upheaval leaving Dubai after three years
but I think you've just trumped me! Kelly's
staying in Dubai. Has Jason moved with you?

To Andy:

Jason and I have split up

From Andy:
Sorry to hear that. Hope you're not too upset.
Good luck with the shop opening. I'll get in
touch when I'm back and we'll find a way to catch
up properly. Take care x

I smiled as I logged off my laptop. I always felt warm and fuzzy with nostalgia after hearing from Andy, even if it was only a brief email exchange. I reached behind the dressing table to draw the curtains, pausing to stare for a moment into the inky blackness. The wind had picked up and the sounds of the approaching storm echoed round my bedroom: a garden gate crashing, a dog barking, trees creaking. I shivered. Storms weren't my friend. They transported me immediately back to Uncle Alan's flat and the flash of lightning that revealed his decomposing body. Another storm had raged on the night of his funeral. I could vividly remember backing myself into a corner of my room after he was cremated, clutching onto Mr Pink, and sobbing for Uncle Alan's lonely soul.

Why had Mum and Dad gone out tonight of all nights? I didn't want to be alone. I leapt as a burst of rain pelted the window. Yanking the curtains shut, I dived under the duvet fully dressed, curled up in a foetus position, and hugged Mr Pink tightly, willing the storm to end.

Think nice thoughts. Think about Andy and the good times we had. But a storm had also raged the night that our relationship ended and, as my bedroom lit up with lightning and the thunder crashed, I felt the pain of goodbye all over again.

Andy was my first in every sense of the word and I really believed I'd found The One. Our three years together at university were so happy and after graduation we jetted off for a week's holiday in Rhodes. It was an incredibly romantic week, but also an emotional one as we prepared to face our toughest challenge yet: embarking on our new careers two hundred miles apart. I'd secured a job in Manchester but Andy's job was in London. We knew it wouldn't be easy but we'd already experienced the challenges of a distance relationship each university holiday when we both returned home to our families. Having survived that greater distance, we were confident that London to Manchester wouldn't tear us apart.

The first few weeks were fine. We'd already decided we wouldn't meet up as we had new homes and jobs to settle into and new friends to make. We spoke regularly on the phone and talked about how much we loved and missed each other.

Then things changed. Andy began sounding irritated each time I phoned. He only managed the occasional one-sentence email in reply to the reams I'd write to him, saying he was too busy with work to write more. We made arrangements to meet on three occasions and, each time, he cancelled.

I started to wonder if he'd met someone else. Once the idea popped into my head, I couldn't shake it. After the third cancelled weekend, I caught the train to London anyway. I phoned Andy from outside his office, desperately hoping he was there and not out with my replacement. It was half eight on a Friday evening but he was still at the office. Feeling relieved – but scared as he didn't sound at all pleased to hear that I was outside – I asked him to come down for ten minutes. The cold look he gave me as he burst through the revolving doors was a far cry from the emotional reunion I'd imagined on the train down. I'd naively thought that, if I could just see him, everything would slot into place.

I asked if we could go for a meal and talk. He refused. 'I told you I was busy, so I don't know what you're playing at by coming here and making a scene.'

'I'm not making a scene,' I protested. 'I was worried about you.' I reached out to take his hand but he took a step back.

I saw his eyes flick to the overnight bag beside me on the step. He sighed then reached in his pocket, pulled out his keys and dangled them in front of me. 'I hope you've got a good book in there because you're going to have to entertain yourself all weekend. I told you I was busy. I'm working. We're at a critical stage in this project. It's more important than...'

It would have killed me to hear the end of the sentence. I remember staring at the keys then at the face of the man I'd thought

I'd be with forever. As he stared back at me, dark eyes flashing with what seemed to be contempt, I couldn't see anything of the Andy I loved. I gently pushed the keys away, shook my head then said, 'And here was me thinking I was the most important thing in your life.'

'My career's important,' he snarled. 'I told you not to come. Why didn't you listen?'

'I did listen. But I stupidly thought you might be missing me as much as I was missing you.' I swallowed on the lump in my throat as I willed him to take me in his arms and say, 'Of course I miss you. I'm glad you came really.' Instead, he just put his keys back in his pocket, looked at his watch and tutted. The sound pierced through my heart.

'It's okay,' I said. 'I won't waste more of your precious work time. If you haven't got the time to see me or speak to me, what's the point in being together anymore?' I paused, hoping he'd say something to convince me there was still hope for us but he just stared back, frowning. I picked up my bag. 'I'll be off, then. I hope you and your career will be very happy together.' It was a stupid line but it was the only thing I could think of at the time. 'Goodbye, Andy.' I paused again, my eyes pleading with him to recover this. Silence. With shaky legs, I walked back towards the underground, head held high, tears streaming.

My resolve crumbled within about ten paces. I stopped and turned around, half expecting to see Andy slumped on the steps, crumpling with regret, or – even better – chasing after me and begging me to take him back. Instead, he'd gone inside, presumably back to his 'important' work. The knife twisted deeper. In a daze, I caught the tube to King's Cross and boarded the next train to York, anxious to be surrounded by people who really did care about me. I was too late for a connection to Whitsborough Bay, but my parents drove to York to collect me. Mum sat in the back and cuddled me like a child while I sobbed all the way home.

It had taken two years before I felt strong enough to compose an email to Andy. At a loose end one weekend, I'd decided to sort through a box of photos and put them in albums. I came across the one of Andy and me in Rhodes that I used to have stuck on the fridge. Tanned and radiating with happiness, I'd thought it was only a matter of time before he proposed. I'd never have predicted that we'd split up by the end of the following November.

Looking at the photo, I realised I didn't feel angry or hurt anymore. Instead, I felt happy with nostalgia so I sent a quick 'hi-how-are-you?' email. Andy replied immediately saying it was good to hear from me. The emails got longer and more regular and the friendship was gradually restored, our messages even becoming quite flirty. I was convinced that we'd get back together one day, when the timing was right.

It was a year before we broached the subject of meeting up for a drink, but by the time we finally co-ordinated our diaries, I'd met someone else and he'd been offered a short secondment overseas – the first of many. And so began the pattern of it never being the right time to try again.

'And now he's finally coming back to the UK for good and I'm single,' I whispered into Mr Pink's fur, 'but I don't know if he's single or still with Kelly. Or someone else. And anyway, I'm not exactly local. It would never work.'

Even if he was single, was it too late to try again after all these years? Eight years was a hell of a lot of water under the bridge.

I reached out and switched off my bedside lamp. 'Location isn't the only problem,' I whispered to Mr Pink. 'He isn't called Steven.'

13

I had a fitful night's sleep and was wide awake shortly before half six. My head felt hangover-fuzzy yet I hadn't touched a drop. Drawing back the curtains, it was still dark but, from the tranquillity, I knew the storm had passed... for now. The sun would be rising within the hour: a stunning spectacle. There was nothing I loved more than being on the beach when the sun peeped over the horizon then steadily rose into the sky behind Lighthouse Point. It was a sight that was way overdue for me.

Twenty minutes later, I steered Mum's car down the approach road to South Bay. The gradually lightening sky was speckled with pink and orange in stark contrast with the silhouette of the lighthouse and harbour. To top off the picture-perfect scene, lights twinkled around the curve of the bay. Absolutely beautiful. Why had I traded this for big cities for so many years?

I parked the car on the seafront and headed down a few steps onto the sand. Seaweed and driftwood strewn across the beach and promenade hinted at the storm that had raged hours earlier, but all other signs were gone as the gentle waves lapped onto the sand a few hundred metres out. I perched myself on the edge of the beach wall and inhaled the salty air.

Soon after, I was treated to an orange arc peeping over the horizon, casting a welcoming glow across the calm sea. Sunrise on the beach: stunning. Absolutely stunning. And suddenly I had an over-whelming compulsion to run. Me. The person who'd shunned exercise for a year. It was going to hurt but I wanted to do it.

I had the beach almost to myself as I jogged slowly along the hard sand, dodging round lumps of seaweed. I could make out the silhouettes of a couple of people walking dogs and two more runners in the distance. The peace gave me time to think and, by the time I'd made it back to my starting point, I'd reached a decision. I was *definitely* going to give online dating a try. Targeted online dating as Clare suggested: only Stevens. Andy returning to the UK and us both being single could have meant something if I'd still been in London, but my present circumstances made it a non-starter. So we'd just continue as friends who occasionally emailed each other and I'd bury any thoughts of it finally being the right timing for us – since it clearly still wasn't. If I was ever in London, I'd look him up, but with a business to run and weekends committed to doing that, me being in London was a very unlikely scenario.

Bending over, hands on my thighs, I gulped in deep breaths of cold air while my heartbeat steadied. I sat down on the cold sand and smiled as I drank in the blazing ball of fire behind the red and white striped lighthouse.

With another deep breath, I lay back on the sand, eyes closed, feeling trickles of sweat run down my hairline and into my ears. How very attractive. I hoped none of the joggers or dog-walkers were Stevens because sweaty, beetroot-red, and breathless wasn't the most alluring of looks.

I lay there for a few minutes listening to the distant waves, the cry of gulls, and feeling the slowing of my heartbeat. Despite the physical exertion, I felt more relaxed than I'd felt in a very long time.

'Sarah? I thought it was you.'

Nick? I snapped open my eyes. He was silhouetted against the sun, but it was definitely him. My heart began beating faster again as I propped myself up on my elbows and put my hand up to shade my eyes as I squinted at him. 'Hi. What are you doing here?'

'Same as you by the looks of it.'

'Sweating buckets and having a coronary on the beach?'

Nick laughed and reached his hand out to me. 'Want a hand up?'

I nodded. 'Your hands are very warm,' I said as he pulled me to my feet. *And very soft.* An image filled my mind of those hands cupping my face, and then his fingers running through my hair as he kissed me. *Whoa! Where did that come from?*

'And yours are very cold,' he said. 'Here.' He encased my hands in his and rubbed them quickly. I looked at our joined hands, then into his eyes. In that brief moment, it felt like everything around us stopped. I was oblivious to the lapping of the waves and the cries of the gulls that had been so clear moments before. I was, however, still very aware of the thud-thud of my heart as I lost myself in his twinkling blue eyes. He reached up to my face with one hand and gently caressed my cheek as I held my breath... and his gaze. 'You have some sand on your cheek,' he said but he didn't move his hand and I didn't want him to. He was going to kiss me. And I didn't want to stop him.

'Ebony! Stop!'

We both turned as a large black Labrador leapt up at Nick, knocking him sideways.

'I'm so sorry. Ebony! Here now!' An elderly woman gave us an apologetic glance before she chucked a ball for Ebony who bounded after it. Peace was restored but the moment was lost. *Damn bloody dog.*

Nick cleared his throat. 'All warm now?'

'Yes. Thanks. Erm, so, erm... you've been running too? Is this a regular thing?' I set off towards the steps onto the promenade in the hope of averting attention from whatever it was that had just happened between us.

Nick followed me. 'I try to come down two or three mornings a week. I hate gyms and I used to hate the idea of running, but a couple of years ago I looked after Skye and Stuart's Spaniel while they were on holiday. She ran so fast and I was scared of losing her so I used to run to keep up with her. When they came back, I realised I missed the exercise so I took it up properly. I've no interest in running anywhere other than the beach, though. There's something exhilarating about running with waves crashing round you. What about you? Regular runner?'

'God, no! I used to be in a club at college, running along the seafront at North Bay twice a week, but I fell out of the habit when I went to university. The only running I've done since then has been a half-hearted jog on a treadmill.'

'So what made you go running today?' Nick asked.

'I had a bad night's sleep and woke up with an overwhelming urge to see the sunrise, which somehow turned into an over-whelming urge to run. I haven't done much exercise for well over a year so I'll probably need a Zimmer frame to help me get around tomorrow.'

He laughed. 'You might want to do a few stretches just in case. Do you think you'll do it again?'

I thought for a moment. 'You know what, I think I will. It was hard work, but I really enjoyed it.'

'If you ever want company, I'm usually here for sunrise a few mornings a week although I don't have set days as I'm often away with work.'

We reached the steps and ascended onto the promenade.

'I might take you up on that,' I said, heading towards where I'd parked the car. 'If you can put up with seeing me in this state again.'

'What state?'

'Sweaty, bright red and far too fat for a pair of leggings.'

Nick stopped.

'What's wrong?' I asked, stopping too.

'I wish you could see yourself through my eyes,' he said. 'Because that's not what I see at all. Far from it.' He held my gaze until I had to look away, feeling suddenly shy.

'I'd better go,' he said. 'Hope to see you again soon.'

I waved as I watched him jog towards his car, a grin on my face at his compliment and the almost-kiss.

My cheeks hurt from grinning by the time I got out of the car at Mum and Dad's for a shower and change.

* * *

On Monday morning, I was at Seaside Blooms waiting for some workmen to arrive to fit my new floor when a text arrived.

✉ From Nick
Hope you've had a good weekend. It was great to
see you on Saturday. I'm working away for the
next few days but, if you're not too achy, can
face it again and don't mind some company, I'm
aiming for a run at 7.15 on Friday. See you if I
see you

I was about to reply when there was a knock on the door. Thinking it would be the workmen, I was surprised to see Auntie Kay instead. I hadn't seen her or even spoken to her since Wednesday. Her hands-off approach was starting to concern me as I'd assumed she'd have been by my side every step of the way. I voiced my worries to Mum at the weekend but she reassured me that the reason I'd seen so little of Auntie Kay was specifically to avoid the hand-holding. I needed to pursue my own vision for Seaside Blooms and get used to making the decisions on my own. After all, it was my business now.

'It's the elusive Auntie Kay,' I said, giving her a hug. 'Wow! I'm honoured by your presence.'

'Don't be so cheeky,' she said, wagging her finger at me playfully. 'I've got a mountain of things to sort out and so have you. You don't need me getting in your way.'

'Do you have time for a cuppa?'

'Always.'

We headed through to the kitchen and I switched the kettle on. 'Let me guess why you're here.' I folded my arms and gave her a stern look. 'I bet you're dying to know the outcome of your little bit of matchmaking and it has probably killed you not knowing for the past few days.'

'I don't know what you're talking about. What matchmaking?'

'Auntie Kay!'

'Okay. You win. I had to do it. I know you think you're destined to be with someone called Steven but you and Nick are perfect for each other. I've always thought it. Now that you're single and back here, I realised there'd still be nothing I could do about it if I was on the other side of the world so I had to give things a little nudge before I left. You're not mad at me, are you?'

I took one look at her mischievous twinkling eyes and laughed. 'You're so naughty.'

'I know, but I'm still your favourite auntie.'

'You're my only auntie,' I said, 'which is just as well as I don't think I could cope with more than one like you.'

'Are you going to put your favourite auntie out of her misery, then? Are you going to see him again?'

The kettle clicked off and I quickly turned my back on her under the pretext of making the drinks. I needed my cheeks to lose some of their colour before I turned and faced her once more.

'Yes, but only as friends.'

'No! Why?'

'Because you were right. He's a really lovely guy and I like his company.'

'You know that's not what I mean. Why just friends? Why not more?'

'It's bad timing. As you just said, I've got loads to do with the shop. Plus, I've just come out of a long-term relationship and he's not called Steven.' I turned back round and handed her a mug. 'So I'm not going to rush into anything with anyone just yet. Maybe in the New Year.'

'With Nick?'

'You never give up, do you?' I ushered her towards the desk and perched on it while she sat on the chair.

'Finding out about Nick isn't the only reason I came in. Do you have any plans for Thursday night?'

'No. Why?'

'I'm cooking a farewell meal for you, Ben, your mum and dad. Thought I might as well take advantage of your brother being home for a long weekend. Seashell Cottage for half six?'

'Sounds good. I'm guessing I won't see you until then?'

She smiled as she shook her head. 'You know I'm at the end of a phone if you have any burning questions, but you're doing brilliantly without me, exactly as I expected.'

'I just don't want you to feel pushed out.'

'Believe me, I'd never feel like that. It's not my business anymore, sweetie. It's yours. Oh, and I have something for you.' She rummaged in her bag and handed me an A5-sized envelope. 'You were asking about a photo with the lighthouse...'

'You found it?' I fumbled with the envelope, pulled out an old black and white photo, and gasped. Standing in front of Whitsborough Bay's lighthouse were three figures. I'd seen their childhood photos before so immediately recognised the children as Mum and Auntie Kay. If I didn't know better, I'd have sworn the adult with them was me, not my grandma. My heart thumped as I reached out and gently touched Grandma's image. *Is it true about Steven, Grandma?*

'I was sorting through an old box of papers last night and came across it. I had to do a double-take. The likeness is uncanny, isn't it?'

I nodded slowly, mesmerised by the photo.

'What made you ask about it?' she said.

'Madame Louisa mentioned it.'

I watched her frown. 'No! So I've just found something that's going to make you believe in that prediction even more. Which is going to make you believe Steven's your destiny and Nick isn't...'

'I'm afraid so.'

'Damn!'

There was another knock on the door. 'That'll be the men fitting the floor,' I said.

'I'll leave you to it, then,' Auntie Kay said, standing up and following me to the door.

I let the workmen in and offered to make them drinks while they brought in their tools. Waiting for the kettle to boil again, I stared at the photo. What was it with things miraculously turning up? Was it a sign? I made a mental note to check behind Mum and Dad's sofa one more time in case the bracelet decided to make a reappearance too. Then I picked up my phone and replied to Nick's text:

✉ To Nick

Could barely move this morning but it's easing! I'm going to Auntie Kay's for a family farewell meal on Thursday so think I will be too full of food and drink to run the next morning. Another time maybe? Thanks for asking

14

Seaside Blooms was a hive of activity all week. The wooden floor looked amazing – so much better than lino – and I'd also had a large counter and preparation table fitted.

Auntie Kay had never bothered with a computer at work, doing everything on paper or by phone. There was therefore no broadband connection and, unfortunately, no free Wi-Fi from any surrounding businesses. With The Outback cleared and organised, there was little more I could do at the shop so I left the fitters to it and worked on my laptop at home, sourcing and ordering the shop fittings and several gift ranges. It had been a really productive week and it felt like big steps had been made in getting ready to re-open.

On Thursday evening, I'd only just set off walking towards Seashell Cottage after work when a text arrived:

✉ From Nick
Met a Stephen this week and thought of you. Hope you have a good time at Kay's tonight x

✉ To Nick
Thank you x

As the message sent, I felt a pang of anxiety. Should I have added the kiss? He'd started it. Did it mean anything or was it just one of those things you do on texts? Was it because of what happened on the beach? A little shiver of pleasure ran through me as I recalled the intensity of that brief moment before that stupid big dog leapt on him and ruined things. Would we really have kissed? I knew I'd wanted to at the time with every fibre of my being, but I also knew that, for the whole of the drive home, there was only one thought going round and round in my mind: What the hell are you playing at? He's not called Steven; he's not called Steven...

Nick's texts had given me butterflies but Monday's reaction had been down to the excitement of the almost-kiss after a year of no affection from Jason, and my reaction to his text just now was only because he'd mentioned a Stephen. That was all. It wasn't Nick causing the butterflies. Was it?

When I arrived at Seashell Cottage ten minutes later, I knocked on the door then walked straight in, as I'd always done.

'Hello?' I shouted. No answer. 'Anyone home?' My stomach rumbled at the tantalising aroma of home-cooked chilli.

A familiar mewing sound made me look down. 'Kat? What are you doing here?' I bent down to give her a fuss. Her brother appeared from the dining room and rubbed round my legs. 'I know Auntie Kay wanted to say goodbye to everyone, but I didn't realise the invitation extended to you two. Where is everyone?'

I opened the lounge door. Nobody there. I was about to close it again when something grey and fluffy on the sofa caught my eye. Were those my cushions? I frowned and stepped into the room. My candles and photos adorned the mantelpiece. What the...?

'Hello?' I called again. 'Where are you?'

The dining room was empty. The kitchen was empty. But both rooms housed more of my belongings.

Running up the stairs and into Auntie Kay's bedroom, I found it full of my bags and boxes. Mr Pink had pride of place on top of the bed. I wandered over to touch him just to make sure I wasn't imagining things when Mum, Dad, Ben and Auntie Kay jumped up from behind the bed and yelled, 'Surprise!'

I clutched my heart dramatically. 'I was beginning to think I'd boarded the Mary Celeste.' I hugged them all.

'Have you had enough of me already?' I asked Mum and Dad. 'What's all my stuff doing here?'

'You're moving in,' Auntie Kay said.

'How come?'

'While I'm away, I'm a little concerned that my beloved Seashell Cottage may get cold and neglected. I thought we may be able to do each other a favour.' Auntie Kay looked at Mum and winked. 'To save you from the insanity of my sister's compulsive meal-making, clothes-washing, and clock-watching, I want you to move in here. Rent-free, of course. But, in return for this considerable generosity on my part, I'd ask that you keep the garden tidy, stop the junk mail from piling up, and keep the place clean. What do you think?'

I looked at Mum and Dad. 'You wouldn't be offended if I moved out?'

Mum smiled. 'You need your own space. And, no offence, but your dad and I have got used to having the peace and quiet of the house to ourselves.' Dad put his arm round her and kissed the top of her head.

I looked at my brother's eager smile and my heart sank as I turned to Auntie Kay. 'Thank you, but I can't accept. You've given me too much already with the shop and the loan. It's not fair on Ben if I get a free house too, even if it's only temporary.'

'Don't be so daft,' Ben said. 'Did you never wonder how I managed to buy a house on my salary?'

'I...' I shrugged. I hadn't given it much thought but, now that he mentioned it, a two-bed terrace in a fairly nice part of Leeds did seem a little out of the reach of Ben's low-paid day job working for a missing persons charity.

'Auntie Kay gave me the deposit,' he said, shaking his head. 'So I think we're evens. Can we eat now?'

I looked from him to my parents to Auntie Kay. Everyone seemed to be nodding encouragingly. 'Does the invitation stretch to Kit and Kat?'

'Of course,' she said. 'They've already made themselves at home.'

'As long as everyone doesn't mind, it's a big fat yes, then,' I squealed. 'Thank you so much.'

'You're very welcome.' Auntie Kay gave me another hug.

'You're not going for another ten days,' I said. 'My stuff's everywhere. It'll be in the way.'

'Ah. Slight change of plan. Linda and I are leaving on Monday now.'

I gasped. 'This Monday? As in four days' time? The shop's not ready yet. What if I have questions?'

'Then email me them. I'm moving into Linda's this evening so we can sort out the last-minute details. I'm around for three more full days and I promise to be more available in that time if you need me. I've done all my clothes shopping now.'

'But...'

'I hate to break up this riveting discussion,' Ben said, 'but I'm wasting away. Man need food. Now.' He pushed past me and bounded down the stairs like a little kid, followed by Auntie Kay, then Mum and Dad.

I looked around the bedroom trying to take in what had just happened. A new business opening in two weeks' time and a new home from this very minute. Shocked as I was by Auntie Kay's announcement, I knew she was right; I'd done most of it on my own so far. How spooky that I'd been talking to Elise less than a week ago about moving out and now it had happened. If felt like everything was slotting into place. Of course, moving in meant I had absolutely no excuse for putting off registering with a dating site and going all out with my search for Steven.

Kit launched himself onto the bed and I nuzzled into his fur. 'Do you think it's time we found you a new daddy?' I whispered. He purred loudly. 'I'll take that as a yes.'

My phone beeped. Nick again?

✉ From Nick
Forgot to say in last text... do you have any plans for 2 weeks on Monday? I have a proposition for you. Will stop by the shop one day next week to explain x

✉ To Nick
No plans so far. Sounds exciting. See you soon x

Eek! Kisses again. Was he asking me on a date? No. You don't ask someone on a date for two-and-a-half weeks' time and you don't use words like 'proposition'. But a little part of me quite liked the idea of a date.

'Sarah! Food's ready,' Ben shouted up the stairs. 'Get your arse down here.'

Nice. 'Coming.' I stood up and was momentarily blinded by a flash from a chest of drawers. Moving a little closer, I saw a large and very sparkly photo frame that must have caught the light. Instinctively I picked it up to look at the photo: a large print of the lighthouse picture Auntie Kay had shown me on Monday. She must have had it enlarged while she was in town. Blown up to A4 size, my resemblance to my grandma was even clearer.

'Sarah!' Ben shouted again.

'Coming,' I shouted back, reluctantly putting the photo back on the drawers. Something else in the larger picture caught my eye: Grandma's bracelet. When Grandma died, Auntie Kay as the elder sister inherited her wedding and engagement rings and Mum inherited the bracelet.

She also says your mum will be devastated in the future when she can't find your grandma's bracelet. It's not lost. It's under the sofa...

I'd already looked under Mum and Dad's sofa but what if it was under Auntie Kay's instead? I raced out the room, down the stairs and into the lounge.

'What *are* you doing?' Ben said, making me jump as I lay on the floor.

'Do me a favour and lift up that end of the sofa.'

'Why?'

I glared at him. He sighed but did as he was asked. I bent down and looked underneath. *Fluff... coins... hair-grip and... oh my God!* I grabbed at the object.

Ben lowered the sofa back down with a grunt. 'What is it?'

I stared at the item resting on my palm. 'Grandma's bracelet. The one Mum thought she'd lost years ago.'

'No way. How did you know it was there?'

I smiled and shook my head. 'You wouldn't believe me if I told you.' Suddenly feeling very weak, I sunk back against the sofa, breathing deeply. Wow! The bracelet under the sofa and the lighthouse photo, exactly as predicted. There was no way she could have guessed at those things. There was just one thing left to happen, then: meeting Steven. Oh. My. God!

15

'How cute is this place?' Clare said, looking at the roses round the door on the double-fronted white-washed cottage. 'I can't wait to see it in daylight.'

I ushered her into the narrow hallway the following evening and closed the door on the bitter November night. 'Glad you found it all right. I've got a fire going in the lounge.'

'A real one?'

'Of course. Now, do you want to be all cutesy cottage and have hot chocolate with marshmallows or can I tempt you with a glass of wine?'

'After the drive I've had, what do you think?'

'I'll get the glasses. Make yourself at home.'

I grabbed a bottle of wine and glasses from the kitchen and headed back to the lounge.

Clare was talking to Kit and Kat. 'Hi cats. How's your new home? Jesus. I must be going soft. Will you listen to me talking to two stupid moggies?'

I laughed as I put the glasses down on the coffee table so I could pour the wine. 'I thought you might be expecting an answer from them.'

'Scarily enough, I think I was. It's been a long day.' She took a glug of her wine then looked around the room full of my books and other belongings. 'Nice room. Looks like you've settled in well already. Where's all your auntie's stuff?'

'In my old bedroom. Dad and Ben did a huge swap round yesterday while I was at the shop. I'd been thinking that I should look for somewhere to rent so it's worked out perfectly. It's been lovely being back at home, but I'm used to my independence. I don't think I could have lived with my parents long-term but they seemed so pleased to have me back that I didn't want to offend them by saying so.'

'Can't say I blame you. If I moved back to Ireland, I'd hate to live with my parents.' Clare stared into the fireplace for a moment, fiddling with the Claddagh ring she always wore on her right hand. 'Will you listen to me? What a stupid thing to say. I have no intention of *ever* moving back to Ireland – *whatever* happens in my life – and, seeing as I don't even exchange Christmas cards with the parents, the mere idea of me being in a situation where moving back in with them is even an option is absurd, so it is.'

'More wine?' I asked as Clare gulped hers down in one.

'Please.' She held out her glass. I noticed her hand shaking. I'd noticed the rambling too. It was odd how we shared the same nervous tendency to talk too much.

'You know I'm here if you ever want to talk about what happened with you and your parents, don't you?'

'I know. But I'm grand, thanks. I don't know what came over me. Must be the sea air or something.'

'Must be. It can have a strange effect on them city folk what aren't used to it.' I put on my best yokel accent and smiled.

The subject of Clare's past was closed again. Every so often, she let something slip. I'd pieced together that she'd been brought up in a strict catholic family in a village not too far from Cork. There'd been some major family fall-out when she was a teenager resulting in Clare moving to Cornwall to live with a distant relative. She'd never returned to Ireland or spoken to her parents. There were siblings but she wasn't in touch with them either. She never mentioned her guardian in Cornwall so I suspected ties had been severed there too. I'd never seen any family photos or pictures of her home.

When we were at university, I tried to get Clare to open up and tell me about her family but she always refused. The bits I knew had mainly come from drink-fuelled nights out, but the minute she revealed something about her past that I tried to probe, she clammed up completely and avoided me for a couple of days. I soon wised up and realised it was none of my business and I'd rather have Clare as a friend with a mysterious past than know all about the skeletons in her closet yet no longer have her as a friend.

'So,' Clare said getting to her feet, 'where's your laptop?'

'Why?'

'Will I be right in guessing someone hasn't registered on a dating site yet? It's my mission this weekend to make sure they do.'

'Now?'

'Now's just grand. Sure, if we get your profile up and running tonight, you could line up a few dates for next week.'

'I...' But I had made the decision to register and I was all out of excuses for delaying it. It would be good to have Clare with me for support. 'Sod it, let's do it.'

* * *

'Do you really think I'll get any responses?' I locked the door to Seaside Blooms the next evening after an exhausting day of assembling display units, while Clare painted some stunning floral images onto the walls.

'For the fiftieth time today, *yes!* I'm convinced of it.' She rummaged in her bag. 'And not only that, I reckon you'll have several responses by the time we get back to the cottage. Now will you be quiet? I'm concentrating.'

We set off up Castle Street. 'What are you looking for?' I asked.

'My phone.'

I stopped. 'The phone you said you'd left at the cottage charging?'

Clare pulled it out of her bag. 'I lied.'

'Why would you do that to me?'

'It was for your own good. You'd have been checking your messages constantly, on a high if you heard from anyone and on a low if you didn't and either way, would have got nothing done. Instead, you've put together more flat-packs than an IKEA store, which, I have to say, was quite impressive to watch.'

'Can I check my messages now?'

'No.'

We walked for a while in silence as Clare fiddled with her phone. She was right to have hidden it because I *would* have been checking it every five minutes. Broadband was getting connected the following week so my lovely new work Mac had been sitting there all day, teasing me with its inability to do anything online.

'Do you think it was a bit sad marking all those Stevens as my favourites?'

Clare sighed again. 'Will you shut your trap, now? I'm trying to read something. We'll be home in ten minutes.'

Sulking slightly, I dug my ancient phone out of my pocket and was surprised to see a text from Nick. I hadn't heard it beep.

✉ From Nick

Not going to be able to stop by this week and won't be running either. Last minute job in Edinburgh. Working for a Steve! But he's twice your age & 5 times divorced! Keep that Monday free still. Will catch up soon to explain my proposition. Also had some ideas for your website xx

Damn! I'd been looking forward to seeing him. *Whoa there, Sarah! Stop it. You may have messages at home from a stack of Stevens begging for a date with you. Think lustful thoughts about them, not about Nick.*

But he did sign off his text with two kisses this time. What did that mean?

* * *

'Oh my God!' I squealed fifteen minutes later. 'Five messages. I can't believe it.' Hands shaking, I clicked on the first one.

'What does it say? Will you angle your laptop so I can see?'

I did as I was told. 'This one's pants – just a welcome message from the-one.com.'

'So read it later then.' After acting so relaxed about it all day, Clare now had her excited head on. 'Who's the next one from?'

I clicked on the next message. 'Crap. Not a Steven. It's from someone called Dave Peacock. Let's see.' I scanned the message then screwed up my nose. 'Ew! That's disgusting. And he can't spell.'

'What does he say?' Clare grabbed the laptop from me.

```
Hi, I'm Dave. I see your new. Your gorgeous. I
bet your a dirty bitch. I want to lick cream off
you. If you fancy a shag, get in touch. I'm hard
for you. I want…
```

'Ew!' she agreed, clicking off the message. 'Dirty, dirty man. I'm sure they're not all like this.'

'Did you change my profile back to one of your mucky ones?' It was a battle last night to get something I approved of on my profile. Clare insisted on being in control of the laptop and kept selecting hobbies like 'pole dancing' and 'erotica' as well as compiling indecent summaries about what I'd like to do to any Stevens out there.

'Of course not. I was only messing with you last night. You know I wouldn't do that to you for real.'

I tentatively looked at the next message when she clicked on it:

```
Hello Sarah, my name's Chris Taylor. I'm 25 and I
live in a small hamlet called Greavedon between
Whitsborough Bay and York. I work in the planning
department at York City Council. I love old
buildings. You say you live in a 200-year-old
cottage so you probably agree!
```

'He sounds normal.' I could hear the relief in Clare's voice. 'A bit young perhaps, but quite nice. Although there's no point reading the rest.'

'Why not?'

'He's not called Steven. Remember, the whole point of this was to target Stevens.'

* * *

'I'm gutted,' Clare said over drinks in Minty's later that evening. 'I thought it was a really grand idea.'

'You weren't to know. Please don't feel bad.' I took a sip of my wine and wondered what else I could say to lift Clare's spirits and make our night out fun rather than the sombre affair it was turning out to be.

'Great, that's just what I need,' Clare muttered, staring towards the entrance.

I turned round to see what had caught her attention. 'Elise! I thought you were going to your grandma's.'

'I was but she's had a better offer. One of the men in her retirement home is taking her out to the theatre. Grandma's really excited, bless her. It's so sweet.'

'Ew – old people getting it on? Disgusting.' Clare shuddered.

'Hi Clare, nice to see you as always. Thanks for sharing.'

'Ladies,' I warned, 'play nicely.'

Elise sat down in one of the spare chairs at our table. 'Don't worry, Clare, I'm not going to crash your night out. Gary and I are meeting friends for a Chinese, but I spotted you in the window and thought I'd come in to say hello to Sarah and see if she's had any messages now that she's finally registered with a dating site.'

'How do you know she's registered?'

Uh-oh.

'Sarah texted me last night to tell me, of course.' Elise turned to me. 'Any news?'

'Five messages.'

'From Stevens?'

'Four non-Stevens plus a message from a Steven I'd picked as a favourite saying he was flattered but he'd met someone and was about to remove his profile.'

'That's a shame.' She shrugged. 'Consider it teething problems.

Maybe give it until Christmas and, if it's more of the same, change to another site or give it up as a bad job.'

I nodded and smiled.

'In that case, I'll leave you to it.' Elise gave a nod towards Gary who was loitering outside the window, pointing to his watch. 'Don't give up,' she whispered, giving me a hug. 'Call me when your house-guest has gone. Clare, as always, it's been a delight.' And, with that, she sashayed out of Minty's.

I looked at Clare. 'Before you say anything nasty, remember that Elise thinks it's a good idea.'

'Wasn't going to say a word. Is it your round?'

'Yes.'

'Grand.'

* * *

'Did she get away okay?' Elise asked over the phone on Monday evening.

'Who? Auntie Kay or Clare?'

'Ha ha. Kay, of course.'

'Yes. She'll be on the plane right now. Dad got back from the airport a couple of hours ago.' We'd all had Sunday lunch together and said our goodbyes then before Ben caught the train back to Leeds. Mum, Auntie Kay and I all got upset so there were lots of hugs and promises of regular contact. Mum and I had intended to join Dad for the airport run but Auntie Kay decided it would be too emotional to say goodbye two days in a row and, on a practical note, five adults was going to be a squeeze alongside the luggage.

'She'll let us know when she lands,' I said. 'And, not that you're interested, but Clare left this morning.'

'Dare I ask...?'

'Two more messages. And I have a date.' I couldn't keep the excitement out of my voice as I did a little dance round the lounge.

'Really? When? Who?'

'He's called Steve Turner. I'd put him in my favourites and he got in touch last night. We've exchanged a few messages this evening and we're going to the cinema tomorrow night.'

'Can I come round and help you get ready?'

'If you want. I could probably do with some wardrobe advice.'

'We can discuss a strategy for what to do if he's creepy or boring and you want to escape. Not that he will be, of course,' Elise said, 'because he may well be *the* Steven.'

'I know.' I did another little dance round the room. 'I'm so excited.'

'What about the other message?'

'Some bloke called Darren. He sounds nice, but I haven't replied yet because I was too excited about hearing from one of my Stevens. I might wait until after the cinema then get in touch.'

'Remember he's not a Steven, though.'

'I know. But he sounds nice.'

'Sarah!'

'I know. I need to be strong.'

'I know it's tough, but if you spend time with Darrens it's time you're not spending with Stevens. And if you're deviating into non-Stevens, I suspect there's a Nick who may be top of your list.'

As usual, she was right.

16

✉ From Auntie Kay
Good flight over to Canada and settled in our
hotel in Vancouver. Have you and Nick got your
act together yet? I know he's not called Steven
but surely you can see he's perfect for you xx

✉ To Auntie Kay
Can't believe you're thousands of miles away and
you're still meddling! I have a date tonight.
With a Steven. So ner! xxx

I checked my watch as I hurried down the cliff path to the seafront. Whose stupid idea was it to wear high-heeled boots? Hurrying in heels wasn't easy and I was late. It wasn't even my fault. As I was leaving the street, one of Auntie Kay's neighbours stopped to congratulate me on being the new owner of Seaside Blooms and ask me whether Auntie Kay was enjoying her travels. Despite my protests that I had to meet someone and that Auntie Kay had only left yesterday, Mrs Bailey kept me for nearly fifteen minutes talking about the time she'd *almost* booked a long weekend break to New York before deciding on a static caravan in Cleethorpes instead – not quite the same thing.

As soon as I rounded the corner, I spotted Steve, immediately recognisable from his online photo. He raised his hand, stared at his watch, shook his head then turned to stare down the seafront in the opposite direction from my approach. Hmm, if my interpretation of his body language was correct, Steve Turner was not a happy little bunny at being kept waiting.

I took a deep breath and tapped him on the arm, declaring brightly, 'Steve? I'm Sarah.' I put my hand out to shake his and felt very small when he didn't take it. Years of working in business made this a natural reaction on meeting someone new, but perhaps it wasn't appropriate. Especially for a date I'd kept waiting. Especially a date with a face like thunder. Especially a date who was looking at me as though I was something unpleasant he'd just trodden in. Oh pants. It was going to be a long night.

'You're late.'

I self-consciously put my hand back down by my side. 'I'm so sorry. I got held up. One of my—'

'It's about to start,' he interrupted. 'You owe me £7.75.' He put his hand out.

'Sorry?'

'£7.75. I've already bought the tickets.' He moved his outstretched hand slightly closer to me and repeated, '£7.75.'

'Erm, okay.' I rummaged in my bag for my purse and handed him a tenner.

'I haven't got any change.'

'It doesn't matter about the change,' I muttered, feeling like I was paying a taxi-fare.

'Okay.' He pocketed the note. How rude. It was only £2.25 but I had expected at least a little objection or perhaps an offer to buy some popcorn. He thrust a ticket into my hand and headed into the lobby without even holding the door for me. I watched him through the glass, heading towards the usher. Was he even aware I wasn't with him? Or bothered now that he'd been paid – with interest – for the ticket? I hesitated for a moment wondering whether to follow or run. Sod it. I'd paid and it was a film I really wanted to see so I might as well go in.

I caught up with Steve as he reached the door to screen two. 'I hope we can get some decent seats,' he said, finally acknowledging me again. He then surprised me by stepping back and holding the door open with a big smile that lit up his eyes and transformed him from Mr Grumpy into Mr Pretty Hot Actually.

I relaxed, putting his earlier rudeness down to a combination of nerves and frustration at my lateness. I'd have been the same. Well, not rude, but I'd have been fed up if a date was late, especially if I'd already paid for tickets.

The opening credits were rolling and, as my eyes adjusted to the gloom, I saw that the cinema was packed.

'Shit. We're going to have to sit right at the front. Nice one, Sarah.' He spat my name out in disgust then stormed down the slope.

I was mortified as I took in the curious gazes of the cinema-goers sat in the closest seats to our disturbance. 'Sorry,' I whispered, scuttling after him.

'Sorry,' I whispered again as I pushed past several pairs of legs to slide awkwardly into a seat beside him in the middle of the second row. 'Sorry,' I whispered to Steve as I sat down beside him.

He shushed me. The cheeky git actually shushed me.

* * *

As I slowly walked back towards the Old Town, I switched my phone off silent and noticed several missed calls from Clare. I decided to wait until I was back at the cottage before ringing her but she beat me to it, no doubt desperate for a progress report and probably even more desperate to score points by knowing everything before Elise. If I were a betting woman, I'd put money on her having had me on solid redial for the past half an hour.

'How was it?' she said, the moment I answered.

'Absolute disaster...'

'What an eejit,' she cried after I'd told her about his reaction to me being late. 'Why didn't you just walk out?'

'To be honest, I was so surprised at his reaction, I just followed him and sat down but I kept going over his reaction, getting angrier.

I'd finally plucked up the courage to leave when he completely threw me by taking hold of my hand.'

'No!'

'Yes. Can you believe the nerve of the guy?'

'What did you do?'

'Faked a sneeze and put that hand over my mouth. He wasn't so keen to grab it after that.'

Clare laughed. 'You're learning. I hope it hasn't put you off.'

'No. I'll stick with it. Maybe the next Steven will be The One.' I hoped so anyway. Because I didn't want too many repeats of this evening. I cringed as I recalled shuffling out of the cinema with the crowd, trying to ask Steve what he thought of the film. He looked at me as though I'd asked him what he thought of shooting a few ducklings for fun. 'I'd have enjoyed it far more if we'd got a decent seat.'

Well and truly put in my place yet again, I began rehearsing how I could bring the evening to a swift close. He beat me to it. 'I'm going to the gents',' he said. 'You don't need to wait for me. In fact, I don't want you to wait for me.' Then he disappeared in the direction of the toilets. Rudey McRude from Rudesville.

17

'I had a visit from a rep this afternoon,' I told Elise when she dropped by on her way home from school a few days later. 'He was called Steven.'

Her eyes widened. 'And...?'

I smiled. 'He was lovely.'

'Are you going to see him again?'

'On a work basis, yes. On a personal basis, no.'

'Why not?'

'Because he's already married.'

'Happily married?'

'I'm guessing so seeing as he and his wife are about to renew their vows to celebrate their ruby wedding anniversary. He tells me he's never known a day's unhappiness since he met his wife except when he had to spend a week on a training course away from home.'

'Ah, that's so sweet.'

'Isn't it? That's what *I* want – to meet someone whom I can't bear to be away from and who can't bear to be away from me. It must make you feel so special.'

'Yeah,' Elise said. 'It must be nice.'

'What are you talking about? You've got that with Gary.'

'I meant the longevity. It must be nice to still feel that way after so long.' She turned away and gestured round the shop with her arm. 'So, one week tomorrow till opening day. The place looks amazing, Sarah. Are you pleased?'

I looked round the shop and felt a tingle of pride. The wood floor and silver light fittings were classy, the soft cream walls added warmth, and the various glass and silver shelves and display units oozed quality. Rows of brushed silver tubs and vases eagerly awaited their first delivery of flowers, and the dark granite counter and preparation table seemed to sparkle with excitement for the first bouquet to be created on it.

'It's even better than I imagined,' I admitted. 'Although I did spend more than I hoped to get this look.'

'I think it was money well spent. I like these.' Elise pointed to a display containing wooden christening gifts. 'I haven't seen anything like these in town.'

'Good. I wanted things that were different.'

'What's going on there?' She pointed to a circular display unit.

'Teddy bears, which are coming on Monday. I'm expecting two card deliveries on Tuesday, more gifts and vases on Wednesday, first flower delivery on Thursday, then it will be flat out on Friday making bouquets ready for opening on Saturday.'

'You've certainly got your work cut out.'

'I know. I'm trying not to panic but it feels like there's so much to do. Are you sure you don't mind helping out next Saturday?'

'I wouldn't miss it for the world.'

I smiled. 'Thanks. I'm glad you and Mum will be here.'

'Is Clare coming?'

'No. She's got a work event that she couldn't get out of.'

'That's a shame.'

'Don't start...'

Elise held her hands up. 'It wasn't a bitchy comment. I genuinely meant it's a shame after she helped you paint and get things ready. It would have been nice for her to be here for opening day.'

I nodded. 'That's more like it. Life is so much less stressful when the two of you can play nicely.'

'It's not me who starts it. It's—'

But a knock on the door saved us.

'Hi, stranger,' I said to Nick. 'How was Edinburgh?' Those damn butterflies were back. Why did he have to be so attractive?

'Edinburgh was great, thanks. How's progress?'

'Getting there. Do you want a sneak preview?'

He nodded eagerly. 'Do you mind? I haven't caught you at a bad time, have I?'

'No. But you can only come in if you promise to say nice things.'

'I promise to say nice things. And I'll mean them.'

I swung the door open and inhaled deeply as he stepped past me. Whatever he was wearing smelt divine.

'Hi. I'm Elise.' She scowled at me as she wandered over and shook Nick's hand. 'Thought I'd better do the intros seeing as somebody's forgetting their manners.'

'Sorry,' I said. 'Elise, this is—'

'Steven,' Nick interrupted.

Elise's eyes widened and she looked from Nick to me and back to Nick again. Her mouth opened but no words came out.

'Sorry,' Nick said, grinning. 'Couldn't resist. I'm Nick.'

'Oh, so you're Nick.' Elise smiled widely and I knew she was appraising him. She turned to me. 'I didn't realise Nick knew about Steven.'

'I wanted the male perspective. Plus he plied me with alcohol and kind of dragged it out of me.'

'Interesting. And what was your verdict, Nick?'

'I thought Sarah should give her search a try. There's a lot in this world we can't explain or can't prove. Just because I can't see into the future, it doesn't mean that nobody can. But I also suggested she doesn't waste years on the search. If Steven doesn't turn up in, say, three months she should look elsewhere.' Nick looked directly at me as he said the last part. Heat rushed to my cheeks and I couldn't hold his gaze. I pretended to find some muck on the immaculate counter and rubbed at it with my thumbnail.

'Good idea,' Elise said.

'Thank you. Anyway,' Nick said, 'I came in to tell you about my proposition, Sarah. I know you'll only have been open a couple of days and probably have loads to do but are you still free a week on Monday night?'

'I am.' At last. I'd been dying to hear about the mystery proposition.

'Fantastic. If you don't like the sound of this, just say so and I won't be offended, but I promise it's not as geeky as it might sound.'

'I have an open mind,' I assured him.

'A few years ago, I set up something called Bay Trade with my best mate, Skye, and her fiancé, Stuart. It's a trading service for small businesses in Whitsborough Bay. Members promote each other where they can and we trade our skills for free or for a discount. I recently did a website and designed some fliers for our plumber and he fitted a new shower for me. Saved each other a fortune.'

'Sounds like a great idea,' I said.

'Glad you like it because we wondered if you'd like to be our florist. We only allow one person from each type of business to join us so it doesn't become competitive.'

'Was Auntie Kay a member?'

Nick shook his head. 'Stuart knows Evie who runs Blossoms but, as she's closing down, she's dipped out.'

'Would it cost me to join?'

'No.'

'And would I have to come to regular meetings?'

'Come when you can. It's the second Monday of each month and it's very informal. We ask if anyone needs some help or advice, or if there's news, then it's a few drinks and a chat.'

'Could be good for business,' Elise suggested.

I pondered for a moment then nodded. 'Okay. I'm in. So is a week on Monday an extra one because that's the end of the month?'

'It's something different. One of the group, Bob, is emigrating to New Zealand so it's a leaving do for him.'

'And what does Bob do?'

'He's our builder.'

'No! Bob the builder? Seriously?'

Nick laughed. 'No. He's a physiotherapist but it was too tempting to let it pass. We're meeting in The Old Theatre at seven then we've got a table booked at The Bombay Palace at nine.'

'Okay. It's a date,' I said. 'Well... not really a date... just me and you being out at the same place, and...'

'It's fine,' Nick said. 'I know what you mean. I'd best leave you both to it. Nice to meet you, Elise.'

'And you,' she said.

I walked Nick to the door. 'Are there any Stevens in Bay Trade?' I asked.

He shook his head. 'Sorry. See you soon.' He waved as he headed down the street.

'He likes you,' Elise said after I closed the door.

'Rubbish.'

'And you like him.'

'I do. As a friend. Because—'

'I know,' she said. 'Because he's not called Steven.'

'Well, he isn't and I'm sure Steven's about to knock on my door.'

A knock on the door made us both jump. Steven? I unlocked the door again.

'Nick?'

'I forgot to give you this.' He handed me a black leather portfolio.

'What is it?'

'Some website ideas.'

I flicked through the portfolio to see several pages of sample layouts with little boxes explaining the logic and flow of what he'd done.

'Nick. These look amazing. You must have spent hours on this.'

He shrugged. 'I enjoyed it. Evenings alone in a hotel can get boring so it was refreshing to have something to do other than stare at the TV.'

'I don't know what to say. Thank you. Can I hang onto these?'

'They're yours. There's no rush to look at them. If you like a design, let me know. If you want to pick and mix from several, I can do that too. And if I've completely missed the mark, please say and I'll do some more.'

I continued to flick through image after image. 'I think it's going to be a case of being spoilt for choice rather than not liking them. Thank you.'

'Pleasure. I'll see you at Bob's leaving do, if not before.'

'How sweet is he?' Elise said when I locked the door again.

'I know.'

'You wish he was Steven, don't you?'

'No!'

'Sarah?'

'Yes. Yes, I do.'

'Then why don't you give it a go with him?' she asked. 'You know I believe the CD but I can also see that your Auntie Kay was right about you two. What if Madame Louisa got the name wrong? What if you push Nick away and Steven never materialises? What if Nick's moved on and found someone else by the time you accept that?'

'And what if I go for it with Nick and Steven *does* appear? The poor guy's best friend ran off with his fiancé the day before their wedding. He's been wary of relationships ever since. Imagine if we had a few dates and things were going really well and then Steven walked into my life and swept me off my feet. If Nick's as keen on me as you and Auntie Kay seem to think he is, imagine what that would do to him. I couldn't put him – or me – through that. Plus, selfish as it may sound, I really like him as a friend. You're the only friend I have who still lives in Whitsborough Bay. I like the idea of having two.' The more friends I had, the less likely I was to end up alone like Uncle Alan.

Elise nodded. 'Perhaps it's too soon to rush into things with Nick. But I think you should seriously consider his suggestion of putting a timescale on it. How about two months starting from the New Year? That would mean you've been home for about five months. If Steven doesn't appear in that time, I suspect he never will. And maybe then you can start considering people with other names. Like Nick. Agreed?'

'Okay, okay. It's agreed. Two months from New Year it is, then.'

But as I flicked through the portfolio after Elise had left, I couldn't help thinking about Nick and wishing he had the right name.

18

✉ From Nick
Hope your first day is perfect and you sell
loads. Can't believe how much you've done to the
place. Look forward to hearing about it all on
Monday xx

✉ From Auntie Kay
Thanks for photos. The shop looks amazing. You're
amazing. So proud of you. Let me know how it goes
xxxxxxxxxx

✉ From Clare
Keep the customers locked in till they spend a
fortune. LOL! Wish I could be there doing PR for
you instead of for this bunch of numpties. Good
luck! You can do it! xxx

'I'm nervous.' I squeezed Mum's hand on opening day a week later.
'What if nobody comes?'

'They will. I know of at least a dozen of Kay's regulars who've
said they'll be in today to give you their support.'

'What if they're the only ones?'

'Sarah,' Elise scolded, 'you can't fail. The place looks amazing. You've sent discount vouchers to all Kay's regulars. You've done a stack of advertising. You've even been on Bay Radio. I think you'll be run off your feet. I've already seen several people looking through the window this morning.'

'So have I. Squashing their greasy noses on my nice clean glass.' I turned to Mum again. 'Do you really think Auntie Kay would like what I've done to her shop?'

Mum squeezed me tightly. 'She said so in her text, didn't she? We're all so proud of you.'

'And keep remembering that it's not her shop anymore; it's yours,' said Cathy who'd jumped at the offer of her old job back. 'She deliberately gave it to you as an empty shell so you could create this. I'm so excited to be working here with you. I bet Kay wishes she was here. She'd be beside herself with excitement and pride.'

I swallowed hard on the lump forming in my throat. Today was not a day for tears; I'd scare the customers away if I started. I surveyed what the last five weeks of hard work had achieved and couldn't help but be impressed. Half the shop was devoted to fresh flowers including a range of more daring modern blooms that I wanted to test on the market. The other half of the shop was now devoted to gifts. My teddy bears had arrived and looked so adorable with their pudgy tummies and cute faces, ready to be hugged. I'd spent the last week unpacking deliveries, arranging any surplus in the stockroom, and doing a final clean before a busy day of bouquet preparation.

Christmas was a month away so I'd ordered some Christmas gifts and made the shop look festive with red and white poinsettias, holly, wreathes, and beautiful Christmassy-looking bouquets and baskets. I'd decorated a small tree and hung a stack of red and white fairy lights around the shop to create ambiance.

Mum looked at her watch. 'Nearly time. Are you ready to face your public?'

'As ready as I'll ever be.' I took a deep breath, wiped my sweaty palms down my uniform – a dark green apron with the shop name and a white rose embroidered on the bib part – and picked up the keys. Placing them in the lock, I grinned at my team as I announced,

'It gives me great pleasure to declare the newly-refurbished Seaside Blooms open.'

* * *

Mum had been right; I needn't have worried about a lack of customers. All my hard work in promoting the shop, plus loyalty to Auntie Kay, meant there was a constant stream of customers, old, new, and just visiting the town for some Christmas shopping. I'd prepared twenty or so simple inexpensive red and white Christmas bouquets and displayed them on a wooden barrow outside the shop. They sold out within an hour so Mum and Cathy spent the next hour or so making more that sold out again by lunchtime.

The cards and gifts also sold really well, I took bookings for two wedding flower consultations, a request for a large floral arrangement for a couple's Golden Wedding Anniversary party, and a booking for a funeral.

Dad dropped in to see how it was going and ended up staying for three hours to help us out. He became quite tearful, muttering about how proud he was that I'd returned home and accomplished so much, which set me off.

'I don't know about you three, but I'm exhausted,' I said as the last customer of the day left and I was finally able to lock the door. 'I don't think I've ever worked so hard in my life. Thank you all so much for your help.'

'You're welcome,' Elise said. 'I've really enjoyed it.'

'Busier than I've ever seen it,' Cathy gushed. 'Well done, you.'

I stretched and rolled my head to try and relax my stiff neck and shoulders. 'I have a proposal for you all. How about I get cashed up, one of you sweeps the floor, one of you puts some fresh water in the flowers and one of you washes the mugs, then I take you all out to Mario's – my treat.'

* * *

'Can I propose a toast?' Mum raised her glass in Mario's a little later. Elise and Cathy nodded in agreement and grabbed theirs. 'To my beautiful daughter on the incredibly successful opening of her new business. To new beginnings at Seaside Blooms.'

'To Sarah.'

Mum took my hand in hers as she continued. 'You know your dad and I have always been supportive of you wherever you've lived and if you'd stayed in London and asked Kay to sell the shop, we'd have supported you in that decision. But can I just say how proud and delighted we are that you decided to come home because we've loved being part of this and we've missed you so much.'

'Hear hear,' Elise said.

I blushed as I raised my glass. 'To Seaside Blooms. And to you all for your amazing support today. I couldn't have done it without you.'

A waiter cleared our plates and advised us that our main courses would be along shortly. 'I think I'll just nip to the ladies before our mains arrive,' Mum said.

Cathy stood up. 'I'll join you, Sandra.'

Elise twisted in her chair. When they were clearly out of earshot, she said, 'While your mum's not here, what's the latest online news?'

'I've been so busy getting ready for the shop, I've hardly looked.'

'Liar.'

I laughed. 'I've genuinely been too busy for the past few days.'

'When was the last time you looked?'

'Monday night.'

'Were there any messages then?'

'A few.' I drained the last few sips of wine and raised an eyebrow at Elise who promptly refilled my glass.

'Messaged anyone?' she asked.

'No. I've put a couple more Stevens down as favourites but I haven't made contact. I thought I'd better get opening week out the way.'

'Good plan. Are you all set for your hot date with Nick on Monday?'

'Behave,' I said. 'It's not a date.'

'Of course it isn't.'

'Elise! It isn't. And you know why. Stop looking at me like that.

I've got Auntie Kay nagging me by text, Clare on at me over the phone, and now you.'

Later that evening, on my way back from the ladies, I had a strong sensation of being watched. I turned slightly and caught the eye of a man two tables away. He looked to be in his mid-to-late-thirties with greasy hair and a dodgy goatee. He wore a deep maroon shirt that was at least two sizes too small if the bursting buttons were anything to go by. He stared for a bit longer then raised his hand and waved, revealing a large sweat patch under his arm. I frowned and looked round to see if he was waving at someone behind me but there was nobody there. He waved again and smiled. It was a sinister smile, the sort you'd expect to see on a photo-fit on the news. I shuddered.

He stood up, still staring at me. *Oh my God, he's coming over. Do I know him? Maybe he was a customer today.*

'Sarah,' he said, 'it is you, isn't it?'

'Erm, yes.' *And you are...?*

'I thought it was. You're even more beautiful in real life.'

'Than what?'

He laughed loudly and snorted. Several diners looked in our direction and I felt my whole face flush. 'Than your photo, of course,' he said.

'My photo?'

'I like to look at it before I go to sleep each night.'

No! He isn't...?

'I meant to get in touch when you added me to your favourite list,' he continued, 'but I hoped you'd message me first. I'm not great at making first contact.'

I could hardly bear to ask the question. 'Your name's Steven?'

'Yes! Steven Bell. Ta-dah!' He waved jazz-hands at me, the dandruff on his shoulders bouncing up and down as he moved. 'How did you know? There's no photo on my profile.'

'Lucky guess.' I tried to sidestep him but he had my route blocked.

'Seeing as we've met now, would you like to go out tomorrow night?'

Eek! Saying no online was one thing but being confronted with the anti-Steven on a night out with my mum was quite different. 'I've just opened a new business today,' I said. 'I've got stacks to do tomorrow to get ready for my second day of trading.'

'Monday night then?'

'Sorry, I've got plans with friends.' Thank goodness for Bay Trade.

'Tuesday?'

'Sorry, Steven, but this week really isn't good for me.'

'Next Saturday then?'

No. Not next Saturday. Not ever. Please get the message. You're creepy and telling me you look at my photo before you go to bed is not a chat-up line I'd recommend. Please leave me alone. But I was too polite to say any of that. I settled for a non-committal, 'Maybe.'

'I'll take that as a yes then,' he gushed, showering me with spit.

'It's not a yes.'

'But it wasn't a no so that's good enough for me.'

Where was straight-talking Clare when I needed her? Why couldn't I be strong like her? 'Message me,' I muttered. 'I must go.' I finally managed to squeeze past him and return to my table.

'Who was that?' asked Mum.

'Just some guy who thinks he knows me.'

'Does he?'

'No. Definitely not.' I didn't dare catch Elise's eye.

I sat back in my chair and took a long glug of my wine as I listed off my Steven encounters in my head. My search for Steven hadn't got off to the best start. Could I cope with a few more months of it? Or should I just give it all up as a bad job, conclude that Madame Louisa has given me the wrong name, and make it clear to Nick at the Bay Trade thing on Monday that my search was over. And if he'd like to retry that moment on the beach – without the playful Labrador – I wouldn't push him off.

19

✉ From Nick
Hi you. Tomorrow night's been rescheduled for a
week on Thursday. Hope you can still make it
then. I've been offered another week's work in
Edinburgh which I'd turned down for Bob's do but
might as well take seeing as it's changed date. I
need to do some prep or I'd have suggested a
drink. Can't wait to hear about your first day xx

Damn! I slumped back on the sofa at Seashell Cottage on Sunday
afternoon. Feeling my shoulders sag with disappointment, I had to
check myself. 'So much for re-living the beach moment,' I muttered.
But at least it gave me another week to search for Steven. I kept
blowing hot and cold on it. One moment, I drifted into a fantasy
about kissing Nick, but then I thought about the discovery of the
lighthouse photo and Grandma's bracelet and started fantasising
about *the* Steven appearing imminently.

✉ To Nick
That's a shame. Have fun in Edinburgh. Next
Thursday's fine. Same time and place? First day
exceeded expectations. Exhausted now xx

✉ From Nick
Glad you can still come. Everything's the same
but the date. Hope you get to relax today after
all that prep for opening day. Have an amazing
full first week. Will be thinking of you lots xx

'Will you be thinking of me because you fancy me or thinking of me because it's my first full week?' I said to the phone. Auntie Kay and Elise were convinced he was into me, but I kept having doubts about that too. What if he just wanted friendship? I could make a fool of myself if I wasn't careful. I shook my head and put the phone down before I typed an appropriate text for my pro-Nick moments that would be completely inappropriate for my search for Steven.

Lying back on the sofa, I phoned Clare, figuring she was probably home from her working weekend.

'Sounds like your first day was grand,' she said. 'So why do you sound so down just now?'

'I'm not down. I'm just tired and stuffed full of Sunday lunch, courtesy of my Mum. I was fine when I was there but, now that I'm back at the cottage, I don't really know what to do with myself.'

'Once you get into a routine at the shop, I guarantee you'll be grateful of Sundays off. No Elise?'

'I don't see her every day, you know. She helped in the shop yesterday but I probably won't see her again till the end of the week.'

'You know what you need?' Clare said. 'A night on the beers with me. I'm seeing my Leeds client on Friday so I'm coming to stay for the weekend whether you want me to or not. What time can you be home on Friday?'

'Shop shuts at half five so about six.'

'I'll be there for six.'

'I might have other plans.'

'*Do* you have other plans?' she asked. 'Because I'd love to hear that you had plans for a night of steamy sex with a stranger.'

'I might have.'

'Hmm.' Clearly dismissing that as a possibility, Clare continued, 'Make me something full of calories for dinner.'

'You're on.'

* * *

'I should let you cook for me more often.' Clare spooned another huge dollop of lasagne onto her plate on Friday night. She'd already devoured an enormous plateful, a jacket potato, a side salad and most of a garlic ciabatta. 'You're not too shabby at it.'

'Thanks. I think. Have you not been fed this week?'

'I get sick of living off hotel food and pre-packed sarnies. This is real food. Lots of cheese. Lots of garlic. Yum.' Clare broke off another piece of garlic bread. How the hell she stayed a perfect ten was beyond me.

'So one of your online favourites turned out to be a sex offender?' she said.

'The bloke from Mario's? I didn't say that. I just said he was creepy.'

'Have you had any more messages?'

'I had a bad dream about creepy bloke and it put me off. I haven't checked them all week.'

'Sarah!'

I grimaced. 'I was a bit too busy the week before too.'

'*Sarah!*'

'It was opening week this week so it's not like I haven't been busy.'

'And the week before?'

'Getting ready for opening week. I looked on the Monday night but I honestly haven't had the time since then.'

She narrowed her eyes at me and sighed. 'I suppose you do have a legitimate excuse, but the shop is open now which means excuse time is over. It's time for a serious action plan, but before we log on, have you got any pudding in?'

'Syrup sponge and homemade custard; your favourite.'

'Oh my God, Sarah. Not only do you cook the most amazing lasagne in the world, you get old school puddings in, make your own custard and have a fridge full of wine. I think I may change my name to Steven and marry you myself.'

* * *

'Thirty-eight messages.' Clare whistled when we sat down on the sofa with my laptop a little later. 'That's a lot of admirers, young lady. We may have to forfeit a night out as it looks like we have a full evening's work ahead of us, so we have.' She grabbed the laptop off me and balanced it on her knee. 'Are you sitting comfortably?'

'Why are you in the driving seat again?'

'Why do you bother asking? Ready?'

It was a bit more promising this time. 'This one's from a Steven.' Clare scrolled down the page. 'And, at first glance, he seems fairly normal.'

We both stared at the screen, reading the message:

Dear Sarah, I've never joined a dating site before and was a bit dubious until I read your profile. There are some strange women out there but I'm sure you've come across some strange men too!
Why did I join? I'm 32 and was happy with my single life until my friend Ade's wedding a couple of weeks ago when it dawned on me that I was the only single one there.
I'm an engineer and work is male-dominated and it's not easy to meet someone when you're out and none of your mates are single.
I like your profile. We sound very similar. I'm intrigued as to what your business is.
A week on Friday, I'll be on a stag do in Whitsborough Bay. The stag is a massive Dr Who fan so we're doing a pub crawl in Dr Who costumes. Don't panic that we're a bunch of geeks because I'm not into sci-fi myself. The stag is a Dalek and I'm Tom Baker's version of Dr Who (if you've never watched it, he played the fourth Doctor in 1974–81 – I Googled it! He's the one with the long striped scarf and

```
curly hair). If you're around, please come and
say hi. We're meeting at 7.30 and working our
way down town. If you can't make it or don't
fancy it, it would still be great to hear from
you. In fact, even if you can make it, it would
be great to hear from you first; break the ice
and all that!
If you do come, remember the hair is a wig — I
don't have a huge curly bouffant normally! I'm
waffling so I'll say goodbye. Steve.
```

What do you think?' Clare asked. 'Not that I need to ask given that huge cheesy grin.'

'He sounds nice. A week today, eh? Could be tempted.'

'Er... no. It's tonight your man's talking about.'

'It can't be. He said a week on Friday.'

'Look at the date.' Clare jabbed the screen. 'He sent it last week. That'll teach you not to check your messages for nearly two weeks.'

'Pants.'

'How would you like to meet your doctor tonight?'

'Sod it, why not? Is there a photo?'

Clare clicked on the link back to his profile. 'Not yet.'

'Oh well, I guess I won't be able to miss the scarf and bouffant. Who else have we got?'

'Don't you want to get ready to meet him?' Clare asked.

'Yes, but it may look a bit desperate if we're there right at the start. There's a standard pub crawl down town so we'll easily find him a few pubs in. And I'm dying to read my other responses. There may be someone even better.'

'You're the boss,' she said. 'But I'm still in control of your laptop.'

An hour or so later, we had a shortlist and an action plan. My search for Steven was starting to feel more positive although I did feel my resolve crumbling when I spotted a message from someone called Nick, which instantly got me thinking about Nick Derbyshire.

There were some tempting messages from non-Stevens, but Clare put her foot down and refused to let me even finish reading them, let alone make contact. I didn't argue. I knew exactly who my first port of call would be if I deviated from Stevens.

I didn't tell Clare about Nick because it would provide her with the perfect excuse to call off the search for Steven. Despite the strong attraction to Nick, I still wasn't ready to make that step. I wasn't ready to dismiss the CD and I wasn't prepared to risk hurting him and losing him as a friend.

The shortlist read:

1. *Check out Steve Dennison on pub-crawl tonight*
2. *Go to The Coffee Corner for take-out on way to shop tomorrow to check out the manager, Stéphan Marcell*
3. *Message Stevie Barnes, Steve Berry, Ste Parker, Steve Masterson and Stephen Fitzpatrick*
4. *Arrange dates with one or more of the above*
5. *Get very drunk tonight. And probably tomorrow night too*
6. *Buy bacon for sarnies on Sunday morning. Buy ketchup for Clare*

Clare grabbed the list and marched into the kitchen. I followed her and watched as she stuck it to the middle of the fridge with some magnets. 'This is your rulebook,' she said. 'You do not, under any circumstances, deviate from the list. You're allowed to add new Stevens but you do *not* correspond with or meet anyone who is not called Steven or some variation of. Agreed?'

'Agreed.'

'It's now eight-forty-five. I already look gorgeous but you seriously need to whack some make-up on as we're off out to meet your man Dr Who.'

My pulse quickened. Was I ready for this? 'You don't think it's too late to go out?'

'You were the one who wanted to wait. Don't you dare think of bottling it now.'

'But—'

'But nothing. Look, you, there's no need to be nervous. Auntie Clare's with you every step of the way. If he's grim, we'll leave. If he's gorgeous, we'll stay and I'll help you clinch the deal.'

I smiled gratefully. 'Okay. Steve Dennison, here we come.'

'You have an absolute maximum of fifteen minutes to get ready. We need to be in our first pub by quarter past.'

'I love it when you're masterful.' I winked at her as I headed for the stairs.

20

'I spy a Dalek.' Clare nodded towards the group of men crowded near the bar of The Old Theatre. It was the third pub we'd tried but there was no way the group could be missed. Steve was easy to spot amongst them, thanks to the scarf and wig. 'What's the plan?'

'We'll get a drink then do a spot of person watching. See what he's like and, if he seems okay, follow him to the next pub and introduce ourselves.'

Like any stag do, the group attracted lots of female attention.

'Any observations so far?' Clare asked after about fifteen minutes of spying from a discreet distance.

'He never approaches women. He seems more comfortable when it's just the lads.'

'Worth stalking?'

'I think so.'

We followed the stag party to the next pub.

'So, what's the plan here?' Clare asked.

'Another drink? I need a bit of Dutch courage before I speak to him.'

'You'd better not be bottling it.'

'I'm here, aren't I?'

* * *

'I can't believe it's the third pub,' Clare said half an hour later, 'and you haven't made the slightest move. I'd forgotten how crap you are at all of this.'

She was right. I could probably fill a billboard poster with a list of all my failed flirting attempts over the years. 'I'm going to screw this up, aren't I? Help.'

'I think you need the charm of the Irish. Let the professionals do the work.'

Standing awkwardly on my own against a mirrored pillar, clutching my empty glass and wishing I didn't look so conspicuous, I watched Clare approach Steve Dennison and say something in his ear. He looked surprised and turned in my direction. He shook his head and said something to Clare. *Oh God, he doesn't like the look of me. I want to leave. Right now.*

There was another exchange of words, Steve looked across again, shook his head once more and shrugged. Clare said something else, they both laughed, then she returned to me.

'It can't be good or you'd have shouted me over,' I said.

'Well, I pointed you out—'

'And he thought I was ugly? Or fat? Or both?'

'Don't interrupt and of course he didn't think you were ugly or fat. You're gorgeous and you've lost weight since you moved here, not that you were fat before.' She looked at me sternly. 'You have to stop putting yourself down.'

I shrugged. 'What did he say?'

'He thought you looked lovely.'

'But?'

'But he met someone else online. They met up on Tuesday and he's meeting her in the next pub. He says he's really sorry but he assumed you weren't interested when you didn't message him back.'

'Did you explain that I'd only just picked up his message?'

'Yes, but he seems keen on this other girl.'

'You're the PR expert. Couldn't you have come up with something?'

'Like what? I wasn't going to beg him to date you.'

Fair point. 'What were you laughing at?'

'I made some daft comment about his costume which tickled him.'

'You were flirting with him?'

Clare grabbed her drink and took a swig. 'I know you're upset so I'll ignore the implication.'

I stood quietly for a few moments, fidgeting with my watchstrap. 'Sorry, Clare. I didn't mean that. Would you mind if we called it a night?'

She shook her head. 'We can leave this pub but we're not going home while you're upset.'

'I'm not upset. I'm just... Oh, I don't know.'

'Maybe you're not upset but you're disappointed, so you are. And I know you'll be taking it personally, even though he thinks you look lovely and the only reason he's not interested is bad timing.' She moved my head so she could look me in the eye. 'It's not about you, Sarah. It's circumstances. You *are* taking it personally, aren't you?'

'I can't help it.'

'Which is why we're not going home where I know you'll brood and convince yourself you're fat, ugly, will never get married and have children, and will end up a mad spinster with cats.'

'Am I really that predictable?'

'You'll meet the right person; I'm sure of it. Just don't expect it to be instant and do expect there to be knocks along the way. What's that bollocks they say about the path to true love never running smoothly or something like that?'

I smiled and wiped at the tears that were about to run down my cheeks. Clare reached for my hand and gave it a squeeze. 'Let this be a lesson to you, though,' she said.

'In what?'

'Checking your messages more often. If you're serious about finding Steven, you need to be on the ball. If you're going to do it half-heartedly, you may as well go back to hoping he'll walk into the shop one day.'

I nodded. It was true. You snooze, you lose.

'Come on,' she said. 'Where to next? Where do all the hotties hang out in Whitsborough Bay?'

'God knows. I haven't been on the pull here since I was eighteen.'

'We still have a list to get through, haven't we?' Clare said as I steered her back up the precinct towards Minty's. 'Starting with the lovely Stéphan Marcell in the morning. And once we've exhausted the list, there are stacks more profiles we haven't looked at and more Stevens in your favourites who haven't contacted you so you can drop them all a message. Plenty more options.'

I stopped walking. 'Do you really think I'll meet someone special?'

'I'm sure of it. He may not be on your current list and he may not even be on a dating site, but I'm absolutely convinced that, one day soon, you'll meet someone who sweeps you off your feet – just like in the soppy movies you love so much – and you'll get your happy ever after. I'm just not convinced he'll be called Steven. In the meantime, why don't you try and relax and enjoy the moment?'

'What do you mean?'

'You've just relocated back to somewhere you love but haven't lived for twelve years and you've become the owner of what promises to be a grand business. Why not just take a while to enjoy being the new you?'

'The new me?'

'Sarah, the entrepreneurial florist instead of Sarah, the other half of a couple. What you've achieved in the past six weeks is amazing. Stop kicking yourself for being single and congratulate yourself for being successful.'

She had a point. A very good one. When did my two best friends become so wise? And when did I become so tunnel-visioned and obsessed with meeting The One at the expense of appreciating all the great stuff I had going for me? Things needed to change. *I* needed to change. I was nothing like Uncle Alan so I needed to stop obsessing about ending up like him.

21

'One cappuccino and a skinny latte, please,' I said in my friendliest, most cheerful voice as I leaned on the counter of The Coffee Corner on Saturday morning.

Stéphan Marcell was serving and he was lush. His online photo really didn't do him justice. Deftly handling the espresso machine, he was the epitome of tall, dark, and handsome. His online profile said he was half-Portuguese, half-French. Stunning. Even more gorgeous than Stephen Lewis the plasterer. And this time there were no fluorescent green prams in sight.

'Coffees.' He slammed the paper cups on the counter. 'Anything else?'

I flinched. 'Er, yes, two croissants please.' Hmm. Not so friendly. Nice accent, though.

'Heated?'

'Yes, please, if it's not too much trouble.'

Without acknowledging me, he opened a small oven behind him. 'Christ!' he muttered before shouting, 'Sammie! Here! Now!'

Clare and I exchanged concerned looks.

A young girl in her late teens burst through a door marked 'staff only' looking terrified.

'What did I ask you to do last night?'

'Clean the oven?' She cast a sideways glance at us.

'Does this fucking look clean to you?' He shoved her towards the oven.

'I cleaned it last night. I promise.'

'Someone broke in last night and covered it in crap, did they?'

'I don't know how it got like that. I'm sorry. I'll do it again now.' Sammie headed for the staff only door again.

'Where are you going now?' Stéphan shouted.

'To get a cloth.'

'What's this then? An arma-fucking-dillo?' He picked up a cloth and threw it at her.

'I didn't see it there.'

'That's your problem, Sammie. You don't see anything. Like these customers *you've* kept waiting who *I've* had to serve. Didn't see them, did you?'

The poor girl looked close to tears. 'It's okay,' I piped up. 'We'll just take these.' I dropped some coins on the counter and grabbed our drinks.

'I'm guessing you won't be messaging him?' Clare said as we made a swift getaway.

'Absolutely gorgeous. Absolutely amazing accent. Absolute git. Two down, five to go.'

Having Clare in the shop for the day was an eye-opener. Elise had been friendly and helpful with customers on opening day, but Clare was something different. She was a genuine asset to sales and I was fascinated to see that side of her in action. She could charm anyone and everyone, swiftly adapting her behaviour according to the age and gender of the customer. She managed to secure three wedding bookings, convince five or six customers to spend way more on bouquets than they'd planned, sell an additional product like a card or gift to about three quarters of the customers who'd only come in for flowers, and complete on several gift transactions where the customer was clearly browsing and would likely have left empty-handed without her intervention.

I printed off the impressive daily sales report after locking up and whistled. 'Can you work here every day?'

She laughed. 'You couldn't afford me, but I'll train you if you want.'

'I could never be as brazen as you. Besides, I think it's a lot to do with your accent and your personality. It wouldn't work with me.'

'It would. Yes, I play on the cheeky blonde Irish thing, but it's about reading people and saying the right things, all of which can be taught. With a few lessons from me, you could be a pro by Easter.'

'Would you really do that for me?'

'Of course. I know you're going to be a huge success anyway, but if I can help in any way, I'm more than happy to.'

'You're on.'

'So what do you want to do tonight?' I said as we walked back to Seashell Cottage. 'Takeaway and film?'

'No way. We're going on a double date.'

'What?'

'You heard me. As you said this morning, it's two down, five to go. So let's contact one of the five when we get home and see if he has a nice single mate he can drag out tonight.'

'I thought you said I should relax and enjoy the business more.'

Clare laughed. 'You should. But it doesn't mean you have to call off the search for Steven. Just don't get so obsessed with it that you ignore the amazing things you're doing in your day job and don't get so stressed about the disappointments along the way because they're inevitable.'

Who was I to argue with such logic? A double date with a Steven it was.

* * *

'I can't believe you've talked me into this.' I pulled my coat tightly around me as we walked from Seashell Cottage into town for the second night in a row. I reached into my pockets for my gloves and gratefully thrust my icy fingers into the soft fleece.

'Stop moaning. We'll have a great time. And stop being such a wimp; it's not that cold.' As Clare spoke, her breath hung in the air. 'Okay. I lied. It's bloody freezing. But I'm not lying when I say we'll have a great craic.'

We were meeting Stevie Barnes from Little Sandby, a cute

village about ten minutes north of Whitsborough Bay. According to
his profile, he'd recently turned thirty-three. He'd married and
divorced young, had one dog and no kids.

'I'm nervous,' I admitted.

'There's no need to be, especially when I'm here to hold your
hand. I reckon you two will get on brilliantly. Although isn't he the
IT geek?'

I nodded. 'Something to do with IT and publishing but he said
on his profile that he won't put off prospective dates by explaining it
because it's not that interesting.'

'Just as long as he doesn't try to explain it tonight or we may
have to walk out. IT geeks bore the hell out of me.'

'Most people bore the hell out of you.'

'True. Which makes it odd that I've put up with you for so many
years.'

'Rude!' I playfully whacked her with my bag.

The plan was to meet Stevie and his best mate Rob in Minty's at
eight. Stevie had messaged to say that Rob had recently moved back
to the area after splitting up with his long-term partner. He was
happy to make up the numbers providing Clare knew he wasn't
looking for a relationship.

As soon as we walked into Minty's, I recognised Stevie from his
photo online. He wasn't gorgeous – just very pleasant-looking in a
boy-next-door kind of way. He had short, sandy coloured hair, dark
brown eyes, dimples when he smiled – something he did the second
we walked through the door – and was slightly overweight, which
suited him. I just hoped that, unlike Stéphan, he would have a
pleasant personality to match his pleasant looks.

'Sarah?' He smiled warmly again and confidently placed a
gentle kiss on my cheek. 'I'm Stevie. It's great to meet you. And you
must be Clare?' He kissed Clare too then introduced his friend. Rob
was also very nice-looking rather than gorgeous, but the opposite
of Stevie in colouring and build – a mop of dark wavy hair, blue
eyes and a very toned-looking physique. He looked a lot like my
brother.

'Thanks for meeting us at such short notice,' I said.

'It's our pleasure. Can I get you both a drink?'

'He's lovely,' whispered Clare when the boys headed for the bar. 'Nice one.'

'First impressions are very positive. And his mate seems pretty nice too.'

'Absolutely,' Clare said. 'Probably not Britain's Next Top Model but you'll hear no complaints from me. And if he needs some help getting over his relationship breakdown with no commitments, I'm the woman for him.'

'You're terrible. You should come with a warning.'

* * *

It was a lovely evening full of warmth and laughter. Before we left shortly after midnight, I arranged to meet Stevie again on Monday night for the cinema and drinks. He kissed me then Clare on the cheek again before heading in the opposite direction with Rob.

'Disappointed?' Clare linked my arm as we headed towards the Old Town.

'With Stevie? No. He was great fun.'

'I mean with not getting a goodnight kiss.'

I pondered for a moment. 'Actually, no. It wouldn't have seemed right. We were there as a group and it was good that way. What did you think of Rob?'

'Seemed like a nice guy.'

'Did you think he looked like my brother?'

'I guess he did a bit,' Clare said. 'Did Saint Ben tell you we went for a curry when I was in Leeds last month?' Clare had christened him 'Saint Ben' thanks to his charity job and all the volunteering work he did. In return, he always called her 'Irish' – highly original.

'It's becoming a bit of a regular thing, you and our Ben.'

'Oh behave, you. Saint Ben has a girlfriend and, even if he didn't, there'd be nothing going on. Your brother's always been a good laugh and it's nice to eat in company when you're on the road as much as me. I'm spending more and more time with my Leeds-based client and I'd rather meet up with your brother than stare at a hotel TV all night. That's all.'

'Sorry. I was only joking.'

'Food.' Clare pulled me into a packed kebab shop. 'Enough about Ben and back to tonight. Did you fancy Stevie?'

'Not sure. He's attractive, I enjoyed his company and we've got loads in common, but... I don't know... I think there was something missing.' It didn't feel like it felt with Nick. But he had the right name, which was incredibly frustrating. 'Maybe he's not *the* Steven. Or maybe he is and I'll fall for him slowly. Why do you ask?'

'There was something about the two of you together that I couldn't quite pinpoint and it just hit me what it was when you said Rob looked like Saint Ben. Watching you and Stevie was like seeing you and Ben together. You had that same easy banter.'

I mulled her observation over. 'You could be right. I guess we'll see how it goes on Monday night. Maybe it will be different when it's just the two of us.'

'Maybe,' Clare said. 'Now, are you going to order anything cos I could kill a chicken kebab right now? I've got the munchies real bad.'

* * *

After the previous cinema fiasco with Steve Turner, I made sure I was on time for my date with Stevie. In fact, I was twelve minutes early. But so was he. We laughed as soon as we saw each other, since one of the things we'd discussed on Saturday night was our shared contempt for people who weren't punctual.

'How long have you been here?' I said.

'Seconds. Honest. I've got something for you.' Stevie fished into his pocket and handed me a candy-striped paper bag.

I peeked in it. 'You angel. You've bought me gummy bears.'

'You said you liked them and I know the pick 'n' mix here doesn't have them. Look what I've got.' He pulled out another paper bag and opened it for me to take a peek.

'Rhubarb and custards? Can we share?'

'We certainly can. Ready to go in?'

I smiled as Stevie held the door open for me and asked me where I'd like to sit. What a contrast to my last cinema date.

* * *

'This is me,' I said as we arrived at Seashell Cottage after a quick post-film drink on the seafront. 'I've not taken you too far out your way?'

'I'm parked five minutes' walk from here so it's perfect.'

We looked at each other slightly awkwardly. Should I invite him in? I was tired, though. He'd understand. 'It's work tomorrow and it's late. Would you think I'm rude if I don't invite you in for coffee?'

'I have to get home to walk Bonnie so it's perfect for me,' Stevie said. 'I've had fun, though. Fancy doing it again soon?'

'I'd love to.'

Stevie smiled, flashing his cute dimples. Adorable. But fanciable? I still wasn't sure. He didn't give me butterflies. Not like Nick.

'I've got a couple of things on at the end of the week,' he said. 'Is Wednesday too soon?'

'I've got no plans so it sounds good to me.'

'Great. I'll message you to confirm a time and film.'

I nodded. 'Do you want to leave your car here so we can walk together?'

'Good plan. I'll do that. Goodnight, then.'

'Goodnight, Stevie.' I tried to sound flirty but I'm not sure I pulled it off.

We stood there staring at each other, Awk-ward! It had been easy to avoid a first kiss on Saturday when Clare and Rob were there, but surely not kissing at the end of our second date – a successful date – would be wrong. I looked into his eyes. He was going to kiss me. Yep, he was definitely going to do it. Any minute now. But I didn't lean in to make it any easier for him.

'Right, goodnight then,' he said.

'You've already said that.'

'So I have. Come here you.' He reached out... he was so going to kiss me... and enveloped me in a huge bear hug. 'Sleep well, Sarah.'

He turned and headed towards town to collect his car. That was odd.

* * *

'That was odd,' Elise said.

'My thoughts exactly. What do you think it means?'

'You're asking the wrong person. I've only had two first kisses and one of those was with Ricky Williams when I was six. With Gary, it happened really easily and naturally.'

'I was wondering if he was just a bit shy.'

'Could be. If he's been single for a while, it could be a pretty big thing.'

* * *

'That was odd,' Clare said.

'That's exactly what Elise said.'

'You told her first?'

Oops, hadn't meant to let that slip.

'I thought you'd have told me first. I'm the one who set up the date. I'm the one who's met him.'

'Hey, it's okay. I was about to phone you when Elise called me. I could hardly not tell her. Besides, she wasn't much help and I knew you would be. What's your verdict?'

'Well, it could be any number of things,' Clare said. 'He could have been single for a long time and be out of practice. He could be gay.'

'No! You don't really think that, do you? He's been married.'

'And divorced. Maybe that's the reason?'

I could tell by the sarcastic tone in her voice that she was messing with me. 'You're hilarious.'

'Bad breath?'

'I'd have noticed.'

'Wind?' Clare giggled. 'Maybe he was about to do a huge belch and was scared of doing it while kissing you.'

'Yuck. I don't think that was it.'

'In that case,' she said solemnly, 'I go back to my question from Saturday night; do you fancy him?'

Did I? 'No, I don't think so. I feel as though I should fancy him because we seem so compatible. I thought the kiss might confirm things either way.'

'You know what else it could be?' Clare said.

'What?'

'That he's feeling exactly the same as you.'

* * *

Must kiss Stevie. Must kiss Stevie. Must do it now. Can't sit all the way through the film wondering if he's the Steven. Must kiss Stevie.

'Are you okay?' Stevie stopped walking down the cliff path on Wednesday evening. 'You seem distracted.'

'Sorry, miles away. What were you saying?'

'I was telling you about Bonnie eating the wrapping paper last Christmas then trying to munch the tree baubles, but it's probably not amusing enough to tell twice.' He laughed. 'In fact, it probably wasn't amusing enough to tell once so I don't blame you for not listening. Are you sure you're all right?'

'Sorry. I'm fine.' I stared down the path again. Over the roofs of the houses in the Old Town, I could see the flashing light at the top of the lighthouse. The photo of Grandma in front of it came to mind. I needed to eliminate Stevie as *the* Steven once and for all and a kiss was the only way of doing that.

'You're not acting very "fine",' he said, sounding concerned.

I took a deep breath. 'You're right. There's something bothering me.'

'Anything I can help with?'

'I hope so.'

I turned to face him. 'There's something I need to do before we walk any further. I hope it won't annoy you.' I leaned in and kissed him full on the mouth, gently at first, then harder. Thankfully he responded. Being pushed away would have been mortifying. I closed my eyes and tried to make myself go with the moment. But there wasn't really a 'moment' to go with; it just didn't feel right. I pulled away and we stood looking at each other. My mouth started twitching in the corners. His did too. Within seconds we were both laughing.

'Was it just me, or did that feel wrong?' I fought the urge to wipe my mouth.

'I don't know what it was,' he agreed, 'but it felt like kissing a relative. Not that I've ever kissed a relative like that, mind you.'

'You don't fancy me do you, Stevie?'

He let out a big sigh and looked at me sadly. 'No. I'm so sorry. I want to but I just don't. You don't fancy me either, do you?'

I pulled a sad expression too. 'No. Which is strange because I *do* think you're attractive and we have so much in common so you should be perfect for me. At the risk of sounding like a six-year-old, will you be my friend?'

Stevie laughed and gave me a hug. 'I'd be honoured. We can be cinema buddies. What do you think?'

'Sounds perfect.' I exhaled loudly as I linked his arm and pulled him in the direction of the cinema. 'I'm so glad we got that out in the open. So, tell me new bezzie mate, is there anyone else online that you like the sound of? Maybe we can help each other find The One.'

'Well, there is this woman called Rachel...'

* * *

✉ To Clare
Back from my date with Stevie. Kissed him. Felt nothing. He was the same. Agreed we'll be good friends as there's no chemistry. I guess that means he's not The Steven either. Pants

✉ From Clare
Who's next on the list?

I rolled off the sofa and headed for the fridge. Taking a pen, I updated my list:

1 Check out Steve Dennison on pub crawl tonight

Go to The Coffee Corner for take-out on way to shop tomorrow morning to check out the manager, Stéphan Marcell

Message Stevie Barnes, Steve Berry, Ste Parker, Steve Masterson and Stephen Fitzpatrick

> *Arrange dates with one or more of the above*
> ~~*Get very drunk tonight. And probably tomorrow night too*~~
> ~~*Buy bacon for sarnies on Sunday morning. Buy ketchup for*~~
> ~~*Clare*~~

Next on the list? Steve Berry. He'd messaged a few days ago and I got distracted by the whole Steve '*Dr Who*' Dennison thing and meeting Stevie. The man deserved a reply...

But then my phone beeped.

✉ From Nick
Hi from a freezing Edinburgh. Windy city? It's
like a constant hurricane! I swear I'm so
battered by the wind that my body is covered in
bruises! Are you still on for Thursday? Can't
wait to catch up with you xx

Aw, bless him. I'd kiss those bruises better. *Whoa there, Sarah! Where did that come from? You seriously must stop thinking about Nick like that. You've got a list of Stevens to contact and you're about to get in touch with one of them.*

But making contact with Steve Berry didn't seem quite so urgent anymore.

22

I turned the music up a notch to try and drown out the depressing sound of rain hammering against the shop window. 'My first quiet day,' I said to Mum. 'I don't like it.'

She put down the vase that she was dusting. 'You're not worried, are you?'

I shrugged.

'Don't be, sweetheart. Shops always have a mix of quiet days and busy days, but I think we can definitely put today's lack of customers down to the weather. Would you go shopping in this?'

'No chance.'

I glanced at the clock. Two hours and forty minutes to go until Bob's rescheduled leaving do when I'd meet the guys from Bay Trade. And see Nick again. Butterflies! *Stop doing that. He's not Steven.*

'That's the dusting done,' Mum said. 'I'll just give the kitchen and toilet a clean. Shout if you need me.'

'Thanks, Mum.'

With no customers and no orders to create, I checked the dating site but there were no new messages, so I clicked onto Facebook. Nick had updated his status.

Nick Derbyshire Looking forward to a night on the beers with the Bay Trade guys and the lovely **Sarah Peterson**
4hrs
Skye Harris The LOVELY Sarah Peterson? Is there something you want to share with us Mr Derbyshire? Are you finally off the list of Britain's Most Eligible Bachelors?!
Nick Derbyshire I wish. See you tonight

My heart thumped faster. 'I wish...' 'I wish...' What did that mean? What did he wish? Did he wish he were with someone as in anyone? Or did he wish he were with me? It could be taken both ways. Seriously people, make your messages clearer.

I read the message over and over again, butterflies going mad in my stomach. What was happening to me? Every time I heard his name or thought about him, I fell to pieces. I couldn't have fallen for him. It was wrong. He was wrong. *Argh! He is not called Steven!*

* * *

I wiped my sweaty palms down my coat and tried to ignore the gymnastics routine in my stomach as I thanked the doorman who held the door of The Old Theatre open for me at about quarter past seven. Nick had texted me just as I left the shop to say they'd probably be towards the back on the first floor and to remind me they were meeting at seven. Despite my preference to be punctual, I'd been too nervous to risk being first.

I took a deep breath and headed for the stairs. Hesitating at the stair head, I could see what I figured had to be the Bay Trade crowd, given the mix of ages, but no Nick. My phone beeped and I fished it out of my bag.

✉ From Nick
Running a bit late. So sorry. See you really
soon xx

Damn! I'd have to approach someone. Scary. I stared at the group, trying to decide who looked the most approachable. A tall, slim woman with long blonde wavy hair caught my eye and headed towards me. 'Are you Sarah?' she asked.

I nodded.

'I thought so. You look just as lovely as Nick described. I'm Skye.'

'Hi.' Eek! Nick's best friend.

'I'm so pleased you've come tonight,' she said. 'I know Bay Trade doesn't sound like the most exciting of concepts but I promise you it's great fun and fantastic for business too.' She beamed at me and ushered me towards the bar. 'Nick's running a bit late I'm afraid. Domestic crisis. He asked me to look out for you. Can I get you a drink?'

'It's all right, I'll get it.' I reached for my purse, not wanting to impose.

'Nonsense. Put it away.' Skye laughed gently. 'You can get me one later if it makes you feel better. Now, what would you like?'

'Dry white wine please.'

I studied Skye while she placed the order. I instantly felt comfortable in her presence, possibly because she reminded me of Elise. She wore the same sort of clothes – long floaty cream dress, bolero-style turquoise cardigan, some chunky silver and turquoise beads and a turquoise flower in her hair – and was the same tall, slim build.

'What sort of domestic crisis?' I asked tentatively while we waited for the drinks. I suddenly had a vision of a wife and children at home that he'd conveniently forgotten to mention.

'I'm not sure of the full details,' Skye said. 'Something to do with his new puppy and some feather pillows I think.'

I heaved a sigh of relief that I hoped wasn't obvious to Skye. 'Nick says you paint?'

'Yes. I'm an artist first and foremost but I also love making jewellery and have probably spent more time doing that than painting recently. I enjoy anything creative.'

I pointed at her necklace. 'Did you make that?'

'I did. And these.' She pushed her hair behind her ears to show me some stunning silver and turquoise earrings.

'They're gorgeous. I might need a pair myself.'

'Thank you,' she said. 'With compliments like that plus a glowing reference from Nick, I already adore you.'

Glowing reference? Look just as lovely? What had he been saying about me? My heart raced.

Skye was the perfect hostess, introducing me to various members of the group and asking me lots of questions about my background, the shop and how I was finding life back in Whitsborough Bay after so many years in big cities. She couldn't have done more to make me feel at ease. She made me laugh with anecdotes of nights out with Nick. Each time she told a story involving him, I found myself hanging onto her every word. It was obvious that Skye – and everyone else in the group – thought the world of him, which made me like him even more.

About twenty minutes later, I saw Nick out of the corner of my eye and my legs went momentarily wobbly. He made a beeline for me, grinning. 'You came!' He gave me a big hug and a peck on the cheek then looked embarrassed as he pulled away. 'Sorry. It seems like I haven't seen you in ages. Was that a bit full-on?'

'No, it's fine,' I reassured him. 'I liked it.' *Uh-oh! Where did that come from?*

He looked momentarily surprised then winked and said, 'In that case, I'll have to do it again.'

'Feel free,' I responded before I could stop myself. It must have been that large glass of wine on an empty stomach. 'So, tell me about this puppy,' I said, keen to change the subject.

Nick rolled his eyes at me. 'He's a six-months-old golden Retriever called Hobnob and he went on a rampage while I was out today. He shredded my pillows and there were feathers everywhere. I half expected to find some dead geese. Then he managed to grab a toilet roll and trail it around the house.'

I laughed at the image. 'Did you get it cleared up okay?'

'Yes. It took ages. But that wasn't the worst. When I was ready to come out, I discovered he'd taken a dump in my best pair of shoes.'

'No!'

'And do you know how I discovered that?'

'You didn't—'

'Thank God for socks is all I can say. Even so, it was pretty grim.

The shoes and the socks are now in the bin, my best jeans are in the wash and I had to jump in the shower again. That's why I'm so late, the little sod.'

'Nightmare. What's he doing now?'

'When I left, he was in his bed feeling very sorry for himself. I hope he's still there reflecting on his behaviour when I return tonight. I can't be too hard on him, though. I've been away for two weeks on the trot and when I finally brought him home from my sister's, I had the audacity to nip to the supermarket. I think it was a dirty protest for being such a rubbish owner. Do you have any pets?'

'Two cats. Kit and Kat are brother and sister but thankfully they've been pretty well behaved despite all the disruption they've had with three homes in less than two months.'

'What do you think it says about both of us that we've named our pets after chocolate biscuits?'

'I dread to think,' I said. 'I used to have a goldfish called Smirnoff so that probably isn't a good sign either.'

Nick laughed. 'You're not going to believe this but I had a hamster called Guinness. Speaking of which, I must do a trip to the bar. You've got an empty glass so that needs rectifying.'

Nick reached for my glass and his hand gently grazed mine. We both looked up and directly into each other's eyes. Had he felt that jolt of electricity too? It felt even stronger than on the beach. This wasn't meant to be happening but I didn't think I could stop it. I didn't want to.

'Bar,' muttered Nick, disappearing quickly into the crowd.

The group moved from the pub to The Bombay Palace. The hours whizzed by, getting to know the different Bay Traders and chatting to Nick. Everyone was so welcoming and friendly but I found myself longing to be alone with Nick. Something had definitely started on his sister's wedding day, continued at the pub, deepened on the beach and, now... Well, there was no denying it. I wasn't just falling for him; I'd fallen. No matter how much I believed in the predication, there was no room in my mind for thoughts of any Stevens; my mind was filled with Nick.

Bob wanted to settle the bill for the whole group as a goodbye gift before emigrating. While some of the group were busy pinning him down so he couldn't hand over his credit card, I leaned on the table and allowed my thoughts to drift into a fantasy of a romantic walk home with Nick. I'd shiver in the cold night air, he'd put his arm round me to keep me warm and I'd rest my head on his shoulder. He'd gently kiss the top of my head and tell me he'd had an amazing evening and it was all thanks to me. I'd tell him I was sorry it was at an end. He'd stop, take my face gently in his hands, tell me it was just the beginning and not the end, and kiss me. And it would feel nothing like the asexual kiss I'd shared with Stevie. And it wouldn't matter that he wasn't a Steven. It would be perfect.

'Sarah. Hello. Wake up.' Skye waved her hand in front of my face. 'Penny for them?'

'What? Erm... I was just thinking of something I have to do in the shop tomorrow.'

'Must have been something serious. You were miles away.'

Pants! 'It was... erm...' *Think! Fast! Nick's looking at you.* 'It was a bouquet a customer wanted and I... erm... don't think I have the right colour gerberas.'

'Well, I reckon that's a big fib and you're really thinking about a man,' Skye said, her eyes twinkling mischievously. 'I've seen that look before. And you hardly touched your food. Must be love.'

My cheeks flushed and I cast a nervous glance at Nick. He laughed and put his arm round me.

'Of course she's thinking about a man,' he announced. 'She's thinking about me, what a great evening she's had in my scintillating company, and how she can't wait to do it again.'

We all laughed, nervously in my case. Sitting so close to Nick, my head against his chest, I felt weak at the knees. He smelled so good. He felt so good. I could hear my heart thumping frantically and wondered if he could hear it too. I felt disappointed when he removed his arm although I couldn't help thinking that he'd held me a little more closely and tightly than needed. Had he been aware that the words he spoke in jest were true?

Bill finally settled, everyone pulled on their coats and headed outside.

'Would you mind if I walk you home?' Nick asked.

'I'd love that,' I said, perhaps too quickly.

'No need for that,' piped up Bob. 'I'm just round the corner from Sarah. Tony and I are both heading that way. We'll see her home safe.'

I opened my mouth to protest but what could I say? Nick lived in the opposite direction. If I created a fuss, it would be obvious that I wanted to be alone with him and I'd feel pretty damn stupid if I'd misread the signals from him and he was just being a gent with his offer – not saying it because he wanted to be alone with me too.

'Okay, if you're sure you don't mind...' I caught Nick's eye and he smiled sadly and shrugged his shoulders. That intense look was there again and I knew. I just knew. He felt the same way as me. Auntie Kay and Elise were right.

Bob, Tony and I reached Seashell Cottage and parted. I stood on the doorstep for a moment, imagining what I'd be doing if it had been Nick who'd walked me home instead. Would he have kissed me? If he hadn't made a move, would I have dared kiss him? Oh well, I'd never know. I opened the door just as my phone beeped. Spotting his name on the screen, my heart skipped a beat. I opened his message and grinned.

⌧ From Nick
I had an amazing night thanks to you. I think you might have guessed that I hoped to walk you home so I could give you one of these in person so here's 3 by text instead — xxx — I know I'm not a Steven, but if you give me a chance, I promise I'll treat you better than 20 Stevens! I think we could be great together. Hope you feel the same. Let me know if you do. Goodnight, Sarah xxx

Aware I was letting all the heat out, I quickly closed the door then leaned against it as I read Nick's text over and over again. By the time I found my way to the sofa, my face ached from smiling.

Kit and Kat appeared and rubbed round my legs. 'Mummy will give you a fuss in a moment,' I said. 'First, I have a very important text to write.'

To Nick

I've been trying to ignore my feelings cos of the Steven thing but I do feel the same. How about a rain check without Bob and Tony to cramp our style? Come to the shop at 5.45 tomorrow if you're free. Can't wait to see you again and collect those kisses in person. Steven who? xxx

23

Beep... beep... beep...

I groaned and rolled over in bed, groped around on the bedside cabinet for my mobile, and blindly pressed a button to snooze the alarm. Relief flowed through me that the most hideous sound in the world had ceased, quickly followed by panic; I'd fallen asleep before Nick replied.

Sitting up, I squinted at the screen, expecting to see a little envelope, but it was blank. I switched the bedside lamp on and stared at the phone again. Still blank. My heart sank.

I reluctantly heaved myself out of bed and padded across the landing to the bathroom. Maybe he'd just turn up after work. I didn't say he needed to reply. Yes, that was it. He'd pick me up at 5.45.

But I didn't feel convinced.

At the shop that morning, I found myself constantly staring at my phone. I checked my inbox. I checked it wasn't on silent. I checked my inbox again.

Shortly before eleven, I breathed a sigh of relief when a text envelope appeared with Nick's name on it.

✉ From Nick
Hi Skye, are you free for coffee at some point

today? Have a dilemma and could do with your
advice

I leaned against the counter and re-read the short message.
Skye?

✉ To Nick
Hi Nick, Sarah here. You've just sent me that
text — not Skye. You OK? Anything I can help
with? xx

I had a bouquet to make but I couldn't bring myself to work.
Instead I just stared at the screen. Dilemma? What sort of dilemma?
Could it have anything to do with me? I willed him to reply.
Quickly.

✉ From Nick
Sorry about that. I'm fine. Hope you're OK and
didn't have a sore head this morning! Have a
good week

No kisses? Not even a smiley face? No confirmation to meet up
tonight? No acknowledgement of the text I sent him? No mention of
the text he sent me? What was he playing at? I shoved my phone
back in my pocket and stormed towards the flower buckets to get
what I needed for the bouquet.

'Hey! What have the flowers done to upset you?'

I spun round to face Mum. 'What?'

'The flowers you're grabbing. You've already snapped one.'

I looked at the crushed stalks in my hand. I'd actually snapped
three.

'Are you okay, sweetheart?'

'Yes. Sorry, Mum. Just a bit annoyed.'

'Anything I've done?'

I shook my head. 'Of course not. Ignore me. Bad morning.'

'Do you want to talk about it?'

'Thanks, but I'm fine. And I'd better get on with this bouquet or

I'll have an angry customer on my hands to make a bad day even worse.'

Mum reached out and took my empty hand in hers. 'Remember that I'm here if you need me.'

'Thanks, Mum, but I really am fine.' It was tempting but I didn't feel like opening up at that moment. The anger had subsided and I felt silly. Nick's text last night must have been the drink talking. Clearly I'd imagined the chemistry and he wasn't interested. I should have ignored his text and not sent that ridiculous reply. I shouldn't have deviated from the search for Steven... look where it had got me.

I finished the bouquet and tied a piece of raffia round the bottom. So what if Nick wasn't interested? I had a load of Stevens on my list so I didn't care. In fact, I'd contact them all as soon as I got home. That's what Clare would do. She'd say bollocks to Nick and set up her next date.

I lay the bouquet on the counter. Maybe I'd see if he appeared at quarter to six, though, before I rushed into anything...

I waited over an hour after closing time, just in case. I must have gone through every emotion in that hour from excitement (maybe he'll turn up?) to devastation (he's not going to come) to apathy (I don't care anyway; I'm a successful woman in my own right and don't need a man in my life) to anger (why the hell would he lead me on like that?)

The anger became the strongest emotion and eventually spurred me home and into decisive action. As soon as I closed the door at Seashell Cottage, I stormed into the kitchen and grabbed my list off the fridge, scattering the magnets to the floor.

I threw myself onto the sofa with my laptop and logged into the dating site. 'Goodbye Nick Derbyshire. Stand me up, will you? Well, I don't need you.'

* * *

An hour later, I closed my laptop, feeling exhausted but a lot calmer. I reflected on my updated list:

Ste Parker (original list) – Casual 'hello' message sent, apologising for the delay in getting in touch due to setting up new business

Steve Masterson & Steve Berry (original list) – Both profiles had been removed

Stephen Fitzpatrick (original list) – Messaged him. Immediate response back to say he'd got back with his ex-girlfriend at his work's Christmas party last week but wished me every success in finding someone

Steve Collins – Had added me to his favourites (very flattering). Messaged to thank him for this and say 'hi'

Stephen Webb & Steven Fox (both new) – Casual 'hello' messages sent

I retrieved the magnets from the kitchen floor and stuck my new list to the fridge door. Kat squeaked at my feet. I picked her up and gave her a hug.

'It was the right thing to do,' I said to her. 'What if I'd got involved with him and Steven came along? We'd both end up getting hurt. This way's better. He's obviously not interested in me or he wouldn't have sent me such a casual text. I have a silly little crush on him, that's all. It will go away soon and maybe one of these Stevens will be your new daddy. Would you like that?' Kat purred and nuzzled closer. 'That's right. Nick and I were never meant to be. The man of my dreams is called Steven. Nick was a blip. Madame Louisa said it wouldn't be plain sailing. This is obviously what she meant. From now on, we're searching for Steven. We're not dreaming about Nick.'

But a tear slipped down my cheek.

* * *

A week passed and I didn't hear a peep out of Nick. Seaside Blooms thrived and trade kept increasing as Christmas crept closer. Mum was helping out full-time and Cathy's sixteen-year-old daughter, Jade, had started working Saturdays and a few weekday shifts when she wasn't at college, which relieved the pressure.

Auntie Kay kept us posted on her travels with regular family emails and photos. Every so often, she texted me to ask for a progress report on Nick but I evaded the subject.

The final week of school term arrived and, by Friday evening, there was still no word from Nick.

I'd barely seen Elise for the past fortnight as she was tied up directing a pantomime at school and various other Christmas activities. Stevie was tied up with a few big work projects and Clare was unavailable due to weekend work commitments although she was expected in Whitsborough Bay on Saturday night.

Mum and Dad seemed to be out every other night with friends, leaving me all alone with just two cats for company. And my troubled thoughts. Despite my resolve to forget about Nick and just search for Steven, I couldn't get him off my mind. I didn't think it was appropriate to text him again but I ventured down to the beach at dawn for a run five times during that fortnight in the hope that we'd run into each other – literally. We didn't.

I spent a ridiculous number of evenings staring blankly at the TV, checking my laptop every fifteen minutes or so to see if I'd received any new messages or to check Nick's Facebook status. I hated being like that. I kept opening up my lovely silk beaded notepad and trying to focus on ideas for developing the business, but the next priority really had to be my website, which got me sidetracked looking at the portfolio Nick had pulled together, which got me thinking about Nick again, which drew me back to the laptop to check his Facebook status. Vicious circle.

Ste Parker from my original list hadn't been in touch but the three new Stevens had. I'd stupidly entered into online conversations with all of them which created a massive challenge in remembering who'd said what. Even though I could scroll up to previous messages, there soon became too many messages to work through. I ended up allocating Post-it notes of a different colour to each Steven, scribbling down the key points, and sticking them to the dining room wall in coloured columns in an effort to keep track.

Around mid-afternoon on Thursday, we hit a lull. I watched Jade dusting the shelves in the glass display cabinets while she sang along to 'Last Christmas'. In The Outback, I could hear Mum singing while she unpacked a delivery of gifts. Cathy, making a

Christmas wreath next to me, hummed away quietly and I smiled as I watched my team in action. *My team.* I liked it.

I decided to take advantage of the lack of customers and check to see if I had any messages. There was one from each of the three new Stevens and, as I quickly scanned through them, my heart sank. *No! I don't believe it!*

'I need to nip out, Cathy,' I said, logging off the site. 'Will you be okay without me for a bit?'

Cathy laughed. 'Of course. It's not like I'm on my own. I've got George Michael in here and Andrew Ridgeley out there. You take a break.'

'I'll only be ten minutes. Maximum.' I grabbed my coat from The Outback, telling Mum I had an errand to run. Clutching my mobile, I headed for Castle Park at the end of the street and sat on one of the benches, overlooking South Bay. The biting coastal wind made my eyes stream but at least it was dry. I called Clare, hoping she was free.

'Clare. Please say you can talk.'

'Sure. We're at an exhibition, but I've seen what I need to. Let me go somewhere quieter.' The background chatter died down and her voice came over a bit echoey. 'I'm in the entrance hall now. What's the craic? You sound worried.'

'I am. I've heard from Steve Collins and he's asked me to meet him.'

'That's grand. When?'

'Tomorrow night.'

'So what are you worried about?'

'I've heard from Steven Fox and he's asked me to meet him too.'

'Oh. Dare I ask...?'

'Tomorrow night.'

'Bummer.'

'I've also heard from Stephen Webb.'

'No! Tomorrow night too?'

'Yep.'

'Christ, Sarah, you're in demand. What will you do?'

'I was hoping you'd tell me.'

'You could try meeting all three of them,' she said. 'Pick three pubs close to each other, arrange to meet them at three different times, then keep making excuses to leave one and go onto the next.'

'You're joking.'

'Of course I am, you eejit. Imagine what a nightmare that would be for someone like you.'

'What do you mean "someone like you"?'

'You know exactly what I mean. Someone nice and polite and a bit anal.'

I couldn't take offence as she was absolutely right. 'So what should I do?'

'Several options spring to mind. You could pick your favourite and keep the others warm, you could pick your favourite and reject the others, you could say you can't make it to any of them, or you could suggest Friday night to one, Saturday to another, and Sunday to the other. Although I'm with you on Saturday night so that scuppers that plan.'

'Which would you do?'

'I'd date all three on the same night.'

'And if you were me?'

'I'd pick one. Do you have a favourite?'

'I like them all so far. It's hard to judge from a handful of messages.'

'You must be leaning towards one of them.'

I thought for a moment, trying to separate them in my mind, mentally picturing my columns of Post-it notes. 'Steven Fox. I think. Perhaps.'

'Foxy it is then,' Clare said. 'But I'd keep the other two warm; tell them you already have plans for the weekend, but would love to meet up after Christmas, and hope they don't catch you out with Foxy.'

I thanked Clare and headed back to the shop, feeling slightly more relaxed. I'd give it till the end of the day and message Steven Fox. No point in looking too keen.

Cathy was serving a customer, Jade was still cleaning, and I could hear Mum on the phone in The Outback.

'Did anything exciting happen while I was gone?' I asked Cathy and Jade when the customer left.

'I sold another of those silver teddy bear money boxes for a christening,' Jade said before shyly adding, 'and I talked her into a really cute teddy bear, a card, and some gift wrap.'

'That's brilliant, Jade. Thank you.'

'The customer who just left wanted two bouquets; a twenty-pound and a ten-pound one,' Cathy said. 'She's coming back in half an hour.'

'Thank you both.'

'What about that guy, Mum?' Jade said.

My stomach lurched. What guy?

'Soup for brains,' Cathy said. 'Nick came in looking for you.'

Oh my God! 'Did he leave a message?'

'He looked a bit disappointed that he'd missed you and said he'd probably see you after Christmas.'

'Anything else?'

'No. That was it.'

'Is he your boyfriend?' Jade asked.

'Jade!' Cathy scolded.

'No. He's not my boyfriend.' *But I wish he was.*

'Are you okay?' Cathy said. 'You look a bit peaky.'

I waved my hand dismissively. 'I'm absolutely fine. Just a bit tired from the whole opening a new business near Christmas thing. I'm just going to make a cuppa. Do either of you want one?'

Drink orders taken, I headed into The Outback where I pulled my phone out my pocket and quickly texted Nick.

✉ To Nick

Hi. I hear I've just missed you. So sorry. Would love to have seen you. Don't suppose you're still in town?

I stared at the screen in nervous anticipation while I boiled the kettle, but no reply came.

Two hours later, cashing up complete and the team on their way home, I stood by the counter in the darkened shop and looked at the messages from the three Stevens. I realised I couldn't face meeting any of them. The only person I really wanted to go out with was Nick. Maybe I blew it when I told him about Steven that first day in the pub.

I slowly typed in a message for Steven Fox then copied and pasted it into the other two message threads:

Thanks for your suggestion to meet up. Can I take a rain check for after Christmas? I've recently moved back here. My best friend from London is coming to stay for the weekend. We haven't seen each other in ages and we've had this booked in for some time so it would be rude of me to cancel. Really sorry. Hope you have a fantastic Christmas. 'Speak' soon. Sarah

✉ To Clare
Thanks for your advice earlier. Decided not to meet any of them just now. Long story. Don't suppose you can give that work do a miss and come up tomorrow night instead? Need cheering up xx

✉ From Clare
Sorry. Would love to but will get sacked if I miss it. Bunch of very important eejits to enter-tain. Biggest event in the company calendar. Promise to be up by 11 at the latest on Saturday. See you in the shop. Cheer up or I'll give you a slap xx

24

Elise Dawson

49 mins

Was intending on having ONE quick glass of bubbly before a night out with the Kayley School team but on my 3rd glass already. Could be a messy night!

Clare O'Connell is at The Dorchester, London…

1 hr

Works Christmas party and prize-giving. Free bar. Nice

Kay Summers

5 hrs

Think I was born to travel the world. Heading to New York tomorrow till 3rd Jan. New Year in New York! So excited

I sighed as I read through my Facebook newsfeed that evening. Mum and Dad were off for Christmas cocktails with the neighbours and Ben was out with his mates in Leeds. It was less than a week till Christmas and everyone had a packed evening of entertainment. Except me, the spinster with cats, all alone like Uncle Alan. The thought made me shudder and I had to reprimand myself: 'You have friends. You're not alone like him. You're just on your own tonight and a bit lonely. It's a different thing.'

I checked Nick's newsfeed for the umpteenth time but there was still nothing since the comment about going out with 'the lovely Sarah Peterson' from before Bob's leaving do. I sighed again and checked my messages. Nothing there either.

Back on Facebook, I typed in:

Sarah Peterson

Billy No Mates tonight. Feeling very sorry for myself and distinctly Bridget Jones-like, especially after seeing what all my friends and family are up to this evening – particularly you Auntie **Kay Summers**! Thank goodness **Clare O'Connell** is coming to visit tomorrow to entertain me. Going to dig out the romcoms, make some hot chocolate and trough a large bag of Doritos

I re-read my message and toyed with not posting it. Did it sound too 'woe is me?' But it was how I felt and Madame Louisa said I needed to share more. Sod it! I'd post it. I was lonely and bored and I needed some sympathy.

It was only 8.17 p.m. but my PJs, slippers, and fluffy dressing gown called. I removed my make-up and released my hair from its clip, feeling much more relaxed.

Downstairs, I stoked up the fire, lit some scented candles, put *Pretty Woman* on and threw myself onto the sofa with a soft red throw.

Richard Gere had just invited Julia Roberts into the Regent Beverly Wilshire Hotel when a loud knock on the door made me jump. I reluctantly peeled back the throw and padded into the hall.

'Who is it?' I shouted.

'Nick.'

'Nick?' *Oh. My. God!* It wasn't even nine and there I was in my PJs with no make-up on and hair everywhere.

'I wondered if Billy No Mates would like some company before she's found on her floor eaten by Alsatians?' he shouted. 'But I can leave if it's a bad time.'

I smiled at the *Bridget Jones* reference. So, he saw my Facebook status and came straight round, did he? My knight in shining armour. I unlatched the door and opened it an inch or so. 'I have to warn you, I'm in my PJs. It's not a pretty sight.'

'I don't believe that for a minute,' he said.

With my stomach doing somersaults, I opened the door wider and ushered him in out of the cold.

'Nice PJs,' he said.

'They're comfortable. I know men have this fantasy of women in little satin numbers, but it's freezing tonight and fleecy PJs with teddies on are exactly what's needed.'

Nick laughed. 'I'm being serious. I really do like them. Surprisingly, they're kind of sexy. I'm not so convinced about the slippers, though.'

Eek! I'd forgotten about the teddy-shaped slippers. 'Oh well, you've seen me at my worst. The least I can do is offer you a drink for the shock.'

'I've brought you this.' He handed me a bottle of wine. 'I know you were planning hot chocolate, but I thought you might prefer something stronger.'

I smiled again. 'Thanks, Nick. I'd best get this open then.'

'I'd have brought you some flowers too, but I figured petrol station flowers for a florist could be an insult.'

'I can't remember the last time someone bought me flowers.'

Nick smiled. 'We'll have to rectify that soon, then.' He held my gaze. Stomach gymnastics time again. What was he doing to me?

'Make yourself comfortable in the lounge and I'll get some glasses.' I headed towards the kitchen. I wasn't sure how I managed to sound so cheerful and casual when I was falling to pieces inside. All I wanted to do was scream at him, *'Why didn't you reply to my text? Have you any idea how hard the past fortnight has been? And now you're here acting all heroic. What's going on?'* But, of course, I didn't have the guts to say it.

'Pretty Woman,' Nick said when I walked back into the lounge. For a fleeting moment I thought he was complimenting me. Then he added, 'Great film.'

'Oh, yeah, let me stop that.' I handed him one of the glasses then grabbed the remote, put the TV off, and sat beside him on the sofa.

'Are you really sure you don't mind me being here? I should probably have phoned first. You just sounded so down on Facebook that I came straight round.'

'It's fine.' I gently touched his arm. 'I'm glad you're here.'

'Really?'

'Really.'

He held my gaze again. It was definitely there; there was no denying the chemistry between us. So what happened after Bob's leaving do? Should I say something? Should I do something? I found myself staring at his lips and imagining what it would feel like to kiss him. *Good grief, Sarah, get a grip.*

'So,' I said, 'I really enjoyed Bob's leaving do. You were right about the Bay Trade guys. Great bunch. Did Bob enjoy his send-off?'

Nick grinned. 'He absolutely loved it. I can't believe he's already been in New Zealand for a week. What about you? Things going well in the shop?'

'Really good. Sales have been far better than expected which is a relief as I was worried that I didn't have what it takes to run the business after so many years in a big corporate.' I was rambling. Could I just blurt it out and ask him how he felt? Eek! Maybe I could start with a simpler subject: my business worries. I already knew he was a great listener and, being self-employed too, he was bound to get it. Yes, business worries were a much safer – and far less embarrassing – subject.

'Sounds great,' Nick said. 'So why don't you look happier?'

I shrugged. 'Are you sure you don't mind listening to my woes yet again?'

'I'm here, aren't I?'

Plumping my cushion, I changed position on the sofa to get more comfortable. 'I promise I'm usually an optimist but this is unchartered territory for me. I've never been self-employed with the worry of an erratic income stream. I know I should relax and enjoy the great sales but I can't help feeling worried that the current success of the shop is the novelty factor of me being a new business combined with seasonal trade. What if it goes pear-shaped in the

New Year and I destroy everything Auntie Kay worked so hard to achieve? What if I can't afford to pay my team because I don't make the business successful enough? What if I can't earn enough to pay back the loan Auntie Kay gave me to refurbish and stock the shop? I'd feel like such a failure.'

Nick smiled sympathetically. 'As one self-employed person to another, I completely get where you're coming from with the financial security thing. I learned to budget and make sure I have a buffer fund for those tighter months. You'll probably need to do the same. However, I don't think you've got anything to panic about. You're making better sales for two major reasons. Firstly, you offer more choice because you have gifts as well as flowers. Secondly, and more importantly, you've got you.'

'What do you mean?'

'I love your auntie and she's a really talented florist, but, even to the untrained eye, I can see that her style is very traditional like most of the other florists in The Bay. *You* bring something different. You can do the traditional stuff, but you also do all these really current designs that look amazing. Plus, the shop looks so classy now that it stands out against all the other florists in town and makes yours the place to be. So that's probably three reasons. Must return to school and re-take my maths.'

I laughed. 'Thanks Nick. That's really sweet of you.'

'Credit where credit's due. You're exceptionally talented. You need to believe in yourself more. Kay would never have given you the shop if she didn't think you were brilliant. I mean that.'

As he fixed those gorgeous blue eyes on mine, I felt my worries drifting away. Too much time on my own was definitely not good for me; I managed to over-think absolutely everything and create problems that didn't really exist.

'Thank you. I needed to hear that.' I kissed him on the cheek. 'Thank you so much.' I gave him another kiss on the cheek but his head turned as I went for a third and I caught his mouth slightly.

'Sorry,' I whispered, but I couldn't bring myself to pull away from him.

The next moment, Nick kissed me on the lips and I felt my

whole body tingle with delight as I melted into his kiss. Oh. My. God. So worth waiting for.

'I wanted to do that after Bob's do,' Nick said, holding me tightly some time later.

'I wanted you to but my chaperones scuppered that.'

'I could have killed Bob and Tony,' he said. 'But part of me was relieved they'd stepped in.'

'Why?'

'If I'd walked you home, I wouldn't have been able to stop myself. I'd have had to kiss you goodnight and I was worried you might reject me because I'm not Steven. I really thought I'd blown it when I texted you those kisses and you didn't reply.'

I sat upright. 'I did reply and I thought I'd blown it because you didn't reply to me.'

'I didn't get a reply,' Nick said.

'You're joking.' I grabbed my phone off the table and started scrolling through my sent items. 'It's not there.'

'Try your outbox?' Nick suggested.

'It's there. I don't believe it. Damn ancient phone and useless network. I could have saved myself a lot of stress and heartache if I'd thought to check my text had actually gone. I hate this thing. You don't get this with an iPhone.'

'What did it say?'

I chewed on my thumbnail as I re-read my text. 'Here. You can read it.' I passed the phone to Nick.

I watched his lips move slightly as he read it. '"Steven who?"' Nick lowered the phone and looked at me, eyes shining. 'Do you still mean that?'

I nodded. 'I can't believe you didn't get it. I thought you weren't interested because I'd messed things up by telling you about Steven.'

'Come here, you.' He kissed me again.

'I was definitely interested.' He kissed the top of my head as I lay against his chest. 'If I'd got your text, I'd definitely have turned up at the shop.'

'I waited for an hour, then I came home and cried my way through a romcom fest of *My Best Friend's Wedding* and *He's Just Not That Into You.*' I pointed to the *Pretty Woman* DVD box on the coffee table. 'Can you spot the theme?' I decided not to mention the hour spent on my searching for Steven frenzy first. There was such a thing as too much honesty.

'I'm so sorry.' He stroked my hair.

'It's not your fault. It's that damn phone. And to make matters worse, the next time I heard from you was that text you meant for Skye instead. When I texted to say you'd sent it to me by mistake, your reply was all formal with no kisses or anything.'

Nick groaned. 'What a pair we are. When you didn't reply – or rather when I thought you hadn't – I thought I'd blown it for pushing you when I knew you wanted to search for Steven. I needed to talk to someone which was why I texted Skye.'

I cringed. 'Did you tell her about the Steven thing?'

'Sorry,' Nick said. 'I couldn't avoid it. Are you angry with me?'

I shook my head. 'She won't tell anyone else, will she?'

'No. She's great with secrets.'

I sat up, reached for my wine, then passed Nick his. 'What did she say?

'She understood. She's quite into clairvoyance.'

I smiled. 'That doesn't surprise me.'

'She said the attraction between us was obvious. She's a great believer in fate, just like you, and she reckoned that if it was meant to be, it would happen.'

'Sound advice,' I said. 'When you came into the shop yesterday...'

'It was to follow Skye's advice and make sure we were still friends.'

'I sent you a text in the hope I'd still catch you. Did you get that one?'

Nick nodded. 'I was nearly home when it came through.'

'You didn't reply, though.'

'I didn't know what to say. I didn't know how you felt about me and I was worried I'd text something that might scare you off if you weren't interested.'

'I was very interested. Believe me.' I kissed Nick again.

'I don't want to ruin the moment, but...' he said when we pulled apart.

'But what about my search for Steven?'

Nick nodded. 'Sorry. I have to know.'

'It's over.' I paused. 'I've been in touch with three Stevens during the past week and they all asked if they could meet me tonight. The only person I really wanted to be with was you and, even though I thought there was no chance of that, I still turned them all down. I chose you.'

'So you don't believe in the CD anymore?'

I shrugged. 'I can't dismiss the CD because of that stuff about my uncle, the picture and the bracelet. But I have to assume she was wrong about Steven. I liked you when I first saw you looking all dashing in your morning suit and I've been fighting it ever since. After Jason, I wanted to believe I was going to meet the man of my dreams and I was so happy to believe that he was called Steven, I had my eyes closed to the Nick right in front of me. If you'll have me, I don't think I need to search for Steven anymore.'

'Of course I'll have you.' Nick kissed me again. 'Do you really mean that? It's over with Steven?'

'I really mean that. If a Steven walked into my shop tomorrow, I don't think that there's anything he could say or do that would make him more perfect for me than you.'

25

'I've missed you so much.' Clare almost knocked an elderly couple flying in her effort to get to my side of the shop counter late the following morning.

'Sorry,' she said, vaguely acknowledging them, 'but she cannot serve you until I've done this.' She dropped her bag on the floor and hugged me tightly. 'Ah, that's grand. You can serve these nice people now. I need a wee and a coffee. Hi everyone.' With a dramatic wave towards my team, she disappeared into The Outback.

'I'm so sorry about that.'

Thankfully the customers laughed. 'I assume she's a good friend,' the man said.

'You'd think so, but I've never seen her before in my life.' They looked so shocked that I felt I had to quickly add. 'I'm joking really.'

'What's the craic?' asked Clare, reappearing with a drink after the couple left. 'I hope you've organised a night on the town with your man Stevie and the delightful Rob.'

'I haven't organised anything but I can text Stevie to see if they're free.'

'You're busy creating.' She indicated the half-made bouquet on the counter. 'Why don't you give me your pathetic excuse for a phone and I'll text Stevie while you finish? He won't be able to say no to me. No man can.'

Grinning at her outrageous display of self-confidence, I handed over my phone.

Five minutes later, she emerged from The Outback and thrust my phone in front of me. 'What's this?'

I glanced down at the message from Nick from earlier that morning and blushed.

⌑ From Nick
Good morning I only left you 6 hours ago & I'm
missing you already. Wish I could see you
tonight xxx

'Care to explain?'

'Shh.' I nodded towards Mum and Cathy who were busy re-stocking the flower buckets. 'Who said you could look through my texts?'

'It's the obvious thing to do when some daft muppet hands over their phone,' she whispered. 'Am I correct in thinking you've ditched the search for your man Steven and shagged some bloke called Nick?'

'I haven't shagged him as you so delicately put it but, yes, the search for Steven has been called off.'

'You dark horse. I didn't think you'd ever dismiss that CD as bollocks. Good on you.'

'I haven't dismissed it as bollocks.'

'But you're seeing a non-Steven.'

'Yes, but it isn't that simple. I'll explain why later.'

'Go on. Admit it was bollocks.'

My phone beeped, saving me from a further debate, but Clare grabbed it off me.

'Oi!' I tried to retrieve it but she held it high, giggling.

'It's from Stevie,' she said when I gave up and she was able to lower the phone. 'Not lover-boy. Yes! They were planning to go out tonight anyway and would love to meet us.'

'Great. You've got your answer so give me my phone back.'

'Say please.'

'Please.'

She stuck out her tongue as she handed it over.

'You're being very childish today and suspiciously upbeat.' I shoved my phone deep into my jeans pocket.

'But I make you laugh,' she said. 'Now spill. I have to know everything about you and your man Nick. Who is he for a start and how is it I've never heard of him?'

'Shh! I promise I'll tell you every last detail but you have to be quiet.'

'Why?'

'I don't want my parents to know yet. Mum will tell Auntie Kay and she'll start planning the wedding. I just want a bit of time to enjoy being with him without the family drama.'

'Okay. I'll zip it, but don't blame me if something accidentally slips out.'

'Can I have this please?' A short woman in her mid-twenties placed a soft pink bunny on the counter.

'Aw. It's so cute.' Clare shoved me aside. 'Will you be wanting this for a special occasion?'

The woman beamed proudly. 'My cousin's just had her first baby.'

'Congratulations. Now I don't wish to be stereotypical, but would I be right in thinking the pink means she's had a girl?'

'Bethany Lily.'

'What a beautiful name,' Clare gushed. 'Have you bought a card yet as we have a lovely selection of unique cards at fabulous prices.'

'Well, I...'

'Let's just leave this little fella here and I'll show you. No obligation, but you might as well look. Stay in the warmth a bit longer. And I tell you what else would make this gift even more special...'

By the time the customer left ten minutes later, she'd also bought a card, an expensive gift box, a photo frame and a bouquet for the new mum because, as Clare put it 'baby gets showered with gifts and poor mum who's done all the hard work and is absolutely exhausted gets forgotten'.

I gave Clare an appreciative round of applause. 'You could sell ice to the Inuit.'

'I keep telling you, watch and learn. But I admit I am good. Very good. In fact, that's why I was named as Prime's PR person of the year last night and received a rather fat bonus to say thanks. Hurrah for me.'

'Clare! That's fantastic. No wonder you're so giddy this morning.'

'It might have something to do with it.' She looked down the shop towards where Cathy and Mum were still busy with the flower delivery. 'Seeing as you won't tell me about your night of passion with your man Nick, I'm going to see if your mum or Cathy have anything interesting to tell me. And I think it's about time you did some work. I don't know, just because you're the boss, you think you can spend the day mooning after your new man and everyone else will do all the hard work.'

'I'm not mooning and I've not stopped all morning but I'm sure Mum and Cathy would appreciate your help. Just *don't* tell them about Nick.'

Less than ten minutes later, my plan to keep Nick a secret was well and truly scuppered. I was making a bouquet for a waiting customer when the bell tinkled.

'Special delivery for Ms Sarah Peterson. Who can take it?' I looked up to see a young girl wearing a uniform from The Chocolate Pot, holding a large box tied up in cellophane with a big red ribbon round it.

'Ooh, what is it?' Mum asked.

My heart thumped as she took the box and peered at the large card on the front. She frowned, then smiled, then looked across at me. I could almost see the question marks spinning round her like in a cartoon. Cathy, Clare and Jade also gathered round the box, whispering and giggling.

'Hand it over,' I said the second my customer left with her bouquet.

'"I can't send you flowers so here's the next best thing. Thinking of you. Nick," plus lots of sloppy kisses,' Clare read. 'Who's Nick, Sarah?'

'Yes, sweetheart, who's Nick?' Mum asked.

'Nobody.'

'Doesn't sound like nobody,' Mum said.

'Is it Nick Derbyshire?' Cathy asked.

'It might be. Hand them over.'

Mum passed me the box.

'Ooh, Kay will be delighted.' Cathy turned to Mum. 'Your sister always thought Nick and Sarah would make a perfect couple.'

'Do I know him?' Mum asked.

'I don't know,' I said. 'Maybe when he was little. His grandma lived next door to Auntie Kay.'

'She's turned pink,' Clare said. 'I think our Sarah's pretty smitten.'

'Are you going to open it?' Jade asked.

'Not with you lot watching.'

'Aw, go on,' Clare said. 'Don't be such a meanie.'

Scowling at her, but inwardly delighted that Nick cared enough to send me something, I turned my back to them and put the box on the counter. I carefully unfastened the ribbon and peeled back the cellophane. Inside the box were two compartments: one filled with cupcakes with flowers decorated on the top and the other filled with beautifully iced flower-shaped shortbread biscuits. They looked and smelled divine. What an absolute sweetheart.

'Don't be a spoilsport. Turn around and show us,' Clare said.

I turned round, rolled my eyes at her and then lifted up the box so they could all see. 'Who's for elevenses? And then, if you're all nice to me and we're not too busy, I might tell you about Nick. But it will be *very* brief.'

'Don't panic, everyone,' Clare said. 'I'll get the unabridged version out of her later and text you all.'

Clare followed me into The Outback. 'Are you going to phone this Nick to thank him?'

'I might. Why?'

'I wondered if you might like to invite him along tonight.'

'Really? You wouldn't mind?'

Clare shook her head. 'I'd like to meet the guy who you've given up on Steven for because he must be pretty damn special.'

I blushed again. 'I think he might be.'

Clare smiled. 'He can only come on one condition: strictly no

PDAs. You know I hate it when people are constantly snogging and pawing each other.'

'It's a deal. No PDAs. Are you absolutely sure?'

'Stevie and Rob will be there so it's not like I'll be a gooseberry so, yes, I'm sure. I can't wait to meet your new non-Steven.'

Almost as soon as I brought the drinks and goodies out, things went crazy in the shop. My mug of tea went cold and it was two hours before a lull allowed me to take a bite of my cake.

Around mid-afternoon, two women stepped into the shop and I recognised one of them immediately. 'Skye! What a lovely surprise. How are you?'

'Really good, thanks. I'm sorry to turn up on a Saturday but there's something I want to ask you. I don't suppose you can spare ten minutes?'

I nodded. 'You've actually timed it perfectly. We've hardly stopped all day and it's just this minute calmed down.'

'I know,' Skye said. 'We passed about an hour ago and the shop was packed so we went to The Chocolate Pot for a cuppa instead. By the way, this is my sister, Kate.'

'Hi, Kate.' I smiled at her. The family resemblance was striking but Kate had short blonde hair instead of tumbling curls and wore a smart black shift dress with a cerise pink belt around the waist; very chic in comparison to Skye's flowery maxi dress.

'Hi Sarah, good to meet you.' Kate offered her hand and shook mine enthusiastically. 'There's something I wanted to speak to you about too.'

'Really? Sounds intriguing.'

We moved away from the counter, leaving Cathy and Clare in charge of customers, and wandered to the end of the shop.

'I know you're busy,' Skye said, 'so I'll be really quick and, if you like the sound of it, we can talk some more when the shop's closed. I'm organising an arts and crafts exhibition in The Ramparts Hotel over the Easter holidays. The theme is "Less is More" and it's all about simple but beautiful crafts. I wondered if you could create some modern minimalist floral displays to complement my paintings and jewellery which I will, of course, pay you for, but could you also create some arrangements to sell?'

'Wow! That sounds amazing. Yes, please.' The Ramparts Hotel was Whitsborough Bay's only five-star hotel and was huge. Events like this were very well-attended.

'I'm the manager at The Ramparts,' Kate said. 'The floristry contract is up for renewal. Our current florist has served us well but we want to move in a different direction, creating displays that wow rather than just look pretty. I've been keeping an eye on your work and I'm impressed.'

'Thank you.' My head was spinning. I'd only been in The Ramparts a couple of times but I remembered there being flowers everywhere. A contract with them would be extremely lucrative.

'As an independent hotel, we like to work with local suppliers so you tick that box. I personally work off a combination of gut-feel and talent. Early indications are positive. If you're interested in pitching for the contract, let's set up an appointment for the New Year. If you can meet our needs at the right price, I won't approach anyone else for a quote.'

'No pressure then,' Skye said, laughing as she gently nudged her sister.

'Wow again! I don't know what to say. That's an amazing opportunity. Thank you.'

The shop had filled up again and we were getting jostled. Kate reached into her jacket pocket and handed me a business card. 'If you call my PA on Monday, she can set up a meeting for the New Year.'

'I will. Thank you again, both of you. This is amazing.'

Kate smiled. 'You're very welcome. We'll let you get back to your customers.'

I walked them to the door and stepped out onto the cobbles. 'Can I ask you something, Kate?'

'Of course.'

'I'm flattered and excited to have this opportunity, but I'm curious as to what made you think of me. I thought most businesses would have wanted a more established florist for something like this.'

'That's a good question, but someone sang your praises so highly that I felt I had to come and see for myself.'

I grinned at Skye. 'Thank you. I think I owe you a drink or two.'

Skye shook her head. 'It wasn't me.'

I frowned. 'Then who?'

'It was Skye's friend Nick,' Kate said.

My heart raced. 'Nick? Really?'

Kate nodded. 'He was designing a new brochure for us and he asked who supplied the flowers. I told him the contract was up for renewal so he asked if I'd considered you. I told him I was aware that Seaside Blooms had changed hands and I wasn't going to give such a big contract to a new business but he nagged me for days and I realised he wasn't going to shut up until I agreed to visit your shop. Once I'd seen your work I knew it was exactly what we wanted so I think it's Nick you owe a few drinks to.'

The door opened and Jade poked her head out. 'Sorry, Sarah. Mum needs you for a minute.'

'Be right in,' I said.

Kate shook my hand again. 'I look forward to seeing you next year. I think this could be the start of a great partnership.'

As they set off down the cobbles, Skye turned round, gave me a thumbs up and mouthed the words, 'It's yours.'

Back inside, I dealt with Cathy's query then picked up my mobile, smiling widely.

✉ To Nick
```
Skye & Kate have just been to the shop. You might
have just won me a huge contract at The Ramparts.
I owe you so much thanks that I don't think words
will cut it… I may have to show you my apprecia-
tion later xxx
```

I hesitated as I re-read it. It was quite brazen for me. Oh, what the heck... send.

✉ From Nick
```
So pleased for you. I knew you'd wow her. I'd say
you don't have to thank me… but on re-reading
your text, perhaps you do! Can't wait xxx
```

The shop continued at a steady pace for the next couple of hours but at 5 p.m., things finally slowed down so I gathered my team round me. 'Thank you all for working so hard today. The rush is over so I want you all to get your coats and bags, grab another cake, biscuit or both, and go home early. Clare and I can cope, can't we Clare?'

'I can,' she said. 'Not sure about Sarah, though. I think she may be the weak link in this otherwise extremely strong chain.'

They all protested about leaving early, but I insisted. Five minutes later it was just the two of us.

'I don't know about you,' I said. 'But I'm definitely ready for a relax and a few drinks tonight.'

'Now you're talking,' Clare said. 'I thought my job was demanding but I don't mind admitting that it feels pretty easy compared to today. How do you cope?'

'By turning my hobby into my career. Yes, it's busy. Yes, it's physically exhausting but it's mine and it's a success and I love it. And, if I can secure that contract—'

'Which sounds like it's in the bag.'

'Fingers crossed. The future for Seaside Blooms is looking pretty good.'

'That's more like it. Does this mean you're relaxing and enjoying the experience more?'

I nodded. 'I appreciated the pep talk. Helped me get my act together.'

'I think this town and this shop complete you,' Clare said. 'You have a glow about you.'

'That's a lovely thing to say.' Tears pricked my eyes. 'Would you mind holding the fort? I trashed the stock cupboard earlier looking for a teddy. I feel an urge to re-organise.'

She nodded. 'Any excuse to play with the soft toys.'

As I stood on the small stepladder, re-organising the cuddlies, I heard the bell tinkle in the shop and felt a cold breeze around my ankles as the door opened and closed.

A loud male voice exclaimed, 'Oh my God! Clare Siobhan O'Connell. I came to see Sarah, but this is an unexpected added bonus. I haven't seen you since graduation. How the devil are you?'

My heartbeat quickened. *Surely that's not...?*

'Andrew Steven Kerr,' responded Clare. 'I thought you were in Dubai. What the hell are you doing here?'

I froze. *Andrew Steven Kerr? Steven. Oh my God! Why didn't I think of that before?*

26

'Let me see if Sarah's free,' Clare said. 'Can you be trusted not to steal out the till while I'm gone?'

I gripped the stepladder with one hand, the other clenched around a teddy bear.

Moments later, Clare poked her head round the doorway. 'You'll never guess who's just turned up.'

'Andy?' I squeaked. 'What's he doing here?'

'I've no idea but I don't think he's here to buy flowers.'

'What should I do?'

She frowned. 'Come out and say hello of course. I thought you two were friends.'

'We are. But...'

'But what?'

'You said it yourself, Clare.'

'Said what?'

'His name.'

'Andy?'

'His middle name.'

'Steven? Jesus! Steven! You don't think...?'

I sighed. 'I don't know what to think.'

The bell jingled again. 'Well, you can't hide in here forever,' she said. 'You've got a customer and an ex-boyfriend wanting you. And can you put that poor teddy down before you rip his head off?'

I looked down. My knuckles had actually turned white. Releasing my grip, I gently placed him in the crate. *Focus, Sarah! You have a business to run and a friend to face. Neither of them are scary prospects.* 'Can you see to the customer while I see to Andy?'

'I'll have to steal you back if they want flowers.' She leaned over and gave my hand a reassuring squeeze. 'Time to face your past. It'll be grand.'

She headed back into the shop and I took a few deep breaths before following.

'Andy! Long time no see.'

'Sarah!' He gave me a kiss on the cheek then moved in for a hug. 'It's been too long. It's so good to see you.'

I hugged him back but pulled away laughing when he held on a little too long, muttering something about PDAs scaring the customers and Clare away. I could tell from the hug that he was carrying a little more weight these days but it suited him. Gone was the floppy fringe from university, although his hair was still thick and dark. A very tanned face – out of place in a northern seaside town a few days before Christmas – highlighted the years spent living and working abroad.

'Welcome back to the UK. But what are you doing here?'

'I said I wanted to take you out for a catch-up when I got back from Dubai so here I am. You look fantastic, by the way.'

I blushed. 'Thank you. When did you—?'

But the bell jingled and yet another customer came in. And another. And another. So much for the last half an hour being quiet.

'I can see you're busy.' Andy headed towards the door. 'What time do you close?'

'Half past.'

'I'll be back then.'

I was about to protest that I had plans, but he'd already gone and an elderly lady was wittering something about chrysanthemums. Or was it christenings?

'What did he want?' asked Clare when the shop finally emptied.

'To have a catch-up.'

'What? He came all the way back from Dubai for that?'

'He's back in the UK,' I said.

'London to here is still a trek. I take it you weren't expecting him.'

'Definitely not.'

'Then why's he turned up out of the blue? People don't travel several hours without warning just to catch-up with their ex. Hey, do you think he's about to tell you he made a mistake by letting you walk out of his life eight years ago and he wants you back?'

My legs felt quite weak at the prospect. I leaned against the counter to steady myself, hoping Clare wouldn't notice.

But Clare missed nothing. 'Sarah! I know that look. What are you thinking?'

'Nothing.'

'*Sarah!*'

The bell jingled and another couple of customers came in. I quickly made up a bouquet for one of them while Clare sold and gift-wrapped a teddy bear for the other. The unfinished conversation hung heavily in the air.

'Okay,' she said the minute the shop emptied again, 'start talking now. What's going on in that head of yours? You don't seriously think he wants to try again, do you?'

'I don't know. I always thought Andy and I would get together again one day but the timing never seemed right. Now he's back in the UK for good, I'm not with Jason anymore, and he's called Steven.'

Clare put her hands over her mouth and shook her head at me. 'You need to stop that train of thought this minute.' She took her hands away and started counting on her fingers. 'Number one – he's not Steven; he's Andy. Number two – he's back in the UK, but he lives in London. Four hours away. And number three – the most important one – you may not be with Jason anymore but you *are* with Nick. I haven't met the guy but I like him already. You need to hang onto *him* instead of hanging onto your past.'

I put my arms on the counter and cradled my head in them, my stomach churning.

'Madame Louisa predicted this was going to happen.'

'Did she?'

I twisted my head to look at her. 'She said I'd have to decide between the familiar or the new and should follow my heart, not my head.'

'What will your heart be telling you? Andy or Nick? And can I just emphasise again that Steven is Andy's middle name. *Not* his first name but his *middle* name.'

'It's still his name.'

'And you still fancy the pants off Nick so don't you be forgetting that,' Clare cried. 'Oh Jesus! He's back.'

The door opened again. 'Hi. Only me.'

What was I going to do? I'd told Nick the night before that no Steven could be better than him then in walks the 'Steven' I always thought I'd be with forever. I could not, in a million years, have predicted that. But maybe it was nothing to worry about. Maybe Andy really had come for a drink and a catch-up with an old friend. It'd be nice to do that. As friends. Nothing more. I was with Nick, and Andy was no threat to that. The butterflies in my stomach were nothing unusual. I always had them when Andy got in touch and today they might be more intense because I was surprised to see him and a little thrown by the Steven thing.

'Right, I'll be going back to yours just now to get ready for our night out,' announced Clare loudly when Andy closed the door. She pointed at him. 'Don't you keep her long or you'll have me to answer to. We have plans.'

I couldn't help but smile at her bluntness. Poor Andy, already put in his place.

'Hi,' I said when the door closed. 'You're back.'

'As promised. You obviously have plans for tonight but do you have time for a drink first?'

I smiled. 'A very quick one. Let me lock up and sort myself out. I need five minutes to cash up.'

'How about you direct me to your favourite bar and I get the drinks in? You can join me when you're done.'

'Minty's,' I said. 'It's back up—'

'I saw it earlier. I'll see you in there shortly. Dry white wine still?'

'Please.'

I had to count the till eight times before I finally managed to balance it.

27

Andy had secured a couple of comfy armchairs at the back of the bar. He was engrossed in something on his phone so didn't look up. I paused in the doorway and took a moment to watch him, convincing myself he was really there and not an apparition from my past. He wore dark blue jeans, a deep purple shirt and a black cashmere sweater. It all looked very expensive. And very gorgeous.

Eventually he looked up then smiled as he spotted me. 'I was beginning to think you'd stood me up.' He rose and moved in for another kiss on the cheek then a hug although he didn't hold on so long this time. A wave of nostalgia swept over me as I inhaled the familiar smell of his body spray. I'd always loved that scent.

'Sorry. It took longer than expected. Thanks for the wine.' I sat down and took a gulp.

'You're welcome. It's good to see you, Sarah.'

'You said that earlier.'

'Then you'll know I'm not lying. You look great.'

'Thank you. You look good too. Very tanned.' I smiled apologetically as I posed the obvious question: 'Why are you here?'

His eyes widened then he laughed. 'Straight to the point. You've obviously been taking lessons from Clare.'

'It's nothing to do with Clare,' I said, shaking my head. 'I just can't imagine why you've come all this way on the off-chance I may be free for a catch-up.'

'I tried to phone but it was your old work number.'

'Of course. Sorry about that. Why didn't you email me then? My email address hasn't changed. Or Messenger? Why come all the way up here?'

'Isn't it obvious?'

'No.'

He smiled, but the smile didn't reach his eyes. For a moment, he looked tired and vulnerable.

'I've missed you,' he said.

'You've missed me?' It was barely a whisper.

He nodded. 'Living overseas away from friends and family gives you lots of thinking time and you're all I've been able to think about recently. I always thought we'd get back together one day, but that was never going to happen while I was abroad and you were with Jason. But now I'm back and Jason is out of the equation. I know I should have emailed but I just had to see you and...' He stopped and ran his hand through his hair. 'Kelly and I... well... it was never like it was with you. Nobody has ever come close to what we had together. You're the only woman I've ever loved, Sarah. I wanted to see you in person to ask you if there's any chance we can try again?'

For eight years, I'd longed to hear those words. I'd imagined dozens of movie-perfect scenarios where Andy would come back into my life and sweep me off my feet. The trauma of our break-up would be instantly forgotten. I'd see the pain and regret in his eyes for letting me walk out of his life and we'd share a kiss so passionate that those wasted years would melt away and we'd know that our future together was sealed forever.

Only this wasn't one of those moments. I genuinely didn't know how to react.

'Say something,' he pleaded. 'You're making me nervous.'

'I don't know what you want me to say.' I took another gulp of my wine as I tried to gather my thoughts.

'I want you to say you feel the same but I'm guessing that's not the case.' He stood up. 'I'm sorry. I should go. This is probably the stupidest, most impulsive thing I've ever done.' He picked up his coat.

'Andy! I didn't exactly wake up this morning with a speech prepared in case you turned up out of the blue and announced you wanted to try again. It's very unexpected. But I would like to hear you out.'

He didn't look convinced but sat down anyway. 'Okay. I'll stay. Where do you want me to start?'

A burning question popped into my mind and, as soon as it did, I knew it was the most important question and whatever happened next depended on his answer. 'There's something that I need to know.' I looked deep into his eyes. 'I need to know why you changed. Why did you throw three happy years away, just like that?'

He took a sharp intake of breath but managed to hold my gaze.

'We've never talked about it,' I continued, 'and I've always felt like it's the elephant in the room each time we've met up. I need to know what happened to us.'

Andy returned my stare for a short but agonising moment. I felt my resolve slipping and bit my lip. *Don't flinch. Don't tell him it's fine and there's no need to open old wounds because you need this. He owes you this.*

Finally, he spoke. 'You're right.' He took a swig of his pint and sighed. 'I got a bit too career-driven and ambitious. It's not a great explanation, but it's the truth.'

'Okay,' I said slowly, nodding at him. 'But that doesn't actually explain anything. What does that even mean?'

He sighed again. 'The graduate programme I joined was for two years and I thought there was a guaranteed job at the end but it turned out that they would only take on the very best performers. There were some really talented grads and it quickly became a competition to out-do each other. I thought I was good enough to get away with working a nine-to-five day and going out drinking every night. No chance. I made a couple of careless mistakes in my first month and my manager gave me a "pull your socks up or you're out by Christmas" pep talk. I realised I couldn't piss about anymore so I threw myself into my career.'

'And being with me was pissing about, was it?' I snapped, cringing at the volume of my voice.

'No! I didn't specifically mean you. I meant in general. I needed to focus on the job but that meant putting in long hours and working weekends to prove I was the best which, ultimately, meant losing you.'

'You should have told me what was going on, especially about the mistakes at work. I might not have liked it but I'd have understood if we'd needed to cool it while you got back on track.'

He smiled weakly. 'I'm sorry about the way it ended. I should have at least let you stay that weekend to talk it over.'

'I was just thinking about that recently,' I said. 'I cried all the way home that night.'

'You looked so hurt. It's haunted me ever since.'

'Really? I didn't think you'd noticed.'

He reached for my hand. 'I wanted to run after you that night.'

A little shiver of pleasure ran through me at his touch and my heart started racing again. 'Why didn't you?' I whispered.

'I've asked myself that question so many times. I just wasn't in a good place. As awful as it sounds, you were a distraction. I risked my career being over before it even started if I didn't keep that focus. At the time, it seemed easier to let you go. I never stopped thinking about you and regretting what happened. Look what I carry around with me.'

He let go of my hand, reached into his wallet and handed over a creased photo. I gasped and those butterflies went wild again. It was the picture of us in Rhodes that prompted me to get in touch with him again and rebuild our friendship. How romantic.

'It's been in there for years,' he continued. 'Every time I feel down or lonely I take it out, look at your smiling face and I feel better.'

Tears pricked my eyes at the thought of him being so sentimental. It was the sort of thing the old Andy would do. 'I have another question,' I said. 'Why now?'

Andy flashed me a dazzling smile – the kind of expensive-looking smile that Simon Cowell would be proud of. 'My manager took me aside in the summer and told me that I'd done a great job with my project. I could either commit to phase two which meant another three years in Dubai or I could return to the UK for good. Kelly and I were over so I had nobody to factor into any decision-making. I went home that evening and got your photo out. It struck me that, for years, I'd been talking to your photo when I really should've been talking to you in person. I picked up the phone, but then I had this lightbulb moment. I realised I didn't just want to speak to you; I wanted to be with you. Reading between the lines on your emails, I didn't think you were happy with Jason, which meant me being abroad was the biggest barrier to us trying again. I'd just been handed the opportunity to remove that barrier so I gave my boss my decision the next day and hoped you still felt the same way about me. Unfortunately, I had to do four agonising months in Dubai to hand over the reins, but I came to find you as soon as I got back.'

I watched Andy visibly relax now that he'd confessed all. In the romantic movie of our lives, I'd cry and tell him I'd loved him all these years too and we'd both live happily ever after, but something was holding me back. I suddenly felt quite overwhelmed by the huge amount of unexpected information he'd shared. A beep from my mobile made me jump.

⊠ From Clare
Where the hell are you? We're meant to be meeting
the boys at 7. Get your arse home NOW!

'I'm sorry Andy, I've got to go.' I stood up. 'Clare's here. We're meeting friends. I'm late.'

He stood up too and held my coat for me. 'I understand. I wouldn't dream of asking if I can join you as I'm sure you don't want me disrupting things...'

He was clearly angling for an invite but there was just no way. Imagine that conversation: 'Andy, meet Stevie who I met online when stalking men called Steven because, when I was eighteen, a clairvoyant told me that the man of my dreams would be called that. Stevie could have been my boyfriend because he's got the right name, but when we kissed there was no chemistry so we're just great mates. And meet Nick who currently *is* my boyfriend and who I strongly believe could be The One although I resisted him for ages because he isn't called Steven. Guys, meet Andy. Andy was the first love of my life who has now just told me I'm the only woman he's ever loved and he wants me back. And, guess what, his middle name's Steven. I'm sure you're all going to be the best of friends. Can I get anyone a drink?' I shuddered.

'So, I'll just finish this and head off then?'

I nodded. 'Sorry. If I'd known you were coming... will you go back tonight?'

'I booked myself into The Ramparts Hotel for a week.'

'A week? It's Christmas. I'd have thought you'd be spending it with your parents.'

'Spending time with you right now is more important. I know it may have been impulsive turning up but I want you to know I didn't expect an immediate answer which is why I've booked a week. If it's okay with you, I'd like to spend a lot more time with you and see if there's any chance of picking up where we left off all those years ago.'

'I'm sorry, Andy. You're probably not getting the reaction you were hoping for. Surprised would be an understatement.'

'I understand.' His dark eyes twinkled and my stomach did another flip. It was the way his eyes danced with excitement and passion that first attracted me to him.

'I'll stay for as long as it takes for you to realise I'm the only one for you,' he said. 'Always have been. Always will be.' He reached forward and tucked a loose strand of hair behind my ear while I held my breath.

Oh. My. God! This couldn't be happening. After all these years. How long had I waited for him to say those words? How many times had I replayed that fantasy in my head? And every single time it had ended with a kiss. And a fair bit more. But now that it was finally happening, was it more of a case of be careful what you wish for? Something wasn't right. I couldn't deal with it right now. I had an irate Clare at home and my new boyfriend to meet.

'I'm sorry, Andy. I have to go...'

28

'The arrogant little shit.'

'Eloquent as always, Clare.' I pulled my scarf tighter around my neck as we headed back into town later that evening, brollies doing battle against the wind and rain that had whipped up since meeting Andy. I hoped a storm wasn't on its way.

'Well, he is,' she said. 'I really liked him while he was at university, but I think that guy is long gone. I think his high-flying career and huge pay packet have gone to his head and he reckons he can get whatever he wants at the click of his fingers. Plus that line about you knowing he's always been and always will be The One? I think you may need a paramedic to get his head out of his arse.'

'I liked it. It felt romantic at the time. You really think he's arrogant?'

'And you don't? It takes some major arrogance to turn up unannounced to see your ex and book yourself into a hotel for a week while you try to worm your way back into her life without even checking whether or not she's single. I hope you told him you were seeing Nick.'

I stopped walking.

'Sarah! Why the hell not?'

Because I've dreamed of that moment for years and saying nothing was a million times better than jumping on him and dragging him home to bed for old times' sake. But, of course, I didn't say that. 'Lack of opportunity? I felt sorry for him? I thought he might judge me for moving on so quickly? And...' I paused.

'And?' Clare glared at me.

'He's called Steven.'

'How many times? He's *not* called Steven. He's called *Andrew*.'

'But Steven's his middle name.'

'So what?' She grabbed my arm and started walking again. 'If he's the one for you, why didn't your clairvoyant say your future husband would be called Andrew? She was *very* specific on that point. If you're going to believe it then you have to believe it all. A middle name is too tenuous.'

'Maybe, but I can't stop thinking about that and the fact that, even before I knew the clairvoyant CD still existed, I always believed we'd get together one day.'

'Even during your first year with Jason when things were going well?'

'Well, maybe not then...'

'You want to know what I think?'

'Do I have a choice?'

Clare gave me 'the look'. 'I think you loved Andy at uni. He was your first serious boyfriend and you were good together, but you both changed when you graduated and it fell apart. Instead of remembering why it fell apart, you're remembering all the good times to a point where you've built him into this perfect being who you somehow believe you're meant to have a second chance with. You've been thinking about this second chance for so long that you've made it a fait accompli. The fact that his middle name links with your search for Steven just adds credence to your beliefs and now you're willing to jeopardise your new relationship with someone who could be your future for someone who was your past and should remain in your past for all the reasons it ended in the first place. Am I right or am I right?'

Was she?

'I'll take your silence as a sign that I'm either spot on or I'm close. Is this the pub?'

I nodded and started to lower my brolly.

'Your lovely new man, from what you tell me, is in there waiting for you. Keep remembering that you've been swept off your feet by him. You think that much of him that, until a few hours ago, you'd completely given up your search for Steven to be with him. I'll emphasise again that Andy's in your past and he should stay there, but Nick could be your future. If you don't screw it up.'

Before I could say another word she pushed me through the door of The Old Theatre.

'You've already met?' I was surprised to find Nick at a table with Stevie and Rob, half-empty pints in front of them all.

Nick stood up and gave me a quick, but very soft and lovely peck on the lips, setting the butterflies away again. 'Stevie and I have met before,' he said.

'No! How come?'

'I'm a mate of Stuart's,' Stevie said.

'Skye's fiancé? Small town.' I shook some rain off my brolly and leaned it against the table.

Clare coughed behind me. 'Sorry. Clare, this is Nick. Nick, Clare.'

Introductions over, we shed our coats and scarves while Stevie headed to the bar for another round. I sighed shakily as I sat down next to Nick.

'Sorry we're late. Did you get my text?'

'Yes, thanks. It's been good to catch up with Stevie. Are you okay? You look a bit stressed.' He tenderly touched my arm, making my heart race. I wanted nothing more than to cuddle him tightly and remove the last few hours from existence. But it wasn't that simple. Andy's reappearance had stirred up a whirlpool of hidden emotions and I had no idea what to do next.

'I'm fine.' I was aware that my voice sounded high and squeaky. 'Busy day and you know how much I hate being late.'

Nick gazed into my eyes but I couldn't hold eye contact. 'I'm not going to push you, but I'm here for you if you want to talk about it, whatever it is.' He gave me such a warm, reassuring smile that my heart melted. Damn Andy for re-appearing and throwing a spanner in the works. And damn him for having the right name. Nick didn't deserve this. Neither did I.

'Thanks, Nick.' I squeezed his hand. 'I may take you up on that offer later.'

'Oi you two, stop canoodling and pay attention to your friends,' called Clare across the table. Her eyes caught mine and the expression asked if I was okay. I nodded and smiled weakly.

'Is Stevie brewing these drinks himself?' I joked, craning my neck to see him trying to get served at the bar. 'A girl could die of thirst in here.' Or of guilt.

Despite the emotional turmoil presented by Andy's reappearance, I still managed to have a great evening. Nick met with Clare's approval, which was a relief after her contempt for Jason. 'I can't believe you'd even consider Andy when you've got a man like Nick,' she said on a visit to the toilets. 'Nick's a keeper. He clearly idolises you and I can tell you feel the same. If that eejit Andy hadn't shown up today, you wouldn't even be questioning your relationship. You were so right to ditch the Steven search for him. Don't let Andy back into your life. I beg you.'

Nick walked us home. The rain had eased a little but the wind hadn't. I felt a storm brewing, physically and metaphorically. Clare announced she'd make drinks then head up to bed with hers and several rounds of toast to soak up the alcohol.

Left alone in the cool lounge, I curled up on the opposite end of the sofa to Nick and pulled a throw over our legs for warmth. Twenty-four hours earlier we'd been snuggled on the sofa and I'd felt like I hadn't a care in the world. What a difference a day could make.

I looked at Nick's concerned expression. I didn't want to hurt him but I had to tell him. 'Something happened this afternoon. I don't know what to make of it but I think honesty is really important in a relationship so I'm going to tell you even though it might hurt you.'

Nick sighed. 'This sounds ominous. Should I be worried?'

I couldn't reassure him. 'I don't know where to start.' My eyes filled with tears.

'The beginning?'

Clare poked her head round the door, passed me two mugs of tea, then headed upstairs, leaving the enticing aroma of toast hanging in the air. Bloody Andy. The three of us could have been laughing and joking over tea and toast instead of Clare feeling banished to her room while I had one of the hardest conversations of my life.

'When we went to the pub after Auntie Kay tried to set us up, do you remember me telling you about Andy?'

'Your boyfriend at university? The one in Dubai?' Nick blew on his tea.

'I haven't seen him for about fifteen months, but he emailed me recently to say he was coming back to the UK for good. I told him I'd split up with Jason and moved back home. He turned up at the shop this afternoon.'

Nick put his tea on the coffee table. 'I'm guessing he wasn't after mate's rates on a bouquet?'

'No. He wants to try again.'

'And you said...?'

My cheeks flushed. 'I said it was out of the blue and I didn't know what to say or think.'

'Did you tell him about us?'

'No,' I admitted in a small voice, hanging my head in shame.

'Any reason?' He didn't sound mad, just hurt.

'Clare asked me the same thing. She's furious with him, by the way, for thinking he can just walk back into my life. I don't know why I didn't mention it. We only had a brief conversation and I couldn't think how to throw it in. I mean, he travelled all the way here to tell me he loves me. I didn't want to hurt him by throwing it back in his face.'

'He told you he loves you?'

Too honest, Sarah. Why did you have to say that?

'Not in so many words,' I muttered. I knew I was doing the right thing in telling him about Andy. I also knew that Nick meant the world to me and, if the pained expression in his eyes was anything to go by, I was breaking his heart. What I really didn't know was how I felt about Andy anymore. Half of me was screaming that it felt so right with Nick and he really could be The One despite being a non-Steven. But the other half was screaming that I'd always believed Andy was The One and, here he was, begging me to get back with him... and he was a Steven... well, sort of.

'How did you leave things?'

'He's staying at The Ramparts. I didn't ask him to. He'd already booked himself in. I guess I'll meet him at some point to talk.'

Nick studied my face for what felt like a lifetime. 'There's something else, isn't there?'

How could he possibly know?

As if reading my mind, he said, 'Remember that I volunteer with children who have seriously messed up lives. I'm not saying you're seriously messed up or anything. I just mean that I can spot when someone's not telling me everything.'

I stared at the empty fire. 'I hadn't thought about it until he walked into the shop and Clare said it aloud.'

'Said what?'

'His name.'

'What about it?' I turned to face him and saw realisation dawn.

'Andrew Steven Kerr,' I said. 'Clare and Andy always wound each other up by saying each other's full names because Clare hates her middle name. They did it today.'

Nick looked as though I'd punched him in the stomach. 'I thought you'd given up on the search for Steven.'

'I had. It's just... I...' A tear rolled down my cheek.

He reached out and took my hand. 'Please don't cry. I get it. I do. It sounds like you need some time and space right now so I'm going to make things easy for you and say let's just park what happened last night.' He swallowed hard. 'I think the world of you and I believe we have something pretty special. In fact, I'd go so far as to say I think we could have a great future together. But you and Andy have a past together. If you don't explore the Steven connection and whether the timing is finally right for you both, you and I won't survive for long because he'll always be there in the background like a ghost and you'll always be wondering *what if?*'

'But...' The words caught in my throat as another tear trailed down my cheek. Nick tenderly wiped it away.

'It's for the best. I should go.'

I nodded, unable to speak as more tears fell. I followed him to the door in a daze. I hadn't made a decision about Andy. I hadn't wanted to push Nick away; I'd just wanted to be honest with him. I'd only wanted him to know I was going to meet with Andy to understand more about why he was here; I wasn't planning to run off with him.

'Goodbye, Sarah.' Nick hugged me tightly then disappeared down the garden path into the darkness and the rain.

I shivered as I leaned against the doorframe, the wind whipping my hair across my face. I had to fight hard against the urge to chase after him and beg him to stay because I knew he was absolutely right; not exploring things with Andy would leave too many unanswered questions and too much pressure on my fledgling relationship with Nick.

The sky lit up followed by a deep rumble. The storm had broken and I started to shake.

'You'll freeze if you stand there all night,' said a soft voice right behind me. Clare reached around me and gently closed the door. 'Come here, you.'

'He ended it,' I whispered as I sunk into her arms and sobbed.

A knock on the door a few minutes later made us both jump. Clare released me and opened it cautiously. 'Can I speak to Sarah?' asked Nick.

Clare moved aside. Rain trickled down his face and his dark hair lay flat against his head.

'You've changed your mind?' I asked. *Please say yes. We'll find a way through this. I want you in my life.*

'No. But I couldn't leave without saying something. I really am going to give you the time and space you need to decide whether you want to try again with Andy. But I don't want you to make the decision thinking it's been easy for me to walk away from you because I'm not that bothered or because we only got together last night. I said you mean the world to me but that was a cop-out. Andy says he loves you. Well, so do I. I didn't want to say it because I didn't want to scare you by being too serious too soon. I know we only met ten weeks ago but I already can't imagine my life without you in it. You're amazing, Sarah. You're beautiful, funny, kind and intelligent. I'm so impressed with what you've done with Kay's business and I was excited about supporting you as you go from strength to strength. The minute I met you before Callie's wedding, I knew I wanted to spend the rest of my life with you. I'm not someone who believes in love at first sight but it happened to me that day.' He paused for breath.

You love me? I opened my mouth to speak but no words came.

'Please don't say anything,' he said. 'You need to meet Andy to talk but you need to have the full picture first. I'm not going to get in touch with you again. It's up to you to make the next move if you want to. If you decide that this thing with Andy was over years ago, it's just a coincidence that Steven's his middle name, and you do want to be with me after all, you know where I am. But you need to be completely over your search for Steven because I definitely can't do this again. I hope you will come back to me. I'll be waiting for you, Sarah. However long it takes.'

As another bolt of lightning illuminated the sky, he leaned forward and tenderly kissed me on the cheek. 'However long it takes,' he whispered. Then he retreated into the darkness again, his footsteps drowned out by the thunder.

'I don't care what that stupid clairvoyant said. You should be with your man Nick.' I turned around. Clare was sitting on the stairs, crying. Clare never cries. 'If you really believe in fairy-tale endings, how can you not see that Nick's yours? I can see it and I don't even believe in all that crap.'

29

✉ From Auntie Kay
Just spoken to your mum. She told me about you
and Nick. Beside myself with excitement. Knew you
two were perfect for each other. Glad you've come
to your senses and called off your Steven search.
When you have a moment, please email me with all
the details. Don't leave anything out! Is it too
early to buy a hat?!!! xxxx

My heart sank. She was so right. We *were* perfect for each other. But was Andy also perfect for me, just like he was when we got together twelve years ago? Or was he still the Andy who treated me like crap as soon as he started his fast-track career? Or perhaps someone even worse? But what if he was The Steven? I had to find out or, as Nick said, I'd be forever wondering 'what if?'

'Another text from Andy?' Clare asked as we relaxed on the sofa after a late breakfast on Sunday.

'No. Auntie Kay.' I blew on my tea. Andy had already texted me twice to ask if we could meet to talk.

'Are you going to meet him?'

'Not today,' I said. 'I'm too confused. I need some space before I jump into something I might regret. Do you fancy a walk around The Headland?'

'Is there a pub at the other side?'

'Yes.'

'I'll get my boots on.'

✉ To Andy

Sorry for not replying sooner. Can't meet today. Got plans with Clare. Can you pick me up after work tomorrow? 5.45pm

* * *

Andy knocked on the shop door bang on 5.45 p.m. the following day. 'I've got something for you,' he said when I closed the door behind him. He reached into a large paper carrier bag. My stomach churned as he pulled out a familiar-looking brown box tied up with cellophane and red ribbon. 'I didn't feel it was appropriate to give my business to someone else and get you flowers so I got you these.'

It can't be. Please don't let it be the same as Nick's gift. I reluctantly undid the bow and opened the lid to reveal the same mix of floral cupcakes and biscuits.

'What's wrong?' Andy asked. 'Is it a bad gift? You're not on a diet again, are you?'

I blinked the tears away and tried to look pleased. 'No. Nothing like that. They're great. Thank you. It's a lovely thought. Really. I'll just pop them in The Outback. Wait here a second. Don't move. Back in a sec.'

With an overwhelming feeling of sadness, I placed the box on the worktop in the kitchen area, next to the half-empty box from Nick. I swallowed hard on the lump in my throat as I re-read Nick's message, wondering what he was doing at that very moment and whether he was thinking about me.

'Where do you fancy going?' Andy's shout brought me back to the present.

I shook my head and threw a tea-towel over the two boxes. Out of sight, out of mind. Maybe. *Pull yourself together, girl. Andy's here and he could be Steven. You've dreamed about getting back with him for years so stop moping about someone you've known for five minutes. Nick's given you the time and space to explore this so stop hiding in the kitchen and get exploring.*

'I don't mind,' I shouted back. I grabbed my coat and bag and headed back into the shop. 'Food or drinks?'

'I was thinking both. Maybe we could start with a drink then I can take you out for a nice meal?'

I smiled. 'I think we'll play it by ear. It's work tomorrow so I can't do a late one. Exactly how long I stay out may depend on how quickly I've had enough of you.'

'Then we may be out for a long time. I'll treat you so well tonight you'll never want to go home. My aim is to make sure you've never had enough of me.' Andy flashed his most dazzling smile.

I shook my head. 'That has to be the cheesiest thing I've ever heard you say.'

He grimaced. 'Sorry. It's been a while. Maybe I need to work on my lines.'

'Maybe.' I pushed him towards the door. 'Let's start in The Purple Lobster and take it from there.'

Despite my best intentions to only give Andy a couple of hours of my time and get an early night, one drink turned into four. Tucked away in a booth in a quiet corner of The Purple Lobster, we reminisced about the night we got together, the rest of our time at university, our graduation, and that last holiday in Rhodes before things went downhill. I confessed about my disastrous last year with Jason and Andy told me about his on-off relationship with Kelly. It was one of those nights where the conversation flows and the hours whizz by... just like it used to.

'This is me,' I said when we reached Seashell Cottage shortly before eleven. 'I'd invite you in, but...'

'I know. It's too soon.'

I nodded. 'I've had a great time, though. My sides actually hurt from laughing so much.'

'Mine too. Could you bring yourself to do it again tomorrow night? Perhaps we can manage something more sophisticated than a bag of chips on the way home?'

'The chips worked for me,' I said. 'But tomorrow doesn't. It's Christmas Eve.'

'I know. Oh. I bet you have plans.' Andy's eyes looked full of hope. 'Do you?'

'Sorry, Andy. Ben's coming home and we're having a family get-together at Mum and Dad's. It'll be the first time in years it's just been the four of us.'

'Sounds nice. I'm assuming you'll be spending Christmas Day there too?'

I nodded. 'I'd invite you, but—'

'I'm the git who broke their daughter's heart?'

'Something like that. Sorry. Plus, I don't want to tell them about... this... until I know what this is.'

'Stop apologising. I'm the one who appeared out of the blue four days before Christmas. I'm the one who should be apologising. I realise my timing sucks. I was so desperate to see you again that I didn't think about the time of year. Any chance you're free on Boxing Day? Or the day after? Or the day after that?'

I studied Andy's disappointed face. The glow from the moon made him appear so young and innocent... yet incredibly alluring. Why did he have to be so damned attractive? Oh, what the hell. Mum wouldn't mind if I was a little late. 'Pick me up at the same time tomorrow night. I can only give you an hour, absolute max.'

His face lit up. 'You're sure?'

'I'm sure. Now get out of here before I change my mind.' I pointed back up the road.

'I'm going. But first I have to give you one of these.'

Andy reached out and gave me a hug. It felt good to be held by him, familiar and comfortable. He gave me a gentle kiss on the top of my head. That felt good too.

'Tomorrow, then.' He cupped my face in his hands and gave me a soft and gentle peck on the lips. 'I'll be counting down the hours. Goodnight, Sarah.'

Mmm, that felt good too.

But so did kissing Nick.

* * *

Christmas Eve in Seaside Blooms was crazy. Thankfully I'd enlisted Elise to help and I don't think any of us stopped all day. She'd been so busy at school that we hadn't even spoken for the past two weeks so she knew nothing about the Nick and Andy situations. I was desperate to get her take on it but there was no chance of conversation in the shop. We'd have to catch up later in the week.

Andy appeared at five-forty-five on the dot again, after everyone had gone, and took me to The Purple Lobster where the hour whizzed by. Surrounded by Christmas revellers, we got swept away in the festive spirit talking about Christmases we'd loved as kids, our favourite traditions and the best and worst presents we'd ever received. When Andy described his three best gifts, I blinked back the tears as I said, 'I bought you all of those.'

'I know. And that's why they're so special. Like the person who gave me them.'

The butterflies went into overdrive as I held his gaze. 'I still have that bear you gave me for our first Christmas. I nearly wore a hole in him from hugging him after we split up.'

Andy smiled. 'I'm glad you still have him. I thought you might have shoved him in a charity bag.'

I had done on several occasions but, each time, had been overcome with an attack of the guilts and retrieved him. I had, however, shoved him at the back of the wardrobe.

'Wait here a second,' I said when we reached the gate of Seashell Cottage. I ran down the path, unlocked the door and headed to the kitchen.

'Here you are.' I handed Andy a set of spare keys. 'I can't bear the thought of you spending Christmas Day alone in a hotel room. I know I won't be here for most of the day but surely a cottage with a DVD player, a real fire, and a fridge full of lager is better than a hotel room?'

Andy beamed. 'You lifesaver. I was dreading tomorrow.'

'I'll probably be back around teatime so, if you're still here, we can spend some time together then.'

'Sarah, you're the best. Happy Christmas.'

He gave me another brief peck on the lips. Then another. I knew he was testing me to see if I'd respond. I didn't pull away but I didn't encourage him either. Normally I wouldn't read such a big deal into a kiss but I knew that the minute I kissed Andy properly, it wouldn't just be a kiss; it would be me saying I wanted him back too. Yet something seemed to be holding me back from taking that step, which was a little strange considering the Steven connection, the obvious chemistry, and how many years I'd fantasised about that scenario.

* * *

✉ From Andy
Morning gorgeous. About to have xmas full English then going for long walk on the beach before a DVD fest at yours. Have a lovely day with your family. Can't wait to see you later xxxxxx

✉ From Auntie Kay
Happy Christmas from New York to my favourite niece. Missing you all. Are you spending today with Nick? Hope so xxx

✉ From Clare
I hate xmas but I know you love it so season's greetings and all that bollocks. Bah humbug xx

✉ From Nick
I know I promised not to get in touch but I had to wish you a Happy Christmas. I hope all of your Christmas wishes come true. Thinking of you xx

It was lovely being home for a family Christmas although it felt strange not having Auntie Kay with us for the first time ever. The arrival of Nick's text set the butterflies going again but so did Andy's. Was it possible to have strong feelings for two men at the same time?

'How's it going with your new man?' Mum asked over a post-dinner glass of Baileys while the men washed up. 'Nick, is it?'

'Yes. Nick,' I said, ignoring the first question and hoping she was too full of Christmas spirit to notice.

'I Skyped Kay on Sunday and she wouldn't tell me about her travels until I'd told her what I knew about you two. She was so excited. She speaks very highly of him.'

'I know.' I kicked my shoes off and curled my legs up under me on the huge leather armchair.

'He sounds like a lovely young man.'

'He is. He's the best.' I sipped my drink then slurped an ice cube into my mouth.

'Then why's it over already?'

I spat the ice back into my glass. 'How...?'

'You couldn't wipe the grin off your face on Saturday when he sent the cakes and you were glowing all day. But something happened on Saturday night or Sunday because you've been distracted for the last two days and, when I mentioned his name just now, instead of lighting up, you just looked sad. Do you want to talk about it?'

I sighed. 'It's a long, complicated story.'

'Would it have anything to do with Andy being here?'

'Andy? How...? Have you developed a sixth sense or something?'

Mum put her drink down on the coffee table. 'I saw him in town on Sunday. Major déjà vu moment. He hasn't changed much.'

I closed my eyes and held my cool glass against my aching forehead. 'Oh Mum, it's such a mess. I don't know what to do.'

'You could start by telling your mum all about it before the men finish their chores.'

I reached for her glass. 'You might need a top up on that.'

* * *

'And he's at Seashell Cottage now?' Mum said when I'd finished, leaving out the part about Steven.

I nodded.

'You can go if you want. I understand.'

'No, Mum. I'm staying. Part of the deal was that I wouldn't

change my plans. I was always going to head home early evening to feed the cats and that's what I'll still do.'

'How do you feel about them both right now?'

I drained the last of my Baileys. 'Very confused. A few years ago, if you'd asked me what I'd do if Andy Kerr walked back into my life and asked to try again, it would have been a no-brainer.'

'And now?'

'I don't know what's stopping me. Am I scared of getting hurt again? Am I worried it won't be as good second time round? Do I think he's just on a charm offensive to get me back and he's really still the guy he became after uni? Or is the truth simply that I like Nick more?'

Mum gave me a sympathetic look. 'Do you know what you need?'

'Another drink?' I rattled the ice cubes in my empty glass.

Mum laughed. 'Time. I know it's a cliché, but let's face it, Andy couldn't have picked a worse time of year to walk back into your life. Don't let the fact that he's going home in a few days push you into any decisions. Tell him he can stay longer – if that's what you want – or tell him he can go home without a decision but, whatever you do, don't rush into anything you may regret.'

30

I left Mum and Dad's at half four and texted Andy to say I'd be home in fifteen minutes. Ben had evening plans back in Leeds so he gave me a lift home.

Opening the door to Seashell Cottage, the aroma of mince and garlic hit me. He'd never cooked, had he? He'd always been hopeless in the kitchen.

Andy bounded down the hall, gave me a hug, wished me a Merry Christmas, and said I wasn't allowed into the kitchen while he was creating. He directed me upstairs into the bathroom where he'd run a hot bubble bath. Scented candles glowed and soft music played. He'd even perched a glass of wine on the window ledge.

'Don't panic,' he said. 'It's not a ploy to get you drunk and naked. I just thought you might like a relaxing bath after rushing around for the last couple of months. Although,' he added wickedly, 'I'd be more than happy to scrub your back... or anywhere else for that matter.'

Blushing, I threw a towel at him and ordered him out of the bathroom.

Lying back in the mandarin and jasmine bubbles five minutes later, I felt incredibly relaxed, although the wine and Baileys had probably helped. I love baths and hadn't had time for one since moving home. What a lovely thought and just what I needed.

Closing my eyes, my mind drifted back to the first time Andy had run me a bath. It had been our first Valentine's Day together. We'd been to a Valentine's Ball along with most of the students from our flat. It had been a lovely evening until a scuffle broke out on the next table and I somehow ended up wearing a pint of Guinness. Soggy and smelly, I had no choice but to leave. Andy ran me a bath while I peeled off my ruined dress then he perched on the side and gently poured jugs of water over my head, rinsing out the stout.

'I can't believe our evening's ruined.' Tears of frustration poured down my cheeks. 'It was our first Valentine's together and some drunk idiots messed it up.'

'Hey, it's not messed up. If anything, they've made it better.'

'How can you possibly think that?'

'I get you all to myself.' He moved his soapy hands onto my tense shoulders and expertly massaged them. 'We'll have other Valentine's Days to celebrate together.'

We'd never spoken about a future together. 'Will we?' I whispered. 'Does that mean you can see me in your life for a bit longer?'

Andy stopped massaging my shoulders and shifted his position so he could look into my eyes. 'I can see you in my life forever. I love you, Sarah.'

I hadn't wanted to be the one who said it first. Elise told me she'd always regretted being the first to say she loved Gary, wishing he'd said it first. I was glad I'd waited as it truly was a magical moment. 'I love you too, Andy.'

Baths are great but the average bath isn't quite big enough for two adults and our demonstration of how much we loved each other caused a little bit of water displacement. Okay, a lot of water displacement. Which ran through the floorboards into the lights in the kitchen below and shorted the electrics in the whole flat. And the one next door. And the other buildings in our quad. Oops.

I opened my eyes and reached for my glass of wine, grinning at the memory of us scuttling down the corridor to my room, Andy holding onto a pile of soggy clothes and towels and me clinging onto my bottles of toiletries; we couldn't leave any evidence behind to show who'd caused the blackout. Grabbing my hand towel from the sink, I sent Andy back out into the dark corridor to mop up the wet trail. He only just made it back into my room, stark naked, when the lights came back on. There'd been an investigation, but we got away with it. Clare was the only person who ever knew it had been us who caused chaos that night. Well, I had to tell someone.

I lay back in the bubbles sipping my wine. It had been an amazing night. But our whole relationship had been brilliant, which was why it hurt so much when it ended. I'd loved him so much. Did I still?

* * *

'Are you covered?' Andy called from outside the door about ten minutes later. 'I wondered if you were ready for a top up.'

I glanced towards my half-empty glass. 'Go on, then. But no trying to peek through the bubbles.'

Andy pushed open the door and kept his eyes firmly fixed on my face as he headed towards the bath and topped up my glass.

'Is it hot enough for you? I know you like it boiling.'

'It's perfect.'

'What are you grinning at?'

'Don't read anything into this,' I said, 'but I was thinking about the first time you ran me a bath.'

He smiled. 'The Valentine's Ball. I was thinking about that earlier too. I wasn't sure if you'd remember.'

'Of course I remember. It was the first time you said you loved me.'

'I don't know why I took so long to say it.' He kneeled down by the bath. 'I loved you the moment I saw you.' He smiled tenderly and my heart started racing. 'That night, I seem to recall telling you that I could see you in my life forever. Fast forward less than three years later and I let you slip away.' He looked so vulnerable again and also so very attractive in the candlelight.

'You have to stop punishing yourself,' I said. 'You're forgiven. Let's stop focusing on what might have been and focus on the here and now. One day at a time.'

Andy sighed and stood up. He tucked a curl behind my ear. I held my breath at his touch and my stomach flipped. 'You're an amazing woman, Sarah Peterson. Thank you for being so under-standing.'

I smiled and nodded. I didn't trust myself to speak in case I let my alcohol-fuzzy head take control and suggest we relive the night of the Valentine's Ball.

* * *

'I'm confused.' Fifteen minutes later I stared at my plate of beans on toast. 'Don't get me wrong, Andy. This looks delicious, but I was sure I could smell mince earlier. Am I going mad?'

'Ah! Slight change of plan. I tried to impress you by making a chilli. You know how I was never great at cooking? If it's possible, I've got worse. I burnt the chilli. I may owe you a new pan. I think I welded it to the bottom.'

I laughed. 'Don't worry about it.'

'I didn't think there'd be any takeaways open with it being Christmas Day so I had a bit of a panic. Then I realised making you a big meal was a stupid idea because you'll have had a huge dinner and probably only want something light. So, voilà!'

'I'd definitely have struggled with a big meal. This is spot on.'

'Did you enjoy your bath?' Andy asked, when we'd finished eating. 'Was it the right thing to do?'

'It was unexpected but perfect. I mean that. Thank you.'

'It looked pretty good. I was tempted to join you.'

'You should have.' *Oh my God! Engage brain first.*

Andy laughed. 'You should see the look on your face. I take it you weren't meant to say that aloud?'

'No.'

'Well, I'm glad you did. I know you're not promising anything but for that thought to even cross your mind, it shows that you're thinking of me as something other than a friend. If only for a brief moment.'

'I...' Maybe I should have stayed sober. My decisions when inebriated were frequently ill-advised. The phrase, 'It seemed like a good idea at the time' was invented for me after a few drinks.

'Do you have any plans for tomorrow?' Andy asked when we moved into the lounge.

It dawned on me that I'd been so busy that I hadn't planned beyond Christmas Day. I wanted to see Elise but we hadn't confirmed a day. 'Not yet. Why?'

'Would you do me the honour of spending the day with me?'

I smiled. 'If you're as good company as you've been the last couple of days, I might be able to cope with it.'

'That's a relief. I've organised a surprise for you.' He looked very pleased with himself.

'What is it?'

'It won't be a surprise if I tell you, will it? I'll pick you up at half five.'

I spluttered on my wine. 'In the morning?'

He nodded. 'You should dress warmly. Lots of layers. And wear sensible shoes. Oh, and you'll need a hat.'

'What are we doing? Conquering Everest?'

'Patience. You'll find out tomorrow. I think you'll like it. In fact, I *know* you'll like it.'

Andy insisted on doing the washing up and leaving by ten so I could get a good night's sleep. He gave me a gentle kiss on the lips again as he left. It was slightly longer this time but the fact that he wasn't pushing me earned him massive Brownie Points.

My head felt fuzzy from a steady flow of drink across the afternoon and evening and my whole body felt weary. I blew out the candles, spread the dying embers in the fire, and was about to switch the lamps off when I spotted my laptop on the coffee table. Maybe just a quick look on Facebook...

My newsfeed was full of Christmas best wishes and comments from friends and acquaintances about their Christmas Day, predominantly referencing too much food, too much drink, too many sweets, and too much money spent. Surely that was what Christmas was all about; too much of everything. One of the entries was from Nick.

Nick Derbyshire
5 hrs

Happy Christmas to all my friends and family

How was he? Was he sad? Had I ruined his Christmas? Feeling an overwhelming desire to connect with him I clicked onto his timeline and scrolled down it, building up a picture of the past week.

Skye Harris > Nick Derbyshire

22 December at 20:38

Are you OK? Tried phoning a few times & keep getting voicemail. Stuart says you seem down and your last post is very unlike you xx

Nick Derbyshire I'll text you

Marcus Jones > Nick Derbyshire

22 December at 10:11

Thanks for finishing that job for us. Have a great Christmas break. We'll catch up in the New Year

Nick Derbyshire

21 December at 23:46

I've had enough of this year. How long till the next one?

Skye Harris Cheer up you xx

Callie Michaels You OK big bruv? I'm only a phone call away if you need me xx

Nick Derbyshire

21 December at 01:33

Just had the most amazing evening ever

Callie Michaels Spill!!!!

Skye Harris This wouldn't have anything to do with a certain young florist, would it?

Nick Derbyshire Might have!

Skye Harris YEEAAAHHHHHHHH!!!!!!!! You're so perfect for each other. Fancy a coffee later to catch up?

Nick Derbyshire 2 p.m. in The Chocolate Pot, **Skye**? **Callie** – will call you soon x

I scrolled up and down between the few short entries that told such a story from elation to devastation. 'Have I really caused all that? I'm so sorry Nick.'

With a heavy heart, I shut down my laptop and slowly padded upstairs to bed where I lay for the next two hours cuddling Mr Pink and staring into the darkness, trying to work out how I felt about the two men in my life. When fatigue finally overcame me, I still hadn't reached a conclusion but I had realised one thing: I hadn't replied to Nick's text. It had come through while I was basting the turkey for Mum and I'd made a mental note to reply later when I had time to think of an appropriate message that didn't come across as a brush-off. I wanted to show him I still cared. *Yes, Sarah, you showed you really cared by forgetting to reply altogether. You absolute muppet.* I hoped that my rudeness hadn't caused him any further distress.

I reached for my phone and started but abandoned several replies. Nothing seemed right. I'd left it too late and I was too tired, drunk and confused to send something acceptable. I'd maybe try tomorrow instead.

31

'Denbury Castle?' I asked as Andy directed the sporty two-seater he'd hired off the York road at about six the following morning.

'What makes you think that?'

'Unless you're planning to ditch me in a field in the middle of nowhere, Denbury Castle's the only place of consequence down here.'

'Then we might be going to Denbury Castle. Or we might not.'

'You're so frustrating, Andrew Steven Kerr.' My stomach lurched as I said his middle name. I hated this. Was he *the* Steven or not? Was he the heart or the head decision?

'And you are so impatient, Sarah Louise Peterson.'

A few more turns and we were definitely on our way to Denbury Castle, a magnificent eighteenth-century house and 1000-acre estate at which I'd enjoyed many a family day out over the years. Can't say I'd ever been there before sunrise, though.

'You were right. Denbury Castle it is,' Andy said, pulling onto the approach road to the estate. A few minutes later, we stopped in the large, empty car park. 'Wait here a moment,' he said. 'I just need to check that it's happening.'

'Check that what's happening?' But he was already out of the car and heading towards the visitors' entrance. I sank back in my seat, enjoying the heat and the low soothing music on the radio. I must have dozed off as the door opening startled me.

'Good news,' Andy said. 'It's on.'

I pulled on my hat and he offered a hand as I heaved myself out of the car.

'No more questions,' he said, still holding my hand. 'All will be revealed shortly.'

We made our way across the deserted courtyard. I was so used to being there in broad daylight surrounded by tourists that I felt like an intruder. We skirted round the path to the left and I could just make out the dark silhouette of the house in the distance.

'Are you sure we're meant to be here?' I whispered. 'It's so quiet.'

Andy squeezed my hand tightly. 'I'm sure. It's all arranged.'

We headed down the drive towards the house. And then I saw it – a flash of orange. I stopped dead, mouth open. 'Is that what I think it is?'

'It depends what you think it is.'

'I daren't say in case I'm wrong.'

'Then let's move a bit closer.'

Mesmerised, I crept down the drive towards the lawns. With every step, the sky seemed to get a fraction lighter until my eyes could clearly see something I'd always dreamed of but had never had the funds nor opportunity to experience: a hot air balloon.

'You remembered.' Andy had once asked me what would be at the top of my bucket list and I said a hot air balloon ride. Ideally it would be over The Grand Canyon although I'd happily do it over Spaghetti Junction for the experience.

'I always swore to myself that, when I could afford it, I'd be the one to fulfil that dream for you. Happy Christmas, Sarah.'

'Oh my God! Andy!' A lump caught in my throat. 'It's the best present ever. I can't believe you've organised this. For me.' I turned to give him a hug.

'I'd do anything for you. You must know that.' His voice was so tender, making my heart race.

I didn't want to let go and clearly Andy didn't want to either. I'd been holding back on him as it hadn't felt right but, at that moment, everything seemed to click into place and every sense was screaming at me to kiss him. I couldn't fight my instincts.

It felt like we'd never been apart; so familiar and yet new at the same time.

'Oi, Andy, do you want a ride in this thing or not?' The unexpected shout broke us apart. We looked at each other and laughed.

'Thank you,' Andy said.

'For what?'

'For that. I know it doesn't guarantee anything but you wouldn't have kissed me like that if I didn't mean something to you.'

'Andy, you've always meant *something* to me.'

Andy smiled and gave me another brief kiss. 'We'd better hurry. Last one to the balloon's a rotten egg.'

I squealed as I raced after him down the drive.

* * *

Andy couldn't have organised a more perfect day. The sunrise champagne balloon flight was followed by a mooch around the grounds of Denbury Castle, lunch in a quaint country pub then a romantic walk along the seafront back at Whitsborough Bay.

He dropped me off at Seashell Cottage late in the afternoon, saying he'd leave me in peace for the evening after hogging me for most of the last twenty-four hours.

'Are you free tomorrow night? he asked as we stood outside the cottage.

Seaside Blooms would be open again and I'd been looking forward to an evening on my own, or perhaps catching up with Elise. If I agreed to see him, that would be five days in a row that we'd spent time together and I suddenly felt quite stifled by it. He'd promised me I could have time to think about what I wanted but he wasn't giving me that time.

'Please,' he said, clearly spotting my hesitation. 'I've got another surprise planned. Not quite as impressive as a balloon flight, but it's something you'll love.'

I'd never been able to resist his puppy dog eyes. Smiling, I nodded. 'Okay, then, but I can't give you all evening. I need an early night.'

He smiled seductively. 'I'm sure that can be arranged.'

I stiffened. 'Andy! You know that's not what I mean. I'm shattered and I need some sleep.' I could hear the irritation in my voice and softened my tone. 'Thank you for an amazing day. That really was a dream come true.'

'You're welcome.'

When he showed no signs of leaving, I placed the key in the lock and pushed the door open slightly. 'Have a good evening back at the hotel.'

'I'll miss you,' he said, wrapping his arms around me and kissing me goodbye. I could tell from the urgency behind his kiss and the way he pulled me close that he wanted me to invite him in and take things a bit further. Had he not listened to what I'd just said? I felt quite annoyed at him for yet another contradiction – saying he'd leave me in peace then making it clear that he didn't want to.

I pulled away and gave him a playful push. 'Thanks again and I'll see you tomorrow.'

He looked momentarily disappointed, then smiled, waved and headed off down the path.

Closing the door behind me, I leaned against it and a sigh of relief escaped from me, which wasn't the reaction I expected following such an amazing day. Mum had told me not to let him rush me into anything but rushed was exactly what I felt. He'd turned up without warning on Saturday, had bombarded me with texts on Sunday, and had managed to talk me into spending time with him every day since Monday, even getting me to change my Christmas Eve plans with my family.

I peeled off my various layers then phoned Elise to see if she was free for a catch-up. She said she'd drive over as soon as she finished her dinner, which meant I had half an hour – plenty of time to catch up with Clare. I frowned just before I phoned her. If I'd just invited Elise round and was about to call Clare, I obviously wasn't that desperate for some alone-time. What did that mean?

'Sorry, Sarah,' Clare said when I finished my update. 'I know you had a great relationship back in the day but I don't trust him now. I know you'll think I'm being cynical but it strikes me that your man Andy's trying a bit too hard.'

'In what way?'

'It seems to me that he's doing everything he can to tap into your best memories of your time together and is flashing his cash trying to spoil you.'

'Because he took me on a hot air balloon?'

'For starters, but it's also the free things like running the bath to remind you of the power cut incident. Don't you think that's a bit planned? That was the night you said you loved each other. Pretty big moment. I bet he ran the bath just to get you thinking about it again.'

I laughed. 'Maybe that was his motivation but what's so bad about him making a bit of effort? He's got a lot of making up to do.'

'It's hard to explain what I mean.' Clare sighed and paused, obviously trying to find the right words. 'It all seems too engineered, too romantic-movie-perfect. A balloon flight, a walk around a stately home, a posh lunch in a country pub with a roaring log fire, a walk along the beach... I bet he chased you along the sand then picked you up squealing and threatened to throw you into the sea so you clung tighter to him. The laughter stopped as you both looked deep into each other's eyes and kissed as the wind whipped your hair and the waves crashed around you like Whitsborough Bay's answer to Cathy and Heathcliff.'

'How...?'

'Jesus, Sarah, you did, didn't you? Will you not see my point? It's like he's been watching back-to-back romcoms – probably worked his way through your DVD collection on Christmas Day – and he's contrived a day full of movie-perfect moments. I think the only thing he missed out was some fireworks, which was a missed opportunity because he must remember how much you love them.'

Could she be right? Did I also think that deep down? Was that why I felt relieved when he left earlier?

Clare continued. 'Something doesn't add up. I think there's more to his sudden declaration of undying devotion than he's letting on.'

'Like what?'

'That's the part I can't get my head round.'

When Elise arrived, I brought her up to date on what had happened with Nick and then Andy's unexpected appearance putting a spanner in the works. She was particularly keen to understand how I felt kissing Nick then kissing Andy and empathised with the messy situation I'd found myself in.

'Today really does sound perfect,' she said. 'You're obviously feeling something for Andy at the moment, but is that based on nostalgia for your lost love or have you fallen for the present-day Andy?'

I shrugged. 'That's what I'm struggling with.'

'Are your feelings for him stronger or weaker than your feelings for Nick?'

'I can't work that out either. Nick was so new and exciting and stirred something I hadn't felt in so long. I keep thinking about him. A text from him on Christmas Day had my stomach in knots and I found myself checking out his Facebook page in the evening just to have some contact with him. But Andy is familiar. I know it's been eight years but kissing him felt like we'd never been apart. And, yesterday, my thoughts only drifted to Nick a few times. I was far more focused on Andy. But was that just because I was with him and he'd organised the dream date?'

'Then I put a question to you,' Elise said. 'If Andy had just taken you to The Old Theatre or The Purple Lobster for lunch and a bracing walk around The Headland, would you have kissed him?'

I thought for a moment. 'You're thinking the only reason I kissed him was because I was swept away with the romance of the balloon flight rather than because I'm falling for him again?'

'Could it have been? I think it would take a pretty strong person not to be moved by such a massive gesture.'

'Possibly. Oh, I don't know. I'm confused. Help!'

Elise slurped on her herbal tea for a few moments. 'How about we play a little game? I saw something like this on *Friends* once. Don't laugh at me but I want you to lie down on the sofa, close your eyes and try to relax.'

'Seriously?'

'Have you got a better idea for solving your current dilemma?'

'No.' I figured anything was worth a try so I did as I was told. Elise dimmed the lights and waited for me to stop fidgeting.

'When I ask you a question,' she said, 'I want you to give me the very first thing that comes into your head. Okay?'

'Okay.'

'What do you enjoy most? A shower or a bath?'

'A bath.'

'Which is best? *Poldark* or *Outlander*?'

'*Outlander*.'

'What do you prefer? Chocolate or crisps?'

'Crisps.'

'What's stopping you from telling Andy to leave?'

'He might be *the* Steven.'

'Do you prefer summer or winter?'

'Winter.'

'Night out or night in.'

'Night in.'

'Jeans or PJs?'

I laughed. 'PJs. Definitely.'

'London or here?'

'Here.'

'What's stopping you from going for it with Andy?'

'Nick.'

'Toast with butter or jam?'

'Butter.'

'Cinema or DVD?'

'Cinema.'

'Why's Nick stopping you?'

'I love him.' I opened my eyes and sat up. 'Oh my God!'

Elise smiled knowingly at me. 'Finally!'

I frowned at her. 'You don't look surprised.'

'I'm not. When you told me about Nick, your face lit up and your eyes sparkled. When you told me about Andy, you had a wistful look on your face, as though it was all about the memories.'

'Why didn't you say that?'

'You needed to realise it for yourself.'

I shook my head, my stomach churning. 'That's it, isn't it? I love my past with Andy and he'll always be special to me because he was my first love, but I want my future to be with Nick.'

'What about Steven?'

'Obviously not as important as being with Nick,' I said. 'It mustn't be. Let's face it, the ex who I always thought was The One has walked back into my life, told me he loves me and he happens to be called Steven. He takes me on the date of my dreams and it's all lovely and romantic, yet I'd still rather be with Nick.'

'Then you need to tell him,' Elise said. 'When?'

'Now.' I stood up. 'Right now.'

* * *

'Nick, I'm so sorry for what happened last weekend with Andy. I'm so grateful to you for being such an amazing person in putting your own feelings aside to give me the time to work mine out. As you rightly said, I'd always have wondered "what if?" if I hadn't spent time with Andy but I know now that he isn't right for me. I now know why things ended so I've finally got closure. I had to give Andy a chance but I realised that, every minute I spent with him, I'd have rather spent with you. I know I've hurt you and I don't deserve you back but you said you'd be waiting for me, however long it took. I'm hoping you meant that. Is there any chance you could forgive me and we could try again?' I looked at Elise. 'It's naff isn't it?'

'No. It's heartfelt,' she said. 'Did you say he lives on Fountain Street?'

'Yes.'

Elise turned the car right to head across town.

'What if I'm too late and he's met someone else?'

'I very much doubt that. Not if he loves you as much as he said.'

Nick, I'm so sorry for what happened last weekend... I rehearsed the words over and over again in my head. They really did sound naff. *Oh God! We're nearly there. Too late to change it.*

'What number?'

'Sixty-two.' I wound down the window for a better look. 'Apparently it's a few doors up from a newsagent's.'

Elise cruised slowly up the street of three-storey terrace houses, all with Christmas tree lights twinkling in bay windows. Shortly after the shop, she did an impressive reverse parking manoeuvre into a space on the opposite side of the road, turned off the lights and switched off the ignition.

I counted up from the newsagent's. 'It must be the one with the light outside.'

'Ready?' Elise asked.

'No, but I have to do this. Will you wait for me in case he's not in? Or in case he doesn't want to speak to me?'

'Of course I will but I'm sure he'll want to speak to you.'

'Am I hypocritical doing this after spending the day kissing Andy?'

Elise squeezed my hand. 'Don't think about that. It's not like you've slept with him or anything. You've just been on a journey of discovery and you've discovered that Andy isn't the one for you, but you could only have discovered that if you'd let him in a bit, couldn't you?'

I smiled. I was so lucky to have a thoughtful and understanding friend like Elise. It was time. I took a deep shaky breath. 'Right. This is it. Do I look okay?'

'Gorgeous.'

I'd just put my hand on the door handle when Nick's door opened. I retracted my hand. 'Movement.' Sliding down in my seat, I stared as a woman stepped out of the house. Tall and slim with messy long blonde hair, she was casually dressed in skinny jeans with a baggy checked shirt over what looked like a white T-shirt or vest-top. The lack of a coat suggested that she probably had a car somewhere close-by. Sure enough, she rummaged in her jeans pockets and dug out a set of car keys.

Maybe it wasn't Nick's house. My hopes were dashed as the woman moved away from the doorway to reveal Nick behind her. Wearing his dressing gown. His hair was all ruffled, as if he'd just got out of bed. The woman reached into her jeans pocket again and handed Nick her keys while she tied her hair back. My heart sank with the realisation that she looked like she'd just got out of bed too. She reached for the keys but Nick pulled her into a tight embrace instead. I held my breath, heart thumping, while he clung onto her, his head nuzzled into her hair. They pulled apart and Nick kissed her. It was only a quick peck but I couldn't see if it was on her cheek or lips. They spoke and there was lots of nodding, a final hug, then she got into a small silver car and started the engine. Leaning against the doorframe, Nick waved. He stood there long after she'd pulled away, looking in the direction in which the car had gone. He ran his hand through his hair then headed back into his house, closing the door.

Crap. I'm too late. Too bloody late.

'Oh, Sarah. I'm so sorry.'

Elise's words told me that she'd read exactly the same into the situation as I had. He'd moved on. And why shouldn't he? I hadn't given him any indication that he should wait for me. I hadn't even shown him the courtesy of replying to his Christmas Day text. Pants. Why couldn't I at least have done that? Why did I have to get distracted with the damn turkey and then forget again today because of Andy?

'You said he had a sister...?'

'That wasn't Callie.'

'You've met her?'

'No, but Auntie Kay says she's about my height with dark hair. That was definitely *not* Callie.'

'A friend?'

'I appreciate what you're doing but did that look like a friend to you? Besides, the only female friend he's ever mentioned is Skye and I've met her.'

'I'm sure there's an innocent explanation.'

'He was in his dressing gown. It's seven-thirty. They hugged for an eternity. They kissed. He stood on his doorstep for ages looking in the direction she'd gone. It didn't look innocent. It looked more like two people who'd just got out of bed.'

Elise's silence spoke volumes.

'Will you take me home please? And would you mind if I had some time alone?'

She squeezed my arm gently then put the car into gear. We headed back towards Seashell Cottage in silence.

32

The shop couldn't have been open for more than five minutes the following day when the bell tinkled. A short woman, probably a similar age to me, headed straight for the counter. She smiled at me and removed a deep pink woollen cap, revealing a mop of shoulder-length dark hair. 'You must be Sarah,' she said brightly. 'I'm Carolyn. But you can call me Callie. Everyone does.'

'Nick's sister?' Eek!

'The very same.'

'You look just like him.'

'I know. I get it all the time and I try not to take offence that people think I look like a man.'

'Oh, I didn't—'

'It's okay. I'm kidding. I've been dying to meet you. Nick never stops talking about you.'

'Really?' That was probably before his evening of passion with Blonde.

'Really,' Callie said. 'I've never heard him so enthusiastic about anyone before.'

'Oh. You do know—'

'That you're not together?' Callie wrinkled her nose. 'He told me you have a few things to work out with your ex. So how's that going?'

'With Andy?'

'Yes.' Callie clapped her hand over her mouth. 'Oh. I'm so sorry. Don't answer that. What an awkward question to ask you. You're hardly going to feel comfortable telling me that things are great when I'm Nick's sister, are you? I have this terrible habit of engaging mouth before brain.'

I smiled. I already liked her. What a shame Nick had moved on. I could have imagined becoming good friends with Callie. 'How's Nick?' I asked. 'Have you seen him recently?'

'Christmas Day. He was a bit tied up yesterday so I didn't get to see him then.'

I bet he was. And then my mind filled with this horrible image of him quite literally being tied up while Blonde walked round him brandishing a whip. *Ew! Stop thinking that.*

'And he was okay?' I asked.

'He put on a brave face with it being Christmas but I could tell he's really upset. I know you'd only just got together but it was love at first sight for him. He told me that on my wedding day. I don't think I've ever seen him so happy. Mum and I were beginning to despair that he'd be single forever then along you came and it was like he'd found his soulmate at last.'

I was saved from responding by the arrival of a young couple who smiled and headed towards the gift section.

'I can see you're busy,' Callie said. 'And I promise I didn't come in here to have a go at you for breaking my brother's heart. Ooh. I didn't mean to say that either because it sounds like you've deliberately treated him badly and I know that's not the case.' She stopped and grimaced. 'I've just implied you treated him badly too which I know you haven't. I think I'm just going to stop gibbering and focus on why I came in. Can I order some flowers for Dad's, Grandma's, and Granddad's graves? We have our annual family pilgrimage to the cemetery on New Year's Day.'

'Nick mentioned it. Three bouquets of white roses, is it?'

'Yes please. Half a dozen roses in each for the graves plus three single roses for Nick. Did you know he throws them into the sea?'

I nodded.

'It's really sweet of him,' she continued. 'He goes down to Lighthouse Point and throws in the roses at two minutes past eleven promptly as that's the exact time and day that Grandma died. She was the last to leave us. He stays there for about ten minutes then he picks Mum and me up, takes us to the cemetery, then the three of us have lunch. It's been the same routine for years.'

'Do you ever go to the lighthouse with him?'

'No. Never. It's his thing. He started doing it the year after Grandma died so he'd have been about seventeen or so but we didn't know about it until years later. Mum and I have always respected his need for a private moment.'

I could picture him standing at the end of Lighthouse Point, lost in thought as he tossed the stems into the water. Suddenly I imagined me in the picture, a few paces away from him to give him space. He'd throw the roses, murmur a few words then turn to me for comfort. I had to stop torturing myself like that. We weren't together. If anyone was going to be there to comfort him, it was going to be Blonde and I had to accept that he'd moved on.

I turned my attention back to Callie. 'When do you want them? New Year's Eve?'

'Yes please. Sometime in the afternoon.'

'Will Nick come in to collect them?' I tried to sound disinterested but I don't think I pulled it off.

'No. Just me, I'm afraid. He's actually in town with me this morning and he wanted to come in but he was worried it would make things awkward for you. He's so lovely like that, always thinking of others. I have a message from him, though.'

'Oh. What did he say?' That he still loved me? That he desperately wanted me to be with him and I should send Andy packing and run away with him instead?

'He hopes that you'll start going to Bay Trade in the New Year. Apparently you made a really good impression and they'd love you to join.'

Was that all? He wanted me to go to Bay Trade? Oh well, I guess I couldn't really expect any declarations of love given that he'd so clearly moved on. Not that I had any right to judge him for that after spending so much time with Andy.

'I'd like to,' I admitted. Aside from the fact that I liked them, it had already proved lucrative for business with Skye's exhibition confirmed and the potential contract at The Ramparts. 'But I don't want Nick to feel uncomfortable. He set it up and they're his friends.'

'Don't be so daft. He'd love you to go.'

'Tell him maybe February or March. Give things time to settle.'

'I'll tell him. I'd better go. I think you're needed.' Callie indicated the couple who were approaching the counter with a photo frame and a soft giraffe. 'It was lovely to meet you. I'll see you next week for the roses. And sorry about all that stuff about you and Nick. None of my business.'

'It's fine. Honestly.' I waved her off.

After the couple paid for their gifts and left, I sat down heavily on the stool by the counter. Why hadn't I asked her about Blonde? But I knew the answer; I didn't want to hear that he'd moved on. To have her confirm it would have taken away the tiniest possibility that it was innocent and I still stood a chance with him.

✉ From Andy
Hi gorgeous. Can I pick you up at the cottage at 6.30 instead of the shop? Wrap up warm again. Can't wait to see you tonight xx

✉ To Andy
OK. See you there

I couldn't bring myself to put kisses or even a smiley face on my text. I didn't feel very smiley. What I felt was very guilty as I watched the little envelope sending my text. Should I be honest with Andy and tell him how I felt about Nick? Or should I keep trying with him and forget about Nick like he'd forgotten about me? But what if it was innocent with Blonde and Nick really was still waiting for me?

The door opened, signalling a welcome interruption to my confused thoughts. 'Crikey, sweetheart, you look like Santa forgot you'd moved. I don't know if I dare ask if you had a good Christmas.'

I smiled at Cathy and Jade. 'Sorry. Miles away. Christmas was great, thanks. What about you two?'

'It was lovely, thank you,' Cathy said. 'But the best bit was Jade's news.'

'Oh yes?' I looked expectantly at Jade, anticipating some news about an exam result or something like that. I certainly didn't expect her to bounce up and down excitedly, thrust out her left hand and squeal, 'I got engaged.'

Engaged? I didn't even know she had a boyfriend. On autopilot, my hand reached for hers and I looked down at the shiny platinum band and sparkling solitaire diamond. It was stunning. Simple. But absolutely stunning.

'When?' I eventually managed to whisper.

'Midnight on Christmas Eve.'

'She's been with Aaron since she was twelve,' Cathy gushed. 'He's a lovely young man.'

'How did he propose?' I asked. The ring was just like the one I dreamed about. I hoped the proposal wasn't though. I knew I was torturing myself by asking but I felt compelled to know.

'He said he had a special present he wanted me to have without my family around. He stood me in front of the Christmas tree and told me to close my eyes. I thought it was going to be something embarrassing like underwear, but when he told me to open my eyes, he was on bended knee. He cried when I said yes.'

'When's the big day?' A huge lump choked the words. Jade looked radiant with happiness. I'd seen that look so many times and it made me feel further and further away from my own hopes and dreams.

'Summer the year after next when I've finished college.'

'I'm so happy for you, Jade.' I said. 'I know a great florist you must use. She'll do you a cracking deal.'

They laughed and Cathy hugged her daughter. 'I'm so proud,' she said. 'I know some people will think they're too young but they're such sensible kids and, as I've already said, Aaron is lovely. Perfect son-in-law material.'

I smiled. 'He sounds great. Congratulations! Look, I know you've just arrived and you haven't even got your coats off, but Mum's running late and I'm dying for the loo. You couldn't hold the fort for a moment while I go, could you?'

'Of course,' Cathy said. 'We don't want any puddles on your nice new floor.'

Tucked away in the toilet cubicle, I sat down and rested my head against the cool wall while the tears flowed. I was genuinely delighted for Jade but devastated at another reminder that it was always someone else, never me, who was getting married. Someone else who wouldn't be all alone like my Uncle Alan. My shoulders sank even further at the terrifying prospect of being alone. Maybe I should forget about Nick and give in to Andy? If he loved me as much as he said, maybe a proposal was just round the corner? But did I want to marry him? I sighed as I dabbed my eyes then blew my nose. If I said yes to trying again with Andy, would it be like Jason all over again, together because it seemed we should be rather than because he really was the only one for me?

* * *

'What are we doing here?' I asked. 'It's freezing.' Andy had picked me up at half six as promised, checked I was wrapped up warm, then drove me down to South Bay.

'Patience,' he said. 'You'll like it, though. I promise.'

He took my gloved hand as we crossed the road and guided me towards Lighthouse Point – a stretch of rocks with a wide path on the top that led to the stripy lighthouse at the entrance to the harbour. It was where that photo of my grandma was taken. And it was where Nick would be throwing roses into the sea on New Year's Day. Of all the places he could have brought me, why did it have to be there? I closed my eyes and breathed in deeply. *Stop thinking about Nick. Focus on Andy.*

'It's a bit cold and dark,' I moaned, wishing I was back at Seashell Cottage in front of a blazing fire. Without Andy. And ideally with Nick.

'It's not *that* cold and I did check you were wrapped up warm before we left the cottage. It's not my fault if you're not wearing enough layers.'

'I didn't know you were bringing me down to the seafront.' I thrust my gloved hands into my coat pockets.

'According to the temperature gauge in the car, it's a couple of degrees warmer down here than it was in town.'

I could well believe it. It was a still evening and I actually felt quite toasty, but I also felt irritated and the weather seemed like a good thing to moan about. Saved me from addressing the real issue.

Andy offered his arm but I shook my head. 'Warmer in my pockets.'

'Are you okay?' he asked, stopping. 'You don't seem yourself tonight.'

'I'm fine.' Except I really wasn't. And what I was doing to Andy wasn't fine either. It wasn't his fault about Nick... well, ultimately it was, but it wasn't his fault how I was feeling so I needed to either be nice to him or be honest and tell him that getting back together was never going to happen and he should go back to London. I took a deep breath. 'There's something I need to tell you...'

My phone beeped in my pocket. Happy to postpone the awkward conversation, I reached for it, muttering my excuses.

✉ From Elise
Just seen Nick and Blonde hugging. Sorry xx

'Everything okay?' asked Andy.

'Sorry. Just a bit of bad news but I'll get over it.'

'Anything I can help with?'

'No. I don't think anything can be done about it.'

We walked in silence for a while. 'You said there was something you wanted to tell me...' Andy prompted.

'Did I?' What was the point? I'd blown it with Nick. I wasn't sure if Andy was right for me but he'd extended his booking at The Ramparts and was around for a few more days. Maybe that was enough time to fall in love with him again. It wasn't like I didn't enjoy his company or find him attractive. I'd loved him once before. With time, it might happen again.

'Sorry,' I said. 'I've forgotten what I was going to say. Couldn't have been that important.' I took my hand out my pocket and linked his arm.

'Wait here a moment,' he said when we'd almost reached the lighthouse. He took several steps forward, put his fingers in his mouth, and whistled loudly. A couple of teens appeared. He handed them something, then they ran past me down the pier.

'What was all that about?' I asked when Andy returned to my side.

'They were keeping an eye on something for me. Come on.' He took my hand and led me to the side of the lighthouse where a picnic blanket covered the ground. There were some cushions on it, an ice bucket holding what looked like champagne, two glasses and a box of expensive chocolates.

'Andy! When did you do this?'

'Just before I collected you. Would the pretty lady like to take a seat?'

He took my hand again as I lowered myself onto one of the cushions. 'I've got something else too.' He rummaged under the blanket and produced a pan with a big red bow tied to it. He held it out to me. 'For the one I killed.'

I laughed as I accepted it. 'You didn't have to do that, but thanks.'

Andy looked a little lost as to what to do next. Feeling my impatience with him ebbing away, I patted the blanket next to me. He looked grateful as he plonked himself down. 'Champagne?' he asked.

'Are we celebrating something?'

'Every day I get to see you is a celebration.'

I looked at him, shocked, and we both started laughing. 'That was one of the worst lines I've ever heard,' I said when the laughter subsided.

'I promise you it sounded better in my head. I'm so sorry.' Andy hung his head in shame. 'Can you forgive me for being so cheesy?'

He reminded me of a naughty puppy desperately seeking approval. Poor Andy. He was trying so hard. I had to stop thinking about myself and think about him and how tough it must be giving everything and getting so little in return. I felt an overwhelming desire to kiss him again but decided to go for a hug instead.

When I pulled away, Andy poured the champagne and offered me a chocolate. Both were icy cold and delicious.

With the champagne bubbles going straight to my head, I finally felt myself relax. As I emptied my third glass in the space of about twenty minutes, there was a momentary pause in our small-talk about what we'd done that day. I looked towards the seafront where the illuminations around the cinema, the theatre, and various amusement arcades twinkled invitingly. It was all very romantic. Gazing back at his profile as he looked up towards Whitsborough Bay Castle, high on the cliff top beyond the harbour, I willed myself to feel something for him. I didn't need fireworks to go off, but I did need a little spark.

'Are we going to sit here for long?' I asked, starting to feel the cold.

I thought he tutted but surely not; that would be rude. He looked at his watch and said a little too brightly, 'Any minute now. Look up towards the castle.'

I did as instructed and jumped as a loud bang resonated and the air filled with red sparks followed by blue then green.

'Oh my God! Did you organise this?'

'Yes.'

'For me?'

'Of course.'

'I love fireworks.'

'I know.'

Despite the cold, a warm fuzzy feeling enveloped me. 'You're amazing,' I said. And I realised I meant it. 'First the balloon flight and now all this.' I moved in for another hug but he unexpectedly caught me in a kiss instead. As the sky filled with explosions, I completely surrendered to the moment, kissing him back passionately.

But as he drove me back to Seashell Cottage half an hour later, a feeling of uneasiness took a hold again. Did I only kiss him because I'd drunk half a bottle of champagne on an empty stomach? Therefore, was it genuine desire for Andy or yet another ill-advised alcohol-soaked decision spurred on by the arrival of Elise's text and the excitement of the fireworks?

As I stared out of the window, I heard Clare's voice in my head from our phone call after the balloon trip: 'I think the only thing he missed out was some fireworks, which was a missed opportunity because he must remember how much you love them.' Oh my God! Was she right? Was it all contrived? And was that a bad thing?

33

✉ From Andy
Last night on the pier was amazing. I don't want
to be pushy but I do have to be back at work on
Monday. I know it's Saturday and you're busy at
work but can we talk tonight? Please xx

I twiddled with a piece of foliage. He was right. He'd been very
patient so far.

✉ To Andy
I've got some stuff to do but, you're right, we
do need to talk. Can we say 8 pm at Seashell
Cottage? Can you eat at the hotel first?

✉ From Andy
Will do. See you at 8 xx

I slipped my mobile back into my jeans pocket and returned to
the bouquet I was making, but it was a struggle to concentrate. My
mind kept wandering to the evening ahead and every time I tried to
visualise us sitting on the sofa having a serious discussion about

what the future may hold for us, my thoughts drifted to an image of
me lying on the sofa kissing Nick. A flush crept up my body.

✉ From Elise
Really hate to say this but I saw Nick & Blonde
together again earlier. Are you free tonight for
a catch up?

✉ To Elise
Serves me right. Would have loved to meet up but
Andy's coming round for a serious talk. Bit
nervous. He's been amazing this week despite me
being hot and cold on him

✉ From Elise
Don't rush into anything because of Blonde. We're
guessing they're an item but we don't know for
sure. Can I suggest you take Nick out of the
equation & ask yourself if Andy really is the one
for you? Can you really imagine growing old with
him? xx

* * *

'Thanks for your help, Mum.' We'd had a run on newborn and
christening gifts so Mum offered to stay back after closing time to
help me re-stock the shelves. Two pairs of hands would make
speedy work of it and save me from coming in early on Monday.
'Can I ask you a question?'

'Of course.'

I unwrapped a silver piggy bank and placed it gently on one of
the glass shelves. 'It's about you and Dad.'

Mum nodded. 'And?'

I carefully folded the tissue to go back in the box. 'When I split
up with Andy after university, you told me that you and Dad split
up for a while when you were younger...'

Mum picked up another box and unwrapped the contents

before answering. 'I was about to do my nursing training and your dad had a joinery apprenticeship lined up so we'd be living two hours apart. Neither of us could afford cars and there weren't the transport or communication links we have these days. There was parental pressure on both sides. It was all, "You're too young, it's too far, you'll meet other people" and we started believing what they said. So we split up.'

'Did you regret it?'

'Of course. We both tried to be mature about it but being apart from your dad was the hardest thing I've ever had to do. We both knew we'd found The One and it didn't matter to us that we'd met when we were fifteen.'

'How long were you apart?'

'About three months. I finished my studies for Christmas, bumped into your dad that evening, and we knew we had to be together.' She picked up another box to unpack. 'I take it this is about Andy?'

I nodded. 'How did you know that Dad was The One?'

Mum put the box down on the shelf and turned to fully face me. 'Because I couldn't imagine my life without him. Being apart was unbearable and, when I thought of a future without him, I wanted to curl up and die. I knew we were going to have a few tough years living so far apart but that was short-term. I knew we'd have a lifetime together afterwards. When I thought of the future, all I could picture was your dad and I growing old together.'

'Thanks, Mum.' I picked up another box and opened the lid then stopped. 'The problem I have is that I *can* imagine growing old with Nick although I think I've blown my chances. But I don't know if I can imagine it with Andy anymore.'

'Then you have a tough decision to make. Come here.' She put her arms round me and held me tightly. 'Like I said on Christmas Day, don't be rushed into making a decision just because he's heading back to London. If he really loves you... and, let's face it, he'd be mad not to, he'll wait.'

'What if I want to get some closure and make the decision tonight?'

'I say do it. But I suggest you think back to the last major life-changing decision you had to make. How did you decide between London and here?'

* * *

I stared at the columns of Post-it notes stuck to the wardrobe in the spare bedroom at Seashell Cottage. A large sky blue rectangular Post-it note posed my dilemma: *SHOULD I TRY AGAIN WITH ANDY?* Beneath it was a column of 'for' arguments on mint green square notes and 'against' on pale pink; the closest colours I could find to replicate stop and go lights.

FOR
> *Used to be perfect*
> *Loved him for years*
> *Always thought meant to be*
> *We've had fun*
> *He's gorgeous*
> *He's rich*
> *He wants to marry me – I think*
> *He's called Steven*

AGAINST
> *He broke my heart*
> *Is it love… or nostalgia?*
> *Clare's comments: why now?*
> *Will the fun last?*
> *Looks & £ – so what?*
> *Mum: grow old together?*
> *Do I want to marry him?*
> *He lives in London – too far*

Stepping back and scanning down the columns, I sighed. Pretty much every 'for' had a corresponding entry in the 'against' column including something neither of us had mentioned until now: location. I had a six-days-a-week job in North Yorkshire. He had a demanding career in London with regular trips abroad. How on earth would that work?

I clicked the pen again and scribbled on another pink Post-it and stuck it at the bottom of the 'against' column.

He's not Nick

I couldn't take my eyes off the two last entries in each column. *He's called Steven but he's not Nick.* I sat down on the edge of the spare bed. *He's not Nick.*

My mobile phone beeped.

✉ From Auntie Kay
Skyped your mum earlier. I made her tell me about Nick and Andy. You must be so confused. She says you're meeting Andy to talk tonight. I've sent you an email and urge you to read it before you make any decisions. Never forget you're my favourite niece and I only want what's right for you xxxxx

I frowned at the text, a feeling of anxiety sweeping over me as I quickly tapped in a response.

✉ To Auntie Kay
Sounds ominous. Will read it now xxxxx

I closed the bedroom door and headed downstairs, curling up on the sofa with my laptop on my knee.

Hi Sarah,
I wish I was at home right now to say this in person rather than by email. Your mum told me about you splitting up with Nick because of Andy re-appearing.
I'm sure you know whom I'd rather see you with but this is your choice, not mine. All I want is

for my favourite niece to be happy and I can
imagine you're having a tough time working out
whether Andy or Nick is the one who can make you
happy long-term.

I'm going to tell you something that I know
you're curious about…

When I was 16, I had a boyfriend called Tim. He
joined the army and was posted overseas after 18
months together. We were young and the distance
was too hard. I was devastated when it ended
because I thought Tim was The One.

But then I met Charlie Blake at a barn dance in
one of the nearby villages and, the moment we saw
each other, something clicked into place for both
of us. He was very different to Tim but he was
perfect for me.

On my 21st birthday, 15 months after we met,
Charlie was going to take me out for a meal, but
he never turned up. He'd been driving along the
coast road to collect me — a road he knew so well
— but he must have swerved to avoid a sheep or a
deer because his car left the road and careered
down the cliff.

The next day, they recovered the car and Charlie's body. In his pocket was an engagement ring
with our initials engraved inside. I had no idea
he was going to propose.

You know that ring I wear? It's not my mum's
engagement ring, it's the one Charlie bought me.
I never wanted to date again. I couldn't face
getting close to someone and experiencing such an
overwhelming feeling of loss ever again and, if
I'm honest, who was ever going to live up to the
high standard Charlie had set?

Everyone kept telling me that time was a great
healer and Charlie would have wanted me to move

on. People say things enough times and you start
to believe them.

Tim's posting ended and he came home. Somehow, we
picked up where we'd left off.

We'd often double-date with your mum and dad. One
evening I was watching them together and it
struck me that they had what I'd had with Charlie
and that it was something I didn't have with Tim.
We'd talked about getting married and having a
family and I realised that I couldn't do it. If I
couldn't have what your parents had — or what I'd
had with Charlie — I'd rather be on my own. Tim
and I split up that evening.

I've been so blessed as I've not missed out on
having a family thanks to you and Ben. Being able
to see the sea from Seashell Cottage has helped
me feel close to Charlie. I feel comforted
listening to the waves and thinking I can hear
him calling me.

I swore your parents to secrecy as I didn't want
anyone to try and talk me into getting over
Charlie and moving on. I'd been there and done
that with Tim and I broke his heart. I didn't
want to put me or anyone else through that again.
So, there you go. I've loved and I've lost and I
never want to do it again. One day, Charlie and I
will be together. Until then, I've got my
extended family of four who mean the world to me.
You may be wondering what this has to do with you
and your present dilemma. There are two men in your
life right now and I want you to think carefully
about who your Tim is and who your Charlie is…
Tim is someone you care for very deeply and have
a great relationship with, but who isn't your
matching heart. Is Andy your Tim who, just like
mine, also represents the past catching up with

you? Or is Nick your Tim: someone who you feel a
strong draw towards but, deep down, you know
isn't the man of your dreams?
Charlie, on the other hand, is the person you
cannot imagine living without. He's the one you
think about first thing in the morning and last
thing at night, and most of the time in-between.
He's the one who makes you laugh but also makes
you cry, the one who gives you butterflies, the
one you want to grow old with. He's your soulmate. You know what this looks like; just look at
your parents.
Who do you have that with? Andy or Nick? If it's
neither, then end it with both before you cause
you or them more heartbreak. And don't panic
about becoming like your Uncle Alan. Even if you
stay single, you'll never be alone like him as
you have a family and great friends who'll always
be here for you. If you do choose one, make sure
you're not settling for second best; your Tim.
I'm going to say goodbye now because I think I've
lectured you enough.
Find your Charlie, Sarah, and hang onto him with
all your strength because he'll be worth it and,
no matter what that CD says, don't let the Steven
thing be your guide. Let your heart be your guide
xxxxxxxxxxxxxxxx

I wiped my eyes with shaking hands then rummaged in my
pocket for a tissue. Wow! That was unexpected. Poor Auntie Kay. I
had no idea. No wonder she got mad when I set her up.

I was about to type in a reply when my phone beeped. Nick.

✉ From Nick
Sorry I sent Callie in yesterday but I did
promise you I'd stay away. It wasn't easy,
though. I came to town with her and must have

walked past your shop 20 times while you were
with her, trying to pluck up the courage to come
in. But a promise is a promise, no matter how
hard it is to keep! I really miss you! Hope
you're happy and Andy is treating you well.
Thinking of you, always xx

He missed me? He was thinking of me? That wasn't a text from
someone who'd moved on. Did it mean Blonde was out of the
picture? Or that she was never in the picture? Maybe she was just a
one-off? But Elise had seen them together twice since.

Sitting back in the chair, I reflected on Auntie Kay's email, what
Mum had said, and my session with my Post-it notes. The one
common theme was whether I could imagine growing old with
Andy. Would he be the one who stopped me being alone?

I typed in a quick reply to Auntie Kay to thank her for her email,
say sorry for her loss, let her know my decision, and tell her I'd send
her a longer reply later.

Almost as soon as I finished typing, there was a loud knock on
the door. Time to face up to things...

34

'Sorry I'm late.' Andy handed me a small cream bag with black rope handles.

'What's this?' I didn't need to ask. I recognised the bag as one from Castle Jewellery five doors down from Seaside Blooms. 'You've been far too generous already.'

Andy grinned. 'You deserve it. Can I come in? It's freezing out here.'

'Sorry. Miles away.' I stepped back to let him pass and gagged as I was hit by an overpowering wave of red wine. Had he showered in the stuff?

Following him into the lounge I hovered in the doorway wondering what the etiquette was in a situation like this. Should I open the gift and act like everything was fine? Should I hand him the gift back and insist that we talk first? Should I just blurt out my decision?

'I don't bite, you know.' Andy patted the spare seat next to him on the sofa. 'And neither do the contents of that bag.'

I looked down and realised I was holding it out in front of me like a dirty nappy.

'Are you okay, Sarah?'

Now there was a question. If I was honest, I was anything but okay at that very moment. I just wanted to curl up in a ball on my bed with Mr Pink and my cats and make it all go away. I hated the situation I was in. Absolutely hated it. Whatever I said or did, someone was going to get hurt.

'Sit down and open your gift,' he said, patting the sofa again, and looking at me with big puppy-dog eyes.

'Okay, you win.' I perched on the edge of the sofa and opened the black jewellery case to reveal a necklace with a brushed silver rose pendant and matching earrings.

'They're gorgeous, Andy.'

'Roses are still your favourites?'

I nodded as I stared at the jewellery, wondering what to do next.

Andy reached for the box and removed the necklace. 'Here. Let me. You put the earrings on and I'll fasten this.'

Too gutless to argue, I removed my silver studs and replaced them with the roses, then lifted my hair and twisted around so he could fasten the necklace from behind. The light trace of his finger-tips against my neck sent a little shiver of pleasure through me. Damn! I couldn't help it; I still felt something for him. Years of loving him followed by years of longing to be with him weren't going to disappear overnight, no matter what I felt for Nick.

A light kiss on my neck made me gasp. My pulse raced as he kissed me again and ran his fingers through my hair. It felt amazing. But we had to talk. I had to be honest with him. I had to... *Oh God, what's he doing to me?* More kisses on my neck transported me back to our university days when he'd kiss my neck and shoulders until I was practically begging for him. It still had the same effect. I wanted him. I wanted him so badly. I twisted round and our lips met with longing and urgency.

The taste of red wine on his tongue jolted my mind from passion to reality. I didn't love him. I was certain of that. It was only lust and nostalgia confusing my feelings. I loved Nick, though. Even though I believed he'd moved on, I felt like I was being unfaithful to him and very unfair to Andy.

'What's up?' he asked when I pulled away.

'I need a drink. I'll be back in a moment.'

Without a second glance at him, I darted out of the lounge and sought refuge in the kitchen. Grabbing a bottle of Sauvignon Blanc out of the fridge, I held it against one flushed cheek, then the other. *Phew! That was close.*

The stairs creaked. Andy obviously needed the toilet, which meant I had a bit more time to compose myself and plan my next steps. Well, they could certainly start with a drink. I unscrewed the lid and poured myself half a glass, which I gulped down instantly.

Andy had clearly had a lot to drink before coming round. I could smell it. I could taste it. I could hear the slur in his speech. How drunk was he, though, because that would have a huge effect on how he'd take the news? He'd never been able to hold his drink. It was possible he'd built up a tolerance over the years, but the Andy I knew at university would get silly, then amorous, then aggressive. Silly – and even amorous – Andy could be fun. Aggressive Andy wasn't. When I say aggressive, I don't mean in a violent way, just in a confrontational arsey kind of a way. Had he had enough to hit that point? Would giving him another glass of wine tip him into it? I could hardly go back with just a glass for me, though, could I?

I sighed as I topped up my drink and poured him a glass. My phone beeped so I fished it out of my pocket, frowning at the name on the screen. A text from Andy? What the...?

✉ From Andy
Hurry up. I'm all ready for you xx

I shook my head as I put the phone back in my jeans pocket. A hallway separated us yet we were communicating by text. It struck me as quite ironic as text had become our only form of communication in our last couple of weeks together, although Andy's texts back then had lacked the kisses and smiley faces.

What did he mean by, 'I'm all ready for you'? Ready for what? My stomach sank. *No! Don't say Amorous Andy is here. Don't let him be...*

I pushed the lounge door open with my foot. Empty. That creak on the stairs? *Oh no! Don't say...* I gingerly made my way upstairs, still holding the drinks. Heart thumping, I opened my bedroom door and gasped at the sight of Andy, stark bollock naked, sprawled out on the bed.

'Oh my God! What are you doing?'

'Waiting for you,' he said. 'You're a bit over-dressed, but we can soon rectify that.' He patted the bed beside him and did a little growl. I think he was aiming for sexy but he fell a little short. I tried to turn my laugh into a cough in case Aggressive Andy made an appearance.

'Are you coming here or do I have to come and get you?' He winked but it made him look psychotic rather than seductive.

I wrinkled my nose as I put the drinks down on the bedside table. 'Would you put some clothes on first?'

'Why?' He squinted at me as if struggling to focus.

'Because I thought you'd come round so we could talk. Not to... you know.'

'We can talk after. Little Andy's ready for his reunion.'

Little Andy? No, no, no, no, NO! We'd never used a pet name before, had we? Surely I'd have remembered. 'Andy! Please.'

He frowned. 'But I thought this was what you wanted. You seemed pretty keen downstairs.'

He was right and it had been very unfair of me. That kiss had definitely been of the 'take me to bed right now' variety but I absolutely couldn't see it through. 'Sorry. I can't, Andy. Erm...' I fished around for an excuse. 'Not in Auntie Kay's bed.'

'Downstairs then?'

I shook my head. 'I can't.'

He stared at me for a while then looked down. 'Okay. You win. Little Andy's gone to sleep now anyway. I'll put my kecks on.'

'And your shirt? And maybe your jeans?' I couldn't stay and watch. 'I'll make us some coffee and meet you back in the lounge.'

When I entered the lounge with two mugs of coffee, Andy was there and had thankfully replaced his shirt and jeans although I could see that he'd brought the glasses of wine down and had already polished off his and half of mine.

'What do you want coffee for?' he slurred. 'Have some wine.' Then he sniggered. 'Oh, I've already drunk most of yours. May as

well have the rest.' Before I could protest, he'd picked up my glass
and taken a few swigs.

'To us.' He clinked his glass against my mug then gave me a
lopsided grin and patted the sofa again. 'I promise not to jump on
you if you sit down.'

I tentatively sat down on the sofa as far from him as I could
manage without sitting on the arm.

'I have to say that I've quite enjoyed my week in Whit- Whits-
The Bay,' Andy said, 'but I'm soooo glad it's over. Couldn't live in the
sticks for long. Don't know how you've coped with it these past few
months.'

I prickled at the use of the word 'coped'. Was he being rude?
*Smile politely. It was probably just a bad choice of word whilst under the
influence. He won't have meant anything by it.*

'I never wanted to move back here,' I said, trying to keep my
voice light and casual, 'but I'm glad I did. I think living in London
has made me appreciate it more. People go on about how much
there is to do there but there's so much to do here too. We've got
the sea, the countryside, the moors, stacks of pretty villages and
market towns, and it's only an hour to York. We've got a good
cinema, a theatre, great pubs and friendly people. What more
could I want?'

Andy laughed. 'You sound like an advert for "Visit Yorkshire".
Have you swallowed a brochure?'

I slurped on my coffee. 'I'm just telling you what I think of the
place.'

'I'm glad you've liked it back here. It sounds like it's been just
what you needed but I bet you can't wait to be living back in
London again.'

'You what?'

'You'll love being back there. I've got this great apartment by the
Thames. It's rented but there are some for sale in the same building.
We can buy one if the commute's okay for you.'

'Commute?'

'I'm assuming you'll want to work until we start a family but it's
up to you after that. I can support us. I earn six figures you know.'
He tried to hold up six fingers but somehow managed eight. 'There

may be a couple of marketing roles at my place. I can put in a good word for you.'

I gasped. How the hell had he jumped so quickly from a few kisses to me moving to London, getting a job, buying a flat and having his babies? Was he winding me up? His serious expression suggested otherwise. 'I've already got a job. I own a shop, remember?'

'You must have had enough of playing shop by now, surely?' Andy laughed and gave me what I'm sure was meant to be a gentle prod on the arm but it actually hurt like hell. I scowled at him. *Do that again and Little Andy will be wearing this coffee.*

'Come on, Sarah, you've got a brain. You should be fast-tracking your career in London, not wasting away in a piddly little shop in some past-its-best northern seaside resort.'

'I can't believe you just said that.' I slammed my mug down on the coffee table before I really did empty it in his lap. 'That "piddly little shop" as you so delicately put it was started by someone who means the world to me – as you very well know – and I've put a lot of time, thought, and effort into developing the business. Could you be any ruder? And Whitsborough Bay isn't some "past-its-best northern seaside resort". It's my home.'

'It's a shit hole. You know it and I know it. But we can leave soon.'

I wanted to slap him. Looking at the smug grin on his face, I saw again the self-assured arrogance he'd displayed all those years ago when he put his career ahead of me. I pictured myself that day outside his office when things ended. Back then, I'd been falling apart inside. Now, I was so much stronger and I wasn't going to take the same old crap from him again.

I shuffled round on the sofa so I could face him fully, arms folded. Taking a deep breath, I said calmly, 'Please forgive me for being a bit slow, but am I correct in thinking that you want me to close the shop, move down to London with you and get a marketing job again?'

'Of course not! You don't have to *close* the shop.' He plumped a cushion and swivelled to fully face me too. 'You could sell it. Or you could get a manager in to run it for you. Yeah. That would be perfect.' He downed the remnants of wine from my glass. 'Anyway, you don't need to decide right now. I think we've done enough talking.' He put the glass down and smiled seductively. 'I'm sure we can awaken Little Andy...' He leaned towards me, lips puckered, but I put my hand out and pushed him back.

'Not so fast, Romeo. I'm not quite done with the talking.' My voice sounded strong and confident – a contrast to the nervous butterflies in my stomach. 'I know you said I had a brain and I should use it, but I'm having a real thickie moment so please bear with me. Did I or did I not tell you this week that moving up here came at just the right time for me because I didn't enjoy living in London anymore, that I hate the thought of ever working for another big company, and that the shop is the best thing that's ever happened to me?'

'You said all of that stuff but I know you didn't really mean it. You love London. You loved your job. You just lost your way a bit.'

'Lost my way? Have you not listened to a word I've said?'

'Of course I have.'

'So what would make you think I'd ever want to leave the shop and go back to exactly the same life I had before? The life I hated.'

'You didn't really hate it, though. You just came to your senses about that loser Jason then panicked and changed everything else.'

'What?'

Andy wagged his finger at me. 'I think this floristry malarkey is like a gap year for you – a chance to find yourself before you return to normality. Anyway, when you move back to London, it won't be *exactly* the same. You'll have me instead of Jason.'

I closed my eyes and covered my face with my hands. 'We split up because you put your career ahead of me. Agreed?' I lowered my hands on the last word and looked at him.

'You know I was at risk of losing my job.'

'Just answer the question. Did you or did you not put your career ahead of me?'

'Yes. I did. And I've said I'm sorry.'

'And are you now telling me that you've changed so much that you'll never work late and you'll always put me ahead of your career from now on?'

Andy hesitated, the smug expression slipping. 'Of course you'll always come first,' he said. 'But my career's really important. You know that. I've come back from Dubai with a promise of a great promotion. It *will* mean long hours at first, but it'll calm down when my boss can see I'm settling down and getting married like he told me to.'

WTF? 'What did you just say?'

The expression on Andy's face told me he'd just revealed something he hadn't meant to. 'I said it will calm down and we can get married. You know you've always wanted to get married.'

'Not that,' I snapped. 'The bit about your boss.'

'Erm... You'll love the apartment. The kitchen's fantastic. You've always said you'd like to do more cooking and you'll be able to do loads when we entertain my boss and our friends. They'll be so impressed, although you may have to step up the sophistication level from lasagne and shepherd's pie. Might help you shed a bit of that lard too if you lay off the comfort food. If you're going to be a director's wife, you need to look the part.'

Ouch! As I stared at Andy, I realised I didn't know him anymore and he clearly didn't know anything about me either. I wasn't sure who was sat on the end of the sofa but it certainly wasn't the Andy I'd fallen for twelve years ago. I'd really thought he was back but Clare had been right all along; it was the charm offensive and not the true Andy that had wriggled under my skin. The drunken gibbering idiot issuing orders and insulting my weight was the real Andy. He certainly wasn't my Charlie. He wasn't my Tim either.

'Christ, Sarah, what's up with you now?' he spat. 'You've got a right face on you again.'

'I think you should leave.' I gave him my stoniest look then stood up, marched to the door, and flung it open.

'Why?'

'Why?' I was shouting but I didn't care. 'Because you don't need a girlfriend. All you're after is someone to cook for you. Call a bloody agency. And if the other thing you want is sex, call an agency for that too.' I pointed into the hall, indicating for him to leave, but he stayed exactly where he was, grinning inanely.

'What are you wittering on about? I *do* want a girlfriend. I want you. Sarah. I already told you you're the only person I've ever loved.'

I blanched at the use of the past tense and a reality hit me. 'Oh my God! *Loved*? You don't love me now, though, do you?'

'I... erm... I could.'

'Andy! What the...? Why did you come here?' I shouted. 'Why the balloon trip and the fireworks and all that other stuff if you don't still love me?'

'I'll ask you the same thing. Do you love me?' he shouted back.

'No.'

'Then why have you been all over me in the past few days?'

'Why? Because I was confused by your sudden reappearance. Because I took years to get over you and I wasn't sure whether I really had. Because I always believed we'd get back together one day. Because I wanted to believe you'd changed and it could be perfect between us again.' *Because you're a Steven.*

When Andy stared at me blankly, I decided to press on. 'Given that we've both admitted we don't love each other anymore, you may as well be honest about that comment about your boss. What was that all about?'

'What comment?'

'Don't play with me. You owe me an explanation.'

He met my stare again.

'Okay. You win,' he said eventually. 'Will you sit down first?'

I felt a bit silly standing in the open doorway but I couldn't bear to be close to him so I sat down on the armchair instead. 'Go on. This had better be good.'

He picked up my empty glass and, frowning, put it down again. I wasn't going to offer him a top-up. He ran his fingers through his hair and stared into the fire for an excruciating minute or so.

'I don't know if you remember, but I work for a Japanese firm where the top guys have very strong family values that their senior team must uphold. To become a director, they expect you to be married with kids in private school and living in a nice property. A few comments were made that left me with no doubt that, if I didn't get married soon, I wouldn't be promoted any further.'

I shook my head. 'Please tell me you're kidding.'

He looked at me and shrugged. 'I know. It's a bit primitive, but it's their culture and I need to embrace it if I want to be a director and earn the really big salary.'

'Not about that. I meant please tell me that you're kidding me about that being the reason you came here and messed up my life all over again.'

'You're the only person I've ever loved. I haven't found anyone since who I can bear to be around for longer than a few months. I don't have time to keep looking. I've never got bored in your company so I thought we could make it work. I thought I might have a struggle if you were still with Jason, but when I found you here working in a shop, I thought it would be easy.'

'You thought wrong.' I shook my head. 'I didn't think you could stoop much lower than that day outside your office, but you've just descended to a whole new level. Trying to win me back just to secure a promotion and a bigger salary? You really think a relationship could work on that basis?'

He nodded vigorously. 'With the right person.'

'And I suppose I'm that person?'

'Yes.'

'Then you're deluded. You really think I'd be with you for those reasons? If I get married, it will be out of love, not to secure a bigger pay packet. Seriously, Andy, what sort of person do you think I am?'

He just stared at me blankly again.

'I think it's time for you to go back to London. Without me.'

'You can't mean that. Not after all the effort I've put in to win you back. My boss has spent a fortune on you, you ungrateful—'

'Your boss paid?

Andy wouldn't catch my eye. 'No. I did. I didn't mention my boss. It was me. My money.'

Another piece of the jigsaw slotted into place. If his boss had organised and paid for it, it would explain a lot of things like how he'd managed to secure Denbury Castle on Boxing Day and fireworks over Whitsborough Bay Castle. His boss would have the influence and connections to have pulled in favours like that. Why would his boss do it, though? It still didn't make sense.

'To be honest, Andy. I don't really care who paid. Even if it was you, you need to understand that I didn't ask you to do any of it. You chose those things. I wasn't holding a gun to your head.'

'But I wouldn't have got your interest without it, would I?'

'You would. Don't get me wrong; all those things were amazing. But they were only amazing because I seemed to be experiencing them with the old Andy but he's long-gone, isn't he? Which means any chance of us trying again is also long-gone.'

Andy looked pale. For a fleeting moment, I thought he was genuinely gutted that he'd blown it with me because he really did care. But then he ruined it. 'What am I going to tell my boss?'

'About what? What is it with you and him?'

'Didn't you wonder how I've managed to get all this time off work?'

I shrugged. 'Not really. It's the Christmas holidays. I assumed you were on annual leave.'

'I might have told my boss that you were my girlfriend before I went to Dubai but the distance caused us to split up. Returning to the UK meant the relationship was back on the cards but I needed to spend a lot of time with you.'

'Might have told him or actually told him?'

He didn't answer the question. 'I might have said a grand gesture was needed to make it up to you.'

'Like a balloon flight?'

He nodded. 'And I might have said I was going to propose to you on the balloon so we'd need it to ourselves. He's all about family and he felt really guilty that posting me to Dubai split us up so he was keen to do what he could to fix it and he organised the venue.'

I covered my eyes. 'All these lies, Andy. What happened to you? You never used to lie and now it seems you do it as easily as breathing.' I took my hands away and looked at him. 'I'm done talking now. We could sit here and talk all night and I don't think I'll ever understand what has happened this week or why you've done this to me or to your poor boss.'

He narrowed his eyes and shrugged. 'What do you want me to say?'

'How about, "I'm sorry, Sarah, for being a lying little shit. I'm sorry, Sarah, for coming back into your life without warning and getting you to split up with an amazing man to see if we could make it work again. I'm sorry, Sarah, for insulting your shop, your home, and your life. I'm sorry, Sarah, for being an ignorant, arrogant, self-centred lying pig".'

'I'm sorry.'

'You could try to sound like you mean it. It's time you left now.'

He got to his feet, wobbled, then looked at me so coldly that a shiver ran down my spine. 'I'll go but answer me one thing first. I still don't get it. Why would you throw away a great career, an exciting life in the city, and a chance to be with me for... for... this.'

'You've just answered your own question, Andy. You just don't get it. And that's the reason why I choose all *this* over you. You don't get *it*. You don't get *me*. We don't get each other. It's over. Forever.'

The coldness in his eyes seemed to drop a few more degrees. 'You say I've changed but you've changed too and not for the better. I'm not sure I even like you anymore.'

'Fine. That makes us quits. And you can have these back.' I swiftly removed my new earrings and unclasped my necklace before dropping them back into the bag.

He snatched it from me. 'You know that photo of you that I said I kept in my wallet? I found it at the bottom of a crate when I was packing, discarded and forgotten. You're not all that special, you know. You've really let yourself go. I'm not sure I want a fat girl-friend showing me up. I hope your business fails.'

'And I hope you never get promoted. Get out!' I picked up his shoes and socks and shoved them into his arms, stormed towards the front door, and yanked it open. 'I'm waiting.'

When I slammed the front door behind him a few moments later, I let out a shuddery deep breath and prepared myself for the floodgates to open. But they didn't. I was still shaking from the confrontation but the only feeling I had was relief. Eight years of wondering 'what if?' had finally reached a conclusion. Our time had been when we were at university and I'd been foolish to think that, with so much happening in both our lives, we could ever be those same people again. Andy was right; I *had* changed but, unlike him, it *was* for the better. He may have the right middle name but he wasn't *the* Steven. I knew who was, though. I picked up my

phone to reply to Nick's text but spotted a message from
Auntie Kay.

✉ Auntie Kay
I knew it! I knew Nick was your Charlie! I'm
beside myself with excitement. Go get him!

✉ To Auntie Kay
I will. But first I really need some sleep. It's
been a tough week xx

And now for my reply to Nick. I just hoped it would work...

✉ To Nick
Andy's gone. I'm so sorry for everything I've put
you through. Hope we can stay friends and maybe
go out for a drink soon xx

35

Elise had offered to work a couple of shifts over the school holidays. She was waiting outside the shop for me on Monday morning and glanced at her watch as I fumbled with my keys in the door. 'Cutting it a bit fine this morning, aren't we?' It was two minutes until opening time.

'Don't,' I mumbled. I felt stressed enough about being late without anyone commenting on it. 'It's been a hideous weekend and I slept through the alarm this morning.'

Getting the door open at last, I flipped the sign round to open and headed into The Outback to get the float for the till. 'Can you watch things? I'll just be a minute.'

'Sure.'

'I'm so sorry,' Elise said when I'd brought her up to date on the Andy situation between serving customers. 'How do you feel?'

'Angry but relieved.'

'You did the right thing. I hate to be the bearer of more bad news but you know the fireworks he said he'd organised...?'

'Another lie?'

She nodded. 'Sorry. The landlady of The Ship was celebrating her fiftieth birthday and twenty-five years of being a landlady with—'

'With a firework display that would have been seen over the castle?'

Elise nodded. 'It was in this morning's paper. I was wondering how to tell you.'

I covered my face with my hands and muttered. 'Oh, Elise, I've made such a mess of things this past week or so.'

'Hey. You didn't make a mess of anything. Andy did this; not you.'

I looked at her sadly. 'But I could have told him to get lost right at the start. I could have stuck with Nick but I had to be blinded by the whole Steven thing.'

'What are you going to do about Nick?'

'I honestly don't know. I know I want to be with him but I can't decide whether he's moved on or not. We saw him with Blonde and you've seen them twice since, but then he sent me that lovely text. You wouldn't send something like that if you were seeing someone else, would you?' Something about Elise's expression concerned me. 'More bad news?'

'I've seen them together again. Twice more.'

'No!'

'Sorry.'

'When? Where?'

'In her car at the lights near the theatre yesterday afternoon and I saw them on foot the night before but I can't remember where.'

I hardly dared ask but I had to know. 'Did they seem... together?'

'Ooh. I was hoping you wouldn't ask that. When I saw them on foot, he had his arm round her.'

'I guess that's that, then.' I swallowed hard on the huge lump in my throat.

'It could still have been innocent.'

'You don't really believe that, do you?'

Elise slowly shook her head. 'I want to, though.'

'Oh well, plenty more fish in the sea. Or plenty more Stevens on the-one.com.'

'And you don't really believe that, do you?' said Elise.

I shook my head and sighed. 'I really do think Nick was The One and I've let him slip away. He was obviously just being nice in his text on Saturday and I've built it up to be something I want it to be. I guess I know why he didn't reply to my text about Andy leaving. He doesn't care.'

'You know that's not true,' Elise said. 'I know the evidence points towards Nick and Blonde being together, but we don't know that for certain and, even if they are, it doesn't mean it's anything serious. He said he'd wait for you however long it takes, didn't he?'

'Words. Only words.'

Elise gave me a hug. 'So what now?'

I sighed and shrugged. The only certainty I felt was that my search for Steven was over. For me, it had to be Nick or nobody. And terrifying as the thought was of being alone like Uncle Alan, I knew that I'd rather be alone than with the wrong person like Jason or Andy. And, as Auntie Kay had pointed out, I had family and great friends so I'd never truly be alone. I hoped.

✉ From Auntie Kay
Not heard from you since you sent Andy packing.
Are you and Nick back together yet? Really hope
so. You're made for each other xxx

✉ From Elise
Hate to say it but just seen them together again.
Don't get down. Obviously not meant to be. It's a
new year tomorrow and that means new beginnings.
Maybe a fresh start on the search for Steven? xx

'You did the right thing, sweetheart.' Mum put her arm around me
the following day. 'You gave him a chance and he showed his true
colours.'

'I know. At least I finally have closure. It only took eight years.'

'Then why don't you look a little more pleased? Is it Nick?'

I nodded. 'I've lost him, Mum.' I tried to blink back the tears but
it was too late. Mum hugged me tightly and I sobbed on her shoulder, hoping no customers would appear.

'I'd better get myself tidied up,' I said when the tears finally
subsided. 'It's quiet enough today without me scaring the customers
off with my panda eyes. Shout if you need me.'

The bell tinkled a couple of times while I was in The Outback but Mum didn't shout so it was clearly nothing too complex.

I wandered back into the shop, feeling better for a good cry. 'Thanks, Mum. Anything sold?'

'Small bunch of spray carnations and a woman collected those white roses.'

My heart sank. 'Callie?'

'She didn't give her name.'

'About my age? Dark hair? Similar build to me?'

Mum nodded.

'That was Nick's sister. Did she say anything?'

'She just said thanks and paid. Seemed in a rush. I'd have shouted you if I'd realised. Sorry, sweetheart.'

'It's my fault. I should have said whom they were for. I didn't think... Oh well, while it's quiet, I think it's time you told me all about Auntie Kay and Charlie Blake.'

Between serving customers, Mum told me everything she could remember, including Auntie Kay's resolve never to date again.

'Do you think she made the right decision?' I asked.

Mum shrugged. 'I think it was right for her. I'd have loved to have seen my big sister get married and have kids, but I saw how she was with Charlie and I saw how she was with Tim. It was chalk and cheese. Kay and Charlie were soulmates. Kay and Tim were friends. Poor Tim would always have been second best and they both knew it. If he'd never joined the army, who knows what would have happened? Maybe Kay and Tim would have married, but if they had, I think they'd have had a rough ride and I don't think they'd still be together today.'

'What about when it ended with Tim the second time? Couldn't she have found someone else? Someone more like Charlie?'

'She didn't want to. She'd already met the love of her life and he'd been taken away too young. Nobody else was ever going to compare. Every time I thought about encouraging her to move on, I'd imagine how I'd feel if, God forbid, I lost your dad. I'd never want to be with anyone else and I'd resent anyone who expected me to be.'

'Do you really think there's only one true match for everyone?'

'I do, sweetheart, but I base that on personal experience. If neither Andy nor Nick are your soulmate then keep looking because I'm sure he'll be out there.'

'What if Nick *is* my soulmate?'

'Then why aren't you fighting for him?'

It was a very good question.

* * *

'Sarah! You've got a visitor.' Nick? My heart raced as I scrambled down the stockroom stepladder an hour or so later.

But it wasn't Nick.

'Clare? What are you doing here?' I rushed at her for a hug.

'I was bored. You know I hate New Year's Eve even more than I hate Christmas. You were moaning that you had nothing to do now that you've sent that numpty packing so I've invited myself to stay. I thought we could stay in, stuff our faces and drink shed loads. I've got enough food and drink in the car to feed an army.'

I hugged her again.

'What's the matter with you?' She wriggled free. 'You know Clare hugs are on a limited supply.'

'Sorry. I'm just really pleased to see you.'

* * *

Clare stretched out on the sofa later that evening while I screwed up newspaper for the fire. 'I still think you should tell Nick straight out that your man Andy's out of your life now for good,' she said.

I shrugged. 'He knows. I've texted him and I've put it on Facebook but he hasn't responded. He's been spotted with Blonde loads so I have to accept that, for now, he's moved on.'

'I'm not convinced he has. Remember I was here when he made that little speech less than two weeks ago. That wasn't a man who was going to get over you this quickly. There has to be another explanation.'

'Can you think of one?'

Clare was quiet for a moment. 'No. But that doesn't mean there isn't one. I couldn't think of an explanation around your man Andy's OTT behaviour but there was one, wasn't there?'

Hmm. Good point as usual.

Five minutes later, the fire was blazing. 'I think it's time.' I picked up my laptop and sat beside her on the sofa.

'Are you sure you want to do this? If it really is over with Nick, surely you should be ramping up your search for Steven, not calling it off.'

'You've changed your tune. I thought you didn't believe in the Steven thing.'

'I still don't but you do.' She narrowed her eyes at me. 'Or have you finally seen sense?'

'I still believe it but I think the name is a red herring. I listened to the CD several times on Sunday. Madame Louisa says that I'll reach a crossroads where past meets present and I have to follow my heart not my head because my heart will lead me to Steven. The crossroads were obviously Andy and Nick. My head was telling me to try again with Andy because I'd always believed we'd get back together one day but my heart wouldn't let go of Nick. Nick's the heart decision and the heart decision is supposed to lead me to Steven.'

Clare frowned. 'So if Nick is really Steven, even though that's not his name, why aren't you fighting for him?'

'Mum asked me the same thing. It's hard to explain.'

'Try me.'

I sipped on my wine. 'Firstly I feel stupid and embarrassed about the Andy thing. Secondly, he's seeing someone else—'

'Possibly.'

'Almost definitely. And thirdly, if we really are meant to be together, it will still happen. He'll have his fling with Blonde and I'll have had my blip with Andy and we'll be on an even footing to start again. Well, sort of even. I didn't sleep with Andy—'

'And you don't know that he's sleeping with Blonde, do you now?'

'I hope he isn't, but it's none of my business.' I switched the laptop on while Clare stared at me. I really didn't have the energy for an argument.

'I still don't get it,' she said. 'Why remove your dating profile? Using your logic, couldn't you just keep it on there and have a bit of fun until destiny finally reunites you and Nick or whatever it is you're expecting?'

'I don't think it would be fair. I don't want to meet anyone else. The only person I want is Nick. I've already messaged the three Stevens who asked me out before Christmas to say I'm removing my profile and concentrating on the business for the foreseeable future. It's my New Year's Resolution.'

'And what will you really be doing?'

'Removing my profile and concentrating on the business.' *And hoping that Nick will come back to me eventually.*

I'd made a decision that the New Year signalled time for a new perspective on things. I was going to be grateful for all the amazing things that had come my way over the past few months. I had a great business, a great team to help run it, my health, a rent-free roof over my head and my friends and family around me. I was incredibly lucky and I needed to start acting like a lucky person instead of a victim.

'Why do you keep staring at me?' I said. Midnight was fast approaching but we'd already agreed not to acknowledge it. I wasn't a fan of New Year's Eve either. I always found it such an anti-climax so was delighted to be spending it at home with one of my best friends instead of squashed in a sweaty pub with a five-deep queue at the bar and a three-hour wait for a taxi home at quadruple the usual price.

'I'm trying to imagine what it must be like being you.'

I laughed. 'Now why would you want to do something scary like that?'

Clare didn't laugh. 'A few months ago, you ended a three-year relationship with Jason because he wasn't The One, right?'

'Yes.'

'And a few days ago you ended a twelve-year on-off relationship with Andy because you finally realised he wasn't The One either, right?'

I nodded.

'But you think Nick is The One?'

'Yes.'

'And, not only that, you think he's *the* Steven your clairvoyant predicted was the perfect match for you, but she somehow got the name wrong?'

'Correct.'

'Then I just don't get it. You've found your man. He feels the same way about you. He told you he'd wait for you as long as it takes. He sent a text to say he misses you. You've removed your online profile because you don't want to be with anyone but him. You decided to say no to Andy even before you learned the truth about him. You can't stop thinking about Nick. You're not eating properly, you're not sleeping properly and you can't imagine life without him. Yet you won't do anything about it. You won't phone him. You won't go round to see him. You're just prepared to – and I quote – "see what happens".'

It sounded so stupid me avoiding Nick when Clare described it like that. But the thought of knocking on his door or phoning him up and having Blonde answer was too much to bear. 'I'm scared of bumping into her,' I admitted. 'She's slim, blonde and beautiful. I can't compete with that.'

'Bollocks!' Clare said. 'You're curvaceous and beautiful and hair colour's got sod all to do with anything. If you put yourself down again, I'll slap you.'

'Ooh, so masterful,' I joked.

Clare shook her head at me. 'If the only thing that's stopping you from getting back with the man of your dreams is the fear of running into her, then you need to think of a time or a place to catch him where she definitely won't be.'

'Like where?'

'I don't know. I've only met him once. Does he have any hobbies? Play any sports? Go anywhere she wouldn't be?'

I shrugged. 'He goes running along the beach a few times a week.'

'Then take up running. Or go for a walk and accidentally bump into him.'

'Been there, done that. Either he's been running on every day I haven't been or he's stopped going.'

'Then think of somewhere else.'

I sipped on my wine as I racked my brains. 'Oh my God! I know! Lighthouse Point.'

'Where?'

'That rocky pier thing in South Bay with the lighthouse on it. He throws roses in the sea at two minutes past eleven on New Year's Day and he always does it alone.'

The clock on the mantelpiece pinged. Midnight. Happy New Year!

'Lighthouse Point it is, then.' Clare raised her glass. 'Perhaps it will be a Happy New Year for you after all. Sláinte.'

'Sláinte.' I was definitely happy with my lot in life but, if I was able to win Nick back, well... that would be the flake in my ice-cream.

* * *

'Christ, this bench is cold on my arse.' Clare wriggled her bum. 'What's the plan? Will you grab him the second he appears and declare your undying love?'

'No. He likes to do this on his own so I'm going to respect that. I'll show my face when he's done.'

'You'll not be bottling it will you?'

'I'm here aren't I?' I looked at my watch:10.58 a.m. If he liked to throw the roses in at 11.02 a.m. on the dot, he was cutting it a bit fine, especially as Lighthouse Point looked slippery so he'd need to watch his step.

New Year's Day had arrived with a thick covering of frost. A bright sun in the clear blue sky made the ground sparkle like crushed diamonds. Clare and I had taken position on a bench over-looking Lighthouse Point ten minutes earlier. We could see the lighthouse clearly but it was unlikely Nick would look in our direc-tion and, even if he did, there was no way he'd be able to tell it was us.

I grabbed Clare's arm. 'That's him.'

'Are you sure?' She leaned forward. 'Bloody sun. I can barely see.'

'It's Nick. I'd know him anywhere.' I took deep breaths.

'You'll be grand. Just be honest with him. Tell him Andy was a mistake. Tell him he's gone. Tell him you love him.'

'You make it sound so easy.'

Nick slowly headed towards the lighthouse and sat down on a bench, looking out towards the sea. What was he thinking? Was he crying? Praying? Thinking about happy times with those he'd lost? I wished I were with him to give my support.

He stood up and took a couple of paces closer to the edge, presumably preparing to throw the roses in. Then he stopped and looked back down the pier. I followed the direction of his gaze to see a figure hurrying towards him. *No, no, no! It can't be.*

'Is that her?' Clare whispered.

I couldn't answer. I watched as Nick and Blonde held each other.

Clare stood up and walked a few paces in each direction. 'I can't tell if it's a hug or a kiss. He's got his back to us and the sun's too low. I'm sorry, Sarah. I honestly can't tell.' She sat down again. 'Hug or kiss, are you still going to fight for him?'

I looked at them, still holding each other. 'Maybe. But not today. Perhaps I'll have to wait a bit longer for my fresh start.'

'It's *not* a Happy New Year after all,' Clare muttered. 'This is one of the many reasons why I hate New Year; too many expectations and too many disappointments.'

'You're wrong.' I stood up and reached for Clare's hand to pull her to her feet. 'Things may not have gone as planned today but it's still a Happy New Year, especially when you compare it to last year. I'm living in a place I love, close to my family. I get to spend six days a week on my hobby and actually get paid for it. I have amazing friends including one who, even though I rudely abandoned her to move back home, has been by my side most weekends helping me build a successful business. I may not have Nick in my life at the moment but I'd still say it's a very Happy New Year.'

Clare smiled. 'Well, when you put it like that, I think it sounds like we have something to celebrate. What time do pubs open round here?'

37

A week passed. Then another. Then another. Before I knew it, January and February had whizzed by, signalling five months since my new home, new business, and new life.

I didn't see or hear anything from Nick. I regularly checked Facebook but he never seemed to update it. Shortly after January's Bay Trade meeting, I noticed a post from Skye on his timeline saying they'd missed him and hoped he was okay. He replied but all it said was, 'Sorry. Hopefully back next month.' There was nothing mentioned about February's meeting.

Skye had sent me a Facebook friend request and, although I accepted, I politely declined her invite to either month's Bay Trade meeting; it didn't feel right when Nick was one of the founder members.

Life settled into a routine. Stevie and I enrolled in the monthly membership scheme at the cinema in South Bay and made good use of it by going every Tuesday and Thursday. He decided he wanted to lose some weight so we started running along the beach a couple of mornings a week with his dog. It was hard going at first as we ran for longer than I'd done on my own but I persevered and, within a few weeks, we'd built it up to every other day and slightly longer distances. I kept hoping but we never saw Nick. On the positive side, I found myself back at the weight I'd been when I started at university which delighted me. I could finally get back into my size twelve jeans although Clare made me put them in a charity bag as they were 'so a million seasons ago'.

Elise dropped by the shop after school every Wednesday for a cuppa and a catch-up. We also went out for drinks or a meal every other Friday or Saturday and Clare came to stay each weekend in between, fitting visits around her meetings with her northern-based clients.

Seaside Blooms settled into a routine too. I recruited a new team and Mum gradually reduced her hours as they settled into their roles. I discovered what sold well and found new suppliers to keep a regular turnover of new gifts.

I was awarded the lucrative contract at The Ramparts Hotel and anxiously displayed my first arrangements there in late January to a barrage of compliments. An unexpected bonus was additional business from hotel guests and business-users after admiring my work.

As promised, Clare patiently trained me in sales and negotiation techniques and she'd been right; I could do it without being gorgeous, blonde, and Irish. I put my skills into practice immediately, visiting all the funeral directors in town to tout for business as well as hotels, guesthouses, restaurants, and tourist hot spots. I had to take on another two team members to help me keep up with all the extra business I generated.

Business was booming, I had a great team around me, I saw my best friends regularly and I had so much to be thankful for. As I cashed up each day, I couldn't help but feel proud of everything I'd achieved at work.

But every so often, I had a pang of loneliness and longed for Nick by my side. Feeling melancholy, I'd get home from work, put on my PJs, then cuddle Mr Pink as I cried my way through a couple of romantic movies, berating myself for throwing my movie-perfect opportunity away.

* * *

In early March, I picked up a large last-minute booking for a medieval-themed wedding.

'That's stunning,' Cathy said.

I inserted the last piece of foliage into the bridal bouquet and stepped back from the counter to admire my handywork. 'Do you think it looks medieval?'

'I'm no expert but I'd say so. That ivy looks gorgeous.'

'Doesn't it? Must use it more often.'

'I've just done that last posy so is that everything finished now?'

I clicked onto the order on the Mac to double check. 'I think so. Bridal bouquet, three adult bridesmaid posies, a headdress, three flower girl baskets and, of course, the stack of window and table arrangements I did at Sherrington Hall last night.' I looked at the clock. 'Half an hour to spare, too. Not bad going.'

'What time did you finish last night?' Cathy asked.

'About half one this morning.'

'Sarah! You should have let me help you.'

'It was your wedding anniversary. I wasn't going to ask you to cancel your plans for a last-minute booking. To be fair, I could have finished sooner but, as it's my first wedding, I was being a bit of a perfectionist. Did you have a nice meal?'

'It was perfect, thanks. You'll never guess where he took me.'

'Where?'

'The Apple and Peach.'

'Wow! It's supposed to be amazing there.' The Apple and Peach was a Michelin-starred restaurant about twenty minutes up the coast.

'Oh, it was,' she gushed. 'You should get Nick to take you if...'

'If we ever get back together,' I said when she tailed off, looking horrified at what she'd said. 'I don't think that's going to happen anymore, Cathy. It's been too long.'

'Erm... Shall I just go to The Outback and pop the kettle on then get a box for this lot?'

I nodded. Poor Cathy looked relieved to make her escape. I fiddled absent-mindedly with a small piece of discarded ivy as I gazed at the bouquet and wondered what the bride was doing at that very moment. Hair? Nails? Make-up? Sipping champagne with a huge grin on her face? *I wish it was my wedding day. I wish I was the* bride and Nick was the groom. I knew he looked gorgeous in a morning suit. Closing my eyes I imagined us at the altar together.

The bell tinkled as the door opened and closed. I reluctantly opened my eyes to see a tall slim woman walking slowly towards the counter. *Oh my God! It's Blonde! She's a potential customer. Be friendly and professional even if you have just been fantasising about marrying her boyfriend and really want to slap her about with a long stem of gladioli. Still in its metal tub, of course!*

'Morning!' I said a little too brightly.

'Hi,' she said. 'Are you Sarah?'

She knew my name? 'Erm, yes.' My stomach clenched. Did she know about Nick and me? Had she come to warn me away? I studied her face for some sort of clue and noticed that she wore minimal make-up. I could see that she was naturally very pretty, but she looked tired. Large bags under red-rimmed eyes indicated someone who'd either been burning the candle at both ends or crying. Maybe she'd split up with Nick. He was certainly worth crying over. I should know.

'Great. Nick said I should ask for you.'

'Nick Derbyshire?'

'Yes. He recommended you. He said you're the best and nicest florist in town. He obviously thinks very highly of you.'

I didn't know what to say. Was that a dig or a compliment? 'Is there something I can help you with?'

'I'd like to order some flowers for a funeral, please.' She ran a slender hand through her long hair and I couldn't help noticing that her hand shook.

'I'm sorry for your loss,' I said gently. 'Someone close?'

'My husband, Alex.'

Husband?

Her pale eyes filled with tears. 'He lost his fight with cancer last Tuesday. He was only thirty-three. It's too young, isn't it?'

I nodded and swallowed the lump in my throat that always formed when I heard about bereavements. Regularly encountering death was a big downside to my new career and I hoped it would get easier with time although I suspected it never would.

'Do you have a date for the funeral?' *And tell me why you were kissing Nick if you had a dying husband.*

'Next week. Monday.'

'Do you want a wreath or something else?'

A tear slipped down Blonde's cheek. 'I'm sorry,' she said, her voice cracking. 'I thought I was strong enough to do this but I don't think I am just now.' She dropped her bag on the counter and started rummaging. I watched in alarm as her tears flowed freely. 'I can't find my tissues.'

'Here.' I grabbed a box from under the counter and offered it to her. 'Help yourself.'

'Thank you.'

'Would you like to sit down for a moment? Can I get you a glass of water?'

'Yes please. To both. If you don't mind.'

I led her to a wooden chair near the entrance to The Outback and removed a few teddy bears displayed on it. Cathy appeared with a couple of mugs of tea. 'Cathy, you couldn't get a glass of water for this customer, could you?'

'I'm so sorry.' Blonde handed me the empty glass a short while later. 'I don't normally lose it in front of complete strangers.'

'It's okay. I can't imagine what it must feel like to lose your husband.'

'It's agony. I hope you never have to go through it. Are you married?'

'No.' My eyes flicked to the bridal bouquet on the counter. 'Always hoping.'

'I always wanted to get married,' she said. 'When I was little, I was obsessed with weddings. I had all my dolls and teddies married to each other. Made my mum mad when I got hold of her veil and cut it into several pieces so all my girl-bears could have one.' She smiled at the memory. 'I was so desperate for my day to come that I nearly married the wrong person. He was more like a friend, though. The chemistry wasn't there and I realised I couldn't keep trying to create it just so I could have my big day. The hardest part was that the person I *did* marry – Alex – was his best friend and that was the end of a brilliant friendship for the two of them.'

Oh my God! She's talking about Nick. She's his ex-fiancée. 'Are you Lisa?'

'Yes. How did you...?'

'Were you talking about Nick just now?'

Her eyes widened. 'He told you about me?'

'Bits. I know about the wedding being called off.'

'Did he tell you he was with Alex when he died?'

'I... I haven't spoken to him recently.' *He was with Alex when he died? That must mean he knew about the cancer. Which must mean Lisa told him. I wonder when she...?* 'Do you mind me asking how he knew about Alex? I thought they weren't in touch.'

'They weren't but I went to see Nick just after Christmas. Alex told me not to but I knew what it would mean to him to get Nick's forgiveness before...' She wiped her eyes again. 'I knew it was a big ask. I must have driven around the block a dozen times before I had the courage to knock on his door. I braced myself for a scene but I should've known I had nothing to worry about. He's not that kind of man. I didn't even need to beg him to visit. As soon as I told him about Alex, he asked to see him. After everything we did to him, he just came straight out with it, no excuses, no hesitations. He visited every day since and...' Her tears started again. 'I don't think he'll ever know how much that meant to us both. We knew we had to be together but regretted every day that we hurt Nick in the process. Watching Nick and Alex together these past couple of months was like old times. He was there right at the end too. I don't know how I'd have got through it all without Nick's support.'

My throat constricted again. I tried to imagine how Nick felt when given the news that the man who stole his fiancée was about to die and how he was feeling right now, knowing that he was with him at the end. I longed to be there to comfort him. I was also acutely aware of the huge mistake I'd made about him and Lisa, which had kept us apart at a time when he could probably have used my support. No wonder they'd hugged for so long on Lighthouse Point on New Year's Day; they'd had a lot of comforting to do.

'I'm keeping you from your work.' Lisa wiped her eyes again and rose from the chair.

'It's no trouble. Quiet day.' But the minute I said it, the door opened and a couple of customers came in. Cathy was able to help one but the other loitered by the counter.

'I'd best do what I came in to do,' Lisa said as we walked to the counter. 'Can I order two wreaths please? A large white and purple one from me and a smaller yellow and orange one from the kids.'

I'd forgotten they had children, poor little mites. I noted down the messages Lisa wanted on the wreaths and discussed delivery arrangements. She thanked me for my kindness. 'Nick's a great guy,' she said as she turned towards the door. 'You're not an item, are you?'

I shook my head. 'We were. Briefly. But I messed it up.'

'You will be again. I'm sure of it.'

'What makes you think that?'

'The way he lights up when he talks about you. You did the same when you said his name. I don't know what happened between the two of you but, if it can be repaired, repair it. Life's too short. I should know.'

'A twenty-pound bouquet when you've finished gossiping.' An angry male voice drew my eyes away from the door for a moment. When I looked up again, Lisa had gone.

'For now or collection later?' I muttered.

'Now. Be quick.'

Yes sir! I quickly set about selecting flowers. To my dismay, the door opened again and another couple of customers came in and loitered by the counter. No chance of me reflecting on Lisa's surprise revelations then.

38

✉ To Stevie
Do you have time for a drink before the cinema
tonight? Blonde came into the shop today! She's
not seeing Nick. Big misunderstanding. Not sure
what to do next. Would welcome some advice xx

✉ From Stevie
Sounds intriguing! Will have to drive straight
there rather than pick you up as I have a meeting. Meet you in The Anchor at 7pm x

The Anchor, five doors along from the cinema, had become a
regular haunt for pre- or post-cinema drinks with Stevie. It was a bit
of a dive but the staff were friendly and it was convenient. After an
invigorating walk down to the seafront, I held my breath as I
opened the door and braced myself against the mix of stale beer
and old socks.

Looking each way, I recognised a few regulars but no Stevie.
Maybe his meeting had run over. I headed to the bar and ordered
our usual drinks. The door creaked open and I turned around
expecting to greet Stevie. But it wasn't Stevie. It was...

'Nick?' I felt as though my heart was going to leap out of my chest.

He looked just as surprised to see me. 'Sarah? What are you doing here?'

'Meeting Stevie for drinks before the cinema. What are you doing here?'

'Meeting Stevie to discuss some business.'

'Really?'

Nick nodded. 'I smell a set-up.'

'I think you may be right. The cheeky little… not that I'm disappointed to see you, of course.' I looked deep into his eyes. 'It's actually really great to see you.'

Nick held my gaze. 'And you too.'

I indicated Stevie's drink. 'It's your favourite too. Care to join me?'

We sat in a secluded corner. 'How've you been?' I asked.

Nick shrugged. 'It's not been the greatest start to the year.'

'I know about Alex. I'm really sorry.'

Tears formed in Nick's eyes. 'How?'

'Lisa ordered flowers for the funeral today, but she got upset and it all came out. It must have been hard on you seeing him like that after all this time.'

'It was awful. I just keep thinking of all those wasted years. Lisa and I weren't right for each other and we'd probably have divorced within a year and, when I realised that, I could have got in touch and wished them well. I could have got my friend back but, instead, I held a grudge and I nearly let him die thinking I still hated him.' Nick rubbed his eyes. 'Sorry.'

'Come here.' I put my arms around him. He clung onto me as he silently sobbed for a friend, husband, and father taken away far too soon.

'Sorry, Sarah,' he whispered into my hair. 'I've managed to hold it together so far. I needed to for Lisa.' He pulled away and I passed him a tissue out of my bag, which he took gratefully. 'Sorry,' he said again.

'Don't be.' I wiped at my own tears. 'I'm crying and I didn't even know him. I can't imagine what you and Lisa must have gone through. You must be an emotional wreck.'

'I am.'

'Don't punish yourself for the missing years, Nick. Your best friend ran off with your fiancée the day before your wedding. I don't know anyone who could forgive and forget in those circumstances. Don't think about the time lost. Remember instead that you spent lots of time with him at the end. He died knowing his best friend had forgiven him.' Another tear slipped down my cheek at that point and Nick gently wiped it away.

'What a pair we are,' he said.

'Do you want to talk about it?'

Nick took a sip of his drink then shook his head. 'I don't think I'm strong enough right now. Do you mind?'

'Not at all. What do you want to talk about?'

'You. How's the shop going?'

'Couldn't be better.' I smiled brightly as a rush of pride hit me. 'I've got a new team who are great. I did my first wedding today and I've got a stack of bookings across the year. I won the contract at The Ramparts. Did Skye tell you?'

'She's phoned a few times but I've been avoiding everyone while I focused on Alex.' Nick squeezed my hand. 'I'm so pleased for you. I knew you'd get it.'

'Thank you.' A slightly awkward silence descended on us. Why hadn't he acknowledged that I was single again? Maybe he was waiting for me to mention it. Then I felt a wave of guilt. He'd just lost his best friend. Re-kindling a relationship with me would be the furthest thing from his mind. He needed a friend. I should just be that friend and stop thinking about anything else.

'Sounds like everything's clicked into place for you,' he said.

Not quite everything. I knew it was selfish of me after everything he'd been through but seeing him again and holding him as he sobbed had sent my emotions into overdrive. I loved him so madly, so deeply that I couldn't help myself. I longed to hear that there was still a chance for us. I couldn't bear the thought of life without him. Just like Auntie Kay said, there was no doubting that he was my Charlie.

'And how's your Auntie Kay?'

Could he read my mind? Did he know I was thinking about Auntie Kay? *Oh God! This is agony. You're my soulmate, Nick. We should be together.* But of course, I just politely answered his question. 'Having the time of her life. They've toured America, Canada and Australia. They fly to New Zealand next week.'

'Sounds exciting.'

Silence. The elephant in the room was so big I could almost hear it trumpeting. I stared at Nick, hoping he'd say something. I couldn't be the first to speak. I didn't want him to think I was selfish by only thinking about me and what I wanted.

Nick downed the final third of his pint in one. 'Another drink?' he asked.

I pointed to my full glass. 'I'm all right, thanks.'

'You don't mind if I get another...'

'No. Go ahead.' I watched him head for the bar with a sinking heart. It wasn't going well.

My mobile buzzed and I fished it out of my bag.

From Stevie
Hope you don't mind my little set up. Someone had
to take action and I knew you wouldn't be brave
enough to make the first move & let him know how
you feel. So here's your chance. You two are made
for each other. Anyone can see that. Call me
tomorrow with good news xxxxxxx

I looked towards Nick leaning against the bar. Stevie was right. I wasn't brave enough but I needed to be. I'd felt brave that day at Lighthouse Point but that was over two months ago. So much had happened since then. What would I say? Should I just come out with it? 'Nick, you do know Andy's gone, don't you?' But what if he said, 'Yeah. So?' It would kill me. I couldn't do it. I couldn't put myself out there for rejection like that.

I took a large gulp of wine. But what if he wasn't feeling brave either? He really put himself out there by telling me how he felt when we split up. He made it pretty clear then that he wouldn't chase me but he'd be waiting for me. Maybe he couldn't bring himself to say anything in case I rejected him again. After what he'd been through with Alex and Lisa, he must be so fragile right now that there was no way he'd risk adding more hurt.

Lisa seemed to think he still cared and we should be together. She said that stuff about life being too short...

I glugged on my wine again, my stomach in knots. I'd never felt more afraid or out of my depth in how to handle a situation correctly. What was more frightening? Potentially making a fool of myself in front of Nick or letting him walk out of my life yet again? It wasn't a hard question to answer.

Nick headed back from the bar. I needed to be brave. *You do know I sent Andy packing, don't you?* That would be a good start.

I noticed his pint was already half empty. His face bore a deep frown. He sat down and looked at the floor. 'So,' he said, before I had a chance to speak, 'how's it going with Andy?'

What? 'Andy?'

'Your ex. The one who... I'm assuming you're still together.'

'I sent him packing before New Year.'

Nick looked up, an expression of hope on his face. 'New Year? Why didn't you get in touch with...?' The hope faded and he looked away again. 'Oh. Because you didn't want to get back with me, of course. This must be what it feels like to be Callie, not engaging brain before mouth.' He took another swig of his drink. 'I'd better go.' He stood up but I grabbed his arm.

'Please don't leave me again,' I begged, tugging his arm to make him sit down. 'I *did* get in touch with you. After Callie came into the shop, you texted me to say you missed me and I replied telling you Andy had gone. I put it on Facebook too. Several times.'

'I've barely glanced at Facebook since hearing about Alex and the last text I had from you told me that things were great between you two.'

'What? I never...' I fished my phone out of my pocket and scrolled through the sent items. 'Here, read this.'

'"Andy's good. I'm so sorry for everything I've put you through. Hope we can stay friends and maybe go out for a drink soon".'

I grabbed the phone off him and scowled at the text. 'No! That should read, "Andy's gone". Damn ancient phone and stupid bloody predictive text.' I slammed my phone onto the table. 'Did you really think I'd send you a message gloating that my relationship was great? That would be nasty.'

Nick shrugged. 'Everything else was crap so it struck me as another thing to add to the pile. Why didn't you text again when I didn't respond?'

I twisted a curl of hair round my finger. 'Elise and I thought you were seeing someone else.'

'No! Who?'

'Lisa.'

'Why would you think that?'

'I realised that I'd made a mistake with Andy and got Elise to drive me to your house so I could tell you how I really felt about you but Lisa came out although, of course, I didn't know who she was at the time. You had your dressing gown on and you hugged and kissed her so we put two and two together and...'

'And you thought I was sleeping with her?'

I covered my eyes, cringing. 'Something like that. Everything like that. Elise kept spotting the two of you together, but Mum and Clare convinced me I should fight for you so I came to Lighthouse Point on New Year's Day to tell you how I felt but Lisa was there too. It looked like you were kissing so we left and...'

Nick laughed and lifted my hands away from my eyes. Still holding them in his, he said gently, 'Back up a bit. You said you were coming to tell me how you really felt? You already know how I feel about you. Those feelings haven't changed. If it's possible, they've got even stronger. What were you going to tell me?'

Be brave. Say it. 'That you're the one I want to spend the rest of my life with.'

Nick took a deep breath and closed his eyes for a moment as if absorbing this unexpected piece of information. 'It's definitely over with Andy?'

'Definitely. It never really started. It was a huge mistake. He—'

'You don't have to explain,' Nick said. 'All I need to know is that he's gone and he won't be back.'

'He's gone and I've told him I never want to hear from him again.'

'And Steven?'

I smiled. 'That's over too. I took my profile off the website on New Year's Eve.'

'I know I should just shut up and kiss you but I'm a bit emotionally delicate right now as you've seen. I have to be sure that I'm not going to lose you next time a Steven walks into the shop.'

'You won't.'

'How can you be sure? I know spending time with Andy was partly a long-held belief that he was The One, but we both know that his middle name being Steven was a bigger pull. You seemed to really believe that CD. What's changed?'

I studied the face I loved so much. He was right to challenge me. I'd been stupid and careless with his feelings and I deserved to work hard to get him back. 'Nothing's changed,' I said. 'I still believe the CD. In fact, I believe it more than ever now except for one key detail. Madame Louisa got the name wrong. I think you're Steven.'

Nick raised an eyebrow. 'Because Nick and Steven sound so similar?'

'Ha ha. Very funny. No. I just think she gave the wrong name because everything else happened exactly as she predicted. She said I'd have to decide between the past and the present and I should follow my heart not my head which is exactly what happened with you, isn't it?'

'I can't say I'm following you, but even if you're convinced that I'm Steven and she gave you the wrong name, how do I know you won't change your mind again if some attractive bloke called Steven appears in the future?'

'Because I choose you, Nick. With or without the CD, I choose you. Over Andy. Over Steven. Over anyone I've ever known or will ever know. I love you, Nick. I don't know what else I can say to convince you.'

Nick smiled. 'Say it again.'

'Which part?'

'The last part.'

'I love you.'

Nick grinned. 'You've never said that before. You're really sure your search for Steven is over...?'

'I'm sure. Now what was that you were saying about shutting up and kissing me?'

PART III

THREE MONTHS LATER

39

✉ From Auntie Kay
Happy moving in day! My favourite niece and my
favourite customer… couldn't be happier for you
both xxx

'Could you use an extra pair of hands?' Elise said when I opened
the door at Seashell Cottage.

'I thought you'd been summoned to the mother-in-law's for
Sunday lunch.'

'I was but I put my foot down. Considering what we found last
time I helped you move, I had to help again to see if we could top
that.'

I ushered her inside. 'Don't remind me. If anything else from my
past re-appears, I'll swear I'm being haunted. Are you feeling brave?'
I led her to the dining room.

'Why? Have you got your pet dragon chained up in there?'

'Worse. You know how we both like things to be really organised
and have paperwork filed neatly away? Imagine the exact opposite.'
Cringing, I opened the door wide.

Elise gasped. 'Sarah Peterson! I think you've been burgled.'
There wasn't an inch of wood showing on the dining table through

a sea of paperwork, post, and folders. More piles sprouted on the chairs and the floor. We looked at each other and started laughing.

'I warned you,' I said. 'I know it's really unlike me. I hate it. If I kept the door shut, I could just about ignore it.'

'Just think how satisfied you'll feel when it's all done, though. How do you want to do this?'

We worked for about half an hour, singing along to Abba.

I picked up what I thought was an empty cardboard folder and was about to add it into a crate of stationery when I felt something stiff still inside it. 'How the hell did that get in there?' I gasped.

'What's up?' asked Elise.

'The clairvoyant CD's in here.'

'Where was it meant to be?'

'In the CD player in the lounge. I swear I've *never* taken it out of there since I moved in.'

Elise did a little shiver. 'Ooh, goose bump moment. That's just like you suddenly finding it in your Treasures Box last time.'

I removed the CD and stared at it thoughtfully. 'Do you think we should listen to it again?'

Elise put down the papers she'd been sorting through. 'Is that a good idea? Won't it stir up the whole searching for Steven thing again?'

I shook my head. 'I don't think so. Nick's The One and I've never been more certain of anything in my life. I was just wondering if we've missed something on the CD.'

'Like what? A hidden track?'

'I don't know but there's only one way to find out.'

Giggling like schoolgirls, we raced to the lounge. Elise hurled herself onto the sofa while I put the CD in the player then curled up on the armchair next to it.

'It started with the CD. It seems fitting to end my little journey with it too.' I pressed play.

We listened in silence until we arrived at the key question:

'Will I ever get married? All I've ever wanted to do is get married.'

Next came the prediction about Steven and the crossroads choice leading to the true Steven.

'Surely there's something else you can tell me about Steven,' [I said on the CD.] 'How will I know it's him? Steven's a common name.'

'The name isn't that important. Your grandma says you'll just know he's The One. I'm going to...'

I sat upright and paused the CD. 'Did you hear that?' Before Elise had a chance to answer, I backtracked it and listened again.

'... know it's him? Steven's a common name.'

'The name isn't that important. Your grandma says you'll just know he's The One. I'm...'

I stopped it again. 'The name isn't that important. The name isn't that important,' I repeated. 'I've never noticed that bit before. Have you?'

'I can't remember. Possibly. I think I was more excited about the Steven thing and wasn't concentrating.'

'What do you think it means? Do you think Madame Louisa was trying to tell me that the man of my dreams might not be called Steven after all? Surely not. I can't have gone through with the search for Steven for nothing.' Thoughts of my various encounters raced through my mind. I could have avoided all that.

'You could certainly take it that way,' Elise said. 'But your search wasn't a waste. It helped you realise that Nick was The One. It helped you finally get Andy out of your system. Plus, you wouldn't have met Stevie. Now that I've *finally* been introduced to him, I can see why you two became such good friends. He's a lovely guy.'

'True.' I smiled. 'Stevie does cancel out the other rubbish stuff. I wonder if we've missed anything else.' I pressed play again.

'... I'm going to give you this CD and I suggest you put it somewhere safe and listen to it on your own in a week or so when you can really think about what I've said. Or perhaps when you hit your crossroads and it finds its way back into your life.'

Madame Louisa talked about the bracelet then the message from Uncle Alan. There were the familiar sounds of movement as I headed towards the door, the point at which I usually pressed stop. 'I'll let it play a bit longer.'

We both cocked our ears towards the speakers, listening out for anything other than static, and both jumped when Madame Louisa spoke again.

'Oh, Sarah, I can tell you something else about Steven.'

My heart thumped faster. *New information!*

'You've already met him.'

'I have? When?'

'A long time ago. Bye Sarah.'

More static. I cocked my head to listen harder, just in case, but the CD then stopped automatically.

'That's definitely it,' I said. 'What do you make of that, then?'

'You've met him already? Not that we needed any confirmation but that just proves that Andy wasn't the real Steven. You hadn't met him when the CD was made.'

'True.'

'Didn't you say Nick's grandma lived next door? Could you have met him when you were little?'

I shrugged. 'It's possible. Nick says he spent loads of time there as a kid, but neither of us remember meeting each other. I'll have to ask Auntie Kay about it when she gets home on Thursday.' I glanced at my watch. 'Are you okay for time?'

'I'm yours as long as you need me. How about I continue in the dining room and you tackle your bedroom?'

'Thanks for this.' I gave her a hug. 'This is twice in less than a year that you've helped me pack and move. If you and Gary ever move house, I promise to return the favour big time. In the meantime, can I shout you to pizza tonight?'

'Don't you and Nick want to enjoy your first evening as official roomies on your own?'

'We'll have plenty of other evenings for that. Tonight, I want to say thanks to you. Pizza?' Elise's stomach grumbled loudly. 'I'll take that as a yes.'

Elise smiled. 'I'll text Gary and let him know I'll be late.'

* * *

'You're back! I've missed you.' Nick gave me a gentle kiss. 'Hi Elise. Looks like you could have a little side-line in removals if you ever pack in teaching.'

'I'm not sure I have the biceps for it,' she said. 'But it's always good to have a back-up plan. Sarah's promised to return the favour if I ever move. And she's invited me for pizza but I can leave if you'd rather be alone.'

'Don't be daft,' Nick said. 'You're welcome here any time. Pizza is the least we can do to say thanks.' He looked towards the two packed cars. 'Is that everything?'

'Yep. All my worldly goods are cluttering up your car ready to clutter up your house.'

'It's not *my* car or *my* house anymore,' Nick said. 'They're *ours*.'

Elise turned round to mouth at me, 'He's so sweet.'

'I know,' I mouthed back, grinning.

Half an hour later, the three of us had unloaded the cars and sat down with hard-earned mugs of tea when the doorbell rang followed by the sound of the door opening. 'Hello? Nick?'

'Mum! We're in here.'

Nick's mum, Sue, poked her head round the door. 'Great. You're both here.' She hugged Nick then me. 'Congratulations,' she said. 'We bought some bubbly to celebrate.' She handed Nick a bottle.

'Thank you,' he said. 'You didn't have to do that.'

'Congratulations!' Callie burst into the room and dished out hugs too. 'Oh, hello,' she said to Elise. 'Who are you?'

Elise laughed. 'I'm Elise.'

'Sorry,' I said. 'Quick intros. Elise and I have been best friends since our first day at primary school. Elise, this is Nick's sister, Callie, and his mum, Sue.'

'Champagne?' Nick asked.

'Why do you think we brought it?' Callie said.

Nick disappeared into the kitchen and came back with five wine glasses. 'Sorry, not posh enough to have champagne flutes.' He popped the cork like a professional and poured a small glass each.

'To Nick and Sarah,' Sue said.

'Nick and Sarah.'

'Did you bring the present in, Callie?' Sue asked.

Callie jumped up off the sofa. 'It's in the hall. Just a sec.'

Moments later she reappeared with what looked like a picture wrapped up in brown paper and tied with a turquoise organza bow.

'Happy housewarming.' She handed me the package.

'You shouldn't have, but thank you.' I pulled on the ribbon and opened the wrapping to reveal a large black and white framed photo. A young dark-haired boy stood side-on to the camera. He had his arms around a younger girl with dark curly hair and was kissing her on the cheek while she smiled shyly towards the camera.

'Aw, that's so cute,' I said. 'Look, Nick.'

Nick moved across to the sofa arm to look at the photo. 'Very cute. Thanks, Mum.'

Callie giggled. 'Look closer.'

I looked at the photo again. 'Hang on.' My jaw dropped. 'That's me. Oh my God! Is it? Is that me?' I put my hand across my mouth. 'Is that Nick?'

'She *finally* gets it!' Callie exclaimed. 'We thought it looked better in black and white.'

My stomach did a flip. *'You've already met him... a long time ago.'* Elise and I exchanged looks.

'Here's the rest of the set.' Sue passed me a few colour photos and I gasped as I took in the images. The first photo showed a young Nick blowing out candles on a cake in the shape of a number six. The next showed him sat on a garden bench eating a piece of birthday cake with a four-year-old me next to him, cake smeared across my face. We were looking at each other, rather than the camera, and laughing. The next one was an inside scene of pass the parcel. There were several children in the photo spread out in a circle but young Nick and I were sat really close together. He was passing the parcel to me and our hands were touching, our eyes locked. The final picture was the framed one.

'I've got goose bumps,' I whispered holding out my arm to show him. 'I can't believe we met... what... twenty-six years ago and we look like we're together.' I passed the photos to Elise.

'Matching goose bumps,' Nick said. 'Crikey, Mum, where did you find these? I bet there aren't many men who meet the girl of their dreams when they're six then get reunited when they're thirty-two.'

'You were so right,' Elise said, looking through the photos. 'He's Steven.'

I nodded. 'It certainly looks that way.'

'Steven?' Callie said. 'Who's Steven?'

'Long story.'

'I'm in no rush.'

I cringed, but I already knew Callie well enough to know she wouldn't let this go. 'This is really embarrassing so I'm only going to give you the short version...'

I blushed once I'd finished.

'She got the name right,' Sue said.

'What do you mean, Mum?' Nick took hold of my hand and squeezed it.

Sue looked very pale. 'When you were born, we named you Steven.'

'Then how come we all call him Nick?' It was Callie who actually said it but I'm sure it echoed what we were all thinking.

'Because that's the name on his birth certificate. Well, Nicholas is. Don't you remember me telling you this?' Sue looked at Nick but he slowly shook his head. She continued. 'When I went into hospital to have Nick, my best friend and neighbour, Jen, was seven months pregnant. Unbeknown to me, she was rushed to hospital the same day and had a premature boy. We were in different hospitals with no way of contacting each other. Coincidentally we both named our babies Steven. Jen and Keith weren't sure if their Steven would live so they registered his birth quickly, unaware we'd named our baby Steven too. When we found out, we hoped and prayed her Steven would survive and, assuming he did, John and I decided it would be too confusing being in the same class at school, having the same date of birth, living on the same road, and having the same name so we went for our second choice instead.'

'Are you sure you told me this?' Nick said. 'It doesn't ring a bell at all.'

Sue nodded. 'You went through a phase of asking everyone to call you Steven when you were about five or six. Then you decided you wanted to be a girl and asked everyone to call you Keeley Fawcett instead.'

Callie gave a snort of laughter from across the room. 'Sorry, everyone. Inappropriate moment as usual.'

'Can I just check I've understood this,' Elise said. *Thank you, Elise!* I was too shocked to speak myself. 'Are you really saying that his birth certificate says "Nicholas" but he was actually born Steven?'

'Yes. Frustratingly, Jen emigrated to South Africa when the boys were two and we lost touch so I could have stuck with Steven after all. Nick, are you sure you don't remember me telling you this?'

He shook his head. 'No. Although, scarily, Keeley Fawcett rings a bell.' He turned to me, frowning. 'Are you okay?'

'A bit stunned. Madame Louisa was right all along.'

'Looks like it.'

'And I was right. You really are *the* Steven.'

He smiled and looked at me so tenderly, I felt like I could melt.

A slight cough from across the room interrupted the moment. 'I think it's time we made our exit, don't you Mum?' Callie stood up and reached for her bag. 'I think these two could do with a bit of alone time.'

'Of course.' Sue stood up too. 'Congratulations to you both again. Nick, I'll give you a call next week. Maybe I could have you both over for dinner when you're settled?'

'And I'll give you a call, Sarah, because I need to know the full Steven story from start to end.' Callie gave me a hug. 'The more embarrassing the better. I think it's important that I know everything about my future sister-in-law.'

'Callie! They're not engaged.'

'Not yet, Mum, but look at them. It won't be long. I bet he's already picked out the ring and been planning the perfect proposal, haven't you, Nick?'

Nick's flushed cheeks made my heart race. *Oh my God! He has!*

'What was that you were saying about leaving, Callie?' Nick put his hands on her shoulders and marched her towards the door. 'I think you'd better do that right now before you say another word.'

'Sorry, Nick. You know what I'm like.'

'I don't know about you,' Nick said once their car had pulled out of sight, 'but my head is spinning after what Mum said. If I'd remembered about being born Steven... I don't know what to say, Sarah.'

'I know. My head's a mess too.'

'Mine three,' Elise said. 'And I think I'm going to leave you in peace so you can stare at that gorgeous picture and get your heads around everything that's happened this afternoon.'

'What about pizza?' I said.

'Maybe another time. I really think you should have some alone time.'

'Seriously, Elise, you don't have to go.'

'Thanks, Nick, but I think I may buy a bottle of wine and have my own romantic night in with Gary instead. I can't remember the last time we did that which must mean it's way, way overdue.'

We waved Elise off and made our way back to the lounge. I looked at the piles of crates and bags. 'I've trashed the place. But I don't know if I can face moving it all. I feel drained.'

'The bags can wait,' Nick said. 'There's something more important we have to do first.'

'What?'

'This.' He put his arms round me and kissed me. 'Welcome to your new home, Sarah Peterson.'

'Thank you, *Steven* Derbyshire. Or should that be Keeley Fawcett?'

He laughed. 'I genuinely don't remember the Steven thing. You know that I'd have told you if I'd remembered, don't you?'

I nodded. 'You do know that I wasn't lying when I said my search for Steven was over months ago, don't you? And that I'd chosen you despite the CD, not because of it. Even if your mum hadn't found the photos or told us about your name, I still knew you were The One. All that stuff today was just the icing on the cake; it's all very nice but the cake is the best part and I already have the cake.'

'Are you saying I'm a cake?'

I laughed. 'I think the analogy worked better in my head. You know what I mean, though, don't you?'

Nick kissed me again. 'I do. There's one more thing. Come and sit down a minute.' He led me to the sofa. 'You've met her enough times now to know that my sister has serious foot-in-mouth disease.

She did another classic this afternoon. I know you'll be thinking about what she said about us getting married...'

'I wasn't. I didn't—'

'Sarah! You know you're a terrible fibber.'

'Okay. I *was* thinking about it. But only cos you looked so guilty. Sorry.'

'You've nothing to be sorry about. I know some people would call it early days but we both know it's forever. I *do* want to marry you, but I want to do it properly. I know how much this all means to you and I want to give you the proposal of your dreams. Doing that takes a bit of planning so it's not going to happen just yet but it'll happen soon. I promise. Are you okay with that?'

A tear slipped down my cheek. 'I'm more than okay with that.'

As Nick wrapped his arms around me and kissed me again, I realised that the perfect proposal actually didn't matter that much to me anymore; it was just packaging. The person who gave it was the important part. I loved him all the more for wanting to please me, though.

There'd been a few dead ends in the journey thanks to Andy and Jason. There'd been plenty of frustrating detours during my search for Steven. But now I'd finally found him and, whatever twists and turns the road ahead held, I knew I'd found my soulmate to navigate them with – just like my parents and just like Auntie Kay and Charlie. Auntie Kay had been right; when true love comes along, you have to hang onto it with all your strength because it's worth it. I nearly hadn't had the strength to fight for Nick and now look at us.

It had taken six years longer than I'd expected when I was 'almost fourteen' but my Life Plan was now finally being fulfilled and it had definitely been worth the wait.

And I knew that I'd never be alone.

ACKNOWLEDGMENTS

Thank you for reading *New Beginnings at Seaside Blooms*. I hope you've enjoyed Sarah's journey to find her Steven. It's the second book in the *Welcome to Whitsborough Bay* series. Don't worry if you haven't read the first one, *Making Wishes at Bay View,* as it's a stand-alone story but I do recommend reading the rest of the series in order because they follow chronologically. *Finding Hope at Lighthouse Cove* is Elise's story then *Coming Home to Seashell Cottage* is Clare's story.

This book is very special to me because it's where my journey from dreamer to author started. The premise is based on a real-life clairvoyant prediction I received that I was going to meet the man of my dreams and he'd be called Steven. I searched and I didn't find Steven... but I did find the idea for my first book. I started writing it while I had my own business, a specialist teddy bear shop, and drew on my experiences of setting up a shop from scratch, searching for Steven whilst doing so.

New Beginnings at Seaside Blooms was previously released under the title of *Searching for Steven* but has now been re-released through my wonderful new publisher, Boldwood Books. The story is still the same, the characters are still the same, but it's been re-edited and has a brand new title and gorgeous new cover.

A huge thank you goes to the team at Boldwood Books for

taking me into the Boldwood family and giving Sarah's story a new lease of life. Particular thanks go to my fabulous editor, Nia, for her valuable feedback which has helped shape the new version.

I owe so much to my wonderful husband, Mark. I'd only just started writing this book when we met. I had no idea whether I would even finish the book, let alone have it published, but he encouraged me to learn more about writing which, in turn, led to me finding my voice. He never moans when I lock myself away for hours in my office, fingers glued to my keyboard. Thanks for being so understanding. And thanks to our daughter, Ashleigh, who tries not to disturb me (too much) when I'm creating.

A huge thank you to my original line-up of beta readers: Clare, Sue, Liz, Nicola, Debbie and Joyce (aka mummy-bear). Their enthusiasm, compliments, proof-reading skills and constructive feedback helped *Searching for Steven* secure his original publishing deal, and ultimately led to the re-birth of *New Beginnings at Seaside Blooms* through my second publishing deal with Boldwood Books.

I can't give enough thanks for the passion, advice and support provided over the last seven years from the talented writers known collectively as The Write Romantics. We've celebrated successes and cried over challenges. Alys, Deirdre, Helen, Helen, Jackie, Jo, Lynne, Rachael and Sharon: you're my writing family and I'll always be grateful we found each other. Sharon, in particular, is my writing rock and I love getting together to share the highs and lows of writing, and discuss future story ideas.

Nearly there! This book went through the Romantic Novelists' Association's New Writers' Scheme (NWS) two years running. I was fortunate enough to discover the identity of my readers. Their reports were invaluable in shaping (and slimming) the original version. Talli Roland and Rhoda Baxter, I'm forever appreciative of your constructive feedback.

And, finally, thank you again for reading this book. If you loved it, it would be amazing if you could take a moment to leave a review on Amazon. It doesn't need to be a long review; a sentence is absolutely fine and can make an author very, very happy.

Big hugs

Jessica xx

MORE FROM JESSICA REDLAND

We hope you enjoyed reading *New Beginnings at Seaside Blooms*. If you did, please leave a review.

If you'd like to gift a copy, this book is also available as a ebook, digital audio download and audiobook CD.

Sign up to Jessica Redland's mailing list for news, competitions and updates on future books.

http://bit.ly/JessicaRedlandNewsletter

ABOUT THE AUTHOR

Jessica Redland is the author of nine novels which are all set around the fictional location of Whitsborough Bay. Inspired by her hometown of Scarborough she writes uplifting women's fiction which has garnered many devoted fans.

Visit Jessica's website: https://www.jessicaredland.com/

Follow Jessica on social media:

facebook.com/JessicaRedlandWriter

twitter.com/JessicaRedland

instagram.com/JessicaRedlandWriter

bookbub.com/authors/jessica-redland

ALSO BY JESSICA REDLAND

ABOUT BOLDWOOD BOOKS

Boldwood Books is a fiction publishing company seeking out the best stories from around the world.

Find out more at www.boldwoodbooks.com

Sign up to the Book and Tonic newsletter for news, offers and competitions from Boldwood Books!

http://www.bit.ly/bookandtonic

We'd love to hear from you, follow us on social media:

facebook.com/BookandTonic

twitter.com/BoldwoodBooks

instagram.com/BookandTonic

Printed in Great Britain
by Amazon